# Meet
## and
# Delete

## Pauline Lawless

POOLBEG

Published 2015
by Poolbeg Press Ltd.
123 Grange Hill, Baldoyle,
Dublin 13, Ireland
Email: poolbeg@poolbeg.com

1

A catalogue record for this book is available from the British Library.

ISBN 978-1-78199-999-8

Printed and bound by
CPI Group (UK) Ltd, Croydon, CR0 4YY

www.poolbeg.com

# About the Author

Pauline Lawless is from Dublin and now lives in Belgium and spends winters in Florida. She is the bestselling author of five previous novels: *Because We're Worth It; If The Shoes Fit; A Year Like No Other; Behind Every Cloud; Birthday Girls.*

For more information on these books visit her author page on: www.amazon.com/paulinelawless
www.amazon.co.uk/paulinelawless

To Gaye Shortland, the best editor on the planet, who has been with me from the start. You have somehow managed to polish my six rough-diamond manuscripts into books of which I'm proud. Thank you.

# Chapter 1

Megan Ross let herself into the apartment she shared with her fiancé, Paul, her arms laden with laptop, briefcase and enormous handbag. She almost collided with the big roller-case and large black-plastic bag standing in the hallway. Puzzled, she made her way into the living room where Paul was kneeling at the DVD stand. The shelf, which usually housed the DVD player and Bose sound system, was bare.

"What's happened?" she asked, her eyes scanning the room to see if anything else was missing.

Paul rocked back on his heels, startled. "What has you home so early? I wasn't expecting you for another hour at least."

"I have a dreadful headache so I left work early. What's happened? Have we been burgled?"

He stood up hastily and stuffed the DVDs in his backpack, shifting from foot to foot, his eyes trained on the floor.

"I'm sorry, hon, really sorry, but I just can't go through with it."

"Can't go through with what?" she asked, mystified. "And what are those bags doing in the hall?"

He glanced at her briefly but looked away again as he dropped the bombshell. "I'm leaving," he said in a low voice. "It's all too much. I'm sorry but I just can't go through with the wedding. I feel like I'm suffocating. I need space."

She looked at him dumbly, blue eyes wide with shock. "What do you mean, you need space?"

"I mean, I think we both need to take a step back."

"Take a step back?" she cried, her voice rising uncontrollably. "But our wedding is less than two months away. Everything's arranged, Paul. You can't really mean this?"

He cast his eyes down again, unable to meet hers, and in that moment she understood that he was serious. The realisation hit her like a punch in the stomach. She doubled over in pain, gasping for breath.

"Paul, please say you don't mean this," she begged him pitifully as she sank down into the armchair.

"I'm sorry, really I am, Meggie," he said in a shaky voice. "I know it's a terrible shock but it would be worse to go ahead with it when I'm not sure." He was edging towards the door as he spoke.

"Not sure?" she repeated hollowly. "We've been together for almost eight years! Can't we talk about it at least? I'm sure we can work it out." She looked at him hopefully, her voice pleading.

"I'm sorry but it's too late for that. My mind's made up." He stuck his chin out obstinately, looking at her for the first time. "It can't be a huge surprise to you, Meggie.

2

Even you'll admit things have not been great between us recently."

"I agree we've been arguing more than usual lately but that's just pre-wedding nerves. Lots of couples experience that."

"No, it's more than that. I'm just not ready to get married. I'm moving out today. I'm truly sorry, Meggie."

"Paul, please, you can't do this!" she cried, jumping up, her voice trembling with emotion as she reached out to touch his arm. She was trembling all over and felt like she might throw up. He moved out of her reach.

"This is our whole future you're destroying, Paul," she whispered. "And what about all the wedding arrangements? Everything's organised. The invitations will be going out next week."

"I know and I'm sorry," he said, looking sheepish. "But I'm sure people will understand. We won't be the first couple to cancel a wedding."

She looked at him, stunned, as her whole world came crashing down around her. How could he do this? Yes, they'd been rowing more than usual lately but with the stress of the wedding it was only natural, wasn't it? It didn't mean they didn't love each other any more.

"I still love you, Paul. Do you not love me?" she asked.

Paul shifted from foot to foot, avoiding her eyes again. "I don't know what I feel any more. I just know that I can't go through with this wedding. It's not you. It's me. I'm sorry. I'll just go now. I really hope you meet someone who deserves you."

She felt her anger rising and wanted to slap him or shake him to try and make him see sense but, before she could say another word, he was gone.

She sat for a long time after, tears streaming down her face as she hugged her arms around her slim body and rocked backwards and forwards.

Finally, she roused herself and did what all Irishwomen do in a crisis: she put the kettle on for a cup of tea.

Wrapping her hands around the warm comforting mug, she thought back over the past few months, looking for signs that could have her alerted her to this catastrophe. She supposed that there must have been some but perhaps she'd overlooked them as she'd planned their future together. Now it was over. What was she going to do? How would she survive?

Was it possible he'd met someone else? She didn't think so, certain she'd have known if he'd been cheating on her. Then again, they say the wife is always the last to know, she thought bitterly. Well, she wasn't quite his wife and never would be now.

This wasn't the first time she'd been dumped. She wondered if there was something wrong with her that compelled men to leave her just when she thought they'd be her life partner. Her thoughts strayed to Sam, her first love. They'd been a couple since fourth year in school and their relationship had lasted all through their college years. Then, after they'd both qualified and she'd thought he might propose, he'd upped and decided he wanted to travel the world. Without her, unfortunately.

It had taken her three years to get over Sam and that was when she'd met Paul. And now he was gone too. She'd been very slow to give herself to him completely but, over time, she'd succumbed to his charm and fallen in love with him.

They were an ill-suited couple, as people had been quick

to point out. She, a responsible career woman; he, laid-back, charming and great fun. Unfortunately, he was permanently unemployed and not too bothered about finding work. When she bought the apartment, it made sense for him to move in with her. Paul was quite content to hang around the house all day, playing games and listening to music. Megan couldn't understand how it never bothered him that she was paying all the bills, but it didn't.

"Definitely *not* husband material," her mother had remarked snidely when she'd first introduced them but Megan had paid no attention.

By then she was in love with Paul. Now it appeared that her mother had been right, although funnily enough she had changed her tune with the prospect of a big wedding on the cards.

Megan had not felt the need to get married until she'd hit thirty and found herself getting broody and thinking seriously of having a baby. Suddenly it became important to her to legalise their relationship. She met with no small opposition from Paul who was quite happy with things as they were and had no wish to change the status quo. It had taken her a year to persuade him to take the plunge and now he wanted out. Had she forced him into marriage? Obviously, she thought bitterly.

She knew now why people talked about having your heart broken. That is exactly what it felt like. It was as if someone had plunged a knife through her heart and it was physically breaking. She was distraught and felt that she was in the middle of a nightmare from which she would wake up any moment. Unfortunately it was no dream, it was a reality. She picked her up her phone and called her friend Viv.

# Chapter 2

Viv Connolly was watching TV in the cosy living room that was hers, on the ground floor of her parents' home. She was thirty-one years old and aware that people thought it strange she was still living at home, but she didn't care – it suited her. An only child, she'd been spoilt rotten by her parents all her life and they were a close-knit trio. They refused to take any rent from her and her mother was happy to cook all her meals and do her washing, as she'd always done.

"What's not to like?" Viv was often heard to say. She loved her parents dearly and could see no reason to move out. She was, unfortunately, a shopaholic and fashionista, and living at home meant that the money she earned as a personal shopper or Personal Stylist, as she was called, was hers to spend on clothes, and shoes of course (she'd stopped counting at a hundred pairs), not to mention bags. She had taken over the two guest bedrooms to store them all, leaving her parents with just their own bedroom.

However, lately her father had started grumbling about the closets packed to the brim with her stuff. He was due to retire at the end of the year and had hinted about needing more space for his hobbies.

Viv had a bubbly personality and a striking, exotic look which men found very attractive. She'd had a string of boyfriends over the years and had actually moved in with two of them at different stages. Sadly, they hadn't worked out and she'd moved back again pretty quickly to the comfort and security of her childhood home. "If you want to know me . . ." was all she ever said about these episodes.

As she sipped a glass of white wine and watched *Come Dine with Me,* her phone rang. It was Megan.

"Hi, sweetie, and how is the bride-to-be? In good form?" Viv greeted her best friend chirpily. She was very excited about the forthcoming wedding as Megan had asked her to be chief bridesmaid.

"I'm not."

Viv pulled back from the phone, frowning. Megan sounded weird. "What are you saying? You're not in good form? Are you okay?"

"No, I'm not. And I'm not a bride-to-be either," Megan replied, a catch in her voice.

"Have you been drinking?" Viv asked, puzzled. She could tell her friend was close to tears.

"I wish! Paul has left me. He's moved out. Says he needs space. He doesn't want to go ahead with the wedding."

"*Whaaaat?*" Viv almost dropped the phone in shock. "He can't do that," she gasped. "The wedding is only seven weeks away."

"Well, he has. When I got home from work he had his

things packed, ready to move." Megan started to cry again. Saying it aloud made the reality hit home in earnest.

"The bastard!" Viv cried. "How could he? What a lousy stroke to pull at this stage."

Megan was blubbering now.

"Hang in there, sweetie," Viv said. "I'm on my way over."

She put the cork back in the bottle of wine she'd been drinking from and took another bottle of wine from her drinks fridge, before grabbing her jacket and bag. She went into her parents' living room where her father was watching *Top Gear*.

"Dad, would you mind driving me around to Megan's?"

He frowned at her. "Can't it wait till this programme is over, Vivienne?"

"No, Dad, it can't. This is an emergency." She looked at him and he saw the worry in her large brown eyes.

"If you say so," he sighed. He was used to his daughter's emergencies, usually over some boy or other. "Very well, go in the kitchen and tell your mother I'll be gone for ten minutes. It really is time you got your own wheels," he grumbled as he took off his slippers.

He had a point and Viv knew that once he was retired she'd have to get a car. She knew she had it easy. Her dad worked in an office right beside the shopping centre where she worked, so she travelled to work with him every day. Not having a car also meant that she had no worries about drinking and driving when she went out in the evenings. Usually one of her many friends drove and there was always the Luas and taxis for when they went clubbing. Besides, it cost a lot to run a car. For now things were fine just as they were but she knew it was about to change.

As the car stopped outside Megan's apartment Viv

leaned over and kissed her father on the cheek.

"Thanks, Pops. You're an angel."

He grinned at her. "Go on outta that, you divil! You have me wound around your little finger." He tweaked one of her long dark curls as she got out of the car. "Call me if you need a lift home and it's not too late."

"Thanks, Pops, but I'll probably stay over. I love you," she said as she closed the door.

She blew him a kiss as he drove away. He shook his head but he was smiling.

Megan opened the door and Viv was shocked to see her eyes red and swollen from crying. That bastard, Viv thought to herself when she saw her friend's stricken face. Megan was one of those cool beauties who never had a hair out of place. Right now she looked a dishevelled mess.

"You poor baby," Viv said as she hugged her, whereupon Megan burst into tears once more.

Viv led her into the apartment and, seating her on the sofa, held her until her sobs subsided.

"Just let me pour us some wine and then you can tell me everything," Viv proposed, heading for the kitchen.

She emerged with two wineglasses. Opening the bottle she had brought, she poured two glasses of wine.

"Now shoot!" she ordered, handing Megan her drink.

"I just don't understand it," Megan told her, sniffing. "I came home early from work and there he was with his things packed. I was so shocked. I just couldn't believe it."

"Did he say why?"

"Just that he can't go through with it," Megan said tearfully. "He needs space."

"Well, he left it a bit late to discover that," Viv pointed

out sarcastically. "Do you think he's just getting cold feet? Maybe you could have a talk with him and get him to change his mind?"

"No. He says there's nothing to talk about. His mind is made up. He doesn't want to marry me."

"The little shit! What an asshole! He doesn't deserve you, you know that?"

Viv jumped up and paced the room, her long dark curls bouncing with her anger.

"I don't know. It must be me. Sam walked out on me too. It's obviously my fault."

"Don't you even dare think that!"

"Well, it's obvious I can't hold on to a man. I must be lacking in something."

"Don't doubt yourself, sweetie. You just haven't met the right guy yet."

Megan shook her head, unconvinced.

"Oh God, how will I be able to face everyone?" she moaned. "My mother will have a fit."

"To hell with your mother!" Viv declared angrily. "It's *your* future we're talking about here." She'd never had much time for the egocentric Mrs Ross.

"I have no future without Paul," Megan snivelled, her nose running.

Viv handed her a tissue from the box on the coffee table.

"Bullshit! You're better off without him if he can treat you like this – walking out just weeks before the wedding. It's disgraceful!"

Viv was absolutely furious with him. She'd never liked Paul very much but even she could never have imagined he'd pull a stunt like this.

Megan had knocked back her wine and Viv took the

11

glass from her and went to refill it. It was going to be a long night!

The two girls had become friends in their first year at secondary school. Megan was the girl everyone wanted to be. Not only was she beautiful, she was also a brilliant student who excelled at sports, dancing and music. This, of course, meant that she attracted much jealousy from the other girls. Not from Viv, however, who admired her enormously and thought she was fabulous.

Viv had inherited her grandmother's Italian genes: jet-black curls, soft brown eyes, olive skin, and a curvy figure that combined to give her a sultry look which attracted much attention from the teenage boys in the nearby boys' college.

Megan, in contrast, was a cool, tall blonde. Viv would have given anything for Megan's hair which fell straight, like a silk curtain, halfway down her back. It was a multitude of different blonde shades from ash to honey and, unlike Viv's, never got frizzy, not even in the rain. She had a pretty heart-shaped face with big blue eyes, the colour of a swimming-pool – as one of her admirers had observed. Viv had been over the moon when the beautiful, talented Megan had chosen to be her friend.

They were as different as chalk and cheese, not only in their looks, but also in their personalities. Megan was serious and ladylike whereas Viv was a tomboy and mad as a hatter. She was the most popular girl in the class because she was always laughing and great fun to be with and, besides, she threatened no one. She detested studying and was more interested in fashion and what celebrities were wearing on the red carpet than who won the Crimean War or figuring out the answer to $9^2 \times 9^2$. She had a quirky sense of style and was the only girl in the school with the ability to make her school uniform look unique and trendy. It was a big surprise to everyone when these two polar opposites became firm friends.

Now, almost twenty years later, their friendship was as strong as ever.

Megan graduated from university with a first class honours degree and was snapped up by an international publishing company where she was now a senior editor. Viv, on the other hand, had dropped out of college and after dabbling in the fashion business for a couple of years eventually secured the job of her dreams, as a Personal Stylist in *the* most upmarket fashion store in *the* most upmarket shopping mall in south Dublin.

"I'm a personal shopper, actually, but Personal Stylist sounds better," she admitted, laughing.

She was surrounded by beautiful clothes every day and was being paid to shop, albeit for other women. She was very much in demand by the Dublin society women who were her clients. They treasured her advice and some of them could not choose an outfit without her help. Best of all, she got great discount and often got free clothes from the designers and fashion companies.

Now, as Viv watched Megan knocking back the wine, she searched for some positive that might comfort her friend. The only positive she could think of was that Megan was well rid of that good-for-nothing layabout, Paul, but she couldn't very well voice that aloud. She doubted Megan would see that as a positive right now.

By eleven o'clock, Megan, who normally drank very

little, was totally pissed and Viv had to hold her up as she led her into bed. Thankfully, Megan fell asleep the moment her head hit the pillow. Tomorrow, on top of a probable hangover, she would have to face the awful prospect of telling everyone that the wedding was off. Viv wondered where Megan would go from here, with her dreams in shreds and her confidence shattered. It wouldn't be easy.

# Chapter 3

Claire O'Dowd sat on the patio of the large house in Dundrum, watching the birds feeding from the bird-feeder she'd hung up the day before. She smiled sadly as she saw the stronger birds push the smaller ones out of the way as they greedily pecked at the nuts. There were bullies and victims in every walk of life, she thought. She should know. She'd been bullied all of her life – by her older sister, Sarah, and also by her mother who had passed away three months previously.

It had taken all of Claire's courage to reinstate the bird-feeder in the first place. When she'd first arrived home with it, her mother had expressly forbidden her to hang it up, claiming the birds made her nervous. There was very little that had not made her mother nervous, Claire thought ruefully. She felt a frisson of guilt as she watched the little birds feeding and hoped that wherever her mother was now, she wasn't looking down (or up!) at the little creatures flitting about her garden. Even from the grave, her mother was capable of exerting her influence. Claire had to stop with this guilt and reclaim her life once more. She was only thirty-two years old, after all. Surely it wasn't too late?

Her gentle father, who had died when Claire was twenty-two, had been browbeaten by his wife all of his life and in the end, Claire was convinced, it had killed him.

The night he died her mother had turned to her daughters.

"Who'll take care of me now?" she'd asked, tears of self-pity filling her eyes.

"Don't look at me!" had been Sarah's response. "I've got a husband and a baby to take care of."

"Well, you'll take Daddy's place now, won't you, pet?" her mother had appealed to her younger daughter.

Claire knew it was inevitable. She had no option but to take over her father's mantle. Aged twenty-two and fresh out of nursing school, she'd had to take on the burden of babying her mother as her father had always done. She ferried her to and from doctors, hospitals and pharmacies, shocked to discover that her mother was a severe hypochondriac. There was also the bridge club, ladies' club, book club, not to mention the shopping that necessitated Claire's attention. The list was endless and took up all of her free time. She now understood what a miserable life her father had had.

During her last three years her mother had got ever more demanding and expected her younger daughter to spend every moment she wasn't working catering to her every need. Claire had lost all of her friends – not that she'd had that many, but the few she'd had got tired of inviting her to go out with them. When she constantly refused, they'd stopped asking.

Her sister Sarah was no help. They'd never been very close and Sarah had distanced herself even further from their mother as she'd become ever more demanding. Sarah was six years older than Claire and now had two children. Her husband Ben was a teacher and a gentle soul. Claire often wondered how on earth he put up with Sarah's moods and demands. Sad to say, the apple hadn't fallen far from the tree, and Claire could see much of her mother's domineering character in her sister.

On her mother's death, the house came to the two sisters. Claire had been born in it and loved the old house and the thought of leaving it filled her with fear. Sarah wanted to sell it immediately but the property market was in such a dire state that Claire knew it would have been crazy to sell at that time. Instead, she'd offered to buy Sarah's share and had secured a mortgage to pay her sister off. The money had been paid to Sarah that very morning.

Now, as Claire watched the birds flitting in and around the bird-feeder, she felt at peace. This lovely house was now all hers and it gave her an enormous sense of security.

Claire didn't ask much of life. She was born to be a carer, although her mother had pushed her caring nature to the limit. She found great fulfilment in her job and adored the sick children that she nursed every day in Crumlin Children's Hospital. Their courage inspired her and she longed to have children of her own. However, it seemed highly unlikely that would ever happen now. She was thirty-two, painfully shy, with not a boyfriend in sight.

She'd been in love only once in her life – with Jamie, a paediatric doctor in the hospital. They'd been working side by side for two years when he'd finally asked her for a date. Claire knew she wasn't a looker like some of the other nurses and female doctors, nor had she their outgoing personalities, but Jamie had seemingly seen past that and, despite her shyness, had come to know the girl underneath. He had a quiet and calm air about him and his dark brown eyes held a serious, honest look that she found most attractive.

Her mother had been dismayed when she'd started dating Jamie and was terrified that Claire would get married and leave her. She did everything in her power to break them up. Eventually Jamie, frustrated and tired of all the cancelled dates when Claire had to stay and baby-sit her mother, issued an ultimatum: "Either me or your mother." What could Claire do? To her mother's delight, she'd finished with him.

That was eighteen months ago and Jamie was now going out with a very pretty neonatal doctor called Hannah. Claire doubted that she would ever fall in love again.

She had gone inside to make a cup of coffee when her phone rang. It was Viv, who she had planned to meet for lunch. She hoped Viv wasn't calling to cancel their date.

"Hi, Claire! I was wondering if you'd mind if I brought Megan along to lunch? She's had rather a bad upset and could do with some company."

"Of course not. I'd be delighted for her to join us," Claire replied. She'd always admired Megan at school and had envied her and her seemingly perfect life. She wondered what could have upset her.

She'd known both girls from school although she hadn't been in their set. They were the 'It Girls' that everyone wanted to befriend. Claire admired them from afar and ached to be cool like them, though she knew she never would be. Her mother and Viv's were in the local ladies' club together and kind-hearted Mrs Connolly had often visited Claire's mother in her last year when she'd taken to her bed. She always came armed with some freshly baked scones or an apple tart.

"You and Viv should get together," said Mrs Connolly on one visit. "You were in the same class at the convent, if I remember rightly. I'll get Viv to give you a call."

Claire could see that Viv's mother felt sorry for her and was just being kind and never expected Viv to bother, so she was more than surprised when Viv rang a week later and asked to meet her for a coffee. Claire had agreed and to her amazement she and Viv had hit it off like a house on fire. Of course, Viv talked non-stop, as she'd always done, and didn't notice that Claire said very little. After a few such meetings, Claire lost her shyness. Viv had that effect on people and they had become good friends. Not like Viv and Megan of course – Claire wouldn't have expected that. She was just grateful to have Viv for a friend. They now met regularly for lunch whenever they were both free and she looked forward to these occasions more than Viv would ever know. And now today Megan would be joining them.

Claire was looking forward to the lunch and took extra care getting ready.

# Chapter 4

Megan woke with an unmerciful hangover and it took her a few minutes to surface and realise why. "Oh, God," she moaned, clutching her head as she remembered what had happened the evening before. Paul was gone and now she had to face everyone with the news that the wedding was off.

She struggled out of bed and into the kitchen where Viv handed her a glass of water and two Neurofen.

"Guess you'll need these," she said drily.

"Thanks," Megan replied gratefully.

"How are you feeling?"

"How do you think?" Megan grimaced.

"Come on! We're alive and the sun is shining," Viv declared brightly, handing her a cup of strong coffee. "Think of all the people who are worse off today."

Megan sighed. She didn't see how much worse off she could be. The man she loved had walked out of her life and shattered all her dreams. How much worse could it get?

"Go and have a shower and things will look brighter," Viv suggested.

Megan doubted it but did as she was told.

When Megan returned half an hour later she looked a bit better but not much.

"Okay, now go and get dolled up," Viv ordered. "We're meeting Claire O'Dowd for lunch at twelve thirty."

"Oh no!" Megan protested. "I couldn't possible make small talk today. I'd be terrible company."

"Look, the alternative is to sit here moping or to face your mother with the news. I think lunch with us is by far the better option!"

Megan had to agree with Viv there.

And so, come twelve thirty, Megan and Viv were greeting Claire in La Mère Zou on Stephen's Green.

Claire was shocked at Megan's appearance. Normally impeccably chic, she looked like she had just thrown on any old T-shirt and jeans and her face was make-up free. When Megan took off the sunglasses she was wearing, Claire could see that her eyes were puffy and bloodshot. It was so uncharacteristic of Megan that Claire felt great sympathy for her. Something awful must have happened to have her looking like this.

"I'm sorry to be gate-crashing your lunch," Megan apologised as she sat down.

"Not at all! I'm delighted you're here," Claire said shyly.

Viv spied the bottle of wine chilling in an ice bucket on the table.

"What's this? Are we celebrating something?"

Claire blushed. "Well, yes. The house is finally mine, as of this morning."

"I take it you convinced Sarah to sell you her share," Viv said to the smiling Claire. "Well done, you!"

Viv then explained the situation to Megan.

Claire's eyes were shining and she was obviously excited. "You're now looking at the sole owner of Shangri-la. I handed Sarah the cheque this morning."

"Congratulations!" Viv said, reaching over and giving her a kiss. "I'm delighted that it's all been sorted."

Megan smiled at her. "That's great news, Claire. Congratulations!"

The waiter poured the wine and they toasted Claire.

Megan began to feel a bit better. Viv was chattering away, as usual, and kept them amused with stories of a client she'd had the day before. They gave their order to the friendly waitress and were on their second glass of wine when Viv's phone rang.

"Excuse me, girls. It's the dickhead. I'll just take his call, if you don't mind." She grimaced, getting up to go outside.

"I gather she means it's her boyfriend, Fergal," Megan grinned. "Once she's started calling him 'dickhead', it's the beginning of the end."

"I thought it was pretty serious."

"You know Viv. Men never last very long with her. She gets bored so easily. I don't think Fergal will last much longer."

"It's never easy, is it? But you're lucky you've met the right man. Your wedding is very soon now, isn't it?"

Megan's face crumpled. "I'm afraid not. My fiancé walked out on me last night. Said he couldn't go through with it." Her voice wobbled as she said it and she bit her lip to stop the tears she felt threatening to fall.

"Oh, I'm so, so sorry," Claire said, visibly shocked. "I can't begin to imagine how you must be hurting."

Her voice held such sympathy that Megan was afraid she might cry, right here in public. "I'm devastated," she whispered.

Claire reached across for her hand. "You know, things happen for a reason and it's much better that it's happened now than after the wedding."

"Viv says that too but it doesn't make it any easier to take. The thought of facing everyone with the news is humiliating."

She looked downcast and Claire squeezed her hand. "To hell with what anyone thinks. You've done nothing wrong. These things just happen."

Megan felt soothed by her words. Claire was right, of course. She understood now why Viv was so fond of this girl. She had a genuine, caring way about her.

"My mother will go ballistic when she hears. I'm going there for lunch tomorrow. I'm dreading it."

"I'm sure your mum will be very sympathetic and supportive when she hears what's happened," Claire murmured.

"You don't know my mother!" Megan said with a grimace.

Viv bounced back in just then. "You won't believe this! The asshole has just cancelled our date for tomorrow. We were supposed to be going down to Powerscourt. I think it's time I gave him his walking papers."

Claire and Megan glanced at each other and grinned.

"What did I tell you?" Megan shrugged. "Poor guy didn't stand a chance with our Viv."

"It's time I deleted him," Viv remarked archly. "Men are truly a waste of time!"

"You can say that again!" Megan said vehemently.

"Please don't ever again let me date someone I meet in a pub," Viv begged them dramatically.

"That's a promise – but does this mean then that you're free to come with me to my mother's tomorrow?" Megan asked hopefully.

"I suppose so," Viv replied, shrugging. This was the last thing she wanted but she could see no way out.

Claire said nothing but smiled as they clinked glasses. It felt good to be with these girls. They were both so beautiful that she felt plain and frumpy beside them but they were really nice and she enjoyed their company.

They had another bottle of wine with their lunch and Megan actually forgot about Paul and her situation for a while as they chatted together.

Claire insisted on paying for it all as it was *her* celebration lunch.

Viv suggested they all go shopping afterwards. "Nothing like a bit of retail therapy to cheer a girl up," she announced as they left the restaurant, giggling like schoolgirls.

They had a fun afternoon. Firstly they crossed to the other side of the road to look at the art that graced the railings of Stephen's Green. It was lovely to chat to the artists about their work and Viv and Megan bought a small painting of a Georgian door for Claire.

"A good-luck charm for your very own house," Viv grinned as they handed it to her.

Claire blushed with pleasure and thanked them as she admired it.

Next they made their way down Grafton Street, popping in and out of the many fashion shops there. Megan was drowning her sorrows, Claire was celebrating her ownership of the house, and Viv – well, she was simply indulging her love of shopping. Laden down with bags, they finally stopped off for a drink in the Westbury before taking the Luas home to Dundrum.

Megan was very quiet and looking glum as they rode the tram home and Claire guessed she was thinking of Paul again.

She herself was very loath to say goodbye to the others after such a magical day. She didn't want it to end. "How about coming back to my house?" she suggested. "I have some prawns and smoked salmon and some nice white wine in the fridge." She looked at the other two hopefully.

Viv thought it was a great idea as she didn't fancy sitting in Megan's apartment all evening, trying to cheer her up.

"Why not?" she cried. "We'll help you christen your house, Claire. Wet the baby's head, as it were." She looked at Megan's despondent face. "What do you say, Meg?"

"Fine by me," Megan replied listlessly.

Viv breathed a sigh of relief. She wanted to keep Megan occupied and keep her mind off Paul and her situation. Tomorrow would be time enough for her to face the music.

Megan brightened up as they reminisced on their schooldays and soon she was feeling in better form. They had a great night and it was near midnight when Viv called a taxi.

As they were leaving, Megan suggested they all get together again soon.

"I'm really grateful to you for today," she said to Claire as they hugged goodnight.

"Good luck with your mother tomorrow," Claire whispered back.

Viv was delighted to see that her two friends had bonded so well and beamed happily as they waved Claire goodbye.

It was the best day Claire could remember and she went to bed glowing with happiness. She had a feeling that this was the start of a new life.

# Chapter 5

For the second day in a row Megan woke with a hangover but Viv was not there to hold her hand this time. After a long shower and a couple of cups of strong black coffee she sat down to take stock of her life.

Viv and Claire had been so positive about her situation last evening and she wished she could believe them but it was easier said than done.

"It would be just awful if you'd gone ahead with the wedding and *then* Paul decided at the very last minute that he wanted out," Claire had said.

She'd had a point.

"Or worse still, if he'd left you at the altar like Big did to Carrie in *Sex and the City*," Viv had chipped in. She and Megan had adored that show in their teens and still watched reruns whenever they were on TV.

Megan had shuddered. "Oh God, I'll never forget that scene. I cried for poor Carrie."

"Exactly! And we might have been crying at the altar

with poor Megan if Paul hadn't pulled out now," Viv had added dramatically.

"Lord forbid!" Megan had cried. The thought had horrified her.

Claire had taken her hand and said softly, "Honestly, Megan, I know you're hurting and feeling let down but it would have been so much worse if Paul had gone ahead with the wedding and, maybe in a year or two, when you were pregnant or even with a small baby, he decided he wanted out. Think about it."

Megan felt a lump come in her throat. Claire was so gentle and caring, yet sensible and pragmatic.

Yes, she would now have to cancel all the wedding arrangements she'd made but it wasn't the end of the world. The first hurdle was facing her mother at lunch and breaking the news. Thank God Viv was able to come along with her. She couldn't have faced the music on her own.

Viv took an age to choose what she should wear to the lunch. She knew Megan's mother and just how critical she could be. She was dreading the lunch almost as much as Megan but knew she had no choice but to go as moral support for her friend. Viv had no doubt that Mrs Ross would behave like the drama queen she'd always been, especially when Megan dropped her bombshell about the wedding. Viv was not looking forward to the meeting but resigned herself for Megan's sake.

She remembered how embarrassed Megan used to be when her mother would turn up to parent-teacher meetings dressed in a mini-skirt and tight top, shaking her Farah Fawcett locks as she flirted with the male teachers. Viv hadn't met her for years but suspected, from what Megan said, that her mother hadn't changed much.

By eleven thirty, full of apprehension, she was ready and waiting for Megan to pick her up.

It was just before noon when Megan and Viv drove up the driveway of the palatial house in Killiney.

Viv let out a low whistle. "My, that's some mansion!" she said in awe, taking in the massive house and large grounds.

"Oh, yes," Megan replied, her voice bitter. "Daphne's third husband left it to her."

It had always amazed Viv to hear Megan speak of her mother as 'Daphne'. She couldn't imagine calling her own mum by her first name but Megan had done this for as long as Viv had known her.

"She doesn't want people to know she has a thirteen-year-old daughter," Megan had explained, way back when they were in first year and Viv had questioned her about it.

"Why not?" the curious Viv had asked.

"Because she tells people she's twenty-five," Megan had explained patiently.

"Boy, that's weird," Viv had remarked.

"That's how she is," Megan had replied resignedly.

Viv had felt very sorry for her and grateful for her own normal parents.

"Hellloooo, my darlings!" said Daphne as she came to greet them, glass of champagne in hand. She air-kissed each of them. "How nice to see you again, Viv." She smiled, looking her up and down critically. It was obvious she did not like what she saw.

Daphne was wearing a very short white dress which showed off her toned, tanned legs. Her long blonde hair – Viv was sure they were extensions – lay in cascading waves down her back as she walked ahead of them on teetering gold platform heels. From the back she looked more like a twenty-something girl than a woman in her mid-fifties.

"You'll join me in an aperitif, darlings," she cooed as she led them out through the French doors to a beautiful terrace overlooking a magnificent garden and beyond that the sea. "Champagne okay?"

"What a lovely house, Mrs Ross," Viv remarked as she sank into a luxurious white armchair.

"Do call me Daphne, dear. Mrs Ross sounds so matronly. Besides, I haven't been Mrs Ross for years."

"Eh, sorry," Viv muttered as she accepted the proffered glass.

"Cheers, darlings!" Daphne raised her glass to them. "Now what's the news?"

"Well, I have some bad news, I'm afraid," Megan started, her voice wavering.

"Oh, for God's sake, do you have to spoil my day with bad news? Surely you have some good news or gossip?"

Megan looked at Viv. Uh-oh, the shit's about to hit the fan, Viv thought.

"I'm afraid my wedding is off, Daphne. Paul has left me." Megan's voice was barely a whisper.

Daphne's hand fluttered to her face, which was devoid of expression due to the amount of Botox there, but Viv could see the anger blazing in her eyes.

"Is this a joke, Megan? If so, it's not very funny."

"I'm serious. Paul says he can't go through with it."

Megan kept her eyes lowered, not wanting to meet her mother's glare.

"That's ridiculous! How could you do this to me? You *have* to go through with it."

"Mother, you're not listening. I have no say in the matter. Paul is the one who wants out."

Daphne was so distraught that she didn't even correct her daughter for calling her mother.

"You simply cannot let him away with this. He *has* to go ahead with it. It's much too late to cancel all the arrangements now. You must force him to marry you."

Megan sighed and looked helplessly at Viv.

"Of course she can't force him to marry her if he doesn't want to," Viv snapped, disgusted at the suggestion and feeling bad for Megan.

"Oh my God! The embarrassment of it. How will I face all my friends? And I've already started dieting for the big day."

Viv looked at her in disbelief. Thinner than Daphne it was not possible to be. Where was she expecting to lose weight? Her fingers? Her toes? The only remotely visible fat was on her lips and boobs and that was due to fillers and silicone. You couldn't lose weight off those, could you?

"You don't need to diet," Megan said, vocalising what Viv had been thinking.

"I do if I want to fit into my rig-out. You *do* remember that I've bought a Prada suit and Philip Treacy hat already, Megan?"

"Yes," Megan mumbled almost apologetically.

Viv could not take it any longer. What kind of a mother was this who had no thought for her daughter's plight whatsoever? All Daphne could think about was her own disappointment.

"I think you might show some concern for Megan, Mrs Ross." She was damned if she was going to call her Daphne now and she didn't give a hoot what her new name was either. "She's been very hurt by all this."

"No doubt it's her own fault," Daphne declared indignantly, glaring at her daughter. "She never could hold on to a man. Men just don't jump ship like that for no reason. There's obviously something wrong with you, Megan."

Viv saw the hurt in Megan's eyes and could take no more. "Come on, Meggie. Let's get out of here. Let's go home," she said, taking her friend's arm firmly.

Megan, her eyes filling with tears, went with her gratefully and they left without another word.

"I expect you to get that wedding back on track," was Daphne's parting shot.

Viv was trembling with fury as she got behind the wheel and instructed Megan, who was crying now, to hand her the keys. Once out of the gate, she put her foot down on the pedal and raced away from Killiney as fast as she possibly could. She drove to Dalkey where she parked on Sorrento Road. Megan's tears had subsided and Viv put her arm around her.

"Pay no attention to her or what she said," she advised her friend gently. "I'm sorry to have to say this but she's a fecking selfish cow."

She said it so vehemently that Megan gave a small smile.

Viv was tempted to say more but she bit her tongue. Daphne was Megan's mother after all and she didn't want to push it.

"Come on. Let's forget all about her and enjoy the rest of the day."

Viv parked the car and they walked arm in arm to Finnegan's Pub. As luck would have it, a young couple were vacating a table outside and the girls pounced on it.

After they'd given their order Megan was very quiet but Viv kept up a monologue until their drinks and food arrived. To Viv's satisfaction, Megan tucked in with gusto, and Viv made sure to keep her glass topped up. By the end of the meal Megan was in better spirits.

"I knew it would be a disaster," she admitted glumly. "I told you she'd go ballistic."

"Well, if she was a normal mother, she would have been more concerned about you."

"She never has been, I suppose," Megan said sadly. "I always was a nuisance to her."

"Silly cow!"

"Maybe she's right and there *is* something wrong with me. I'm just not lovable."

"Bullshit!" Viv exclaimed angrily, furious with Daphne for demeaning her daughter in that way.

Viv thought of her own mother and realised just how lucky she was. Every girl needed a loving mother. Poor Megan didn't have that.

After lunch they went for a long walk down Dun Laoghaire pier and then back to Megan's apartment to watch the DVD of the last series of *Downton Abbey* which neither of them had seen.

Viv's phone rang. It was Claire.

"Just wondering how the lunch went today. I hope Megan's mother took the news okay?"

"Huh! You must be joking! We left after five minutes and went to Finnegan's for lunch."

"That bad, huh? Poor Megan. Tell her I'm sorry."

"Tell her yourself. She's here beside me." She handed over the phone.

"I was hoping it all went well with your mother today," Claire said.

"I'm afraid not," Megan replied. She paused. "Look, we're going to order in an Indian meal later. Why don't you come over and join us? You can help Viv cheer me up."

"I'd like that, thanks. Give me your address."

Megan was pleased that she'd thought to ask Claire over. She wanted to keep her mind off Paul and her mother's reaction, so the more company she had the better. If she could just get through this weekend then tomorrow she could immerse herself in work and try and move past this awful time.

"What a lovely apartment!" Claire exclaimed when she arrived and saw the spacious open-plan design and the minimalist décor. It was exactly what she would have imagined Megan's place to be. Cool and classy.

"Yes, I love it, but I can't stay here much longer. This place holds too many memories for me," Megan admitted wistfully.

"I can imagine," Claire said sympathetically. "Where will you go? Back to live with your mother?"

Viv laughed derisively. "I don't think so."

Claire looked taken aback. "Was it really that bad?"

"It was a disaster," Megan said. "She went ballistic when I told her, as I guessed she would."

"She was downright nasty," Viv commented.

Claire also remembered Mrs Ross from their schooldays. She was always very glamorous and a little intimidating. Her mother had, of course, detested Megan's mother, declaring her tacky and outrageous. Claire had secretly wished her mother had some of Mrs Ross's dash and verve but it now appeared she wasn't all that great of a mother.

"So where will you go?" Claire asked as Megan poured a glass of chardonnay for her.

"I don't honestly know," Megan replied. "There's no point selling in this depressed market so I'll probably rent it out and get a studio for myself or maybe share with someone."

"I've been considering looking for two people to share my house with me." Claire said. "Would you be interested?"

"I certainly would. I don't want to move from Dundrum. I'd definitely be interested, Claire."

"Hey, I'll be looking to move out of my parents' soon," Viv burst out excitedly. "Maybe I could share with you guys too."

"Are you serious?" Claire exclaimed, unable to believe her good luck.

"Yeah. It's a great idea! Much better than sharing with a stranger," Viv pointed out. "Maybe someone you couldn't stand."

"Or maybe a house full of twenty-year-old bimbos." Megan shuddered.

"What do you say, Claire?" Viv asked anxiously. "Of course it would depend on the rent you'd be asking."

"Oh, it would be very reasonable," Claire assured her. She had been apprehensive about taking strangers in so this seemed like a perfect solution.

"We'd insist on paying you the going rate, wouldn't we, Viv?" said Megan.

"Of course," Viv replied, hoping it wouldn't be too much.

While waiting for their meal to be delivered, Megan rang her father in Spain to give him the bad news about her wedding. He now lived near Estepona with his second wife, Betsy, a lovely woman with whom he was very happy. Megan loved her too.

"Hello, Princess, how are you?" he greeted her warmly.

"Hi, Dad, has Daphne been on to you?" Megan suspected that Daphne would have been on to him right away, complaining about his wayward daughter. Funny, but whenever she did something right she was her mother's daughter, when she did something wrong she was his!

"No, sweetheart, what's her problem now?" he asked wearily. His ex-wife only rang when she had a problem.

"Well, Paul has called the wedding off," she told him, a lump in her throat.

"Oh my God, you poor darling! Why did he do that? Are you all right? Do you want me to come home?"

"No, Dad. I'm okay. He says he can't go through with it. He just walked out."

"I'll bloody kill him. What a stupid guy! He wasn't good enough for you anyway. Look, love, I can be on the next flight if you need me."

She felt tears come to her eyes at the kindness in his voice. She tried to smother them so as not to upset him. She didn't want him to know how devastated she really was.

"No, Dad. I'm fine. I'm with friends now."

"Thank goodness for that. Do you want to come over here for a week? It might do you good."

"I can't at the moment. Too busy at work but maybe I'll come for a visit later."

"That would be great. Hang on a minute."

She heard him say something to his wife, obviously telling her the bad news.

"Princess, you take care. Now Betsy wants a word with you."

Her stepmother was upset for her and very sympathetic.

Their reaction was so loving and so different to Daphne's that when Megan hung up she burst into tears. She really missed her father right now.

Viv and Claire did their best to comfort her but she was inconsolable.

# Chapter 6

The following morning, in the store, Viv welcomed her first client, a woman who had to be the biggest gossip in Dublin 14. She was certainly in her sixties but spent a large part of her husband's fortune in an effort to look twenty-five years younger. She'd had so many facelifts that her eyes were now like slits which didn't go well with her trout-pout.

"Good morning, Mrs Quirke. And how are you today?" Viv sounded more cheerful than she felt. The weekend had taken more out of her than she'd anticipated.

"I'm very well, thank you, Vivienne." Then she asked, her eyes glittering, "Did you hear the latest news?"

Oh, now she's going to impart some nugget of unimportant information, Viv thought irritably, not in the mood for this on a Monday morning.

"Megan Ross's wedding is off. Can you believe it? Poor Daphne is distraught. She thought she'd finally got Megan married and off her hands – and *poof!* Just like that, it's been cancelled." Mrs Quirke was relishing imparting this bit of news and watched for Viv's reaction.

Viv wouldn't give her that satisfaction. She yawned as if bored.

"Oh, really? I imagine Megan could have any man she wanted. She probably changed her mind."

"Oh, I don't think so. Poor Daphne was very upset when she called me. I rather think it was the guy who called it quits."

"Oh, did Mrs Ross say so?" Viv was furious with this old bag but kept her cool.

"She's Mrs O'Mara now, not Ross. No, she didn't say so in so many words."

"Well, then. You've obviously got it wrong."

Mrs Quirke felt like the wind had been taken out of her sails. "Oh, of course – you were friends with Megan, weren't you?"

"Yes. We're still friends as a matter of fact."

"Oh, I see. You'd probably know so." Mrs Quirke looked quite crestfallen.

"Now what can I do for you today?" Viv asked her through gritted teeth.

"I'm looking for some cruise-wear for my annual trip to Marbella."

"Didn't you just buy cruise-wear last season?"

"Yes, that was for a cruise, but I couldn't possibly wear that again. People might have seen it then. We live in a very close circle, you know," she added smugly.

Viv felt like telling her that it wouldn't matter a damn what she wore but, ever the professional, she did as she was asked. Mrs Quirke wanted to see low-cut swimsuits and dresses – someone had obviously told her she had a nice cleavage – and she insisted that she wanted the most coveted label of the year. In normal circumstances Viv would have tried to convince the client that she would look better covered up but she was still angry with the woman's gossiping. Her job was to sell clothes and, if the silly cow wanted them low-cut, so be it.

Viv shook her head in disbelief when her client had left, having spent almost two thousand Euros. Some people had more money than sense.

Megan's day wasn't much better. She'd decided the best thing was to tell people straight away that the wedding was off. That way she wouldn't have to fend off the speculation and rumours, should they hear about it from someone else. To her surprise her colleagues in the office were mostly very sympathetic, despite their shock. She didn't go into details but kept up a brave front, smiling and acting normally so nobody could see the pain she was going through. She saw a couple of the younger girls look at her pityingly but her smile became even brighter as she returned their glances. She knew they were all dying to know what had happened but they wouldn't hear it from her.

She almost cracked after the usual Monday morning conference when the managing director pulled her aside and expressed his support.

"We're all sorry to hear about the cancellation of your wedding, Megan, but, to be honest, we think you're doing the right thing."

They had obviously discussed it amongst themselves and thought she was the one who had broken it off.

She was further taken aback when Simon, the other senior editor, stopped into her office.

"Are you okay?" he asked.

"Just about," she replied, giving him a wan smile.

"I know it probably doesn't feel like it right now, Megan, but you've had a lucky escape. I never thought Paul was right for you. I'm just glad you found out in time."

"No, it doesn't feel like it, Simon." She grimaced.

"If you need a shoulder . . . you know I'm right next door."

She nodded, remembering how he'd cried on her shoulder when his wife, Miriam, had walked out on him four years previously. "Thanks, I may take you up on that."

Secretly, Simon thought Paul was a total waster and that Megan deserved much better but he refrained from saying so.

Megan let out a huge sigh after he'd left. "Stay calm," she told herself. "Big deep breaths."

Shaking, she had just sat down at her desk when there was another knock on her door. It was her PA, Emily, bearing a welcome cup of coffee accompanied by her favourite cake, a coffee cream-slice.

"I thought you might need this," Emily said, placing it on the desk.

Megan was touched. The young girl had obviously gone out specially for the cake.

"Thank you, Emily. That's very kind of you." Megan felt a lump in her throat.

"Shall I hold all calls this morning?" Emily enquired, her voice gentle, kindness in her eyes. She was very fond of Megan and was feeling bad for her.

"Please. I have a lot of calls to make. Things to be cancelled." She grimaced.

"I can imagine. Well, if you need me to help, just say so."

"Thanks, I will."

"I hope you don't mind my saying so, Megan," Emily said shyly, "but I think it's for the best." She smiled as she left the office.

Megan sat deep in thought as she drank the coffee, relishing the cream-slice. It was weird but every single person, with the exception of her mother, had said that it was for the best. They'd all met Paul quite a few times over the years and now they were telling her they were glad she wasn't marrying him. Did they see something in him that she hadn't? It was very strange. Strange too that they all assumed she'd been the one to call off the wedding.

Hmmm, she thought, finishing the last delicious bite of the cake. Unfortunately, whatever they thought, it didn't ease the pain in her heart. With a big sigh she settled down to make those calls. She wasn't looking forward to it.

Claire had a spring in her step that morning. Her colleagues in the hospital noticed it and even one of the kids she cared for, Amy, a precocious nine-year-old girl who was suffering from leukaemia, remarked, "I think you have a new boyfriend, Claire." She giggled. "Have you?"

"Why do you say that?" Claire asked, puzzled.

"Because your eyes are smiling all the time and your walk is happy."

Claire threw her head back, laughing.

"You do . . . you do have a new boyfriend! *Claire has a boyfriend, Claire has a boyfriend!*" Amy sang, clapping her hands. "*Claire's getting married, Claire's getting married!*" she cried, jumping up and down.

The other kids in the ward took up the chant.

Just then Jamie, Claire's ex, walked into the ward. He grinned as he took in the situation.

"Aha, so that's why you're looking so happy," he greeted her, smiling broadly.

She blushed a bright red and couldn't answer. He wasn't to know she still carried a torch for him and that she hadn't even been on a date in months. She was about to deny it but he cut her short.

"Congratulations! I'm very happy for you," he said warmly, taking her hands in his.

She blushed an even deeper shade of crimson What could she say?

"Thank you, Jamie," she replied, finally finding her voice. She had *some* pride. She wasn't going to say that no, she didn't even have a boyfriend. God, it was embarrassing!

All that afternoon her mind was on the possibility of having Viv and Megan coming to live with her. She would need to redecorate of course as the house was so shabby. Luckily she had quite a bit of money saved. After all, she'd had nothing to spend it on, all those years that she'd been tied to her mother. Now her mind was alive with ideas but first she'd consult with Viv and Megan. After all, it would be their home too.

By four that evening Megan had more or less cancelled her complete wedding. It had taken her so long to arrange everything and now, in the blink of an eye, it was all over. To her amazement, most of the companies had been happy to refund her deposit. Even the travel agent was happy to cancel the honeymoon to Cyprus but, of course, it was in his own interest as she used him for all their business travel.

The last call was the one she'd been dreading. It was to cancel her dream wedding-dress. She had spent weeks visiting all the bridal boutiques in Dublin and the moment she'd spotted the dress in Bridal Heaven, she knew it was *the* one. The owner, Alison, had been so nice and now Megan had to ring with the news that she wouldn't be needing the dress after all.

"I am so sorry, my dear," Alison said. "You must be very disappointed."

She didn't ask any awkward questions, thank God. She was so nice that Megan almost burst into tears. "I feel really bad about this," she apologised.

"Don't fret about it, dear. It happens all the time. So much so that they don't start on wedding-dresses till six weeks before the big day. So it's no problem. I'll refund your deposit."

Megan was taken aback. It was €200 after all. "Oh no, I don't expect you to do that. After all, you've lost a sale."

"Nonsense, it's bad enough for you having to cancel your wedding without being out of pocket too."

"Everyone has been so nice about this," Megan told her in a wobbly voice. "I didn't expect that."

"Well, dear, we expect you'll be planning another wedding in the future and hopefully you'll remember us then."

"Of course," Megan replied, "and thank you so much for everything."

Megan hung up. "No way," she murmured to herself. There would not be another wedding for her because she would never let herself fall in love again.

Viv was in foul humour when her father picked her up that evening.

"What's the matter, pet?" he asked, ruffling her hair as he always did. "Had a bad day?"

"The worst kind, Pops. Some of these oul' ones drive me nuts."

"Well, we all have days like that unfortunately. Tomorrow will be better."

"How was your day?" Mrs Connolly asked her husband as she dished up the dinner.

"Mine was fine but Vivienne didn't have such a good one."

"Oh?" Mrs Connolly looked at her daughter keenly.

"Well, it's not just the job," Viv explained. "Megan's wedding is off. Paul walked out on her on Friday. Said he couldn't go through with it."

Her mother stood, plates mid-air, a look of concern on her face.

"Oh, poor Megan! What an awful thing to happen. The poor darling! I was wondering why you stayed with her over the weekend. I assumed Paul was away. How's she coping?"

"Well, you can imagine. Still, in a way I'm relieved. I think he would have made a lousy husband and father but I hate to see her hurt."

"The poor dear!" her father chimed in.

"Well, the good news is that I'll be moving out soon. Megan and I are going to move in with Claire O'Dowd."

You could have heard a pin drop as her parents stared at her open-mouthed.

"Are you serious?" her father asked.

"Yes. The house is Claire's now. She bought out her sister Sarah's share. It's all arranged."

"Well, I *am* glad for Claire and it will be good for Megan too but we'll miss you terribly." Her mother looked

48

fondly at her as she took her place at the table.

"I guess it is time for you to move out and stand on your own two feet," her father said. "However, I would naturally prefer if you were moving into your own house with your own husband, pet."

"Fat chance!" Viv cried as she tucked into her mother's delicious steak and onions.

She was going to miss these dinners but he was right. It was time she became independent. Her life would change but she was excited about what the future would bring.

# Chapter 7

Somehow Megan managed to get through the rest of the week. She was touched by all the calls and good wishes she received from her many friends who had heard the news. She was pleased and surprised that many of Paul's friends called her to say how sorry they were and what an asshole he was. The only negative call she got was from her mother, demanding to know whether she'd come to her senses and tried to win Paul back. They had a dreadful row and Daphne ordered her not to contact her again, unless it was to tell her the wedding was back on. Megan hung up on her. She really didn't need this right now.

She closed down her computer on Friday evening, glad that the week was over. She had arranged to meet Viv and Claire after work and she was looking forward to it. She didn't have to keep up a pretence with them. They had decided to meet in Walsh's pub as they wanted somewhere they could hear themselves talk and on Friday evenings that was quite a feat in Dublin pubs. Walsh's was a traditional pub with a country feel to it. It had a main bar mostly frequented by older men and a large lounge area for the younger crowd – so plenty of room to breathe there.

They were both there before her and had a gin and tonic waiting for her on the table. As she sipped it, she could feel the tension leaving her and she started to relax.

"Wow, what a week!" she exclaimed. "I certainly don't want to go through one like that again."

She then told Claire all that had happened that week. Viv had heard it all as they'd been talking every day on the phone.

"I'm so surprised by how kind everyone has been," Megan told them.

"I'm not. I've found that people are genuinely nice and intrinsically kind," Claire observed.

"Huh! You obviously don't have to deal with some of the morons I meet in my work," Viv griped.

The other two laughed at her scowling look.

"Well, I suppose I meet a different kind of person in my work," Claire admitted. "I'm constantly amazed by the courage and acceptance of the parents of sick children, not to mention the kids themselves."

Viv felt suitably humbled. "I'm sorry. You do such fantastic work while I just pander to silly spoilt women. Forgive me – I've just had a bad week."

"Okay, let's put the week behind us and concentrate on this weekend," said Megan. "For starters, where are we going to eat tonight?"

"I quite fancy The Loop for some tapas," Viv replied. "What do you think, girls? Any other ideas?"

"No, that's perfect for me," said Megan. "How about you, Claire?"

"I've never been but it sounds good."

"Great, I'll call and reserve a table," Viv said, taking out her phone.

Claire enjoyed the tapas as she savoured the exciting unknown flavours and sipped a wonderful Ribera del Duero wine. She couldn't help but think how annoyed her mother would be to see her enjoying herself like this. Too bad – her mother wasn't here any more and Claire felt exhilarated by this new-found freedom.

"I'm planning on redecorating the house and I'd appreciate your help," she said as she nibbled on a slice of delicious tortilla. "I'm not very good at that kind of thing."

"Well, I'm great at fashion but I think Megan would be much better at interior decorating than me," said Viv.

Megan was pleased at the compliment. "I'd be delighted to help, if I can."

"That would be great. Maybe you could come to dinner tomorrow evening and could advise me. You too, Viv, of course."

"Oh, damn, I've agreed to meet Fergal," Viv said dismally, disappointed that she couldn't go.

"Oh, have you not deleted him yet?" Megan grinned.

Viv threw her a withering look. "Not yet."

"Well, I'm free, Claire," Megan said, "and I'd love to come. It's amazing how much free time I have now that Paul's not around." She looked glum as she spoke.

"Perhaps I could get away early from Fergal," Viv suggested.

"Great if you can," said Claire.

"Eh, have you thought about how much our rent will be?" Viv asked then.

Claire blushed, embarrassed. "I honestly don't know. I was kind of thinking €60 a week each. What do you think? Is that too much?"

"Good heavens, no, that's too low," Megan said, earning herself a kick from Viv under the table. "I've checked on Daft.ie and the going rate is around €90 to €100 a week."

Viv looked at her in alarm. €60 sounded just fine to her. Megan stared her down.

"I'd be very happy to let you have it for €60. I'm not doing it only for commercial reasons, though your money will help with the mortgage payments, of course. The house is much too big for one person and I'm just pleased that I have two friends sharing instead of strangers. It will be fun."

"Well, if you're sure," Viv said quickly.

"Well then, we'll split the electricity and cable bills three ways," Megan insisted.

"Very well. Is that okay with you, Viv?" Claire asked nervously, biting her lip.

"That sounds fair to me."

"It's a deal!"

They clinked glasses, each of them wondering what the future would bring.


Claire was up at seven thirty the following morning, googling recipes to try and decide what she would cook for Megan that evening. She loved cooking but wanted to make a special effort so she pored over the recipes until she found what she wanted. Then armed with a list she headed off to the shops to make her purchases. She spent the day happily in the kitchen and when all was ready she surveyed the dining room with some satisfaction. She had arranged fresh flowers in every room and the scent of sweet-pea and freesia filled the air.

Megan arrived with a bottle of white Burgundy that Claire suspected was very expensive. She admired the table setting and Claire blushed with pleasure as she opened a bottle of chardonnay and poured two glasses for them. It was such a nice evening that they took their drinks out to the garden and Claire brought out some olives and nibbles she'd prepared.

"It's so peaceful here," Megan sighed as she relaxed in the comfortable garden swing seat. "You know when you walk into a place and it feels just right? That's how I feel about this house."

Claire blushed with pleasure again. She knew exactly what Megan meant. She watched enough of those property programmes on TV. People always commented that a place felt right, or not, as the case might be.

"I felt like that about the apartment too, the first time I walked into it. I'd looked at lots of places but the minute I walked in there I knew it was the one. Strange, isn't it?"

"You'll miss it, I suppose," Claire said gently.

"Yes, but I'm glad to be moving. Too many memories there and I've found a tenant already. A guy I work with."

"That's great. When do you want to move in here?"

"Whenever you say. I'm ready."

Megan's phone beeped just then and she saw it was a text from Viv.

**'Bored stiff here. Watching bloody football. Wish I was there with you two xx'**

Megan laughed. "It looks like Viv is not enjoying herself

much. I have a feeling she'll turn up here yet."

"I made enough for three, just in case," Claire said.

"I never realised this house was so big," Megan exclaimed as Claire showed her round.

Claire explained what she was planning to do with it.

"That way we'll each have our own en-suite. What do you think?" she asked Megan.

"That would be fabulous. Three women sharing one bathroom does not for harmony make."

Claire laughed. "That's what I figured. I'm going to have the whole house painted so you and Viv can pick whatever colours you'd like for your bedrooms."

"Great!"

Megan's phone beeped again. Another text from Viv. **'I'm outta here. Can't stand him another minute. Can Claire feed me?'**

Megan showed the text to Claire.

"Tell her there's more than enough for us all," Claire laughed.

Viv breezed in ten minutes later. "That's it! It's over! I've finished with him. I will not waste another minute of my life on that plonker."

"I figured that was coming. So now we're all single, girls."

"Let's keep it that way," Viv declared.

Claire poured her a glass of wine as Megan explained what Claire was thinking of doing with the bedrooms.

"Mmmm . . ." Viv said when she heard. "I have so many clothes, maybe it would be better to turn the fourth bedroom into a walk-in closet, rather than an en-suite. I can always use the main bathroom as you two won't be using it."

"That makes sense," Megan agreed, "otherwise your wardrobe will submerge the rest of the house."

"Smartass!" Viv retorted, swiping at her playfully.

Claire laughed, thinking it was all coming together famously.

The evening was a huge success. Claire had outdone herself.

"Gosh, this is fabulous, Claire," Viv exclaimed. "You should go on *Come Dine with Me.* And to think I was worried about leaving my mother's home-cooked meals. This is gourmet food by comparison."

"Now, Viv," Megan scolded, "we will all have to take turns in cooking. We can't expect Claire to do it all the time."

"You might change your mind when you taste my food," Viv laughed.

"Whatever, fair is fair," Megan insisted.

"I don't mind doing it. I love cooking," Claire chimed in, anxious to keep the peace.

"I can see I'll have to take you under my wing, otherwise Viv will have you babying her like her mother has always done. This move is so she learns to stand on her own two feet. Right, Viv?"

"Yes, sir!" Viv saluted.

"I'm serious. We'll all have to pull our weight here. Otherwise it won't work."

"You're as bossy as a sergeant major," Viv complained, but she knew Megan was right. It was time she cut the umbilical cord and grew up.

# Chapter 8

The next few weeks flew by as Claire worked furiously to get the house ready for her new housemates. Luckily, she had no problem securing workmen to ring the changes. With so many of them unemployed due to the building cutbacks, they were happy to get the work.

The three girls had gone shopping to choose the paint and paper for the bedrooms and it was all coming together nicely.

"Gosh, I wish I had enough clothes to warrant a dressing-room," Claire remarked as Viv's walk-in closet took shape.

"Well, I'm hoping to change that. You absolutely have to start being adventurous with clothes and dump all those tracksuits and leggings. I plan to do a make-over on you soon." Viv despaired of Claire's dress sense but had resisted saying anything, knowing how sensitive her friend was. She was itching to do something about it.

Claire looked worried.

Megan, who knew Viv's opinion of Claire's style, tried to reassure Claire.

"I don't have a lot of clothes either," she confided. It was true. Her wardrobe was carefully colour-coordinated so, although she always looked extremely chic, she didn't actually have all that many clothes and what she had was expensive and high quality.

Megan was as good as any interior decorator and threw herself wholeheartedly into the project. In truth, she needed to keep herself occupied to avoid thinking of Paul and what-might-have-been. But when she returned to the apartment each night she couldn't escape her thoughts and often cried herself to sleep.

Viv had a new boyfriend so she wasn't available to help. She'd met him in a pub – where else? – and was busy with him almost every night and at weekends.

"Poor Viv, will she never learn? She's always like this when she meets a new guy, always hopeful he's *the one,*" Megan explained to Claire with a resigned air. "They live in each other's ear for about a month and then reality kicks in." She shook her head and her look said she'd been down this road many times before.

Claire felt sorry for Viv.

Megan spent every evening and the following weekend helping Claire and, when they'd finally finished, they went from room to room surveying their work. Claire had to admit it did look fabulous. It looked like something out of one of those house make-over programmes she loved. She was more than happy with the result.

Viv had joined them for once and Claire opened a bottle of Sancerre to celebrate.

It was amazing how different the three bedrooms were. Each matched the occupant's personality exactly, Claire mused, as she went through each one again after the girls had gone. Her own one was done in a blue-and-white Laura Ashley style, pretty and traditional – and safe, she thought to herself ruefully, but it suited her perfectly.

She loved the colour scheme that Megan had chosen for her room. It was aquamarine and slate grey and was sophisticated and modern. It was all simple lines and minimalistic, no clutter. It looked like something from an interiors magazine and was very classy, yet Claire secretly preferred her own room.

As for Viv's! It was zany and over the top – just as she was. Bright neon colours – yellow and lime-green – side by side with blackest-black bedlinen and ceiling. A large modern-art print covered most of one wall. The room would not have been to Claire's taste but Viv thought it was fabulous. So be it! She'd paid for it and she was the one who had to sleep in it.

They were all so different. Claire worried for a moment that their personalities might clash when they were all under the one roof. She sincerely hoped not. They say opposites attract and complement each other, she assured herself. She crossed her fingers and hoped that was true.

She was happy as she sat in the living room later but suddenly, looking around the room, she thought how old-fashioned it was in comparison to the upstairs of the house. That's the problem, isn't it, she thought, once you start on one room the others all look shabby in comparison. She remembered a lady, in one of those programmes where they made over only one room, saying, "Now I'll have to do all the rest of the house." Claire now knew why. She was feeling exhilarated and happy and, in a spur-of-the-moment decision, decided to throw caution to the winds and do the living room too. Why not? She felt like she had finally thrown off the shackles of her domineering mother and broken free. She had just one week to complete it as the girls would be moving in the following weekend.

Megan started to pack for the move. She was not a hoarder and set about it calmly and efficiently. She had ordered a set of packing boxes online and printed off labels to identify the contents of each box. She commenced methodically to fill the boxes and stacked them neatly in the guest bedroom. By Friday evening she was all set and, with her clothes the last things to be packed, she was ready for the move on Saturday morning.

Viv called by after work and was amazed to see the boxes neatly lined up, ready to go.

"My God, Megan, you're so organised," she exclaimed.

"Well, we are moving in tomorrow. Are you packed?"

"Eh, not really," Viv muttered. "I'll just throw my stuff into black bags tomorrow." She looked away, embarrassed.

"God, Viv, I don't know how you can live like that!" Megan shuddered.

"Well, I've been seeing Alan almost every night. I didn't have a lot of time to pack."

"How's it going with Alan?"

"Okay, but he's getting bloody possessive. I told him I wouldn't be available this weekend and he threw a strop." She grimaced and twirled a curl around her finger.

Megan knew that gesture meant her friend was stressed.

"For God's sake, Viv, that's the last thing you need," she said irritably.

"I know." Viv looked downcast.

"Come on, let's have a last drink here. I love this place but there are too many memories of Paul here."

She still could not manage to say his name without a lump coming to her throat. She opened a bottle of red wine and poured them a glass each.

"Have you heard anything from him?"

"Not a word," Megan said sadly as she handed Viv her glass. "I thought he might have contacted me, but not a word."

"Well, here's to closure and new beginnings!" Viv raised her glass.

"To new beginnings," Megan responded, her heart heavy.

At that moment, Claire was surveying the finished living room and she couldn't believe it was the same room it had been a week previously. She had decided on a coffee-and-cream colour scheme and knew she'd chosen well. It was elegant and chic and she loved it. She hoped the girls would love it too but, if they didn't, well . . . it was *her* house after all. Just saying that gave her a thrill.

Megan arrived at Claire's door at nine the next morning with the first of her boxes. She was astounded when Claire showed her into the living room.

"Oh my God! It's fabulous! When did you decide to do it?"

"Well, the upstairs was so nice that this room looked shabby by comparison so I felt I just had to do it. Do you really like it?"

"I *lovvvve* it. It's so . . . chic."

"Well, I learnt a lot from you." Claire was pleased that Megan approved. She could tell she genuinely liked it and that she wasn't just being kind.

"I love the colour scheme. It's so relaxing. It's perfect."

Claire helped Megan in with her boxes, impressed with how everything was packed and labelled. They carried the boxes up to Megan's room and had just finished when Viv rang.

"Hi, Meggie. Will you tell Claire that I'm afraid I won't get over till this afternoon?"

"Why not?"

"Well, Alan rang and wants to meet me urgently for lunch. I don't know what the problem is."

"Oh, for God's sake, Viv, we agreed we'd move in today." Megan was exasperated. "Claire's expecting you."

"I know. Put her on to me and I'll talk to her."

Megan handed the phone over and Viv apologised to Claire, promising to be there by three o'clock.

"It's okay, Viv, I understand. See you this afternoon then."

Megan was furious with Viv. "Honestly, all he has to do is lift his little finger and she goes running. I hate when she does that."

"I suppose she's in love," Claire ventured.

"In love my arse! She's only known him three weeks."

"Come on, let's have a coffee and then I'll follow you to the apartment to pick up the rest of your stuff."

They did that and eventually the last of Megan's belongings were loaded into the two cars. Feeling sad, she took a last look around the apartment she'd shared with Paul for so many years.

She felt the tears sting her eyes as she closed the door

behind her. Maybe this hurt would pass and she'd be able to come back and live here again one day. Right now it didn't seem possible but who knew what the future would hold? She silently said goodbye as she left to start the next stage of her life.

# Chapter 9

Viv felt bad after she'd hung up, knowing that Megan was pissed off with her.

"What's so urgent that you had to see me now?" she asked Alan crossly when she met up with him.

When he told her that his friend was throwing an impromptu party that evening and he wanted her there, she hit the roof.

"Is that the reason you dragged me here?" she demanded angrily. "I told you I'm having dinner with my friends tonight."

"Surely you can cancel them? I need you there. I'll be the only one without a girlfriend." Both his voice and face were sulky.

"I will *not* cancel *my* friends to suit *your* friend's last-minute decision." She was livid.

"You're my girlfriend," he whined. "I need you there."

"Well, I have news for you, Alan. I'm not your girlfriend any more. So just feck off and find yourself someone new because I'm done."

With that she flounced out of the bar.

She decided to walk home, hoping to cool her anger. What a wally! Who did he think he was?

Her parents were out and, letting herself into the house, she grabbed the roll of plastic bags and started to pack. What a headache trying to decide what to take with her and what to leave! She sorted through her wardrobes, trying to be selective. She was surprised to see so many things with the labels still attached. Stuff she'd never worn and didn't even remember buying. It shocked her. She would have to stop. This was ridiculous.

Eventually she had three mountainous piles on the floor: one to take to Claire's, one to leave in her parents' house, and one to discard either to the thrift shop or the clothes bank. She realised that she still had too much to take to Claire's and had to downsize even more, with the pile for the thrift shop growing bigger every minute. She knew she would have to stop buying clothes as she would have nowhere to store them in future and anyway she wouldn't have as much disposable income now. She would need to do some serious budgeting. She finished just as her parents returned home.

Her father helped her carry the bags down to his car. Then he took the remainder of the bags and put them in her mother's little Nissan Micra. She would come back tomorrow and sort the other clothes out. It was time to go. Her mother had tears in her eyes as she hugged her only daughter goodbye.

"Aren't you driving me to Claire's?" Viv asked her.

"No, sweetheart, you're taking my car."

Viv was surprised. "But won't you need it?"

"Now that your dad is retiring," her mother continued, "we won't be needing a second car so we've decided to give my car to you." She was smiling through her tears.

"Are you serious, Mum?" Viv asked, looking to her father for confirmation.

He was smiling broadly. "Time you had your own wheels, pet," he said. "You'll need them now."

"Thank you *sooooo* much," Viv cried, hugging them both. "You're the best parents any girl could have." She was crying now too. "I'll miss you guys so much but I'll be back often to see you, you know that."

With more hugs and kisses she left her childhood home to strike out on her own. She felt scared yet grown-up for the first time in her life. It was time.

Megan and Claire were having lunch when Viv arrived at the house. Her father greeted them briefly as he carried Viv's bags into the hallway. The girls were surprised that she was so early.

"What happened? I thought you were having lunch with Alan?" Megan asked as they moved into the kitchen.

"He's history. Over. Deleted."

Megan laughed. "About time! That's our Viv. Meet and Delete!" Viv was running true to form.

"What was so urgent that he needed to see you?" Claire wanted to know as she set a place for Viv at the table and placed a panini on the grill for her.

"You wouldn't believe this. He wanted me to cancel you guys tonight and go to his friend's party. I needn't tell you what I told him."

They laughed. They could well imagine.

"Come and see what Claire has done in the living

room," Megan said, jumping up. They followed her into the living room.

"Oh my God! When did you do this? It's beautiful," Viv exclaimed, hardly able to believe her eyes.

Claire was delighted with her reaction.

"I love the colour scheme. I can see us having some good nights in here, girls, can't you?" Viv grinned.

"Yes, now that you've dumped Alan maybe you'll spare some time for us, till the next guy appears," Megan remarked dryly.

"Touché," Viv replied, somewhat abashed. "I'm sorry, girls. I swear I will never, ever again date a guy I meet in a pub. Cross my heart," she declared, crossing herself. "Let's enjoy being single ladies together. No men, no complications!"

"I'll second that," Megan agreed.

Claire just smiled.


Claire was overwhelmed as she helped Viv empty her black bags, wondering how she could possibly fit all these clothes in the new wardrobes. Somehow she managed it, loading three and four items on the one hanger. Claire hoped the wardrobes wouldn't collapse. Viv's shoes were lined up around the wall in her bedroom and now they stood three rows deep, leaving very little room for Viv to negotiate the bed. Claire was flabbergasted.

"I can't believe you have so many shoes," she exclaimed.

"Huh! That's only half of them. The rest are back in my parents' house."

Megan had come in on this conversation. "Imelda Marcos is only trottin' after her," she grinned, enjoying the look on Claire's face.

Claire marvelled at the difference between the two girls. Viv was chronically untidy whereas Megan had meticulously organised her belongings with everything in its rightful place where she could locate it in a blink. She was amazing and Claire admired her efficiency.

That trait became more obvious that evening as they sat down in the new living room before dinner. A delicious aroma was coming from the kitchen where Claire was cooking a lasagne, to be served shortly with garlic bread and a green salad.

"Now I think we need to have some rules and regulations here if this venture is to work," Megan declared, opening up her briefcase.

The other two looked at each other, mystified, and Viv threw her eyes up to heaven.

"Yes, sir, Sergeant Major, sir!" Viv replied, saluting.

"No, seriously, Viv. We all want to get along in harmony so I think Claire should lay down some basic house rules, don't you?"

"No, no, that's not necessary–" Claire started to say but Megan interrupted her.

"I know, Claire, but it really is important. I've written out a few things here for you to consider. Maybe you'll want to add or change something. It's just a few ideas." She started to read aloud. "'*€60 each per week rent to be paid to Claire every Friday without fail. €50 each per week to be put into the kitty for food and household expenses. A figure, to be confirmed by Claire, to be paid monthly for electricity and cable TV/WiFi. Each of us to take a turn doing weekly shopping. Each of us to cook two nights per week,*'" Megan stopped and looked at Viv pointedly, "'*or take the others out if she prefers. Each of us to be*

*responsible for the cleaning of her own bedroom/bathroom.
Also to cooperate with keeping communal areas clean and
tidy.'"* Megan paused and looked pointedly at Viv again
and then went on. "As we all have TV in our rooms I don't
foresee a problem if one of us wants to watch something
different to the others so that's okay. Right: *'Friends to be
invited into the living room/kitchen only after okaying it
with the other two housemates. No men in bedrooms. This
last is vitally important.'"*

She took a deep breath.

"Well, what do you think, girls?"

"I think you should be a general, not a lowly sergeant
major, that's what I think," Viv declared sarcastically.

"I-I think you've thought of everything," Claire
stammered. She looked at Viv apprehensively and was
relieved to see that she was laughing.

Megan was grinning too. "I know it's a bit precise," she
said, "but we need to start off on the right foot. We can
always adjust as we go along. I hope you'll both agree."

"I suppose we do need some kind of framework," Viv
agreed.

"None of us have actually done this before so it will
probably be a good guideline," Claire remarked. She was
relieved about one thing. With everything spelt out, she
wouldn't have to ask for rent every week. She could never
have done that. "Thank you, Megan. You did a good job."

"Yes, Meggie, thanks," Viv added, to her friend's
surprise. "Now let's have some food. I'm starving."

And so began their first night as housemates.

# Chapter 10

Thanks to Megan's ground rules, or GRs as Viv called them, the following weeks went very smoothly. Megan had quietly assumed the role of decision-maker and the others were happy to follow her lead. They appreciated her strength and clear thinking. Claire had become increasingly fond of Megan and admired her enormously. And Viv? Well, Viv was Viv! Irresponsible, a little lazy, dreadfully untidy, but always great fun. There was never a dull moment with Viv around. Despite wanting to be grown-up, she was still like a little kid – naughty but adorable.

Claire's life had changed totally and she grew in confidence week by week. She could not have altered her nature if she'd tried and was the perfect homemaker, happy pottering around the house and garden and cooking delicious food for the others.

They were like a regular family: Megan the decision-maker, Claire the carer, and Viv the irresponsible kid they both loved. Claire could not have been happier.

The weather was particularly lovely that summer and they spent many balmy evenings in the garden. After Viv's two disastrous attempts at cooking, the others agreed, for the sake of their health, that it would be better if she would confine her efforts to the barbecue. This she did with gusto and left the gourmet cooking to Megan and the comfort food to Claire. It was a good solution.

Although they had become very close, they each also had a life outside of the house. Claire had reconnected with her old friends and went out for a drink or meal with them every week but refused to go clubbing. She'd outgrown that. She'd been promoted at work and was again in daily contact with her old boyfriend, Jamie. Initially she'd found it awkward but he was so sweet to her that she now looked forward to seeing him every day, despite the fact that he still had a girlfriend.

Her sister Sarah could not believe the changes Claire had wrought in the house and now regretted having sold her share.

"If I'd known this is what you'd planned, I would never have sold to you," she remarked bitterly when she saw it.

"Why ever not?" Claire asked, mystified as to what difference it would have made.

It was obvious to both Viv and Megan that Sarah was jealous and envious of Claire.

"It's hard to believe she and Claire are sisters," Megan confided privately to Viv. "They couldn't be more different."

"She's a bitch," said Viv, never one to mince words.

To their dismay Sarah had started dropping in regularly,

out of the blue, usually just in time for dinner, and Claire was too kind-hearted to say anything. Viv wanted to remonstrate with her but Megan dissuaded her, not wanting to make difficulties for Claire.

"What about my room?" Sarah had asked on her last visit.

"Your room?" Claire repeated, mystified.

"Yes, if I want to come and stay overnight, where will I sleep?"

The three girls looked at each other, baffled.

"Why would you want to come and stay?" Megan couldn't resist asking. She knew Sarah lived only ten minutes away with her husband and two kids.

"Well, you all have such fun here," Sarah replied sullenly. "It's no picnic looking after a family all week, you know. I might like to join you and stay over occasionally. It *is* my home, after all."

Viv almost exploded. "Well, actually, it's not your home any more. You sold your half to Claire, remember?" She faced Sarah head-on.

"Please, no, it's all right," Claire cried, appealing to Viv not to cause a scene. "Sorry, Sarah, but there's only the box-room free as the fourth bedroom is now Viv's dressing-room," she nervously told her sister.

Sarah glared at Viv. "It's far from dressing-rooms you were raised," she remarked.

Viv clenched her fists and was about to retort but, seeing Claire's stricken face, she resisted.

"Viv – come – I want to show you the new dress I bought," Megan cut in, ushering Viv out of the living room.

"God, what a bitch!" Viv exploded. "I'm bloody well

going to disappear the next time she comes round!"

Claire came to Viv after Sarah had left. She looked miserable. "I'm sorry," she said.

"What exactly is her problem?" Viv demanded. "I can't believe her arrogance. '*My home*' indeed!" She was still livid.

"You really should try standing up to her and not let her bully you," Megan advised Claire gently.

"I suppose you're right."

"We'll be here to back you up, sweetheart," said Megan. "I think she's just jealous of what you've done with the house."

"Maybe," Claire replied unhappily.

"You're not alone any more. She has us to contend with now," Viv said grimly.

Claire smiled gratefully at them. Maybe it was time she stood up to Sarah.

Megan had taken on more of a workload in an effort to keep herself busy. Also, her fitness regime had suffered when she was with Paul but now she was going to the gym four times a week. As well as that, she was back swimming and she'd joined the running club attached to the gym. She found she enjoyed running a lot. She could switch off completely as she pounded the pavements and she admired the dedication of the other members, all of whom were in training for the Dublin City Marathon. They persuaded Megan to train for it too and she decided to rise to the challenge.

Megan's relationship with her mother had not improved since she had broken the news about the wedding. Daphne's refusal to accept it had caused a rift between them.

It was with relief that Megan received the news that Daphne was heading to Marbella for the month of September. It would get her mother off her back for a while and maybe by the time she got back she'd have forgotten all about the aborted wedding.

Viv dropped in a couple of times a week to visit her parents and, although they were always delighted to see her, they were happy that she'd become independent of them. She generally left with a big bag of goodies: soda bread, apple tart, casseroles and home-made soups which the girls welcomed with open arms. Viv felt in control of her own life at last and also relished the freedom the car had provided. She'd be forever grateful to her parents for that and their continuing support but it was good that she had cut the umbilical cord.

And, for the first time in her life, she had sat down and made out a budget. Not only that, she had stuck to it and actually managed to save some money. She discovered that saving could be pretty addictive too.

The only fly in the ointment was the lack of men in her life. Viv had rarely been without a boyfriend – not necessarily suitable ones – but she had been as good as her word and, after Alan, had eschewed the guys she met in pubs. But for someone in love with being in love, it was difficult to be without a man. In truth, Viv also missed the intimacy and the sex. She was a romantic and longed to meet Mr Right but she had no idea where to find him.

As the twenty-eighth of September, the date of Megan's doomed wedding, approached she retreated into herself. She became manic about her running schedule and, when she was home, Viv and Claire, who knew she was hurting badly, did their best to keep her spirits up. She knew the others were worried about her but she just wanted to get past the 'big day' and hopefully then she could move on with her life.

A week before the 'big day', Claire and Viv took Megan out to dinner.

"We have a surprise for you," Viv said excitedly, handing her an envelope. Megan took it listlessly, wondering what it could be.

Opening the envelope, she withdrew a ticket. It was for a Ryanair flight. *DUB to CIA*, she read, *FRI, SEPT 27th*. She looked at the girls expectantly.

"What's this?" she asked. "For next Friday? And where's CIA?"

"Ciampino Airport, Rome."

"Rome? Are you serious? I've always wanted to go there." Megan was flabbergasted.

"I know. There's more in the envelope," Viv said, grinning. "Read it."

Megan drew out a sheet of paper. It was a voucher for three nights B&B in Hotel Campo dei Fiori.

"We're coming with you of course," Claire smiled broadly. "A girlie weekend."

"Oh my God, this is unbelievable," Megan said tearfully. "I've been absolutely dreading next weekend. This might help me get through it."

"There's more," Viv told her, pointing to the envelope.

Megan drew out the last sheet of paper. It was three tickets to the open-air opera at the Caracalla Baths for the Saturday. The day she would have been walking down the aisle.

She burst into tears then leaned over and hugged them both.

"Oh girls, this is too much," she blubbered. "You're so kind!"

Claire and Viv beamed at each other, pleased with her reaction. Megan loved opera although Claire and Viv weren't fans. However, they were doing this for Megan so they would grin and bear it for her sake.

"We'll have a brilliant time," Viv declared.

"How can I ever thank you? I'll never forget this," Megan smiled through her tears. "I love you guys." She hugged them once more.

How ironic, she thought, as she lay in bed that night. She had wanted to go to Rome for her honeymoon but Paul had vetoed the idea.

"Rome is full of bloody churches and ancient monuments, not to mention millions of priests and nuns. What do you want to go there for?" he had asked belligerently.

Megan hadn't even tried to explain. Instead she'd booked them on a two-week sun holiday to Cyprus, although lying around a pool all day was not her idea of fun. Now it looked like she would make it to Rome after all, albeit sans husband!

# Chapter 11

Viv had something of a Road-to-Damascus moment that weekend. She was already spending hours on Twitter and Facebook every day, but now she discovered something even better which kept her glued to her iPhone every evening. Online dating! Isabelle, who worked in the shoe department had introduced her to it. It was fantastic! How had she not considered this before? It was so easy. There were thousands and thousands of men out there looking for Ms Right. Why not? Why shouldn't she be the one for them? She was very excited about the possibilities it offered. No more meeting creepy men in crappy bars for her!

Megan was very wary when she mentioned it to her.

"I don't know, Viv – I can't imagine meeting someone online. It seems strange. It could also be dangerous."

Claire was even more doubtful. "I'd be terrified that you might meet a weirdo. I've heard there are all kinds of perverts out there who use these sites to seduce unsuspecting females."

Viv scoffed. "Of course you have to be careful but there are genuine guys who use it all the time. Lots of women are meeting their husbands online. It's brilliant. This site works via direct messaging," she explained, "so nobody can see your personal details unless you give them out."

She was convinced that it was the perfect solution to finding a man and, despite their fears, took to it with enthusiasm. She spent days trying to decide what exactly to put on her profile, both her own bio and the requirements she expected in a suitable partner. She called herself 'Vivacious' which Claire agreed was very clever. It certainly described Viv to a T.

"It's very important that I get it perfect from the beginning," she explained to Claire one evening as she mulled over it.

Claire was fascinated by it all but was very doubtful that Viv would meet the man of her dreams on the internet.

"It *does* work," Viv insisted. "Isabelle, the girl who told me about it, met a guy on this site and they're now engaged. There are loads of success stories like that. It's the modern way of meeting Mr Right."

Megan, who was curled up reading on the other sofa overheard this remark and scoffed.

"It's a load of bunkum, if you ask me." She closed her book and yawned, then stood up and stretched. "Well, I'm off to bed. I'm shattered. Good luck with the hunt!" She threw her eyes to heaven as she left the room. "What next?" she muttered as she climbed the stairs. "Shopping for a husband online! Sheer madness!"

Viv opened up the list of what she was looking for in a man. Claire bit her lip as she read down through it.

"You don't think you're looking for a bit too much?"

she ventured diffidently as she read. "Non-smoker, I can understand. Sense of humour, good fun, that all seems fine. But a man who doesn't like football, likes shopping and can appreciate your passion for shoes? I think he might be a bit difficult to find." She looked at Viv dubiously.

"No point in going out with someone who can't accept me as I am. Better to weed out the unsuitable guys at the start." Viv seemed quite confident that there were men like that out there.

Claire was not so sure.

Still, the photo Viv had chosen to download on to her profile was gorgeous and sexy and Claire guessed lots of guys would respond whether they liked shopping and shoes or not.

Finally, Viv had her profile and her requirements ready, and jubilantly she pressed the *Send* button.

"Now all I have to do is wait for all these lovely men to contact me." She smiled with satisfaction.

Claire hoped she wouldn't be disappointed. "Then what?" she asked.

"Well, we'll message for a bit and if I like them then we'll arrange to meet up. Beats meeting someone drunk in a pub."

"I suppose so." Claire smiled hopefully at Viv.

To Viv's delight, she received three replies the very next day. She showed Claire the photos of the respondents that evening and Claire was surprised to see that two of them were really good-looking. You'd think they would have had no problem finding girls in the normal way. It was all very strange.

They were looking at the photos on Viv's iPhone when

Sarah appeared out of nowhere. She still had a key to the house and had let herself in.

Viv was furious and made a note to ask Claire to take the key back from her sister. She didn't fancy Sarah rummaging through her stuff when they were away.

"What's going on?" Sarah asked, plonking down on the sofa opposite them.

"Erm . . . Viv joined a dating site and we're just looking at the replies she got," Claire told her.

"Really? Let's have a look?" Sarah asked, moving over to see. "Hey, these guys are cute. What site is it?"

Claire told her and realised she shouldn't have said anything when she saw Viv's grim expression.

"Mmmm . . . this is very interesting. Maybe I should give it a go," Sarah mused as she salivated over the photos.

"Why the hell would you do that? You have a husband." Viv glowered at her.

"Oh, lighten up for Christ's sake," Sarah retorted. "You don't know what it's like to be stuck with the same man for years. We all need a little diversion from time to time."

Claire was shocked. Was she hearing right? Was her sister serious?

"You know," Viv said, closing her iPhone abruptly, "there's a site for married couples who want to screw around. Maybe you should join that one." With that she flounced out of the room.

"Christ, what's her problem?" Sarah asked.

Claire just looked at her strangely and went after Viv.

"Sorry, Claire," said Viv, "but I just can't take her and I don't think she should have a key for here any more. She marches in whenever she feels like it."

"You're right, Viv. I'll ask her for it back. I just don't

know what's wrong with her at the moment. Please try and ignore her."

Megan came in from the gym to find Sarah alone in the living room. She wondered where the others were and found herself reluctantly having to make conversation. They were chatting about the Rome trip when Claire came back downstairs.

"You never told me you were all going to Rome for the weekend," Sarah said, turning on her sister accusingly. "I would have come with you if I'd known."

Claire didn't know what to say.

"Yes, well, it was Viv who arranged it," Megan replied smoothly, in an effort to get Claire off the hook.

"Well, it's a shame. I could certainly have done with a break," Sarah said. "Too late now, though, to make arrangements."

Claire let out a sigh of relief. She'd been afraid Sarah was going to insist on coming with them. Thank God she'd let it go. She decided to take her courage in her hands.

"By the way, Sarah, I need the key back."

"What?" Sarah looked shocked.

"Yes, if you don't mind. We need a spare one," Claire said calmly, holding out her hand for it.

Sarah had no choice but to hand it over.

"I must say I don't feel very welcome here," she declared. "I guess I won't stay for dinner after all."

She glared at both girls as she put on her jacket.

"What mother would say I can't imagine," she said stiffly.

"Mother's dead. She won't be saying anything," Claire replied with more bravado than she felt.

Sarah banged the front door behind her and Claire looked at Megan, unable to believe what she'd just done.

"*Yesssss!*" Megan cried, high-fiving her. "Well done! You certainly told her."

Viv came into the room. "Is she gone?" she asked, looking around.

"Yes," Claire said, handing Viv the key. She found that she was shaking.

Megan told Viv briefly what had transpired.

"Well done, you!" Viv hugged Claire.

"I was terrified she was going to insist on coming to Rome with us," Claire admitted, smiling with relief.

"God forbid!" Megan and Viv exclaimed simultaneously.

Viv was very tempted to message the men who'd replied to her, straight away, but thought that might appear too keen. She decided to postpone contacting them until after Rome. It would take all of her time and skill over the next few days to keep Megan busy and her mind off what might have been.

On Wednesday evening the girls had to pack for their trip as they would have no time on the Thursday.

"I really don't know what to take with me," Claire admitted to Megan as the two of them finished dinner – Viv had gone to her parents' to eat.

"Come on, I'll help you choose," Megan said.

They both went up to Claire's room where Megan had great difficulty finding clothes suitable for the trip.

"Whew, I really do need to update my wardrobe, don't I?" Claire observed, abashed when Megan was finally done.

"You really do," Megan replied gently, "but don't worry – Viv is really great at that. When we get back from Rome we'll get her to help."

Claire could see that it was time. "Okay," she agreed.

# Chapter 12

Thursday evening came at last and the three girls, who had all taken a day's leave on Friday, relaxed on the flight to Rome, eager with anticipation. Viv had been there before, on a hen weekend – not that she could remember much about it, what with all that wine – but it was a first visit for the others.

They were pleasantly surprised by the hotel which was in a historic building yet comfortable and spacious. It was also very central. They couldn't wait to explore the city the following day and were up bright and early. Breakfast was served on the roof-terrace and was delicious.

They decided the best thing to do was to take the open-topped tourist bus which would take them to all the famous sights. The city was magnificent and they drank it in with their eyes, marvelling at it all. They'd all seen it often on TV and in films but nothing had prepared them for the reality. They hopped on and off when something took their fancy and stopped for lunch in a restaurant by the Spanish Steps.

Viv had ordered the girls not to let her go shopping and they had their hands full keeping her out of the shops. Not ten minutes passed without Viv passing some comment on the Italian sense of style, particularly the men.

"My God, they're so elegant," she said time and time again as she drew their attention to some beautifully dressed man or other. She was disappointed with Italian women who, she pronounced, were not a patch on their male counterparts.

Claire and Megan exchanged knowing grins. Viv had not left her critical eye for fashion at home.

The Spanish Steps were crowded with sprawling young Italians and the three girls got a lot of attention from the men, who were not bashful about approaching them.

"I think I've died and gone to heaven," Viv declared as another Adonis kissed her hand and told her she was *molto bella*. She'd never seen so many gorgeous men in one place.

Claire and Megan laughed at her but they also had their admirers and had their bottoms pinched too.

"They're nothing if not persistent," Megan remarked as she turned yet another one down.

By the end of the day they were utterly exhausted but happy.

They were sitting in the Piazza Navona having a drink before dinner when Megan said, "Do you know, I haven't thought of Paul or my wedding once today. Can you believe that?" She sounded surprised.

"I guess that means this trip has been a success," Claire observed, smiling.

"I guess so."

"I'll drink to that," Viv chimed in, raising her glass.

They clinked their glasses to hers.

They went to a restaurant in Trastevere where they had a fabulous meal and then wearily dragged themselves into bed, just after midnight.

Megan slept well but was very quiet at breakfast the following morning, on what would have been her wedding day. She turned off her mobile phone, in case some of her friends and family would call. She really wasn't up to talking to any of them today. She wondered where Paul was and if he was thinking of it too.

They were going to visit the Vatican that day and Megan was really looking forward to seeing the Sistine Chapel. Then of course there would be the opera that evening to look forward to.

The day whizzed past and somehow Megan survived it. It was a beautiful summer evening as they took their place amidst the ancient ruins to watch Verdi's *Tosca*. Although Claire and Viv had no interest in opera they were blown away with the setting and the atmosphere. Best of all, Megan was completely engrossed in it all.

They had a pizza on the way home and, as a bell struck midnight, they raised their glasses of Chianti.

"Onwards and upwards now!" Viv said.

"Yes, thank God this day is over," Megan said, her voice trembling. "I never thought I'd survive it, and I wouldn't have without you guys."

Claire felt tears come to her own eyes as she squeezed Megan's hand.

"That's what friends are for," Viv, who was also moved, said quietly.

"We can't very well come to Rome and not go to see the Pope, can we?" Claire asked over breakfast the following morning. She was obviously very keen to go.

"Of course not," Megan replied, sensing her eagerness.

"Whatever!" Viv shrugged. Who was she to object?

So they found themselves in St Peter's Square at midday along with many thousands of others – of every nationality, if the flags were anything to go by. Viv found it very moving and was glad that they'd gone, and told Claire so. She was happy.

Then they went for lunch near the Trevi Fountain and, after throwing in their coins, went shopping in the narrow streets leading off it where they each bought a soft buttery leather bag. Viv bought a belt for her father and a wallet for her mother. That was as far as her budget would stretch.

Tired but happy, they made their way to the bus station on the first leg of their journey home.

It had been a fantastic weekend and a great success, they all agreed, as they boarded the flight for Dublin.

Megan was very emotional. "I can never thank you guys enough," she said.

Well, she thought, that was one big hurdle over. Now it was time to pick up the pieces and face the future. It wouldn't be easy.

They arrived home after midnight and Megan went upstairs to unpack while Claire headed to the kitchen to make hot chocolate for them all.

Viv dumped her case in her bedroom and checked her phone for calls and emails. To her amazement she had eight dating replies. How fantastic was that? Obviously the weekend was a busy time on the site. She glanced quickly at the photos and felt a frisson of excitement. Way to go!

Just then Claire called out, "Viv, Megan, hot chocolate's up!"

Reluctantly Viv signed off, looking forward to reading the profiles and messages in full the following evening. She was too tired now.

As they sat sipping the comforting hot chocolate and chocolate biscuits that Claire had thoughtfully provided, Megan turned her phone back on. As she suspected she had lots of missed calls. Two from her father, others from Emily and Simon and other colleagues at work and also some from friends. It was so kind of them to have thought of her. She then went to her texts and opened the one her father had left on Saturday.

**'Hi Princess, I hope you're okay and having a lovely time in Rome. Tried calling you but you must have your phone off. Clever girl! Thinking of you today and sending you all my love. Hugs from Betsy also. Love Dad xxx.'**

Megan glanced at her watch. It was much too late to call him now. She'd call first thing in the morning.

Scrolling down through her other messages, she gasped with shock. "Oh my God, no!" she cried, her voice anguished. "I don't believe it!"

"What is it?" Viv asked with alarm.

"It's Paul," Megan whispered. "He texted me on Saturday . . . twice."

Viv clenched her fists while Claire moved to put her arm around Megan's shoulders.

"What does he say?" Viv asked.

Trembling, Megan read his first message:

**'I've been thinking of you all this week. We should have**

been getting married today and I am so, so sorry that we're not. I've been such a fool. We need to talk. Please call me, Megan.'

She was shaking so much that she dropped the phone. Claire picked it up and handed it back to her.

'I miss you and still love you. Please, Megan, give me another chance,' the second message said.

"You okay? What does he say?" Viv asked.

"He says he's sorry and that he's been a fool. He still loves me and wants to talk," Megan said hoarsely, her blue eyes dark with anguish.

"*What?*" Claire and Viv exclaimed in unison.

"I don't believe it," Viv cried. "The bastard! *Now* he's sorry. Well, it's a bit late. Too bloody bad!" She was incandescent with rage.

"Are you okay?" Claire asked Megan, her voice full of concern.

"Just when I've struggled through all that pain, survived the past two months and last Saturday. Just when I've decided to move on with my life, he wants to talk." Megan's voice was tearful.

"You're not thinking of calling him?" Viv asked nervously.

"No, it's too late for talking. Much too late. He had his chance," Megan declared bitterly.

"Good girl!" Viv smiled at her, relieved.

Claire squeezed her hand. "What will you do about him?"

"Nothing." She handed Viv her phone, her hand shaking. "Delete them please, Viv, and block him from my phone. I don't need this. He's broken my heart once, that's enough." Her voice trembled as she spoke.

Viv did as she asked with alacrity and handed the phone back. Megan checked the rest of her messages but didn't open any of them. She was too tired and upset, and there was nothing that couldn't wait till tomorrow. There was no call or text from her mother who had probably forgotten that Saturday should have been her daughter's wedding day. No surprise there!

She was more shook than she'd let on about Paul's messages. Did he think he could just sail back into her life after what he'd done? How did he think she could ever trust him again? She never would and so there was no point in even going there.

Strangely, his avowal of love had made her feel better. It was his turn to suffer now.

# Chapter 13

Megan took her messages the following morning over breakfast and was touched by how concerned her friends and colleagues had been for her. She planned to show them now that she was fine and moving on with her life. What else could she do?

Emily, her PA, was acting as if she was walking on eggshells.

"Good morning," she said, then waited for Megan to speak.

"Good morning and thank you for your text," said Megan. "It was very thoughtful of you. Rome was wonderful. I had a great time."

A smile spread over Emily's face. "That's great. I was so worried . . ." she tailed off.

"I know and thank you but I'm fine now, honestly. Now what have we on for this week?"

Emily briefed Megan on the appointments for the week and, when she'd left, Megan rang her father. She could hear his relief that she had come through the weekend in one piece. She promised that she would come and visit him soon.

"How did Rome go?" Simon asked when she entered the conference room for the weekly meeting a short time later. He looked at her anxiously as he spoke.

"Wonderful," she replied, smiling. "I had a great time. It's a beautiful city."

"Are you okay?" he asked, peering at her.

"Sure! It's been a bit of a catharsis actually."

"I'm so glad," he beamed at her. "Now, I got this manuscript in on Friday from a new author and I think it has great potential. Will you have a read of it?" He handed her the ms.

She felt that buzz that always happened when faced with the possibility of finding a great new talent.

"Will do," she replied, flushed with anticipation.

Simon squeezed her arm as the others filed in. "I'm really glad you're okay," he whispered, smiling at her.

Viv had overslept and, grabbing a banana which she ate in the car, arrived at work with one minute to spare. This would be the busiest two weeks of the year as the new Autumn/Winter collections had been delivered and she knew she would be run off her feet. Her clients, wanting to have first choice of the new collections had booked their appointments weeks and even months in advance. She had non-stop back-to-back appointments all week. She groaned, wondering if she could stomach the demands of these spoilt rich women for a whole week.

She had thirty minutes to fly through the store, checking

that everything she expected was in situ. The buyers had shown her their orders in advance so she knew what to expect. As her expert eye roamed over the racks in the different designer departments, she felt the adrenalin bubble up inside her. Beautiful clothes always had that effect on her. Mentally, she ticked off the clothes that she knew would suit the clients she was expecting today. It was going to be a successful season, she thought happily, which would mean more commission for her. In better form, she managed to grab a coffee before her first appointment.

Her seasonal clients were a varied bunch. Mostly they were between thirty-five and fifty-five, and they all had one thing in common: very rich husbands or boyfriends. They all led busy lives and came in religiously at the start of every season to stock up on a whole new wardrobe. They rarely wore the same outfit twice, unlike Kate Middleton. Viv thought they were crazy but it benefited her and kept her in a job.

She also had a few businesswomen, usually in that same age bracket, who didn't have time to shop and these were a lot less demanding and not so extravagant as it was their own hard-earned cash they were spending. They were not slaves to fashion and went more for quality classics than the latest trend.

Occasionally, a young girl would come in, usually the girlfriend or mistress of an older man who was footing the bill and wanted them to dress more conservatively. She found that, generally, most young girls loved shopping and knew exactly what they liked so did not need her services.

Then there were the older ladies who either had developed their own style by now or else didn't care too much what they wore. They came to her only for special-occasion outfits like weddings or cruises.

Her first client this morning was Clodagh, the wife of a builder who had made a fortune during the Celtic Tiger. Despite the fact that he'd gone bankrupt, his wife had no shortage of cash, mainly because he'd transferred all of his assets to her before he got caught out. Viv didn't like her very much but she was not being paid to like her, just to dress her.

"Right, I need four cocktail dresses, two long evening gowns, and three ensembles for the Leopardstown Racing Festival after Christmas. I'll have two horses running there hopefully," Clodagh informed her, smugly. "Oh, and I need a warm winter coat and a couple of pairs of boots. After last winter, that's a priority." She preened in front of the mirror as she spoke, patting her hair and straightening her eyebrows with a wet finger.

"Would you care for a glass of champagne, Clodagh?" Viv asked, knowing full well that the answer would be yes, even though it was only ten thirty. Clodagh had probably already had it for breakfast that morning!

"I shouldn't, but that would be lovely," Clodagh purred.

Fiona, Viv's assistant, poured the champagne as Viv left to whizz around the store, grabbing clothes off rails as she went. She had an innate gift of knowing what clothes would work best on each woman and also how to accessorise each outfit. Ten minutes later, arms laden down, she was back in the Personal Stylist salon.

"Phew!" she exclaimed, as she handed the clothes to Fiona to hang on the rail.

"Oh my God!" Clodagh squealed as she handled the lovely fabrics. "I can't wait to try them on."

She was like a kid in a candy store and just as greedy, Viv thought disgustedly.

For the next hour and a half Clodagh was in and out of the dressing-room, posing and throwing shapes as Viv approved, or not, of the clothes she'd chosen.

"What do you think?" Clodagh asked as she strutted out in a Stella McCartney coat.

"Uh uh. Definitely not, it adds about ten pounds to your frame."

"God forbid!" Clodagh grimaced and rushed back into the dressing-room to throw off the offending article, as if it were contagious.

Viv rolled her eyes at Fiona.

Finally, Clodagh had chosen. Viv totalled up her purchases. The other woman had not even looked at the prices and Lanvin and Donna Karan did not come cheap. She'd fallen in love with a beige Don Goor shearling-lined suede coat which Viv would have given her right arm for. Viv felt she had to point out that it cost in excess of €2000 but Clodagh just waved her hand dismissively.

"It's so warm and will look fabulous over the camel Burberry trouser suit," Clodagh said, rubbing her hand lovingly on the soft suede.

Viv had to agree with her there. She wondered if Clodagh realised how lucky she was to be able to afford this gorgeous coat. Probably not. Even with staff discount, it would have taken Viv a year before she could afford it. Maybe she'd meet someone on this dating site who was filthy rich. Who knew? She sighed. Fat chance!

"It's so exhausting, all this shopping," Clodagh moaned, as she sat down and kicked off her shoe, then rubbed her foot.

"How about another glass of champagne while I go and look for accessories?" Viv suggested.

"That would be lovely. You're an angel."

Viv instructed Fiona to pour as she made another foray through the store, picking up accessories to go with the clothes.

Two pairs of boots, evening shoes, hats and a Balenciaga bag later, Clodagh was done. She didn't baulk at the bill of €9800 that Viv handed her and paid with her Amex Platinum card.

"I don't know what I'd do without you," she gushed to Viv.

"My pleasure," Viv replied. She was only doing her job but the commission she'd earned in one morning had been excellent. After she'd ushered Clodagh out with much air-kissing, she high-fived Fiona.

"A good morning's work!"

Fiona grinned. "What a pain she was!"

Viv was dying for a chance to read her dating messages but she had only ten minutes in which to grab a sandwich before sourcing clothes for her next client, a very successful CEO. This woman had one hour in which to buy her wardrobe for the season and wanted classic clothes. Viv knew exactly what she would like and had it waiting for her when she arrived. Within the hour she had bought the lot and was gone, giving Viv two tickets for a show in the Point Depot. There were some perks with the job.

Megan was excited. She'd sent Emily out for a sandwich and coffee and had spent her lunch hour reading the manuscript that Simon had given her. She was enthralled and couldn't put it down. It was different to anything that had crossed her desk in the past year. It was beautifully written and when she saw that the author was in her sixties she wondered if she'd written anything else. Her name was Gloria Rivers. It was a great name, one that people would remember. Excited, she kept reading until it was time for her appointment with an agent who was trying to pitch a new book by another new author.

She read the first three pages of the manuscript the agent handed her and instantly knew it was not good. There was a huge chasm between it and the book she'd been reading earlier. Knowing she was dashing the hopes of yet another struggling author, she rejected it in the kindest way possible. The agent begged her to take it and read more. She knew it was hopeless but agreed to read more. How could he not know it was bad?

She was very excited about Gloria's book. She had a great instinct for what made a great book and she recognised it in this, from the first few chapters. She knew it would be a bestseller and rang Simon as soon as the agent had left her office.

"Wow! It's great," she told him. "Where did you get it?"

"Direct from the author. It's good, isn't it? I thought maybe it was just me because it was so different."

"No, it's brilliant. Really well written. I can't wait to read it all. Has she sent it to any other publisher?"

"No, she doesn't even know we have it. Her daughter sent it in to us, unknown to her mother," Simon said and she knew he was smiling.

Publishing was a crazy world. You could read three hundred manuscripts, all of them dire and then you came across a diamond like this.

Megan was jubilant. However, the feeling didn't last long.

Her phone rang and she answered without checking the caller.

"Megan, it's Eugene."

It was Paul's brother.

"Hello, Eugene. What can I do for you?" she said formally.

"Megan, I'm phoning to ask you – to beg you – to give Paul another chance. He still loves you and knows he has made a terrible mistake. He is so sorry. Please contact him and at least listen to what he has to say."

"Absolutely not! If he hadn't been such a wimp we'd have been on our honeymoon now. You can tell him that I won't change my mind and that's final."

He sighed. "All the family are furious with him, Megan. He was a fool to lose you. I'm sorry to have bothered you but you know how it is. He's my brother – I had to give it a try." His voice was kind and sympathetic. "Well, goodbye and all the best, Megan," he finished lamely.

"Damn!" she exclaimed as she put the phone down. Would it never be over?

Claire felt rejuvenated after the weekend and happily recounted all she'd seen to the other nurses in the staff canteen. She was also delighted to hear that little Amy was going to be discharged. She would miss the spunky little girl who'd spent so much of her young life in hospital but it was great that she would get to live a normal life again. Claire set about organising a farewell party for Amy for the following day.

"That's a very nice gesture," Jamie commented when he heard about it. "May I come?"

"Of course," she said, blushing.

"How did you enjoy Rome?"

"It was wonderful. It's a fascinating city and very beautiful."

"It's my favourite city, along with Paris," Jamie confessed. "I wanted to go back there this year but Hannah was not too keen so we ended up in Ibiza. Her choice, not mine."

He grimaced and Claire wondered if all was well between him and his doctor girlfriend. She wondered why they were not at least engaged by now. Strange!

She went shopping after work for dinner – it was her turn to cook – and also for goodies for Amy's party. She wanted to get the little girl a going-away present and found a beautiful dress in Monsoon that she knew she would love.

Laden down with bags, she bumped into Viv who had just finished work.

"Here, let me help," Viv said, taking some of the bags from her. "Monsoon? Good girl! What have you bought?"

"No, no, it's not for me," Claire said and explained about Amy.

"Ahhh, that's great!" Viv said as they entered the car park. "God, what a day! I'm bushed. Such drama! I'll tell you all about it over dinner. You won't believe it!"

"I can't wait to hear," Claire grinned.

Viv's days were always dramatic.

Over dinner that evening Viv regaled them with the antics of her day, grossly exaggerated of course.

"These women live in another world, don't they?" Claire commented as she listened.

"They sure do and I don't see why we can't be part of

that world too. These women are no different to us. They were just lucky to hitch up with wealthy men." Viv was feeling more than a little envious of the women who had notched up €30,000 in beautiful clothes in one day. She sighed.

"I wonder where they meet these guys?" Claire speculated.

"Not in crappy pubs, that's for sure," Viv replied. "They're the bargain basements for men. What can you expect to find there only bargain-basement men?" Her last two relationships with Fergal and Alan still rankled. "Online dating is a far superior hunting-ground. Who knows, I might meet, not only the man of my dreams on there, but the *wealthy* man of my dreams."

"Are you saying that you're looking only for a wealthy man?" Megan enquired testily, her eyebrows raised. "You're not looking for a nice man, or a man you could love, but he has to be rich?"

"Hey, I didn't say that," Viv contradicted her. "Just because he's rich doesn't mean that he can't be nice or that I couldn't fall in love with him. The world is not divided into nice men and rich men, Megan. Sometimes they overlap. It *is* possible to have it all. Look at my clients of today. "

Megan rolled her eyes. "Bully for them," she said sarcastically, "but are they happy?"

"I'd be bloody happy if I could have that beautiful Don Goor coat hanging in my wardrobe," Viv replied.

Claire decided to intervene, afraid of an argument developing. "I'm sure Viv doesn't mean she's out to net a rich man, just that if she falls for someone rich it would be nice. Isn't that right?" She looked at Viv helplessly.

"Exactly! I'd rather be happy and rich than happy and poor. What's wrong with that?"

Megan snorted and shook her head. "I can't believe you honestly think that you'll find a husband on the internet."

"Well, I do. What's wrong with that? Boy, you've got a bee in your bonnet this evening."

Megan sighed. "I'm sorry, I'm just a bit upset. I got a phone call from Paul's brother today, asking me to give Paul another chance."

"He never gives up, does he?" Viv said indignantly.

"What did you tell him?" Claire asked anxiously.

"I said no way." Megan tried to sound confident but Claire could tell she was shaken.

"Damn right!" declared Viv. She was a little piqued by Megan's criticism earlier. "Now if you'll excuse me, I'm going now to check on those guys who've been messaging me to see if Mr Nice and Rich is among them."

She flounced out of the kitchen, head held high, iPhone in hand.

"Hey, it's your turn to put the dishes away," Megan called after her.

"It's okay – I'll do it," Claire offered, ever the peacemaker.

Megan rolled her eyes. "I know she's pissed off with me but, honest to God, shopping on the internet for a husband! Is she nuts?"

Viv plonked down on the sofa and went on Facebook first to see what was happening. Then she settled down to go through the dating mails. Gleefully, she saw that she had two new replies. She glanced down through the photos first and had to admit that some of them were really quite dishy.

"Well, have you found Mr Right and Rich yet?" Claire

asked, grinning, as she came into the living room.

"Don't mock me. It's entirely possible I will. Some of them are gorgeous. I'm just about to start reading their profiles."

"Let's see," Claire said as she sat beside her on the sofa.

Viv scrolled back to the start and showed Claire the first reply she'd received. He was one of the ones Claire had thought was very good-looking.

"He's nice," Claire said. "What does he say?" Leaning forward, she read the email.

**'Hey babe, you look hot. Want to party? If so, I'm your man. Looking for a girl to have fun with and I think you're the one. Panting for your reply.'**

"Lord, that's a bit much," Claire said, a bit taken aback.

"Yes, well, *he's* obviously just after sex," Viv remarked as she typed **'No thanks!'** before pressing *send*, then *delete*. "Isabelle warned me. Out of every ten replies I'll probably get two perverts, two nerds, two frauds – usually married – and four genuine guys. Not a bad percentage really. That one was obviously one of the pervs."

From his photo, the next guy was obviously a lot older than the age limit Viv had specified. Reading his profile she could see that he was not her type either.

**'Non-drinker, love country pursuits, hiking, hill-walking, country music.'**

"Look at that, Claire! Definitely a nerd," Viv remarked. She didn't bother replying but deleted him immediately. "Why on earth did he message me?" she wondered. "He's way older than what I stipulated. And into shoes? I don't think so," she added, disgruntled. "Can you see me hiking and hill-walking or line-dancing in my Manolos?"

Claire giggled. "Who's next?"

The next guy was much more promising. He was dark and very attractive.

"Mmmm . . . yummy!" Viv observed.

Claire thought so too. They read his profile together. He sounded very promising. He was French and was the director of a new fashion company setting up in Dublin. As if that wasn't good enough, he also hated football and crowded pubs.

"Now we're getting somewhere," Viv said smugly. "This could be the one. Definitely will reply to him."

Claire was happy for her and fascinated with this whole thing. Was it really that easy?

One by one Viv picked them off, deleting the unsuitable ones. One guy had the nerve to say, '**Love that dress you're wearing in your profile photo. It would look even better on my bedroom floor.**' Viv smartly replied, '**Love the shirt you're wearing. Would look great cleaning my bathroom floor.**'

She swiftly deleted him as Claire giggled. Viv was a right ticket. Claire wished she was as quick-witted as her friend. She only ever thought of witty things to say long after the other person had left.

Another guy was obviously looking for a housekeeper.

'**I'm looking for a woman who is a good cook, a good housekeeper, not afraid of hard work, preferably with her own income.**'

"Jesus Christ! Why the hell has he answered me?" Viv shrieked. "*Delete!*" she exclaimed adamantly, wiping him off the screen.

Claire tried very hard to suppress her laughter.

When Viv had finished deleting the undesirables, she was left with five potential candidates.

Claire watched as she replied to them, wondering if anything would come of it.

Viv was as happy as Larry as she typed furiously. She seemed very positive and looked like she had been doing this all her life.

Claire wondered if it really would work. She couldn't wait to see what would happen. She wasn't as optimistic as Viv but neither was she as sceptical as Megan.

# Chapter 14

Megan stayed up half the night, unable to put Gloria's manuscript down. She was very excited and there was no doubt that they had stumbled on a gem. Tired as she was, she kept reading and couldn't wait to tell Simon what she thought and put the wheels in motion to sign up this author. They had to trawl through so many bad submissions by authors who were convinced their book would be the next big thing that it was a joy to discover one that really could be.

The following morning, Simon was delighted to hear that his hunch had been correct.

"Great, I'm glad you agree with me. Get on to the author and tell her we're interested in publishing her book. Great name, by the way, isn't it?"

"Yes, Gloria Rivers. Almost sounds like a pseudonym," Megan observed.

"Make an appointment to meet with her as soon as

possible," he advised. "We don't want to let this one get away."

Megan rang the daughter's number as soon as she got back to her office. She was thrilled to hear that they liked it and happily gave Megan her mother's number.

Gloria Rivers was shocked to hear that her daughter had submitted her manuscript to them, but overjoyed that they liked it. She agreed to come in to the office the following Friday for a meeting.

Megan felt the lovely glow that always comes when giving the good news to an author that their work would be published and looked forward to meeting the other woman.

There was a lively atmosphere in St Brigid's Ward as the party for Amy got under way. Claire had decorated the ward with balloons and a big banner, and the look of joy on Amy's little face brought tears to her eyes. Amy was wearing a party dress and her parents looked on, smiling, as their little girl enjoyed the festivities. They would be forever grateful to the wonderful doctors and nurses who had nursed their precious child from near-death to the lively bundle she was today. They were particularly grateful to Claire whose love and care had made such a difference to Amy's recovery.

As promised, Jamie turned up – with a gift for Amy. She gasped as she ripped the paper off to find it was a Barbie dressed in a nurse's uniform.

"Oh, thank you, Doctor Jamie. She's lovely. I'll call her Sister Claire," she announced, looking over at Claire shyly.

"That's a brilliant name for her," Jamie said, smiling at Claire who felt her face flushing under his gaze.

Amy's parents handed Claire a present. It was a beautiful gold Claddagh pendant. Claire was overwhelmed.

"I have one too," Amy said as she showed Claire the silver one around her neck. "It's for friendship, Mummy says."

"Thank you so much. It's beautiful," Claire said, touched by the gesture.

And then it was time for Amy to leave.

"That was a great party," Jamie whispered to Claire after they'd hugged Amy goodbye. "Fancy a coffee?"

"Yeah, sure. I'm feeling a bit emotional at the moment. I'll miss Amy a lot."

"I know," he said gently.

They made their way to the coffee shop.

It was packed but they found two seats right near the door. It amazed Claire how easy it was to talk to Jamie as she told him about her trip to Rome.

Neither of them noticed his girlfriend, Hannah, until she was upon them. She'd been with a group of doctors and was just leaving the cafeteria.

"Very cosy!" she remarked in a cold voice, glaring at Jamie. Before he could reply, she flicked back her hair and flounced out.

"Oh goodness," was all Claire could say.

"There'll be hell to pay now," Jamie commented with a shrug of his shoulders.

Claire felt bad. They were only having a coffee. It was purely innocent but Hannah had obviously thought otherwise. Oh dear!

Viv was on a roll. Messages had been flying back and forth between her and her prospective suitors during the day. She sent them whenever she had a break. They were making contact via the dating-site so nobody had her private email address. Her favourite and top of the list was the French guy, Gilles, and she decided maybe it was time to talk to him on the phone. She sent him her phone number and asked him to contact her at seven the following evening. He asked if he could call her straight away but as she was about to leave for dinner with her parents she told him it wasn't suitable. The last thing she wanted was for them to get wind of what she was doing. Much as she loved them, they were a little old-fashioned and wouldn't have understood. Meanwhile she continued to keep in touch with the other four guys who seemed very nice also. No point in putting all your eggs in one basket, as her mother was so fond of saying.

What a great idea this had been! Life was certainly looking up.

Gilles rang her the following evening, on the dot of seven. That was a good sign. His French accent had her swooning. There really was something incredibly sexy about a French accent. To her surprise, they spoke for half an hour. Afterwards, when Claire asked her, she couldn't remember what they'd actually talked about but there was definitely a connection there. He had wanted to meet her that very evening but, as she had arranged to go for an Indian with the girls, she declined. He sounded so disappointed that she almost changed her mind but the thought of Megan's ire prevented her. She promised to meet him the following evening.

Claire was almost as excited as Viv herself.

Megan took it with a grain of salt. "We'll see," was her cryptic remark.

Later, after a super Indian meal, the three of them were relaxing in the living room as Claire downloaded the photos from Rome onto her laptop.

"Oh heavens!" she wailed as she clicked on each photo. "I look so frumpy beside you two." Her two friends looked glamorous and chic in every photo whereas she looked like the plain Jane she knew she was. Was she really as dowdy as all that? She appeared almost invisible in photos of the three of them together as one's eye was drawn to the tall blonde goddess Megan, and the sultry vibrant Viv.

"I think it's time you had a make-over," Viv declared.

"Yes, you have really pretty hair but there's no shape on it and the colour is a tad boring," Megan said. "What you need is to have it properly styled and perhaps the copper tones in it accentuated."

Claire realised she was right. Her hair was a dull mousy shade and she usually wore it pulled up at the back in a clip. Maybe it was time to do something about it.

"Where should I go?" she asked.

"Leave it to me," Viv ordered. "I'll sort you out."

"Better prepare yourself, Claire. You've no idea what she's like when she gets going." Megan rolled her eyes as Viv gave her a dirty look.

"Pay no attention to her, Claire. We'd better go through your wardrobe before then and throw out anything remotely dowdy or frumpy. Then we can go on a shopping spree after we sort out the hair. What do you say?"

"She'll make a new woman of you, Claire," Megan grinned.

"Holy Cow! I'll have nothing left in my wardrobe at that rate." Claire was a little nervous but also looking forward to it. If anyone could help her it would be Viv.

At six thirty the following evening Viv was feeling

apprehensive but excited as she prepared for her date with Gilles. She stood in the centre of her room, clothes discarded on every surface. Claire was helping her choose and was almost as excited as Viv herself.

"I don't want to look too sexy but still I want to look attractive," Viv confided as she tried on yet another outfit.

Eventually it was decided and she was all set. Megan wasn't there to wish her luck as she was still at the gym. They had agreed that Claire would drive her to the meeting place so that she could have a drink.

"I'll need one to settle my nerves," Viv giggled.

She had arranged to meet Gilles in the Radisson Blu Hotel in Stillorgan.

"Are you sure you don't want me to go in with you?" Claire asked, a bit uneasy at the idea of her friend meeting with a total stranger.

"No, I'll be fine. What can happen to me in a crowded bar?" Viv laughed in an effort to put Claire's mind at ease. "Just wish me luck!"

She did agree that if things went horribly wrong and Gilles was weird or vaguely threatening, she would go to the loo and call Claire and Claire would call her back five minutes later. Then Viv could say she had an emergency and would have to leave in a hurry.

She was a bag of nerves as she entered the Orangerie Bar at ten minutes past seven. She spotted him immediately, recognising him from his photo. He was the best-looking man in the room. He recognised her too and stood up to greet her, smiling as he raised her hand to his lips.

"*Ah, Vivienne, chère.* You are more beautiful than I expected. I am so 'appy to meet wiz you."

"Hello, Gilles."

"No, it's pronounced *Zheel*," he corrected her. "*Excusemoi*, it is not like zee Eenglish."

Viv's heart sank. Working in fashion she met gay guys on a daily basis and, gorgeous as he was, there was no mistaking it. Gilles was gay.

Claire was relieved when no call came from Viv and she hoped that the date was going well. She decided to call her sister as they had parted on such bad terms the week before.

It was Sarah's husband Ben who answered the phone.

"Oh, hi, Ben. I'm surprised to find you in. Isn't Wednesday your poker night?"

Ben had been playing poker every Wednesday for as long as Claire could remember.

"Yes, it is, but Sarah decided to go out at the last minute so I had to cancel. I couldn't leave Tash and Owen alone. Tash is only fourteen and God knows what devilment Owen would get up to." His voice sounded down.

"Oh, of course you couldn't leave them alone," Claire agreed with him. "But where's Sarah gone?"

"God knows. She doesn't tell me. We're barely on speaking terms, to be honest."

Claire heard the dejection in his voice and bit her lip. She wondered who Sarah might be with. Her sister didn't keep friends for long. She had a knack of falling out with them.

"Oh Ben, I'm sorry. How are the kids?"

"Owen's fine but I'm afraid Sarah and Tash are at loggerheads most of the time. It's like World War Three here between the two of them. I'm at my wits' end wondering how to deal with it."

"Lord, that's awful, but I suppose most fourteen-year-old girls and their mothers clash." She remembered what a rebellious teenager Sarah had been. She herself had never been the rebellious sort.

"Maybe you could have a word with her, Claire?"

"I doubt she'd listen to me, Ben, she never has but I'll certainly try. How about you all come here for dinner on Friday night? I'll try and have a quiet word with her then."

"That would be great. I hope Sarah is free."

Claire heard the relief in his voice.

"I'm dying to see what you've done to the house," he added. "I hear you've made a lot of changes."

"Yes, I'm pretty pleased with it. Give my love to Tash and Owen. I'm looking forward to seeing them and ask Sarah to call me tomorrow if she can't make it."

"I will indeed. Thanks, Claire. Till Friday then."

Claire was pensive when she came off the phone. Ben was a darling but he'd always been too soft with Sarah. It was obvious their marriage was in trouble. She wondered what the hell Sarah was up to. Claire hoped she was not having an affair. It sounded awfully like it. She wouldn't put it past her sister. She'd definitely try and find out what was going on.

Viv was on her second glass of champagne and starting to relax. Gilles was charming, utterly charming, and very witty. It was obvious he was not boyfriend material but he was terrific company and she was enjoying herself. He was very forthcoming and open and by the time they got to the end of the bottle he had confided in her that he had been betrayed by his last two boyfriends and so had decided to date only women in future.

"I'm so sorry, Gilles," Viv said, aware that she was slurring her words ever so slightly, "but I don't think women are the answer."

"You don't zink so?" he asked downheartedly. "But you are zo beautiful, and a lovely person also."

He looked so glum that Viv reached over and patted his hand.

"We can still be friends, can't we?" she said.

"I would like zat very much," he smiled. "And now, we eat, no?"

Viv ordered the spicy duck salad, Gilles the cheese plate, and he ordered a bottle of St Emilion.

Viv had a hilarious evening as Gilles was a born entertainer and his witty anecdotes about the fashion world had her laughing uproariously. When the evening was over they agreed to keep in touch. She was sad it had turned out like that. If only he'd been straight, Viv thought, as she took a taxi home, it would have been perfect.

Claire and Megan were watching TV when the taxi dropped Viv off after her date with Gilles.

"Well?" Claire asked as she came through the door, dying to know how it had gone. "How was Gilles?"

"It's pronounced *Zheel*, actually," Viv informed them in her best French accent. "He was a pet and I had a brilliant night." Then she added, looking at the two upturned faces, "But, unfortunately, he's gay."

"What?" Claire gasped.

Megan gave a chuckle. "Why on earth did he go on a dating site looking to meet women then?" she asked, perplexed.

Viv sighed. "The poor guy is hoping he can change. He

really was a pet and we're going to meet again. As friends," she added quickly.

"Well, that's something, I suppose," Megan said. "Not a complete waste of an evening."

"Definitely not," Claire jumped to Viv's defence. "Though you must have been very disappointed. But at least you've still got those other four guys to meet."

"Yes. I honestly didn't expect to meet Mr Right on my first date."

Viv was not downhearted. She certainly wasn't going to give up at the first hurdle. Now that she'd taken the first step by meeting Gilles even though it hadn't worked out as she'd expected she was mad keen to meet the others. They seemed nice and what did she have to lose?

"By the way, I've invited Sarah and her family for dinner on Friday night," Claire announced. "You're both very welcome to join us."

"Sorry, count me out," Viv replied. There was no way she was wasting a whole evening with the Ugly Sister, as she secretly called Sarah.

"I'm afraid I'm busy too," Megan said. "My running group are doing a long run on Friday evening and we're going out for a meal afterwards." She was delighted that she had a good excuse for Claire. She was as reluctant as Viv to put up with her sister for an evening.

# Chapter 15

Sarah texted the following morning to say that dinner Friday was fine so Claire shopped on her way home that evening. It was her turn to cook for the girls so she made a huge pot of bolognese sauce and served spaghetti bolognese for dinner. The remainder of the sauce would go into a lasagne that she would assemble on Friday. She also made a large tiramisu for Friday as it was Sarah's favourite and, when Viv pleaded for a spoonful, she declared it was the best she'd ever tasted.

Viv was on a roll and had thrown herself wholeheartedly into this dating game. After the Gilles experience she decided that spending time talking on the phone was a bit of a waste of time. She certainly had never suspected from their phone conversation that Gilles was gay. Better to cut to the chase, meet them and see what they were like in person. So she had messaged the other four guys and set up four dates for drinks, one each for Friday and Sunday and two for the following week. It was all looking good. And there were also two new guys who had contacted her that sounded promising. Honestly, if she couldn't get a decent bloke out of all these men she was a hopeless case. Might as well join a nunnery!

Work was manic. She'd never been so busy and she'd made so much commission this week that she had managed to put by the insurance money for her car for the following year. If her Friday clients, the wife of a wealthy Arab racehorse owner and two footballers' wives, spent as much as they usually did, she might even be able to afford the Jimmy Choo purple shoe-boots that were simply to die for. Could life get any better than that?

The writer, Gloria Rivers, turned out to be a joy and Megan gelled with her instantly when she met her at the office on Friday. She was a grandmother, in her sixties, who had started writing after she retired, to fill in the time as much as anything else. Her daughter had insisted on reading her manuscript and thought it was so good that she had forwarded it to Megan's company, unknown to her mother. Now Gloria was overwhelmed that they were offering her a contract. Recognising a gem when they came across it, Megan and Simon had decided to offer her a three-book contract.

"Thank you, thank you so much," Gloria exclaimed, shocked. "I really can't believe this is happening. This is the stuff of dreams."

"I really loved your book," Megan smiled at the lovely lady. "You have quite a unique style."

"I'm so grateful," Gloria said.

"We're the ones who should be grateful. You're going to

make us a lot of money, hopefully. Now, would you like to have your solicitor look over the contract before you sign it?"

"Not at all. I trust you. I'll sign it now, if that's okay."

Megan smiled. She suspected Gloria was afraid they'd change their mind.

The contracts were signed and on the spur of the moment Megan asked Gloria if she was free for lunch. The new author graciously accepted the invitation and Megan enjoyed hearing the older woman's life story. She was a fascinating companion and the lunch went on much longer than Megan intended. She knew instinctively that they would become friends.

Gloria spoke proudly of her daughters and Megan could tell that she was very close to them. She would like to have had a mother like Gloria.

Viv's day went even better than she'd expected. First up was the sheik's wife who as usual bought a rake of only the best and most expensive clothes, bags and shoes in the store. She was a real lady and a very valuable client. As she left she handed Viv an envelope.

"A little thank-you for all your help," she said, smiling graciously at Viv.

Viv whooped for joy when she opened it and saw that it contained a €200 voucher for the store. She could almost feel the buttery suede of those Jimmy Choos.

Her next client was a mother-of-the-bride who had brought along her two sisters. To Viv's delight the two sisters also bought their wedding rig-outs from her and were very grateful to her for all her help. She took special pride in helping wedding clients who would have been intimidated by snooty salespeople. Viv was anything but that.

She gave up her lunch hour to fit in her next client, a banker who was a regular. She told Viv that she'd just been promoted and needed to upgrade her entire wardrobe. Viv knew her taste and within an hour and thirty minutes she was in and out, having spent a hefty amount.

The whole of the afternoon was taken up with Karen and Lisa, two WAGS, as they were called by the media. Their boyfriends were Irish footballers who had been signed by a top English football club and were earning obscene amounts of money. As a result the two girls had unlimited spending power, thanks to the platinum cards their boyfriends had foolishly given them.

"Oh, I do so love coming in here," Karen exclaimed excitedly as Viv greeted them.

"Yes, it makes me feel so posh having a personal shopper," Lisa giggled.

God help us, Viv thought, are they serious? Posh? She caught her assistant, Fiona's, eye and saw that she too was trying to smother a smile.

Fiona poured them each a glass of champagne and then she and Viv wheeled out two clothes-rails which were laden down with clothes.

"Oh my God!" Lisa squealed, pouncing on a red Hervé Léger dress. "I bags this," she cried, grabbing it off the rail.

Viv knew exactly what they wanted. These girls were highly label-conscious and would not be seen dead in the same dress twice. They devoured the glossy celebrity mags and based their style on what they saw there, so Viv's remit was to find glamorous, expensive designer gear (preferably short and figure-hugging) which would garner them attention, particularly from the paparazzi. Viv had done well. The girls bought everything she'd chosen for them.

They were silly girls and Viv doubted they'd last long, especially as the two footballers were constantly photographed in the tabloids, falling out of nightclubs and even strip clubs, various girls hanging on their arms. She supposed Lisa and Karen were right to make hay while the sun was still shining. Such was life!

Eventually the girls were done, giggling excitedly thanks to the champagne Fiona had plied them with. Women always bought more with some champagne to spur them on. Thanking Viv profusely, they tottered away on their vertiginous high heels, thrilled with their afternoon. The limousine the store used for special clients was waiting outside to take the girls and their purchases home. Viv just had time to dash to the shoe department and pick up the Jimmy Choo bootees before dashing home to get ready for her date. It had been a highly successful day. She hoped the evening would live up to it.


Claire rushed home from work and started preparing the meal. She was serving bruschetta for a starter and she made a salad to go with the lasagne and opened a bottle of Masi Campofiorin, a lovely Italian wine.

She made a special effort with the table settings and had just finished when the doorbell rang.

Ben embraced her warmly and Tash too. Her niece, who was also her goddaughter, had been christened Natasha, but had been called Tash for as long as anyone could remember. Owen, being an eleven-year-old boy, baulked at kissing his aunt. Instead, he grinned cheekily and let her give him a little hug. Both kids were very fond of their

Auntie Claire who always spoiled them, much to their mother's annoyance. Sarah gave Claire a peck on the cheek. She hadn't forgiven Claire for taking the key back off her.

Ben was overwhelmed by the changes Claire had achieved in the house.

"Oh, for goodness sake! Anybody would have done the same," Sarah muttered, scowling. She felt her husband was being over the top with his praise. He'd always had a soft spot for Claire of course.

"Where are Viv and Megan?" Sarah asked, looking around.

"Oh, they're out tonight. I thought it would be nice to have a family night with just us," Claire replied. "Now what can I get you to drink?"

Ben asked for a beer and the kids wanted Coke. Sarah asked for a gin and tonic. "Easy on the tonic," she instructed her sister. Claire and Ben exchanged looks. It was going to be one of those nights!

Claire put the lasagne in the oven and prepared the drinks.

"How was Rome?" Sarah asked, when Claire returned with the drinks. Her voice was brittle. It was obvious it still rankled that she hadn't been invited on the trip.

"Very nice, but tiring," Claire replied. She figured it was better to play it down. She'd intended showing the photos she'd taken but changed her mind. No point in rubbing salt in the wound.

"I'm going to enrol in Italian classes. I really think it's a lovely language," she told them.

"Good for you," Ben said.

"Waste of time," was Sarah's response.

Tash was all chat, telling Claire about the new tap class

124

she'd joined and how she'd been picked for the hockey team. Owen tried to interrupt her flow to tell about his rugby team and an argument ensued.

"For God's sake, Tash, can't you let someone else talk for a change?" Sarah snapped at her daughter who clammed up immediately.

Ben looked helplessly at Claire.

"I'm ready for another gin," Sarah said, holding out her glass.

Claire took it and wondered what she could do to ease the tension. She gave Sarah her drink and asked Tash to come and help her in the kitchen.

"You okay?" Claire asked her goddaughter, giving her a hug.

"Mum is so beastly to me, Auntie Claire. You have no idea."

"I know. I don't know what's bugging her at the moment. I'll try and talk to her," Claire promised as she put the bruschetta under the grill.

"She won't let me get a tattoo or wear make-up or short skirts. All my friends are allowed to do that. She's horrid."

"Well, she's probably just trying to protect you."

"*Protect me?*" Tash shrieked. "When she wears even shorter skirts with thigh boots? It's embarrassing. She's gross! And she's horrid to Dad too."

Claire could see that her niece was on the verge of tears.

"Don't worry. I'll talk to her and see what's wrong. Now will you take in this bottle of wine for me? Good girl!" She gave Tash another hug and handed her the wine.

Sarah came into the kitchen just as her daughter left. "There's very little gin in this," she said, raising her glass.

"Help yourself!" Claire pointed to the bottle of gin and

rolled her eyes as Sarah poured a hefty amount into her glass.

"I suppose Tash has been complaining about me," Sarah said, leaning against the counter while throwing back the gin.

"You should go easy on her, Sarah. She's nearly fifteen and she's a good kid."

"Huh!" Sarah snorted. "Good kid? You've no idea what a nightmare she is. Anyway, you've never had kids. Since when are you an expert?"

Claire stared at her sister, wounded to the core. How cruel could she be? Sarah knew that Claire would have given anything to be married with a family.

"You think marriage is a bed of roses," Sarah continued, oblivious to her sister's hurt. "Well, let me tell you, it's not! It's a frigging noose around your neck."

Claire was too choked up to reply and was saved by the timer telling her that the bruschetta was done.

"Dinner's ready," she said in a strained voice.

Now wasn't the time but it was obvious that a serious talk was called for. She left Sarah throwing back the remains of her drink as she called the others to the table.

The meal was a success as they all tried to ignore Sarah who was getting steadily more drunk as the evening wore on. She ate very little and didn't even taste the tiramisu that Claire had made specially for her. Luckily Ben and the kids lapped it up.

"I'm really sorry," Ben said after he had manoeuvred an almost comatose Sarah into the passenger seat of the car. "It was a lovely dinner, thank you, Claire."

"I told you, she's gross," Tash reiterated as Claire kissed

her goodnight on the doorstep.

"Why don't you and I go out to lunch on Sunday and maybe go shopping afterwards?" Claire suggested, giving her a wink. "Just the two of us?"

"Brilliant, Auntie Claire. That would be cool," Tash said as she skipped out to the car.

She's a lovely kid, Claire thought. Sarah was a fool. She didn't know how lucky she was.

While Claire was dealing with her drunken sister, Viv was having an even worse night. She had agreed to meet her date in the Leopardstown Inn which was jam-packed as it was a Friday night. She barely recognised him as he was older than his photograph suggested. She would have missed him but he recognised her.

"Viv?" he asked as he approached her.

"Bill?" she replied, surprised at his grey hair and heavy physique. Well, beer belly to be honest. Obviously the photo he'd posted had been taken twenty years ago.

"Drink?" he asked, as he led her to a bar stool. "Only seat available," he explained.

"I'll have a brandy and port," she said. She didn't miss the way he raised his eyebrows.

When their drinks were delivered he raised his glass to her.

"How old are you?" he asked.

"I beg your pardon?" Viv squinted at him, thinking she'd misheard.

"I asked how old you are," he repeated. "From your photo I thought you'd be younger."

Me too, you old git, she was tempted to say but she restrained herself. "Actually, I'm thirty-one and that photo was taken last Christmas. I haven't aged that much since then, I hope," she added sarcastically.

"Oh dear," he replied. "I thought you'd be younger. My ex-wife is thirty-one too and I'm really looking for someone younger than her. Just to show her, if you know what I mean."

He then launched into a tirade on what a bitch his ex-wife was and how she was taking him to the cleaners with their divorce. Viv listened flabbergasted as he ranted on and on. The wife had seemingly left him for someone younger which didn't surprise Viv one bit. She was tempted to fling her drink at him but figured that would be a waste of good brandy and good port. He finished his whisky in between his ranting.

"Your round," he said to Viv, pointing to his glass.

She couldn't believe her ears. Knocking back the remains of her drink in one go, she plonked her glass back on the counter.

"I don't think so," she replied, slipping on her jacket and getting off the stool. "Goodbye, Bill, and don't bother to contact me again. Oh, and tell your wife from me that she had a lucky escape." With as much dignity as she could muster, she walked away, head held high.

"Bitch!" he called after her. "All women are bitches," she heard him add.

"Wanker!" Viv muttered under her breath as she strode to her car.

She drove straight to Walsh's pub where she knew the girls from work would be having their usual Friday-night drink, but not before she deleted Bill from her account and blocked him.

She was tempted to have a few drinks and take a taxi

home but instead she stuck to Coke and left the pub just after ten thirty. There was only so much Coke Zero she could tolerate.

She tried to sneak past the dining room so as not to have to meet Sarah but realised that the house was too silent. Could they have left already? Quietly opening the door to the living room she saw Claire sitting forlornly, nursing a glass of wine.

"What happened? Are they gone already?"

"Yes. Sarah got pissed and they left straight after dinner."

"Oh, I *am* sorry."

"How was your date?"

"Don't ask! It was a total disaster." She rolled her eyes and as she recounted her evening she began to see the funny side of it. "I'm sorry now I didn't toss the brandy all over him."

Claire giggled and then the two of them started laughing uproariously.

"Come on, I promised to go through your wardrobe with you," said Viv. "Now is as good a time as any. We might as well get something productive done this evening."

Claire followed her up to the bedroom apprehensively. She suspected there wouldn't be many clothes left in the wardrobe by the time this professional was finished with it.

She wasn't far wrong. As Viv used her expert eye and skills the pile of unsuitable clothes grew bigger and bigger and the suitable one remained very small.

"Better have that credit card ready for tomorrow," she ordered Claire.

"I can't afford to replace my whole wardrobe," Claire wailed.

"Of course you can, if we shop sensibly," Viv assured her. "You don't need clothes for work as you wear a uniform which is a terrific bonus. So you only need leisure-wear. I suggest you get one or two quality pieces from my place – the sale is on and I can get you my discount – so they won't be too expensive, and the rest we'll get in Penneys. You'll be amazed what €200 will get you there. And that includes shoes." Viv was now throwing most of Claire's shoes on the unsuitable pile too.

"If you say so," Claire said, not convinced. However, she was willing to give it a go.

They had just finished piling the unsuitable clothes into black-plastic bags when they heard Megan come in.

"Come on, let's go open a bottle of wine and tell Megan about our evening," Viv suggested. "I could bloody do with a drink."

Arm in arm, they descended the stairs to do just that.

# Chapter 16

Claire was awakened by a knock on her bedroom door as Viv entered carrying a tray with a great-smelling breakfast on it.

"*Ta-Ra!* Rise and shine, baby!" Viv ordered as Claire pulled herself into a sitting position.

Viv placed the tray on her knees as Claire gaped at the bacon, sausage, egg, tea and toast sitting there.

"Wow, what did I do to deserve this?" she asked.

"You need to get your strength up for today," Viv replied, as she sat on the side of Claire's bed and tucked into the tiramisu that Sarah had spurned the evening before and which she'd found in the fridge.

Claire rolled her eyes and bit into a sausage.

"Mmmm . . . this is *soooo* good," Viv declared, licking her lips.

They set out immediately after breakfast. Their first stop was Viv's hairdresser, Anna, who advised that Claire have

131

clip-in extensions to give her hair more body and suggested a colour and highlights to bring out the natural copper tones in her hair. Claire became extremely nervous when Anna handed her the colour chart which had off-the-wall red, purple and even bright orange shades on it.

"I'm thinking of a rich mahogany with copper overtones," Anna said, pointing to a quite normal colour. "Think Cheryl Cole or Kate Middleton. Nothing too outrageous."

Claire heaved a sigh of relief. She'd always admired the glossy hair of both of these famous women. So she relaxed and put herself in Anna's hands.

When Anna had finished Claire could not believe that it was herself looking out of the mirror. She looked like a total stranger. Her hair was full and glossy and fell in layers to her shoulders. It was a gorgeous rich brown shade with copper glints and she absolutely loved it. Secretly she thought she could give Kate Middleton a run for her money.

"Wow!" Viv said, for once lost for words.

Anna smiled with satisfaction as the other stylists and even clients admired it.

"It was expensive but worth every penny," Claire said when she and Viv had left the salon.

Next step was the beauty salon where Viv had booked for Claire to have her eyebrows threaded, eyelashes dyed and gel nails applied. Meanwhile, Viv left to have a scoot around Penneys and A-Wear to see what she could source for Claire's wardrobe.

Viv hadn't realised how pretty Claire actually was. With her lank hair and bushy eyebrows that wasn't surprising, not to mention the baggy tracksuits she lived in. Well, all that was about to change!

They met up for lunch in Brambles and then, energy renewed, set off again. Viv had organised a make-up session with the Lancôme girl in Harvey Nics who was a friend of hers – but better to leave that until after trying on all the clothes. If there was one thing Viv hated, it was women who left make-up all over the clothes they were trying on. Her clients knew better than to turn up caked with the stuff.

The first thing Viv insisted on was that Claire get fitted for a good bra.

"No point in having gorgeous clothes if your boobs are all over the place. A good-fitting bra is an essential."

Claire was shocked to discover that she'd been wearing the wrong size bra all along. She chose three bras, white, black and nude and then, in a moment of daring, opted for a red one too.

Then it was on to Penneys where Viv whisked around pulling clothes off racks for Claire to try on. Poor Claire was dizzy by the time it was over and had a mountain of clothes in her trolley, not to mention shoes and accessories. Viv had been right. The bill came to €227, which was nothing if you considered the amount of stuff she'd bought.

Next they hit A-Wear where Claire fell in love with two tops and a skirt and lastly they made their way to Viv's store.

"You really can't skimp on good boots and you need one good leather bag," Viv advised.

Claire dutifully bought both, using Viv's discount of course.

"Just a couple more things I'd like you to try on," Viv said.

Claire groaned.

"We're nearly finished, I promise you," said Viv.

She led them to her own department where she had put by some things the day before with Claire in mind. First she took out a green Michael Kors cocktail dress.

"I couldn't afford that," Claire cried.

"It's in the sale, plus there's my discount," Viv assured her.

Claire tried it on. It fitted like a glove and, as it was the same green as her eyes, it complemented them.

"You have to have it," Viv insisted.

And she was right – it wasn't as expensive as Claire had expected.

"And the last thing," Viv announced, whisking out a coral velvet tracksuit.

"A tracksuit? I don't believe it!" Claire cried, grinning as she grabbed it.

"Not just any old tracksuit," Viv declared. "It's Juicy Couture. It's also on sale."

It was so comfortable that Claire didn't want to take it off.

They made their way to the beauty counter where Viv's friend did Claire's make-up, explaining what she was using as she did it. The effect was startling.

"Wow!" was all Claire could say when she looked in the mirror." She hadn't realised her eyes were so green but the eye make-up had accentuated their colour.

"You look am*aaaaaz*ing!" Viv exclaimed. "Your eyes are the most amazing brilliant green."

Claire bought the products the girl had used and finally they were done. "Okay, to the pub!" she cried. "I'm parched. Drinks are on me."

They rang Megan who met up with them. She was gobsmacked by the change in Claire. "You look fantastic," she said admiringly.

Claire kept getting a shock every time she caught sight of her reflection in the mirror or in the window. She also couldn't resist flicking her hair, the way Megan always did. It was something she'd never been able to do before.

They picked up a Chinese take-away on the way home and after they'd eaten they sat down to watch the first episode of their favourite programme, *Strictly Come Dancing*.

The comments came thick and fast.

"My God, where did they get her?"

"Wow! He can certainly move."

"I'd die for that dress."

"I thought they were supposed to be celebrities. I've never even heard of her!" This last remark from Viv.

They each had an opinion on every single dancer, praising them or giving them the thumbs-down. They were more critical than the judging panel. However, they were all agreed that the professional dancers were stupendous and each girl had a favourite. They had great craic and it was almost midnight when they dragged themselves up to bed. Tomorrow would be a busy day for all three of them.

# Chapter 17

Claire had arranged to collect Tash at twelve the following day, after Sunday Mass. Ben opened the door to her.

"Wow!" he exclaimed, his mouth dropping open. "What have you been up to? You look wonderful."

His look of admiration made her feel good.

Tash came flying down the stairs. "Hi, Auntie Claire," she cried before stopping dead in her tracks. "Oh my God! Is that really you?" she squealed. "You look fab! Really neat." She walked around Claire, taking it all in.

"Hi, Auntie Claire," Owen called out, sneaking past her in case she might want to kiss him. Her transformation was lost on him. He hopped on his bike, football under his arm, and scooted down the drive and out the gate.

"Come in, come in," Ben said. "Would you like a coffee?"

"No, thanks. I think Tash and I should get going right away."

At that moment, Sarah came down the staircase in a

crumpled dressing-gown, looking very much the worse for wear. She shaded her eyes as she looked her sister up and down, shocked at what she saw.

"What have you done to yourself?" she exclaimed, taken aback.

Claire touched her hair self-consciously. "Don't you like it?"

Sarah shrugged. "That hairdo must have cost a pretty penny – *and* fake nails, I see," she added, taking Claire's hand. "Well, I never! They're not really you, are they?"

"Come on, Auntie Claire, let's go," Tash cried impatiently, pulling at Claire's arm.

"Okay, see you all later," Claire said, feeling a little deflated by Sarah's remarks.

Ben threw her a helpless look.

"Don't mind her," Tash said as they drove off. "Mum's just a jealous cow. I think you look super."

Claire took her niece into Dublin city, knowing how much she loved Grafton Street, and parked the car in the Stephen's Green Centre. They had lunch in Pasta Fresca and she could see that Tash was loving it and feeling very grown-up. After lunch they headed down Grafton Street and Claire enjoyed spoiling the young girl who had very definite ideas on what she liked. A-Wear was a big hit with her and at four o'clock, laden down with bags, they made their way to the Westbury for afternoon tea.

"I think I shopped more this weekend than I have in my whole life up to now," Claire laughed as they admired the tiny sandwiches and pretty pastries the waitress had brought them.

As they enjoyed their tea, Claire told Tash about Amy and how they'd all thought she was going to die.

"But she's a plucky little girl and fought hard to survive. She went home this week and we threw a party for her when she was leaving."

"It must be great to help sick children like you do," Tash declared. "That's what I want to be when I finish school. A children's nurse, just like you."

Claire was touched, delighted that her young niece wished to follow in her footsteps.

"I'm sure you'll make a great nurse. Now, it's after five – I suppose I'd better get you home or your mother will be worrying about you."

"Fat chance! She probably isn't in and, even if she was, she wouldn't care where I was."

Claire felt sad that Sarah's relationship had broken down with her daughter. She planned to have a serious chat with her sister this coming week. It was long overdue.

Megan was also involved with family that Sunday lunchtime. Her mother had returned from Marbella and had invited her to lunch at PJ's in Fitzpatrick's. To Megan's surprise Daphne had seemed in great spirits and hadn't mentioned Paul or the wedding even once over the phone. Megan hoped she'd forgotten about it.

She arrived at the hotel to find Daphne waiting for her, looking bronzed and relaxed.

"Hello, darling, how are you? Good Lord, you've lost a lot of weight."

"Hello, Daphne. I'm fine. I'm training for the Dublin City Marathon and working out a lot – so I haven't actually lost weight, it's just that I'm more toned." Megan could have kicked herself. Thirty seconds in her mother's company and she was already explaining herself and on the defensive.

139

"Whatever," Daphne waved her hand dismissively.

"You look well. How was Marbella?"

"Simply divine, darling. Best holiday I've had in years. I'm seriously thinking of selling up here and moving out. Non-stop partying."

"Why not?" Megan didn't think it would make much difference to her either way. She and her mother just did not get on. She'd finally reconciled herself to that fact.

"Darling, what's happened to your boobies?" Daphne asked, prodding Megan in the chest. "They've practically disappeared. Don't you think that you should consider having a boob job?"

Megan looked at her mother with distaste. "I'm a 34B. That's quite in proportion to the rest of my body."

"I've heard of a fantastic plastic surgeon here in the Rosebay Clinic. Simply everyone who's anyone in Marbella has had work done with him. I've already booked in for a consultation with him this week. Why don't I book a boob job for you? My treat. What do you say?"

"I'll pass. You know how I detest that look. Big boobs over a tiny waist and no hips. It's so unnatural. I'm quite happy with mine as they are, thank you all the same." As always her mother had got under her skin.

"You're not serious?," her mother said, disbelievingly. "I'm sure you'll regret it one day. Men like big boobs, you know."

Megan gritted her teeth and said nothing. She enjoyed the buffet lunch which was always good here and took just one glass of wine. She watched as Daphne polished off the rest of the bottle, regaling her with gossip from Marbella. Megan listened with only half an ear, relieved that her mother hadn't mentioned the wedding.

As they finished eating she noticed her mother look anxiously towards the door several times. Then Daphne's eyes lit up as she beckoned to a young man who had entered the restaurant. He approached their table and Megan could see that he was devastatingly good-looking.

"Megan, I'd like you to meet my friend, Luis. Luis, this is my daughter, Megan."

He was about her own age or even a little younger, Megan guessed, with long jet-black curly hair and dark olive skin. He was wearing dark jeans and a pale blue denim shirt which couldn't hide his muscular physique. He had a wonderful smile which lit up his liquid brown eyes and somehow made him look vulnerable. He was simply gorgeous.

"*Encantada, señorita*," he said as he brought her hand to his lips and held it there a fraction too long. As he did so, he looked up at her from under impossibly long curly black eyelashes and his dark eyes held her gaze.

Megan was mesmerised and shocked at the chemistry between them. She blushed and snatched her hand away quickly, embarrassed. He smelt of Tom Ford's Noir, her favourite men's cologne. She recognised it because it was the one her father always wore. It was *not* cheap!

"Come sit beside me, *cariño mío*," Daphne said, reaching out her hand to him.

He sat beside her, still holding her hand and Megan wondered if it was possible he was her mother's boyfriend. Surely not?

"Can you believe I have a daughter of twenty-three?" Daphne purred.

Megan raised her eyebrows questioningly. Daphne had always looked after her skin and figure and knew she looked younger than her age, but twenty-three was pushing it. Luis appeared not to question it.

"No," he answered. "And a very beautiful daughter," he added, looking at Megan from under his eyelashes, holding her gaze yet again.

Megan blushed as she looked away, disturbed.

"Oh, the apple didn't fall far from the tree," Daphne trilled, a little put out. "Isn't he just divine, darling?" she asked Megan, leaning over to caress Luis's face. "The best-looking man in Marbella. I needn't tell you all my friends were green with envy."

Megan realised with a sickening feeling that Luis was indeed Daphne's latest conquest. It was disgusting to see her mother all over this young guy like a rash. Embarrassed, she decided it was time to leave.

"Sorry, I have to go," she said, getting up quickly.

"Must you?" Luis asked, his eyes showing disappointment.

"Yes, I have to pick up my friend from the airport," she lied.

She bolted out of the restaurant without a backward glance. What a nightmare, she thought as she drove off, angry with herself for being attracted to him. There had definitely been chemistry there, but then all Mediterranean men had a knack of making women feel that way, didn't they? His charm had obviously worked on her mother too.

Viv went to her parents' for lunch on Sunday and later that afternoon went to The Goat to meet her next date, whose name was Conor. He had agreed to meet her wherever was handiest for her which was great. The Goat was within walking distance and was a favourite haunt of hers.

Conor's photo on his profile was very blurred and she hoped she'd recognise him when she met him. She needn't have worried. He came to greet her the minute she walked in the door.

He was not wildly good-looking but had a nice kind face with a smile that lit up his eyes. He was tall and slim and Viv liked him at once.

"I haven't done this before so you'll have to forgive me," he said shyly. "I'm very nervous to be honest."

"I'm pretty new to this too," Viv replied. "You're only my third date."

"How did the other two go?"

"Don't ask! Disaster!"

He laughed then and, when she joined in, the ice was broken. They got on like a house on fire and he told her that he was an engineer who had moved from Dublin to Galway seven months ago. Sadly, his father died suddenly shortly after he'd moved and so he now came to Dublin most weekends to be with his mother, who lived alone in Blackrock. He'd split with his long-term girlfriend nine months previously so all in all he'd had a crappy year. He'd found it very hard to get over the break-up and hadn't dated anyone since.

He and Viv had a lot in common. He was interested in fashion as his ex was a model – with over a hundred pairs of shoes, he confided – and he detested football.

"I do love my golf, however," he admitted.

He was very entertaining and when they were still talking non-stop, two hours later, Conor suggested that they have something to eat. He had a great sense of humour and Viv really enjoyed his company. He obviously enjoyed hers too because at the end of the evening he said he'd like to see her again. He insisted on dropping her home and kissed her on the cheek as he said goodbye.

Viv entered the house, walking on air.

Megan and Claire looked up as she came into the living room.

"Bingo!" she cried. "Third time lucky! I've just met the most adorable man."

The girls listened as she told them about her date.

"See, I told you that it works. You just have to give it time. Sort the wheat from the chaff."

"That's brilliant," Claire exclaimed, hoping this guy was genuine and that something would come of it.

"I hope you're right," Megan remarked cautiously.

Viv was convinced she was.

"Maybe I should try this online dating too," Claire suggested shyly. She'd been thinking that her life was pretty boring and it was time she started getting out and about more.

"You definitely should, Claire. I'm having a ball. Beats sitting in alone every night, and who knows? You might meet someone like Conor too."

"I think you're better off with your own company than some of the weirdos you'll meet on there," Megan advised.

"Don't mind her, Claire. She doesn't need a dating site. She meets loads of men at her running club and at work." Viv glared at Megan. "And what do I meet at work? Spoilt, pampered women with not a man in sight. C'mon, Claire, I'll help you do out your profile right now."

Claire was about to back down as she thought she was not interesting enough and that her CV would be too boring. Viv was adamant and embellished it somewhat. The only requirement Claire wanted in a man was that he be kind and genuine. Viv took her photo and downloaded it. It was quite flattering and Claire was happy that she'd had that make-over at the weekend. If she'd put up a photo of herself before that, she was sure no-one would have replied. Before she knew it she was a member of the dating site and her details were up there for all to see. She was feeling vulnerable and very apprehensive about it.

Viv was delighted that Claire had joined too and looked forward to guiding her. She hoped she would meet someone nice, like Conor.

She had a lovely dream that night where she was walking down the aisle in the most divine dress and waiting at the altar was a smiling Conor.

# Chapter 18

Claire wasn't expecting to create such a stir when she arrived at work the next day but the other nurses gathered around her oohing and aahing at her transformation. She'd never worn make-up to work before and between that and her new hairstyle everyone was amazed by the change in her. Even some of the children told her she was very pretty.

When Jamie came on the ward, he did a double take.

"My goodness! I saw you from behind and thought we had a new nurse. You've changed your hairstyle."

Claire blushed. She didn't think Jamie ever noticed things like that.

"Yes, went a bit crazy over the weekend. My friend took me on a pampering and shopping spree and my credit card is still red hot," she laughed.

"I'm happy to hear that. It's time you started spoiling yourself. You spent long enough pandering to your mother and not yourself," he said with a wry smile.

She blushed again. Don't I know it, she thought, but she

didn't say anything, just smiled.

She called Sarah during her lunch-hour and suspected from her sleepy voice that she was still in bed. At twelve thirty!

"Sarah, can you meet me on Wednesday night?"

"Why?" Sarah mumbled sleepily.

"It's important. I need to talk to you."

"I'm busy on Wednesday."

"Well, how about Thursday then?"

"No, I'm busy every night this week," Sarah informed her.

Claire sighed. "Well, can you please spare me an hour over the weekend? You're hardly busy every single minute then." She was irritated with her sister.

"All right. I'll call you," Sarah agreed sulkily.


Viv decided to go ahead and meet up with her date on Monday night. She was hoping Conor would call, as he'd promised, but just in case he didn't it was as well to keep going. The guy she was going to meet had an English accent and had explained he couldn't really talk for very long. She wondered why he'd chosen that moment to ring her if he couldn't talk. He'd asked her to meet him in Dublin city.

She took the Luas straight from work on Monday evening and soon was squinting in the dark of the small dingy pub where he'd suggested they meet. She couldn't see him but he had seen her.

"Viv, I presume," he said, coming forward and taking her arm.

He led her to a table in the corner and asked what she would like to drink. He was extremely good-looking and

148

was wearing a very smart business suit. Coming back with their drinks, he gave her a dazzling smile as he raised his glass to her.

"Well, tell me all about yourself. Wait – let me guess. Single mother . . . divorcee?"

"Neither," she replied, wondering why he'd asked that.

"No?" He raised his eyebrows in surprise. "Well then, tell me what's wrong with you."

Viv looked at him, baffled. "I beg your pardon?"

"I asked what was wrong with you – such a pretty girl, yet you have to go online to find a guy."

Viv was gobsmacked. He was still smiling so she thought he might be joking.

"There's nothing wrong with me–"

He cut her short. "Of course there must be. All of the women I've met online have been either desperate or ugly, or both. It's not natural for such a pretty girl to be reduced to this. Are you frigid?"

Viv couldn't believe her ears. She was completely floored by the arrogance of this son-of-a-bitch.

"And what's wrong with *you* then?" she retorted. "Do *you* have a problem in the sex department?"

"Definitely not," he grinned. "I can produce lots of witnesses to that."

It was then she saw the white mark on his ring finger and the truth dawned on her.

"Ah, I get it. You're married and you think you'll find desperate girls on the dating site who will be so grateful that they'll hop into bed with you."

He guffawed, a horrible loud laugh. "Well, well, you're clever as well as pretty," he said.

"I guess I am. Clever enough to recognise an asshole

when I meet one and not that desperate that I would waste another second on him." Without another word she poured the remainder of her drink over him. The shock on his face gave her great satisfaction.

"Hey, steady on there. I'm sure we can work something out," he cried, mopping himself with his handkerchief.

Viv gave him a scathing look, then, gathering her bag and jacket, walked out. The barman, who had been watching, grinned at her and gave her the thumbs-up.

What a waste of an evening, she thought, as she waited to catch the Luas home. She couldn't believe her eyes when she got a message from him apologising and asking if she would return to the bar.

"Not bloody likely," Viv said aloud as she deleted and blocked him from her phone.

Another one bites the dust, she said to herself, as the Luas pulled in to the stop.

She kept checking her phone, hoping that Conor would get in touch but he hadn't yet. He was the only decent guy she'd met so far.

"Another pervert," she told Claire later as she recounted what had happened on her date. "Or maybe I should mark him off as a fraud. Bit of both, I guess."

Claire could hardly believe it. "Well, at least your life is never dull," she giggled.

"You can say that again," Viv said, grinning. How true that was!

When Claire logged on to her account on the dating site that evening, she was surprised to find that four men had messaged her. She wasn't as audacious as Viv and wanted to get to know them a bit better before making any dates.

She replied to the men and told them a little about herself. They all seemed nice but there was one man in particular that she liked. His name was Richard and she was looking forward to hearing more about him.

On Tuesday night, Claire had two more replies and was busy messaging them when there was a ring at the door. Megan was out to dinner with her running group and Viv had gone to a cosmetics party with some girls from work.

Claire answered the door and was surprised to find her sister standing there.

"Sarah, what brings you here? Come in."

"Hi," Sarah replied tersely, pushing past her. "I need a drink." She marched straight into the kitchen.

Claire followed and stared open-mouthed as Sarah poured herself a gin and tonic. It was obvious that she'd had a few drinks already.

"What's up?" Claire asked.

"I've had a terrible row with Ben. I need you to put me up for a few days till I sort things out."

"You're not serious?" Claire gasped, wondering if she'd heard right.

"Yes, I'm thinking of leaving him. We just don't get on any more."

Claire was aghast. She wondered what had happened to bring this about. She needed a drink now too. She poured herself a gin and tonic and sat down at the kitchen table to recover from this shock.

"What's happened? What was the row about? You're not serious about leaving, are you?"

"Deadly! My life is so boring with him and I just don't love him any more."

"What about the kids?"

"They'll be fine with Ben while I decide what to do. Tash will probably be delighted. She hates me anyway."

"That's not true," Claire protested. "She's just behaving like all fourteen-year-old girls. It's a phase. She'll get over it. She's a good kid."

"Huh, you should see the way she looks at me. And as for Owen, well, he just lives for football and he's his father's son. That's all they ever think about – football, football, football! I feel totally excluded."

"Oh come on, Sarah," Claire said, suddenly feeling sorry for her. She got up and put her arm around her sister's shoulders. "That's normal. Things can't be that bad. Why don't I call Ben?"

Sarah shook her head vehemently. "No, don't do that! I need space to think. I'm so unhappy with him. I'll be forty next year and life is just passing me by. I keep thinking there must be more to life than this."

Claire didn't know what to say. Sarah had already finished her drink and was ready for a second. She took the bottle of gin and emptied it. Her glass was three-quarters gin with just a splash of tonic, Claire noticed. She was glad the bottle was empty and there was no more. Gin didn't last long with Sarah around.

"Look, why don't I make up the bed in the box-room for you? You'll probably feel differently about things tomorrow."

"I won't," Sarah replied, gulping her drink. She had started to slur her words. "Why can't I sleep in my old room?"

Claire looked at her in dismay. Was she serious?

"It hasn't been your room for over fifteen years, Sarah,"

she pointed out gently. "You know Megan is in it now."

"Why can't Megan sleep in the box-room?" Sarah asked petulantly.

Claire could see that familiar look in her sister's eyes which signified she was drunk.

"Because she pays me for her room and all her stuff is in it. Now I'll go and make up the bed in the box-room for you," she said, exasperated. "You'll have to use my en-suite bathroom, of course, because Viv has the family bathroom now."

"I wish they weren't here. I thought I could rely on you." Sarah looked at her accusingly.

"Of course you can rely on me," Claire assured her.

"I left my case in my car. Could you get it for me?" Sarah dangled her keys in the air.

Claire was appalled. Had her sister driven over after drinking? It was obvious she meant business if she'd thought to pack some things. Oh God, what a problem!

She did as Sarah asked then lugged the case up the stairs and made up the bed for Sarah. When she came back down Sarah was asleep at the kitchen table. Claire woke her with difficulty, then half-carried her up the stairs, undressed her and put her to bed. She was asleep again in a second.

Biting her lip, Claire pondered the problem. There would be hell to pay with Viv when she told her Sarah would be staying. Megan wouldn't be too happy either. But what could she do? She couldn't very well turn her sister away, certainly not in that state. Who knows what Sarah might have done? No, she'd just have to face their wrath. Please God it would only be for a few days. She went to call Ben to let him know that his wife was with her. He was distraught but relieved to know that Sarah was safe at least.

"I don't know what to do," he confided to Claire in a worried voice. "She's out all the time and drinking far too much. I worry about her drinking and driving but, if I mention it, she flies into a rage."

Claire could hear the angst in his voice.

"I confronted her about it tonight and we had a dreadful row. Then she just upped and left," he continued miserably. "I'm so worried about her and it's not good for the kids. They're frightened."

"I can imagine," Claire replied sympathetically. "It's obvious she's going through some sort of crisis. Lots of women feel that way as they face the big four-O. She's safe now anyhow and sleeping, so don't worry. Maybe she'll feel differently in the morning. I'll try and talk to her tomorrow evening and call you."

"Thanks, Claire, you're a gem."

Megan was the first one home. "What's Sarah's car doing in the driveway?" she asked Claire as she came into the living room.

"Oh dear, I forgot. I'd better go and move it so Viv can park."

She dashed out, leaving Megan mystified.

"Well?" Megan asked when she'd returned.

"I parked it around the corner, outside O'Dwyer's." Claire heaved a sigh. "She's sleeping here tonight. She and Ben had a row and she had nowhere else to go. I had to let her stay. She's my sister."

Megan could see Claire was being defensive and understood. "Of course. I just hope it's only temporary. I can't see her and Viv living under the same roof for very long."

Claire bit her lip. "I know. It's just till she and Ben sort things out. A few days at most." She was as worried about the animosity between Viv and Sarah as Megan was. She would help her sister but she would not let her ruin this new life she'd created for herself.

Viv came in shortly after.

"Why the long faces?" she asked as she plonked down on the sofa.

"Well, we have some bad news," Megan started when Claire said nothing. "Sarah is sleeping here tonight. She had a row with Ben and had nowhere else to go."

"Bloody hell!" Viv exclaimed.

"I'm sorry, Viv. I had no choice," Claire said apologetically.

Megan flashed Viv a warning glance, beseeching her not to explode.

"Well, she *is* your sister. I'd have done the same," Viv replied, heeding Megan's request. But she couldn't resist adding, "I just hope she won't be staying for too long."

"No, just a few days, until they can sort things out." Claire crossed her fingers behind her back as she said this. She prayed this would be the case.

# Chapter 19

Viv was very quiet at breakfast the following morning and the atmosphere was a touch awkward. Megan tried to make conversation but it was difficult to talk without mentioning Sarah. Claire knew her housemates were wondering how long Sarah would be staying.

When it was time for Claire to leave for work, she tried to wake Sarah but to no avail. She left her a note propped up on the kitchen table beside a key.

When Claire got home from work that evening, Sarah was sitting in front of the TV, sipping a glass of wine, as if she didn't have a care in the world. Claire was furious that she'd found and opened the only bottle in the house, an expensive one that Viv had bought and that they were saving for a special occasion. Oh Lord, Claire thought to herself, Viv will have a fit. I'll tell her I'll replace it tomorrow.

"Hi, what's for dinner?" Sarah asked, her eyes still on

the screen. She was watching that dreadful reality family, the Kardashians.

"I don't know. It's Megan's turn to cook today," Claire replied irritably, itching to turn off the TV.

"Oh super, I'm sure anything she cooks will be good. I can't imagine you or Viv would exactly be *Masterchef* material."

Claire wanted to slap her sister, hard.

"By the way, where did you put my car?" Sarah asked. "It's not in the driveway."

"No, there's only room for three cars in the driveway and even that's a squeeze. I parked it around the corner, outside O'Dywer's."

"Well, thank you very much," Sarah said huffily. "And why can't I park in the driveway?"

"Because you can't. You're a guest here, Sarah. Viv and Megan live here now." Abruptly, Claire left the room and went upstairs to change.

Megan and Viv came in together.

"Hi, I hear you're the cook tonight, Megan," Sarah said brightly.

Megan didn't get to reply as just then Viv spotted the half-empty bottle of wine.

"Where did you get that wine?" she demanded.

"In the cupboard. Why?"

"Because it's mine," Viv said as she whipped the bottle up.

"Really? I assumed it was Claire's. I didn't see your name on it."

Viv just glared at her.

"When will dinner be ready, Megan?" Sarah asked sweetly. "I'm going out tonight."

"You've been here all day while we've been out working," Viv snapped. "The least you could do was to start cooking dinner."

"I'm a guest here, as Claire keeps reminding me," Sarah replied snootily.

"A guest would at least have good manners and show some respect," Viv remarked before storming out of the room, bottle of wine in hand.

"What's bugging *her*?" Sarah asked Megan who shrugged her shoulders and followed her friend into the kitchen.

"Ooooh! She makes my blood boil," Viv cried, as she put the cork back in the bottle. "I can't be civil to her, honestly I can't."

"Try and ignore her, for Claire's sake," Megan advised, hoping to keep the peace. She hoped Sarah would not be there long. It would cause mayhem if she stayed.

She set about making the pasta carbonara she'd planned for dinner.


The atmosphere round the table was tense but Sarah hardly seemed to notice. She was all aflutter and appeared to be in high spirits. She was heavily made-up and wearing a short dress. She ate little and after ten minutes said, "Okay girls, I'm off out. Thanks for dinner, Megan. See you later."

"Where are you going?" Claire asked. She had been hoping to have a serious heart-to-heart with her sister after dinner.

"I've got a date. You're not the only one who can get dates online," Sarah said, smirking at Viv.

With a flourish she left the room, leaving the three girls with their mouths agape.

"Well, I never!" Viv was the first to speak.

Claire had gone pale. Was Sarah really going out with a man she'd met online? This was more serious than she'd realised.

"Don't worry. I guess she's just a bit cheesed off with domesticity at the moment," Megan tried to reassure her. "It's a phase a lot of women go through as they turn forty. I'm sure it's not serious. She'll get over it."

Viv crowed. She couldn't help herself. "A phase? I'll say! I think she's just a good-time girl. Your sister is a right piece of work, Claire, that's for sure. Maybe some poor idiot will take her off our hands."

Megan, seeing Claire's distress, kicked Viv under the table.

"Oh God, don't say that," Claire said, wringing her hands agitatedly. "I'm sure she and Ben will work things out."

"Poor Ben, is all I can say," Viv remarked.

Megan silenced her with a glare.

The atmosphere in the house had changed with Sarah there and Claire didn't know what to do about it. Megan and Viv did not come home for dinner on Thursday and Claire suspected it was because of her sister's presence. Then on Friday she received a text from each of them. Megan said she'd be home late and Viv said she couldn't make dinner either. Claire was worried. It was all going wrong.

When Claire got home that evening, she went straight upstairs for a shower, only to find her sister ensconced in *her* en-suite. Irritated, she knocked on the door.

"Will you be long, Sarah? I want to have a shower myself."

160

"About half an hour," Sarah replied.

Half-a-bloody-hour for a shower! Claire was annoyed. She put the casserole she'd taken out of the freezer that morning on to heat and potatoes on to boil. They were ready by the time Sarah came down, dolled up to the nines.

"What's for dinner?" she asked, coming into the kitchen.

"Beef casserole," Claire replied.

"Count me out so. I hate stews."

"You have to eat, Sarah."

"Don't worry – I'll grab something later. Might even stick my date for a fancy meal," her sister replied with a smug smile.

"Date? Who are you meeting?" Claire asked with a sinking heart.

"Another guy I met online."

"How are you getting so many dates?" Claire couldn't resist enquiring.

"Easy! I joined three different dating sites."

"Why are you doing this, Sarah? You're married and, besides, it's dangerous. You have to think about Ben and the kids."

"Claire, I wish you could understand," Sarah said plaintively. "I feel like I'm dead inside. I might as well be dead. My life with Ben is so boring, I can't stand it. Life is passing me by."

Claire saw the desperation in her eyes and was shocked. "Do you think this is the way to fix it?" she asked, troubled.

"Yes. It's exciting meeting new people. It makes me feel alive and attractive again."

"Oh God! Please be careful, Sarah. Don't do anything crazy. Please?"

161

The moment of softness from Sarah passed as she laughed. "That's exactly what I do want – to be crazy for a while. What's so wrong about that?"

"What about Ben?"

"What about him? He's getting along fine without me. I called the house today to talk to the kids, and Tash hung up on me. No change there then."

"Oh, Sarah, she's probably upset and hurting. What about Ben? Have you spoken to him? He's very worried about you."

"To hell with Ben! I don't want to speak to him. He drags me down. I want a bit of fun in my life for a change."

Claire took Sarah by the shoulders and shook her. She had never been so angry in her life.

"You're being selfish, Sarah! How can you do this to them? Don't you know what you have? How can you throw it all away for a bit of excitement?"

Sarah pulled away from her grasp. "These men make me feel young again, alive. I'm having fun. What's wrong with that?" She was obviously shocked at Claire's vehemence. She'd rarely seen her sister lose her temper.

"Oh Sarah. How can you be stupid?" Claire wailed.

"I have to go. I'm late."

With a swish of her hair she was gone.

Claire looked after her incredulously. How could she get her sister to see sense?

She sat down to dinner alone but her appetite had disappeared. Then she went up to soak in a comforting bath. Her bathroom looked like a tornado had hit it. Sarah had never been the tidiest of people. Claire cleaned up as she ran her bath and then sank gratefully into it. She lay there, trying to find a solution to the problem. She felt like her life was out of her hands once again and it was not her mother now, but her sister, who was controlling it.

She was sitting in her dressing-gown in the living room when Megan came in. She had been to the gym and was feeling exhilarated, but was quickly deflated when she saw Claire's face.

"What's up?"

"Everything! Why don't I reheat the casserole and I'll tell you over dinner."

"Fine, I'll run up for a quick shower."

"Okay, shoot!" Megan commanded as they sat down to dinner.

"It's Sarah," Claire sighed. "I tried to talk to her but she won't listen. She's meeting guys through those dating sites. She's out with one of them again tonight."

"Oh no! That's so dangerous."

"I know. She says these men make her feel young again."

"But they could be any kind of weirdo! I read an article that said many of these men who go on dating sites are married and just looking for sex."

"I don't think that's happened . . . yet," Claire said glumly.

"I don't know what to advise, Claire. You'll have to get her to see sense."

"You know Sarah – she won't listen to anyone."

"What about Ben?"

"He's going up the walls as it is but I don't think he suspects what she's doing. I promised to call him later but it's not up to me to tell him, is it?" She looked at Megan anxiously.

"No, of course not. Lord, just when everything was going so swimmingly for you, this happens." Megan's voice was full of sympathy.

"I know," Claire agreed, her voice disconsolate.

She called Ben after dinner as she'd promised. He was angry with Sarah now.

"Is she there?" he asked.

"I'm afraid she went out."

"I have no idea what she's up to," he said bitterly. "She won't talk to me. I just don't know what to do. It's pointless to cancel her bank cards because she has the money you gave her for the house, so that won't bring her back."

"How are the kids?"

"Well, Tash is very angry and keeps to her room most of the time. Luckily, Owen is in my school so he can travel in and out with me. I guess he misses her but Sarah was never all that maternal, as you know. I have to talk to her, Claire. Do you mind if I call round tomorrow afternoon when Owen is at Scouts?"

"No, of course not. I should warn you, it's a bit tense here at the moment. The girls are not too pleased Sarah is here."

"I'm sorry. She shouldn't have involved you. Hopefully, I can at least persuade her to come home tomorrow and we can try to sort things out."

"I hope so," Claire replied, but she didn't feel very hopeful.

Viv was in bad form. She'd had a lot of difficult customers at work and was glad the week was over.

It was now Friday and Conor still hadn't called. She'd

all but given up on him and so continued to make dates with other guys. She was very disappointed but she'd obviously liked Conor better than he'd liked her.

As if that wasn't bad enough, there was also Sarah to deal with. Viv decided, if Sarah was going to stay long-term, then she would move out. She went straight to her parents' house from work on Friday evening and over dinner she told them about the problem.

"Poor Claire. That sister of hers is just like the mother was. Domineering and selfish."

Viv and her father were shocked. Mrs Connolly had never been known to say a bad word about anyone before.

Viv left at eight twenty as she had arranged to meet yet another guy in the local pub.

His profile said that he was a foodie and his hobbies were going to restaurants and wine tastings. Viv hoped he would be interesting. His photo was a bit blurred so she was hoping she would recognise him. She entered the pub but could see nobody that looked remotely like the guy she was expecting. She took a seat and ordered a glass of chardonnay. Seconds later a dirty-looking man came into the bar and looked around him. He was so overweight that he could barely lift his feet off the ground to walk and had to shuffle along.

Gross, Viv thought to herself. With horror she realised he was approaching her table.

"Hello, are you Viv?" he asked hesitantly. He was sweating profusely and out of breath.

She couldn't help herself. "No," she replied, "my name is Claire."

"You're not here on a blind date? I'm supposed to meet someone called Viv here."

"Sorry, can't help you," Viv lied glibly. "I'm waiting for a friend."

"Oh, her photo looked a lot like you except that she had curly hair."

Viv thanked her lucky stars that she'd had her hair straightened.

He waddled off and she heaved a sigh of relief. Then she went into the ladies' where she called Megan.

"Megan, you've got to rescue me. I'm in Brown's bar and you've got to come here immediately," she whispered, afraid she might be overheard. "Call out 'hello, Claire' as you approach me. I'll explain everything then."

Megan looked at her phone but saw that Viv had hung up. What the hell! She had no choice but to go and rescue her friend.

"I wonder what mess she's got herself into now?" she said to Claire as she told her what Viv had said.

"God only knows," Claire replied, giggling.

When Megan arrived in the pub and found out what had happened, she gave Viv a good talking-to.

"This online dating is bloody dangerous," Megan admonished her as she sipped the chardonnay Viv had waiting for her. "Have you not read about the dreadful things that have happened to some girls who dated total strangers? You never know what kind of weirdo you might meet."

"Well, he lied on his profile," Viv muttered, sorry now that she'd involved Megan.

"You'll have to be more careful. In future one of us should go with you when it's a first date. I read that somewhere. There are precautions you can take."

166

"Okay," Viv agreed, though she thought Megan was overreacting.

She pointed the man out to Megan as they were leaving the pub. "I kinda see your point," she admitted with a grimace.

Viv's phone rang just then. Megan left her to answer it and walked to her car.

It was the longed-for phone call from Conor.

"I'm so sorry for not ringing earlier but we had a crisis at work and I had to go to the UK with the boss. It's been a nightmare week. I know it's awfully short notice but can you meet me tomorrow night?"

Viv's heart was pounding but she tried to sound casual. "Sure, I've nothing special on."

"That's great. I was afraid you'd be booked up. How do you fancy Thai cuisine? The Baan Thai is good. They do a mean crispy duck." He laughed and she remembered how good it was to be with him.

"Sounds perfect," she told him, smiling.

"Shall I pick you up? Seven thirty?"

"No, I'll meet you there. Seven thirty." She wasn't quite ready to introduce him to the girls yet and especially not to Sarah!

She was walking on air as she arrived home. Megan had already arrived and was alone in the living room, turning on the TV to watch the news.

"That was Conor on the phone," Viv sang out excitedly. "He's taking me to the Baan Thai tomorrow night."

"That's great," Megan replied listlessly.

"What's up? Where's Claire and the other yoke?" Viv asked.

"Claire's gone to bed and Sarah is out, as usual."

"I just don't understand how she's getting so many dates."

"Apparently she's joined three different dating sites."

"Aha! She has probably joined the one I told her about for married people looking to have affairs! We have to do something, Megan. If she stays here she's going to ruin everything for us, not to mention poor Claire. Did you see how Sarah bosses her around?"

"Yes, but what can we do?" Megan asked dejectedly. "Claire can't very well throw her out on the street."

"No, but she can insist she either goes back home or finds her own place."

"Mmm, I suppose."

"Fancy a hot chocolate?"

"Yeah, it might cheer me up."

Viv was in the kitchen making it when she heard the key in the door and Sarah's shrill laugh. She was shocked to hear a deep male voice laughing with her. Viv dropped the cups and whizzed into the hall. Megan had also come out of the living room. They watched speechless as Sarah waved two bottles of wine at them and headed for the stairs. Her companion looked slyly at them, ogling them up and down.

"Very nice," he remarked, smirking.

They could see he was a sleazebag.

Viv was too quick for Sarah who was obviously the worse for wear.

"Where do you think you're going?" she asked, blocking the way to the stairs.

"To my room, if you don't mind," Sarah replied, slurring her words.

Her companion bristled, sensing a confrontation.

"Oh, no, you're not!" Viv said, in full flight. "We have rules in this house and no men in the rooms is one of them." She stared Sarah down.

The man shifted uneasily from foot to foot. Obviously Sarah hadn't told him there would be others in the house.

"Says who?" Sarah asked.

"Says we all," Megan backed Viv up.

"It's not your house." Sarah glared at them both.

"It's not yours either," Viv replied. "It's Claire's."

"C'mon, Sarah. Let's go," the man said, backing away.

"You're just jealous," Sarah hurled at Viv, following him out.

"That's it!" Viv said to Megan. "It's either me or her. I can't live in the same house as that woman. She's a tramp!"

"We'll talk to Claire tomorrow about it. We'll find a solution," Megan assured her, hurrying to the kitchen to rescue the hot chocolates.

# Chapter 20

Claire was last down to breakfast the following morning.

"Has Sarah been down?" she asked as she poured herself a coffee. "I see she's not in her room."

"Sit down, Claire," Megan said quietly. "We need to talk to you."

Claire looked at their downcast faces and realised something was wrong.

"What is it? What's happened?"

Megan told her what had transpired the night before and Claire groaned.

"Oh no!" She sat down putting her hands to her head. "Where did she go?"

"Who knows and who cares?" Viv said bitterly. "She probably booked into some sleazy hotel."

Claire paled. "Oh God, I hope not!"

"You can't let her go on like this," Megan said gently. "It's not on and it's not fair on you either. She's a grown woman and has to take some responsibility for her actions."

Viv was more blunt. "To be honest, Claire, if she stays I'm leaving."

"Please don't," Claire pleaded, wringing her hands. "I'll ask her to leave as soon as she gets back. Heavens, I just realised Ben's coming round to talk with her today. What shall I do?"

"Well, try and put him off, at least till you get in touch with her," Megan suggested. "She'll probably come back at some stage. She'll need fresh clothes."

"Okay," Claire agreed. "I'll do that and I'll talk to her when she gets back."

Megan's phone rang just then. Her mother's number showed on the screen.

"Hello, Daphne."

"Darling, I need you to do something for me." Her mother sounded frazzled.

"Is something wrong?" Megan asked.

"No, on the contrary. I'm calling from the Rosebay Clinic," Daphne said excitedly. "They've had a cancellation, which means I can have my surgery today. Isn't it wonderful?"

Megan recalled that this was the clinic where Daphne's 'brilliant' plastic surgeon was located. She didn't think it was wonderful at all and wished her mother wouldn't do this to herself. There were risks attached to it, as everyone knew. Megan remembered the Irishwoman who'd died in New York having a facelift. And her husband hadn't even known she was going to have it done.

"I had to come in immediately so I didn't have time to pack a case. Could you go out to Killiney and pack one for me? Beauty products, nighties and the like – oh, and don't forget, all my medication. You'll know what to take."

"Sure, but I don't have a key. How will I get in?"

"Well, Luis will be there and he'll let you in."

"Luis will be there? He's not living with you, is he?"

"But of course," her mother replied, surprised. "He has nowhere else to live."

"But you hardly know him!"

"I know him well enough," Daphne laughed. "The best way to get to know a man is between the sheets."

"Gross!" Megan muttered under her breath. She didn't want to picture her mother in bed with Luis, or anyone else for that matter.

"Anyway, I won't need anything until after surgery so it's best to wait until later this afternoon."

"Very well," Megan said resignedly. At least it would be an excuse to get away from Claire's for a while, what with Sarah and tensions running high.

"How did you get to the clinic?"

"Luis drove me."

"Oh, does he have a car?"

"No, silly. He's driving my car."

Megan was shocked. Her mother was allowing Luis to drive the Bentley? He had obviously wormed his way in faster than you could say Jack Flash!

"Okay, I'll do that and see you later. Good luck with the surgery."

"Thanks, sweetie. See you later."


Megan explained to the girls what was happening and they could see she was upset about Luis. Then she went upstairs to get ready.

"It never rains but it pours, does it?" Viv commented when she'd left the room.

173

"You can say that again," Claire agreed. She was worried about Ben coming around that afternoon. What if Sarah didn't come home? What would she say to Ben then? Lord, what a mess!

Claire was a nervous wreck when there was no sign of Sarah by one thirty. How would she explain to Ben that Sarah had stayed out all night? As luck would have it, Sarah rolled in around two o'clock looking like something the cat dragged in. She had the grace to appear penitent.

"Okay, Sarah, I've had enough," Claire stated, feeling strangely confident. "This is my home now and you are abusing my hospitality. Not only that, but you have upset my friends. I heard what happened last night and I'm disgusted. I want you to leave."

Sarah was completely taken aback. Claire had never stood up to her like this before. Where was namby-pamby Claire gone? She seemed to have changed.

"Sorry, it won't happen again," she mumbled.

"That's not the point. You're behaving disgracefully. You have to leave, by next weekend."

"Where will I go?"

"Back to your husband and children, I hope. If he'll have you back, that is."

She was tempted to tell Sarah that Ben was coming around that afternoon but feared her sister might bolt if she knew, so she said nothing. Forewarned was forearmed, they said, and she did not want Sarah forearmed.

Megan went shopping in Blackrock and met an old friend for lunch there. After lunch she headed for Killiney. She went for a long walk down the Vico Road and back along the beach, then made her way to her mother's house.

Luis let her in and once again did his hand-kissing thing, looking up at her with those dark sexy eyes. Megan felt that same frisson she'd felt the first time she'd met him and it unnerved her. She realised he was flirting with her and it irritated her. It was unsettling to see his male attire lying casually around the living room.

"My mother asked me to come and collect some things for her," she said haughtily, moving towards the stairs. "Daphne to you," she threw back over her shoulder, giving him a withering look.

She went straight to her mother's bedroom and tried to avert her eyes from his toiletries in the bathroom. She took Daphne's overnight bag from the closet and started filling it with jars and jars of creams and potions, then the medication from the medicine cabinet. Next she packed a dressing-gown, nighties and underwear. She marvelled at how luxurious all her mother's stuff was. Daphne certainly didn't hold back on pampering herself. Megan almost freaked when she came across a drawer full of sexy Agent Provocateur lingerie, nestling beside a mask and handcuffs. She was shocked. Dear Lord, what was her mother getting up to? Was all this gear for Luis's benefit? Megan didn't want to go there. It was too upsetting.

The thought revolted Megan for some reason. It was all very well for Cher and Madonna to run around with men young enough to be their sons but, when it was your mother, that was a different story. She couldn't help but wonder how they felt about each other. No doubt her mother was using him as arm-candy, to make her appear younger but obviously, if what she'd found in her mother's drawers were anything to go by, there was sex involved too. Daphne had always used men and suddenly Megan felt a little sorry for Luis, which was stupid. He was obviously getting something out of it too but probably had no idea what a praying mantis Daphne was. Well, he'd find out soon enough.

Suddenly she heard a rustle behind her and turned to find Luis staring at her.

"Can I help you find anything?" he asked, advancing towards her.

"No, thank you. I've got it all."

"You are so beautiful," he murmured huskily as he came close.

She was frozen to the spot as he reached up and stroked her hair. Then he took her head in his hands and moved in to place his lips on hers. It took a moment for Megan to realise what he was doing and suddenly she was galvanised into action. She pushed him away from her and slapped him hard across the face.

"How dare you!" she cried. "You're disgusting! You're nothing but a gigolo." She turned and ran from the room, clutching her mother's bag under her arm.

"I theenk you are frigid!" he called after her as she ran down the stairs. "What you need is a real man in your bed!"

She bolted from the house and drove off as quickly as she could, shaking with indignation. What a jerk! Did he really think she was the kind of girl who could be seduced so easily? And would he have taken her in her mother's bed? The very thought revolted her. And to think that she had been feeling sorry for him a short while earlier!

The remark he'd thrown at her as she left rankled. Did he really think she was frigid? That couldn't be true, could it? Though when you thought about it her mother was

176

having more adventurous sex than either she or her two girlfriends at the moment. In fact, more sex, full stop. It was downright unfair and Megan was shocked to find herself feeling just the teeniest bit jealous of Daphne.

She'd enjoyed sex with Paul, and Sam before him, but it was never the earth-shattering explosion that you read about in books. She remembered Paul calling her an ice-queen one time, when she'd refused to have sex with him. Was that what was wrong with her? Was that why she couldn't hold on to a man? The thought frightened her. She wished there was something she could do about it.

She was disgruntled as she made her way into the clinic later that afternoon. Luis's pass and his parting remark were still bothering her. She considered telling her mother but Daphne probably wouldn't believe her, or at the very least accuse her of leading him on. What was the point?

Meanwhile, Ben had arrived at Claire's just after three and Sarah was cornered. Claire went out for a long walk and left them alone together. Thankfully Megan was out in Killiney and Viv was at the beauty salon having her hair straightened and her nails done. Claire hoped that Ben could knock some sense into his wife's head.

"What are you doing here?" Sarah asked Ben sullenly, furious with Claire for letting him in and then disappearing.

He walked into the living room and sat down. She had no choice but to follow him.

"It's time to come home, Sarah. We need to talk."

"There's nothing to talk about."

"I think there is. We've both made mistakes. We have to sort things out."

"I can't go on the way it was. I want a life, Ben."

"You have a life with us, Sare."

"You call that a life?" she cried. "It's boring, boring, boring, just as you're boring!"

He looked hurt. "You don't mean that."

"I do. Look, Ben, I can't live like that any more. Life is too short. Let's face it, we should never have got married. It's not working."

"And where will you live? You can't kip down with Claire forever. She's stressed out about you, you know."

"So she's been running to you behind my back, has she?" she said bitterly.

She wondered if Ben knew that Claire had given her a deadline to get out.

"Maybe I'll get a place of my own," she suggested, looking at him to see how he would take that.

"What about the kids?"

"I'll have them come to live with me once I get a place," she replied.

"Over my dead body. You can't have that life you want and look after them properly. Think about it."

Sarah bit her lip. He was right.

"Why not come home and we'll try and work it out?" he suggested.

She sighed. "I'm not ready to go home. I need time to think about it."

If necessary, Ben would fight her tooth and nail for custody of the children, but he knew it wouldn't come to that. Sarah, as always, would put herself first.

Megan's mother was out of surgery and conscious when she got to the clinic, but she couldn't talk. Her head was swathed in bandages and she couldn't open her mouth. She could almost have passed for a mummy.

"Are you okay?" Megan asked, shocked at how bad she looked. "How are you feeling?"

Her mother nodded and pointed to a pen and pad on the bedside locker.

*How do you think?* she wrote.

Even in this state Daphne still had a sharp tongue. Her face was black-and-blue and very swollen, what Megan could see of it anyway. She'd had a bum-lift too and no doubt her bottom was badly bruised too. She looked a sight. How anyone could put themselves through this torture for vanity's sake, Megan could not fathom. She stayed for a while and then the nurse gave her mother some medication. Within five minutes Daphne was sleeping.

"There's no point in you staying," the young nurse told Megan. "She'll probably sleep right through till morning."

"Okay, I'll call and check how she is tomorrow," Megan said.


When Claire got back she was surprised to find Ben gone and her sister alone in the living room.

"Thanks a lot, sis," Sarah spat at her accusingly. "Going to Ben behind my back!"

Claire was taken aback. "I did no such thing. I never told him anything about what you're doing."

"Maybe not, but he said you were stressed with having me here."

"Well, I am," Claire said honestly. "And so are Megan and Viv."

"You'll be happy to know I won't be stressing you for too much longer."

"What happened with Ben? Are you going back to try and work things out?"

"No, I don't want to go back there." She wouldn't give Claire the satisfaction of knowing that she'd told Ben she'd think about it.

"Will you not try, Sarah? Maybe marriage counselling or something?"

"Why should I? Our marriage is a disaster. I want more excitement in my life. It may surprise you to know that lots of guys find me attractive. It's not too late for me to meet someone new."

Claire looked at her disbelievingly. "How can you be so selfish?" she cried. "Viv is right, you're a bitch. I'm washing my hands of you. I meant what I said. I want you out by the weekend."

Sarah gaped at her. Was this really Claire talking? "What's happened to you? You were always so namby-pamby, always so sweet."

"Well, not any more." Claire glared at her stonily.

"You know your problem?" Sarah came close to Claire and stopped, her face a few inches from her sister's. "You're around Viv too much and you're getting just like her, hard and nasty."

With a swish of her hair, Sarah left the room. She had spoken with more bravado than she'd felt. Obviously she couldn't stay here much longer. What the hell! Anything would be better than living with these morons.

Claire was secretly pleased when her sister said she was getting more like Viv, who wasn't nasty but just a strong character. She was more than happy to leave her namby-pamby – as Sarah called it – self behind and become more assertive. She smiled thinking that, inadvertently, her sister had handed her a compliment.

Five minutes later Claire saw Sarah flash past the living-room door and leave the house, banging the door behind her, without as much as a goodbye.

Sarah had no idea where she would go but she wasn't about to tolerate her prissy sister's sermons all evening. She decided to take the Luas into Dublin city and treat herself to something nice.

She was looking through the dresses in Coast, on Stephen's Green, when she bumped into Kay, a girl she'd worked with before her marriage. Kay had been a real wild card back then and Sarah was pleased to see her.

"You're looking great," Sarah said. "What are you doing with yourself these days? Still married?"

"Long-story-short," Kay replied. "I left him."

"Join the club," Sarah laughed.

"You're joking? That nice what's-his-name . . . ?"

"Ben. Boring Ben."

Kay threw back her head and guffawed. "When?"

"Last week."

Kay found this even funnier. "Come on, let's go and have a drink and we can swap stories," she suggested.

Sarah was thrilled. What she needed more than anything now was a friend. Not judgemental cows like Claire and her friends.

Several drinks later, the two women got a taxi back to Kay's apartment. They stopped at an off-licence along the way and Sarah bought a bottle of gin and some tonic.

Kay's place was tiny and more than a little grotty, Sarah thought with a shudder as she looked around.

"I know it's not much, but it's all mine," Kay said, reading her thoughts. "I can have whoever I like here, when I like, male or female."

She winked and Sarah got her message, delighted to see she was still a wild card.

By eleven the two of them were completely drunk, neither of them having eaten, and Kay suggested Sarah kip down on the sofa. She gratefully accepted the invitation and stayed over.

# Chapter 21

Viv was running late. It was almost seven when she dashed in through the door, hair flying behind her. She had less than forty minutes to get dressed and get to the restaurant to meet Conor. She'd ordered a taxi for seven fifteen.

"Hi, Claire," she called out as she saw her friend in the kitchen. "Have to dash, I'm late!" she cried over her shoulder as she took the stairs two at a time.

She had decided to have a spray-tan in the beauty salon, which had delayed her. She was sick with nerves at the thought of seeing Conor again and wanted to look as good as possible for him. She had finally opted to wear her short white dress which would look great with the tan and was also perfect with the Jimmy Choo boots. Her fingers were shaking so much that she couldn't close the catch on the purple collar necklace which completed the outfit. Grabbing her Michael Kors short white coat she ran down the stairs to Claire.

183

"Can you close this for me?" she asked, handing Claire the choker.

"Wow! You look fabulous," Claire exclaimed as she closed the clasp.

"Really?" Viv asked nervously, smoothing down her dress.

"Honestly, you look sensational. Sexy yet classy. Those boot make your legs look amazing. You'll bowl Conor over, I'm certain."

"Thanks, I hope so," Viv replied.

She heard the taxi honk and, blowing a kiss at Claire, exited to go and meet her prince.


She knew by his face that he was impressed. She had butterflies in her tummy as she went to greet him.

"Wow! You look fantastic," he exclaimed as he greeted her. "You're even more beautiful than I remember."

Viv was ecstatic.

He ordered champagne and Viv reckoned that the money she'd spent getting ready for tonight had been worth every penny. She felt like a princess.

"You've changed your hair," he observed, running his hand over it gently.

"Yes, I've had it straightened. Do you like it?"

"It's lovely, but I think I prefer it curly," he said. "It's more you."

Well, that was a wasted fifty euro, Viv thought, but she was secretly pleased that he liked her curly hair.

She had forgotten how incredibly charming he was and she found herself more and more entranced by him as the evening wore on. He was very tactile and kept touching her hand and arm which she found captivating and exciting. He ordered for them both and afterwards Viv could barely recall what she had eaten, just that the meal was delicious and the whole evening magical. It was as if he had cast a spell on her.

He was witty and entertaining and she listened in amazement as he told her about all the places he'd travelled to and what he'd achieved.

He didn't however mention his ex-girlfriend and Viv was dying to ask him about it but, before she got a chance, he said, "Now, enough about me. I'm dying to hear all about you and your life."

"I'm afraid it's much more boring than yours," she admitted, shy all of a sudden. "I had a happy, uneventful childhood and wasn't very ambitious, I'm afraid. I wasn't very smart at school."

"Well, I find you very smart now," he said as he entwined his fingers in hers.

Viv blushed and longed to reach over and kiss him.

She then told him about her job and moving in with Claire and Megan and he listened as intently as if it was the most fascinating story he'd ever heard.

The time flew by and suddenly they were the last ones left in the restaurant. Conor asked the waiter to call a taxi and she was excited by his nearness in the back seat as they drove home. She kept hoping he would kiss her but, although he kept his arm around her, he made no move to do so.

When the driver stopped outside her house, Conor walked her to the door and kissed her gently on the lips. It was the sweetest kiss she'd ever experienced.

"I really had a good time, Viv," he said, stroking her face.

"Me too," she replied softly. "I really like you a lot."

"Next weekend I'm going to Scotland on a golf trip," he said, "but I hope to see you again. I'll call you. And thank you for a wonderful evening."

Viv was disappointed that she wouldn't see him the following weekend but at least he'd said he would call and that he wanted to see her again. She hugged those words to herself. She had never felt like this before. He was causing her heart to race and her stomach to flutter. She knew that she could easily fall in love with him. She was relieved to find that the girls were already in bed as she didn't want to break the spell that Conor had woven.

Viv was exuberant at the breakfast table the following morning as she told Claire about her evening. Megan had already left to go and visit her mother and would be out all day. She was going for a long run with her running group and then out for dinner with them later.

When Claire suggested they take a trip down to the Kildare Village Outlet Centre, Viv happily agreed.

Before they left, Claire rang Megan to see if there was anything she wanted from there and put the phone on loudspeaker so Viv could hear.

"No, thanks, I don't need anything. How was your night, Viv?"

"Heavenly!" Viv told her.

"She has my ears worn out talking about the wonderful Conor," Claire said. "I'm getting worried about her. She's all sweetness and light. Not at all like our Viv." She laughed as Viv swatted her jokingly.

"I can't wait to hear about it. Just make sure you keep your feet on the ground and don't go crazy spending in the Village, Viv," Megan warned.

Viv stuck out her tongue though Megan couldn't see it.

"Don't worry, I'll take her cards off her if she gets out of control," Claire said, laughing.

"What about Sarah? Is she going with you?"

"No. She didn't come home last night. I've no idea where she is."

"Well, don't worry about her," said Megan. "Don't know when I'll see you. It'll probably be a late night. Our last blow-out before the marathon."

"Have a great time," said Claire.

"Hope the run goes well too!" Viv said, talking over her.

Megan found Daphne much perkier when she got there. The bandages were off so she could at least talk.

"Has Luis been in to visit you?" Megan asked.

"God, no!" Daphne shrieked. "I do not want him to see me like this."

Megan could see where her mother was coming from. She did look a fright. Her face was still swollen and bruised.

"How did you find him when you called out for my things?" her mother asked.

"Okay," Megan replied nonchalantly. "I didn't stay long."

"Oh," was all her mother said. "Did he say anything about me?"

"No. We barely spoke."

Looking at her mother, Megan wondered how she'd feel if she told her that he'd made a pass at her. The thought of her mother and Luis having titillating sex in that bed was disgusting. Somehow, it didn't seem right.

Viv and Claire had a good time in Kildare Village. Claire fell in love with a pink-and-grey wrap-coat in Jaeger which Viv insisted she absolutely should buy. They both stocked up on Molton Brown toiletries but the only other things Viv indulged in were some black fishnet stay-ups in Wolford which she hoped Conor would be peeling off her soon and some opaque tights that she'd be needing for the coming winter.

"These are fantastic," she declared. "They last forever and never run. I guarantee you'll never wear cheap ones again, once you've tried these."

Claire had to agree they were luxurious and bought a pair for herself and for Megan too.

They stopped off for something to eat on the way home.

"You see, it *is* possible to meet a nice guy online," Viv pointed out as she tucked into her food and paused in her praise of Conor for five seconds.

"I guess so. I've been messaging this guy who's really pushing me to meet him," Claire confided.

"That Richard guy?"

"No, this one's called Adam. He seems awfully serious."

"Nothing wrong with that."

"I'm terribly nervous, seeing as it's my first date. If I agree to meet him, would you mind coming along to the bar when I do, just in case?"

"Course not," Viv assured her, grinning. "I'll be there in case he jumps you."

Claire swatted her playfully. "I didn't mean that."

"I know. Go ahead, arrange to meet him. If you could arrange for seven thirty on Wednesday, in Walsh's, that would be great, as I have a date for that night."

"What about Conor? I didn't think you'd want to go out with anyone else now that you've found him."

"I don't, but I won't see him for two weeks and, anyway, I made this date last week so I feel I have to keep it now. He sounds like good fun. Give me something to do while I keep an eye on you and your date. Killing two birds with the one stone, you could say."

They were surprised to see Sarah's handbag on the hall table when they got home. There was no sign of her downstairs so Claire went up to check her room.

"She's fast asleep," she told Viv when she came back down.

"Must have had a hard night, and probably morning too," Viv remarked bitchily. She realised she was being very catty when she saw Claire cringe. Sometimes she wondered how she could be so horrid.

Later, Claire contacted Adam and arranged to meet him the following Wednesday in Walsh's. She hoped she was doing the right thing but she had to start somewhere. It would be good practice for when she met Richard, who had messaged her saying it was time they met up.

And at least Viv would be present when she met up with Adam.

Sarah had spent Sunday with Kay – not quite Sun*day* – as they hadn't got up till one, so half the day was already over. They went out for brunch and met a couple of guys with whom they started drinking. They had a hilarious afternoon and when Sarah eventually got back to Claire's she was delighted to find that she and her friends were out. No third degree from her sister, thank God! She headed straight up to bed and took a sleeping pill. Kay's couch had not been the most comfortable bed the previous night.

# Chapter 22

Megan's Sunday had been brilliant too. The fifteen-mile run had gone amazingly well and she'd posted her best time yet. It had also helped clear her mind of Luis and her mother.

They went back to the gym to change afterwards and she soaked in the hot-tub to ease her tired muscles. They were all meeting up in the pub next door for drinks before going on to dinner. Megan was, unusually for her, feeling reckless and the adrenalin from her run was still coursing through her system. She decided to glam up and wear her short red lace dress along with her towering Louboutin black patent heels. She wore her hair loose around her shoulders and carefully applied her make-up.

Looking in the mirror she knew she was looking sexy and guessed her fellow runners would be surprised. They'd only ever seen her make-up free, her hair in a ponytail, in running or gym gear. Still, she wasn't expecting to cause quite such a stir when she walked into the pub, to be

191

greeted with a chorus of wolf whistles and "Wows!" from the guys.

There was only one other girl, Sylvia, in the group of ten and she was a moaner, forever complaining about something or other and nobody liked her very much. In contrast, Megan trained as hard as any of the men, never once complaining, and they respected her for that. The fact that she was so pleasant and easy on the eye didn't hurt either. Several of them had asked her for a date but she had always politely turned them down, which made her even more desirable. Now, seeing her look so sexy and glamorous, they were practically falling over themselves to buy her drinks and chat her up.

Megan, still high on adrenalin, wallowed in all this attention. Her confidence had hit rock-bottom after Paul dumped her and Luis calling her frigid had been the last straw. She decided it was time to let her hair down and start living again. So she accepted yet another glass of wine although she knew she was more than a little tipsy. What the hell! She didn't care. What was it they said? *Life is for living, death is for dying*. Well, she planned to start living again and she was about to start right now.

Davy was by far the best-looking guy in the club and Megan had seen all the women in the gym vying for his attention. He appeared not to notice them and was very dedicated to keeping fit, which showed in his perfectly toned physique. He was eerily similar to the actor Paul Walker, the *Fast and Furious* star, who had died in a crash the year before. Davy had the same dark-blond hair which was always a little ruffled and a hint of a moustache and beard, just like the late star. But it was his perfect white teeth and startling blue eyes which made people do a double take when they saw him.

Megan was aware of his eyes following her for most of the night but she feigned indifference. He had asked her out the previous month and had seemed surprised and genuinely disappointed when she'd turned him down. When she saw how girls were constantly trying to chat him up all night she realised that he probably wasn't used to being turned down. However, she was very conscious of his presence although he didn't talk to her at all.

It was the best night Megan had had since Paul left and, after the restaurant, they ended up in Club 92: eight guys and Megan. Sylvia, whom the guys had nicknamed MAM – short for Moan-A-Minute, they explained to Megan   had decided not to join them.

Once inside the nightclub they ordered champagne but refused to let Megan contribute. She was never off the floor and danced with every guy in the group, with the exception of Davy. She wondered why he hadn't asked her to dance. Maybe he was miffed that she hadn't gone out with him. What did she care? She sipped her champagne in between dances, unaware that her glass was constantly being refilled.

The truth of the matter was that Davy was very smitten with Megan. He'd never met anyone so cool and oblivious to his charms and it bothered him. He wondered how he could break down that barrier she'd erected around herself. He never took his eyes off her and watched jealously as she flirted with the others. He desired her desperately. He'd always suspected that under that ice-cool exterior was a hot, vibrant woman. He was waiting for his chance and when the last dance, a slow one, was announced, he moved quickly.

She was quite drunk by then and completely uninhibited and pleased that he'd finally asked her to dance. He really was very sexy, she thought as he put his arms around her and drew her to him. She leaned into his body and could feel his erection as he pressed her close. He nuzzled her neck which sent a thrill down her spine. Then he was kissing her and she was kissing him back. They stayed locked together, rocking to the music, and when he took her hand and said, "Let's get outta here," she went with him willingly.

Once outside, they climbed into one of the waiting taxis. They kissed passionately and when Davy slipped his hand under her skirt, she desperately wanted him to keep moving upwards. She knew she was drunk but she didn't care. She wanted to make love to him. She felt sexy and desirable.

As soon as they were inside the door of his house they were pulling the clothes off each other and he took her right there and then, up against the wall. They both came almost immediately and Megan felt exhilarated.

Hah! You call that frigid, Luis? she almost said aloud.

Davy gathered up their clothes and led her up the stairs to bed. There he started making love to her again but this time he was very gentle. He stroked her hair and kissed her face and then her neck as he made his way down her body. She relaxed and went with the flow, abandoning herself to the delicious, sensual feelings. When he touched her breasts she moaned with pleasure and then he made his way further down. She thought she would die with pleasure as he licked her and when she could bear it no longer he moved inside her. They moved together as their desire mounted and then she felt the orgasm sweep over her body just as he exploded inside her. It was the most exquisite, intense feeling she'd ever experienced. So this is what she'd been missing. Those writers had not been exaggerating! Afterwards they both lay panting and then they slowly drifted into sleep, his arm wrapped around her.

Megan was mortified when she woke at daybreak to see the blond head on the pillow beside her. For a moment she didn't know who he was or where she was and then it all came flooding back to her. God, what had she done? She had never done anything like this before. She'd only slept with two men in her life, Sam and Paul, and she'd been in long-term relationships with both of them. She got out of bed as quietly as she could so as not to wake him. Picking her clothes up quietly, she tiptoed out and found the main bathroom. There, she showered and dressed as quickly and quietly as she could, afraid that Davy might wake. The last thing she wanted was to come face to face with him.

Tiptoeing down the stairs she quietly let herself out. His house was on the main road and she called for a taxi. She felt like a prostitute standing there in her red lace dress and killer heels. A couple of men slowed down but when she turned her back on them, they sped off. Thankfully, she didn't have to wait too long and, when her taxi arrived, she gave the driver her office address. Luckily, she kept a spare business suit and shoes in the closet there, along with a wash-bag. She couldn't have faced Viv and Claire and their questions. She was also suffering from a ferocious hangover.

"Had a good night then, luv?" the taxi driver smirked.

She looked at him coldly and didn't reply. He got the message and shut up.

When Simon came into the office at eight fifteen, he was

surprised to see a light on in Megan's office. He opened the door to find her sitting at her desk, staring into the distance. She was paler than usual and dishevelled, which was very out of character for her.

"Are you okay?" he asked, his face full of concern.

She looked at him blankly. Worried, he closed the door and approached her.

"Megan, what's happened?" he asked, placing a hand on her shoulder.

"Oh Simon, I've done something terrible."

His mind raced over all the possibilities. Had she killed someone? Hit and run? He had to get to the bottom of it.

"Have you had breakfast?" he asked.

She shook her head.

"Come on, let's go for breakfast and you can tell me all about it."

He directed her to the café behind the building where it was unlikely they'd meet anyone from the office.

"I got drunk last night and went home with a guy I barely know and had sex with him."

"Phew! Thank God that's all it is." He smiled, relieved. "I thought maybe you'd killed someone."

She gave him a wan smile. "I feel terrible. That's what slappers do."

"Megan, you're single and you've been holding in so much since your split with Paul. Maybe this is what you need."

"You think so? You don't think I'm a slut?"

"Of course not. You could do much worse, believe me. He's not married, is he?" he asked, with a worried frown.

"No."

"Thank goodness for that."

She saw a cloud pass over his face and she remembered that his wife had left him for another man, two years into their marriage.

"Of course, you're right. Thanks, Simon."

"What are friends for? Will you see him again?"

"God no! I'll be running into him at the gym, no doubt, but I won't be going out with him again."

"Well, let's get back to work. We've both got a lot to do. I have meetings all day and you have Gloria's book to finish editing."

"Thanks, Simon," she said again, reaching up to give him a peck on the cheek.

When she got back to the office Megan rang the clinic to tell her mother that she couldn't collect her that day and asked her to get Luis to do it. She just couldn't face her mother and all her drama right now.

# Chapter 23

Sarah was awake earlier than usual on Monday morning. She waited until she was sure the others had left for work before she braved it downstairs. She'd been thinking a lot about what she should do. The thought of going back to Ben was galling but, if she didn't, it would mean giving up on her kids. Ben had left her in no doubt that he would look for custody of them. It was a dilemma. Taking her coffee into the living room she went online to look at apartments for rent. She checked out properties to let in Dundrum and Stillorgan, which was her preferred area to live, but the prices horrified her. They were scandalous! Who could afford €5000 a month for an apartment? It was out of the question.

Although she'd been envious of Kay having her own place, after spending twenty-four hours there Sarah knew it was not for her. She was used to her big house and creature comforts and would never survive in such a small place. She sighed. It appeared she would have no choice but to go back to Ben, but this time it would be on *her* terms.

Claire couldn't believe it that evening when she got home and found Sarah all dressed up and about to go out again.

"Have you given any more thought to what you're going to do?" she asked her sister hopefully.

"I'm thinking about it. Don't worry – I'll be gone before the weekend. I've been looking at apartments for rent."

"So when are you moving out then?" Viv, who overheard the last of this conversation, asked rudely.

"Don't worry – I'll be gone by Friday," Sarah told her snootily.

"Four more days!" Viv said. "Will I survive that long?"

Claire threw her a beseeching look which made Viv feel guilty. She knew she was behaving badly but she really couldn't stand Sarah. However, for four days more she'd make an effort, for Claire's sake.

Viv had been hoping Conor would call but she hadn't heard from him. He was never out of her mind for a minute and she longed to hear his voice. Still, it was only Monday. He was probably busy.

After dinner Claire headed out to visit an elderly neighbour while Viv settled down to watch TV.

Viv was alone in the living room when Megan arrived home. Viv was surprised when she didn't look in to say hello. She went out into the hall to greet her and saw instantly that Megan was upset.

"What's up? Something wrong?"

"No, I'm fine. Just going up for a shower."

Viv knew she wasn't telling the truth and wondered what could have happened. Perhaps she'd had a row with

Daphne. She'd worm it out of her soon enough.

When Megan came down after her shower, Viv had a bottle of wine open on the coffee table. "Have you eaten?" she asked.

"I'm not really hungry," Megan replied, accepting the glass Viv handed her.

"Come on, spit it out. I know you. Something's happened. What is it?"

With her shoulders drooping, Megan told Viv about Davy.

"*Woohooo!*" Viv cried. This was the last thing she had expected.

"You won't tell Claire, will you? She'll think I'm a right slut." Megan looked downhearted.

"Of course she won't. Claire's not judgemental."

"Please don't tell her," Megan begged. "I'd hate her to know."

"Okay. What happens now?"

"Nothing. I even dread having to face him again."

"Fine. What was it like?" Viv couldn't help asking. "Earthmoving?"

"Pretty much." Megan finally gave a rueful smile.

"I'm so jealous," Viv admitted. "It's been so long since I've had sex that I'm afraid, when it does happen, I'll have forgotten how to do it."

"What about Conor? Don't you think it will happen soon with him?"

"God, I hope so! I'd jump into bed with him in a minute but I can't rush him. Although he's touchy-feely, he has behaved like a thorough gentleman. I get the feeling that he's being cautious and wants to go slowly. Afraid of being hurt again, I suppose."

"Did he talk about his last relationship or say why they split up?"

"No, just that he'd found it tough."

"I dare say he'll tell you in his own good time."

"I know but I've never felt like this about anyone before, Meggie. It's scary."

"Not even Ryan?" He had been the first guy Viv had moved in with, though it hadn't lasted long.

"No, not even him. I get butterflies just thinking about Conor, which I do all the time. I love everything about him."

"Lordy, this sounds serious," Megan acknowledged, surprised. "That's how I used to feel about Paul, remember?"

"I sure do. I thought you were crazy. I just hope Conor works out better than Paul did."

Megan looked sad and was about to respond but just then her phone rang. It was Daphne.

"Oh no," she said, taking a deep breath, "I'm not in the mood for any drama right now."

"*What did you say to him?*" Daphne screeched at her daughter down the phone.

"Say?" Megan asked, perplexed

"Yes! What did you tell Luis about me?"

"Tell?"

"*Stop repeating everything I say, like a parrot!*" her mother shrieked.

"If you're asking me if I told Luis that you'd taken a carving knife to Daddy, no, I didn't."

"You're always exaggerate so, Megan. It was only a small knife."

"Whatever! It looked big enough to me as a ten-year-old. But I didn't tell Luis anything. We barely spoke to each other."

"Oh! I assumed you'd said something to him. I just don't understand why he's left me."

"He's left you?" Megan gasped, taken aback.

Viv, who was listening to Megan's side of the conversation, raised her eyebrows dramatically.

"Yes, he collected me from the clinic – I really don't understand why *you* couldn't have done it," Daphne couldn't resist adding. "Anyway, he was very quiet as we drove home. Then he went upstairs, packed his bag and, when he came down, he told me he was leaving. I just don't understand it," she sniffed. "You didn't tell him anything about my past lovers, did you?"

"Of course not."

"Well, I just don't understand it. I know my face is a bit bruised and swollen but surely he should understand it's only temporary."

Megan threw her eyes to heaven.

"Men are all selfish bastards," her mother said, before hanging up.

"Luis has left her?" Viv was eager to hear all when Megan came off the phone.

"Apparently. She thinks I may have said something to him about her."

"You didn't, did you?"

"Of course not."

"Whew! For a minute I thought maybe you'd become closer to him than you wanted to admit to me!"

"Are you mad? He's my mother's lover."

"Not any more apparently, and you did say he was divine."

"Yes, well, I think he's disgusting now. He made a pass at me in my mother's bedroom."

"*Whaaat?*" Viv shrieked, almost spilling her drink. "What happened?" She was agog with curiosity.

"I was gathering my mother's stuff together and he crept up behind me and tried to kiss me."

"You're joking!" Viv gasped, her mouth open. "What did you do?"

"Well, I pushed him away and slapped his face. I told him he was disgusting and a gigolo, then I bolted out of the house."

"How did he react?"

"You won't believe this – he called after me that what I needed was a man in my bed. He called me frigid," Megan grimaced.

"Jesus Christ, I can't believe the nerve of him!" Viv was gobsmacked. "Well, he wouldn't call you frigid if he'd seen you last night," she couldn't resist adding.

"No," Megan replied with some irritation. She was not enjoying this conversation.

"I take it you didn't say anything to your mother?"

"What's the point?"

"I don't suppose you can very well tell her." Viv grinned, thinking it was all quite hilarious. About time Daphne got her comeuppance, she thought smugly.

Sarah meanwhile had met her date in the Shelbourne bar and they then moved on to dinner in the Saddle Room. She had been really looking forward to this but, unfortunately, her companion had turned out to be a shocking bore and much older than his photo had suggested. He hadn't even bothered to hide his wedding ring. It was obvious from the lewd hints he was dropping that he was expecting something in return for the lavish meal. Sarah was wondering how she could escape.

Just before the coffee arrived, she excused herself to go to the ladies' room. As she refreshed her lipstick, debating whether she could make a run for it, she heard someone call her name.

"Sarah! Sarah O'Dowd! It is you, isn't it?"

Sarah turned from the mirror to confront the voice.

"Holy Cow! Orla Casey! How are you? Wow, you look fantastic!"

The two girls embraced.

"God, it must twenty years!" Orla exclaimed.

"Not since you left for London. I heard you'd left there for New York," Sarah said, admiring her sophisticated, glamorous, old school friend.

"Yeah, I did, but I've quit the Big Apple and come home to roost, at last," Orla laughed. "What about you? I heard you were married with a clatter of kids."

"Just two, which is enough, thank you." Sarah grimaced. "My life hasn't been as exciting as yours, I'm afraid."

"Hey, it's great to have met up with you. I only got home last week and I'm dying to catch up on all the gossip. Dublin is *the* happening place again, I hear. I'm heading to 37 now, to meet up with my cousin. Why don't you come with me and dish all the dirt?"

Sarah didn't need to be asked twice. "Sure, I'd love that," she replied, excited.

"What were you doing in the Shelbourne?" Orla asked, as they linked arms to walk the few short yards to Dawson Street.

"Having dinner with a boring old fart. You've just rescued me."

Orla raised her eyebrows. "You're not talking about your husband, I hope?"

Sarah shook her head with a grin.

"Naughty, naughty! You always were a rebel, if I remember rightly. Still the same crazy Sarah, I see."

They entered 37 Dawson Street and Sarah was amazed to see that it was packed to the gills – on a Monday night! It was the trendiest place she'd ever been in and she recognised many celebrities among the crowd.

Orla led her upstairs and over to a booth where a noisy group were laughing and joking.

"Hi, guys, I'd like you to meet an old friend of mine, Sarah."

They all called out hi's and hello's as Orla introduced them. Her cousin, Evan, greeted Sarah with a kiss on the cheek and signalled to the barman who appeared with two Bellinis, as if by magic.

"The best Bellinis in town," she heard someone say in a deep sexy voice.

The speaker was a very attractive man with jet-black hair and dark smouldering eyes. He was staring at her intently and she felt a frisson of excitement run through her body. He moved over on the banquette and patted the seat beside him for her to sit down. She sat and Orla sat down opposite, beside Evan.

"Sarah, you remember Mark, don't you?" Orla asked.

Sarah shook her head.

"Mark Flynn. Pleased to meet you, Sarah." He leaned close to her and offered her his hand.

She took it and felt a quiver as his fingers caressed hers.

"Likewise," she blushed, unnerved by his closeness. His name meant nothing to her and try as she might she couldn't recall him.

"I guess this is my lucky night," he said, as he finally released her hand and gave her a devastating smile.

His teeth were even and a dazzling white and she felt herself melt.

"It's Sarah O'Dowd, isn't it?" he asked, his voice like silk. "I thought I recognised you."

Sarah was taken aback. "Have we met before?" she asked, before tasting the Bellini which was heavenly.

"You probably don't remember me but I remember you from the tennis-club hops. You were the hottest girl there."

His eyes were half-closed as if he was thinking of it and it made Sarah blush.

"All the guys were after you so I didn't get a look-in. I was a bit of a nerd back then," he admitted with a lopsided grin.

"Well, you've certainly changed," Sarah replied with a flirtatious look.

He threw his head back and roared with laughter.

Sarah thought he was the most divine man she'd ever met. The physical chemistry between them was unmistakeable and she wanted him more than anything. He was sleek and polished and oozed glamour but he also had an air of danger about him. His dark eyes never left her face and she was very aware of his body so close to hers.

"How do you know Orla?" Sarah asked him.

"We've always hung around with the same gang so we've offered to baby-sit her till she finds her feet in Dublin again," he grinned.

Orla overheard him and wacked him playfully on the

hand. "Some baby-sitter you'd make! There isn't a mother in Ireland who'd trust her daughter with you," she exclaimed, rolling her eyes.

He roared with laughter once more.

Sarah was in a state of euphoria. This is what she'd been craving. These people were what she wanted to be: glamorous, fun, exciting, and living life to the full, every moment.

There were two more couples at the table, equally attractive and glamorous. She was agog at the girls' jewellery and their clothes and bags were expensive-looking. Although the men were wearing wedding rings, it was obvious from the way they were groping the girls that they were definitely *not* their wives. Who cared? Sarah was having a simply wonderful time as the Bellinis kept appearing in front of her.

Orla kept them entertained with outrageous stories of her life in New York. The night flew by and through it all she was aware of Mark's eyes on her and the heat of his body next to hers. It was thrilling. This was the life!

Orla had worked in PR in New York and planned to open her own PR company in Dublin.

"Now is the time to do it," she confided to Sarah. "Ireland is on the move upwards again."

"What do you do, Sarah?" Mark asked.

"Well, I've been a stay-at-home mum up to now," she told him, thinking how boring it sounded.

"Very admirable," Mark stated. "I can't understand why more women don't do that instead of dumping children in a crèche from the moment they're born."

Sarah basked in his compliment although he obviously had no idea how boring she had found it. "But now my youngest is almost twelve so I'm thinking of going back to work," she added.

"Good for you!" Orla exclaimed. She turned to Mark, disgruntled. "Women have a right to a career too," she stated. "Not all women find being a stay-at-home-mother fulfilling. Look at your own wife! She obviously doesn't."

He grimaced and Sarah guessed all was not rosy in the garden for him either.

"Are you serious about getting back to work, Sarah?" Orla said. "I'm recruiting staff at the moment. Maybe you'd be interested?"

"How would your husband feel about that?" Mark asked.

"He'll have no say in the matter," Sarah replied, a little too brusquely.

He raised his eyebrows quizzically.

"Actually, we're just in the process of splitting up so I really need to be independent."

"Good for you," Orla said again. "If you're serious about going back to work, call me tomorrow and we'll discuss it."

She fished a business card from her bag and handed it to Sarah who looked at it excitedly. This was definitely her lucky night. Everything was coming together beautifully. She could hardly believe it.

"Do you not drink?" she asked Mark, as he ordered another round of Bellinis. She'd noticed that he'd been drinking sparkling water all night.

"No. Alcohol and I don't get on. But I don't need it. There are other pleasures in life." He looked at her under half-closed eyes as he spoke.

She guessed that he was referring to sex. She would

happily have jumped into bed with him that minute.

"Well, I'd better push off," he announced, standing up a short time later. "Some people have to work."

Sarah was disappointed. She'd been hoping that he might instigate something. She was sure he was interested in her.

"Nice talking to you, Sarah," he said, as he bent to kiss her. His lips were soft and hot on her cheek. "Hope I see you again soon," he said softly. And then he was gone.

Sarah felt deflated after he'd left. It was if a light had gone out.

"Did Mark say he was going to work at this hour?" she asked, wondering what business he could be in.

"Yeah. He owns three of the best nightclubs in the city," Orla informed her.

"And also has clubs in Galway, Cork and the UK," Evan added.

"Mmmm . . . interesting," Sarah said.

The other two couples at the table left then. Sarah wondered how they'd refrained from fornicating right there at the table. There was no doubt where they were headed. She wouldn't have minded heading there with Mark. Alas, it was not to be.

"Are you still living with your husband?" Evan asked her when they'd gone.

"No, I'm with my sister at the moment but I have to leave there by the weekend. I don't have my own place yet so I may have to go back temporarily." Sarah looked downcast.

"That's a bummer," Orla sympathised with her. "Listen, if you're stuck, you can kip down with me till you get your own place. I have a spare bedroom."

"Gee, thanks, that would be great!"

"What about the kids? Who will they live with?"

"Ben says he'll fight me for custody." Sarah grimaced.

"That must be awful for you."

"Well, we'll see. If I'm working it might be better if they stay with him during the school week and I can have them weekends."

"How old are they?"

"Tash is fourteen and Owen eleven. Not babies any more."

"Lucky you!" Orla said wistfully. "I was always too busy for kids and now it's too late. My biggest regret."

"Yeah, well, there are pros and cons to having kids," Sarah said. "It's not all plain sailing."

"I suppose not."

# Chapter 24

On Tuesday afternoon, Claire had just finished chatting to Jamie about a small patient who had been admitted that morning when she spotted a young nurse handling a little boy quite roughly. He apparently wanted to go and play but the nurse pushed him back down on the bed. In a flash, Claire broke off her conversation with Jamie and made her way over to the girl.

"Just what do you think you're doing, nurse?" she said, her voice stern. Taking the crying little boy in her arms, she calmed him down. Then she turned and glared at the culprit. "Report to my office at once," she ordered.

She returned to Jamie and excused herself.

He watched her go, his eyebrows raised. "Well, well, so Claire has finally come into her own," he said softly, looking after her admiringly. He was pleased. It was about time.

Sarah had slept late and when she woke had to pinch

herself to make sure that she had not dreamt it all. She looked at Orla's card and knew it was reality. Her sense of excitement returned. Suddenly her future looked bright. She took a long leisurely bath before calling her old friend. She was relieved when Orla asked to meet her that evening to discuss working with her. Sarah had been afraid that it might have only been drink talking, as so often happened at these Irish drinking sessions. They arranged to meet that evening at The Cliff Townhouse on Stephen's Green.

Claire, true to her word, had enrolled on an Italian course which was due to start that evening.

One of her old friends, Pippa, who also lived in Dundrum, had enrolled on it also. Pippa had a new Italian boyfriend and was keen to impress him. They were both looking forward to it and met up for a snack beforehand in a pub close to the Italian Institute. Claire was worried that she might be useless at it and make a show of herself. Pippa, who was full of confidence, told her not to be daft.

"Yes, but I was useless at French at school," she said nervously.

"So was I but Italian is completely different," Pippa assured her as they made their way into Fitzwilliam Square.

Claire need not have worried. She loved it from the first moment, when the teacher had welcomed them saying: "*Buona sera, amici miei!*" She found it to be a very melodic language and was determined to master it.

Pippa felt the same and the two hours flew by. Both girls were happy as they made their way home.

While Claire was being introduced to *la bella lingua Italiana*, Sarah was preening herself in the Oyster Bar of

The Cliff Townhouse. This was another world from the one she was used to and she was trying not to show how impressed she was with everything. Orla seemed right at home and Sarah ordered the seafood platter that her friend recommended. Some of the shellfish were new to her but they were all delicious.

Over dinner she pulled out all the stops to convince Orla that she would be a great asset to her company. Sarah had done a secretarial course on leaving school and worked as a secretary before her marriage to Ben. Nowadays, of course, secretaries were called 'personal assistants'. Orla didn't need much convincing and offered her the job. Sarah couldn't believe her luck.

"You may have to work long hours and possibly nights and there will be some travel involved. Will you be willing to do that?"

"That won't be a problem," Sarah assured her.

"So when are you moving in with me?" Orla asked.

Sarah had been afraid that Orla might have changed her mind and was hugely relieved to hear that. "What day suits you?" she asked.

"Is Saturday okay? Give me a chance to clear out your room."

"Great."

They lingered over dessert and the wine.

"I think Mark has taken a shine to you," said Orla. "I was talking to him today and he was asking me about you. Do you like him?"

"What's not to like?" Sarah laughed and Orla joined in.

"Tell me about his wife," Sarah asked curiously.

"She's Superwoman incarnate. Beautiful, hugely successful, very rich daddy, oh, and skinny as hell."

"She sounds perfect."

"Maybe, but their marriage is a farce. Evan says they stay together for financial reasons."

"Hmmm . . ." Sarah was thoughtful.

"I think he's yours for the taking," Orla said slyly. "I gather you wouldn't be averse to a little fling?"

"Definitely not. He's quite dishy."

"Well, you could do worse than Mark. He's filthy rich too," Orla added with a wink.

Sarah was in seventh heaven. Somebody up there loved her!

When they'd finished dinner Orla suggested they go around to the 37. Sarah readily agreed, hoping Mark might be there. To her delight, he was – sitting with Evan at the same table they'd been at the previous night. He greeted her with a kiss, his lips sending a tingle through her whole body.

"Do you come here every night?" Sarah asked as she sat down beside him.

"Pretty much – when I'm in Dublin anyway," he replied. "It's our local, isn't it, Evan? It's where we all catch up with each other."

There were two other guys with them this time who were also great fun. Sarah was in her element and had another wonderful night. Mark flirted outrageously with her, which thrilled her, but, like on the previous night, he then left to check on his clubs.

"Why don't you call me so we can meet up sometime?" he whispered as he kissed her and slipped her his card.

She took it, her heart racing with excitement. This was the icing on the cake!

"*Wooo-hooo!*" Orla cried when she heard. "But don't

call him for a few days. Trust me, I know Mark. He likes the chase. Don't be too easy, let him wait. He'll want you all the more."

She called Ben on Wednesday at lunchtime to tell him she wanted to talk to him.

He gave a sigh of relief and told her to come round straight away.

She let herself in and found him in the kitchen. He smiled at her.

"I'm happy you're here. I know we can work this out, Sarah."

Her next words floored him. "No, we can't, Ben. I'm sorry, but I've decided that I can't go on. I want a separation."

"You don't mean that, Sarah," he said brokenly, sinking down onto a chair.

"I'm afraid I do. I know it's tough but I've thought about it carefully and it's what I want."

He could see she was deadly serious.

"The kids really need you, Sare . . . and so do I. I'm sure we can work things out."

"There's nothing to work out, Ben. It's over."

"Where will you go?"

"I'm moving in with a friend."

"I presume this friend is a man?" Ben said bitterly, his voice low.

"No, it's a girlfriend. There's no man involved. I just want to be free."

"And what about the kids? I told you I'd fight you for custody." He was near to tears.

"You don't have to. I'm happy for them to stay with you

during the week and I'll have them at weekends."

"Not every weekend."

"Whatever! I've got a new job so I'll be very busy."

He couldn't believe she was being so callous. She hadn't wasted much time, he thought bitterly.

"Well, I guess you've everything worked out," he said. "I don't know how the kids will take it. I'll tell them when they get home from school but I think you need to talk to them and explain what you're doing."

"Okay," she replied, without much enthusiasm. She knew she owed it to them to explain what was happening. But they'd come round. Lots of their school-friends had parents who were divorced. They'd understand. Still, she was not looking forward to telling them.

"I'll call back around four thirty."

She left him sitting with his head in his hands. She felt sorry for him but there was no other way. She wanted a life. He'd get over it and probably meet someone else.

Telling the kids would not be so easy.

She arrived at four thirty on the dot. Owen was playing football in the back garden with his friends and Ben called him in. Tash was in her bedroom but made no appearance when her father called her down.

"Hi, Owen," Sarah greeted her son. "I have something to tell you."

Her son looked down at the ground and scuffed his toe in the way he always did when he was annoyed.

"I know what it is. Dad told me. We're in the middle of a game."

"Well, you'll come and stay weekends with me when I get my new place. It'll be fun," she said, ruffling his hair.

"I suppose," he said, edging to the door, anxious to get back to his friends.

Sarah looked at Ben and shrugged her shoulders. "Not very enthusiastic, is he?"

"He's been missing you, Sarah, but he's a boy. He doesn't show it."

Ben called Tash down once again. She still didn't respond.

"It's okay. I'll go up and talk to her."

Sarah went up the stairs and into her daughter's room.

"My God, look at this mess!" she couldn't restrain herself from exclaiming as she entered.

"You're horrid! I hate you! I'm glad you're not coming home!" Tash cried, running out of the room, then down the stairs and out the front door, banging it behind her.

Sarah sat on the landing step, her head in her hands.

"What did you say to upset her so much?" Ben asked, coming to the bottom of the stairs.

"I couldn't help it. I said something about the mess in her room. That was stupid, wasn't it? But, in any case, I knew I was wasting my time," Sarah said bitterly, upset at the vehemence of her daughter's reaction.

"Sarah! You shouldn't have!"

"I'll call round for my things on Friday morning, if that's okay with you," she told him, shaken, as she got up and started down the stairs.

But Ben didn't hear her. He had run out after his daughter to find and comfort her.

"They'll come round," Sarah said to herself as she drove away. She badly needed a drink so she called her friend Kay and arranged to meet her at five thirty. She couldn't face Claire's right now.

Besides, she was itching to share her good fortune with someone.

Claire was filled with trepidation as she prepared for her date with Adam.

"What will I talk about? What if he finds me boring?" she appealed to Viv, who was helping her decide what to wear.

"You're not boring and as long as you show an interest in him – you know, ask him about his work, travels, what football team he follows – you'll have no problem. Men just want someone to listen, I've found."

"Gosh, I wish I had your confidence," Claire admitted enviously. Viv would never have a problem knowing what to talk about. "Anyway, I'm glad you'll be in the bar. If you see me going to the ladies', you'll follow me in, won't you?"

"Of course. We've agreed on that. Don't worry. Well, I'd better go and get dressed myself."

Five minutes later, she was back.

"Claire, have you seen my suede jacket? I can't find it anywhere."

"No, I haven't . . . Oh, my God!" She remembered seeing a flash of suede as Sarah was dashing out the previous Saturday. "Oh, I hope not!" she cried, pushing past Viv and going up to Sarah's room. There amidst the pile of clothes strewn on the floor was Viv's suede jacket. "Oh, no!" she gasped. "I don't believe it!"

Viv was hot on her heels and saw her precious jacket crumpled in a heap. Claire picked it up and, horrified, they looked at the red stain that covered the whole left side of it.

"Oh my God!" Viv shrieked, taking the jacket from her. "How could she? This is red wine. This will never come out." She felt like wailing but instead, anger set in. "I'll kill her! I swear I'll kill her!"

"I'll take it into the Grafton Cleaners tomorrow during my lunch hour," Claire said apologetically. "They'll get that stain out."

"I sure hope so. I love that jacket. It's Ralph Lauren."

"I know," Claire said miserably.

"I'll kill her when I get my hands on her, I swear!" Viv was absolutely livid.

"If I don't get to her first," Claire remarked grimly. "Come on, we'd better hurry and get dressed or we'll be late."

They arrived at the bar with just five minutes to spare. Viv was meeting her date, Harry, fifteen minutes after Claire's rendez-vous with Adam. They'd arranged that Viv would go in first and when she saw Adam she'd choose a seat near to him.

"Wish me luck," Claire said nervously as Viv left the car.

Viv sauntered in and spotted Adam immediately. He looked exactly like the photo on his profile. Nothing to write home about! He was dressed in a not-very-smart suit with a horrendous tie and was wearing spectacles which he hadn't been in the photo Claire had shown her. Still, she recognised him. He looked up hopefully as she entered the bar and she saw the disappointment on his face that she was not Claire. He was drinking a Ballygowan which didn't bode well.

Viv sat down and ordered a drink. The place was quiet

and she sat daydreaming of Conor as she kept one eye on the door. She was very worried that he hadn't called all week. She was tempted to call him but somehow restrained herself, her instinct telling her that it would be the wrong thing to do. She could not rush him. She was beginning to regret that she hadn't cancelled this date tonight. She was not in the mood for small talk.

Just then her phone rang and her heart almost stopped when she saw that it was Conor. She wanted to play it cool but she was so overjoyed to hear from him that she couldn't pull it off. He was warm and friendly and she was in much better form when he rang off, just as she spied Claire entering the bar.

Viv saw Adam's face light up as Claire approached him. Somehow she didn't think their date would go well. She kept on watching them surreptitiously and saw that Adam was talking non-stop – so Claire needn't have worried on that score. Viv wondered what he was talking about but didn't imagine it could be very interesting.

It wasn't! The first thing Adam had said was, "Can I get you a Ballygowan or would you prefer a juice or something?"

Claire had been about to ask for a glass of wine but figured that wasn't on the cards.

"Maybe we should have met in a coffee house somewhere. I detest alcohol," he confided. "One other thing, I do not believe in sex before marriage. Just thought I'd mark your card from the start."

Claire wished she could have thought of a witty riposte to this, as Viv surely would have, but she was so taken aback that she could think of nothing to say. That was just the beginning! She only half-listened to his conversation, more interested in seeing what Viv's date would be like.

Some more people entered the bar and Viv looked at each of them eagerly, but none of them was Harry.

His messages had been witty and he had assured her that he adored fashion, and shoes in particular. He sounded fun and, now that Conor had called, she was looking forward to meeting him.

She glanced towards the door again and saw a very tall, glamorous woman come in. Viv was checking out her shoes when she realised they were approaching her table.

"Hello, you must be Viv," a deep male voice said.

Viv was so shocked that she dropped her glass, spilling the contents. Looking up, she saw that underneath the make-up and wig, *she* was a *he*, and it was indeed Harry, her date.

"I'm sorry if I have shocked you," he said, whisking out a man's handkerchief to mop up her drink.

Viv regained her composure. "Well, yes, you have rather surprised me."

"I'm sorry but I was afraid if I told you I was a cross-dresser, you would have refused to meet me," Harry admitted bashfully. "May I sit down?"

"Please do," she said, moving over on the banquette to make room for him. Out of the corner of her eye she could see Claire's shocked face as she took in the situation. Adam was also staring at them, as was everyone in the pub.

"You've caused quite a sensation in here," Viv remarked.

"Oh, I'm used to that," Harry laughed.

He had twinkling eyes and a jolly laugh and if he'd been dressed as a man she had no doubt but that they'd have hit it off brilliantly but she wasn't sure she was quite ready for this.

"You're not gay?"

"Good Lord, no. I just like dressing in women's clothes. It's so much more glamorous and interesting than what's available for my own gender, don't you think?"

Viv roared laughing and he joined in. When Claire saw how Viv was enjoying herself, she wished she could have joined them. It would certainly have been more fun than listening to the boring Adam drone on.

It didn't take her long to discover that he was a religious fanatic and, after an hour listening to him spouting his beliefs, she could bear it no more. She stopped him in mid-flow.

"Excuse me, Adam, but I have to go into the bathroom to take a call."

"I didn't hear your phone." He looked at her accusingly.

"It's on silent. I felt it vibrating," she lied.

She went into the ladies' with a nod to Viv who excused herself and followed her.

"My God! Is that Harry?" Claire couldn't contain her curiosity.

Viv laughed. "Isn't he a howl? He asked me to call him Harriet actually. Takes all sorts but he's great fun."

"More than I can say for Adam," Claire groaned and told Viv what she'd had to suffer through. "I'm going to tell him I have to go. What excuse should I give him?"

"Tell him your housemate has accidentally cut herself and you have to go home to take her to A&E."

"Now why didn't I think of that?"

"I'll stay with Harriet for another half-hour or so. He's very entertaining."

"Lucky you," Claire said grimly. "I'll head down to

224

Tesco. Give me a call when you want me to collect you."

"Great!"

Adam was not pleased when Claire told him that she had to go.

"Why does this happen every time I meet a girl on that site? Honestly, I think it must attract the wrong sort of women."

Claire would love to have told him that it was because he was a crashing bore but did not want to spend another minute in his company.

She had already left when Viv came out of the ladies', grinning as she saw a disgruntled Adam pay for the Ballygowans.

The time flew by as Harry entertained her and it was only when Claire rang to say she was outside that Viv realised the time.

"Sorry, Harriet, but I have to go. My friend has arrived to pick me up."

"What a shame. I've so enjoyed talking to you."

"Me too."

"Do you think we could meet again?"

"You're a dear sweet person but I don't really think so," Viv told him regretfully. She wasn't quite ready to have a Harriet in her life right now.

"I understand," he said, "but thank you for a great evening. Don't be surprised if I turn up at the store someday, to have you style me." He laughed wickedly.

"No problem. If I hear I have a client called Harriet, who's six-foot four, I'll know it's you."

They laughed as she kissed him on the cheek, both aware of the weird glances they were getting from the other customers in the bar.

Claire had pulled up outside the door and Viv popped into the passenger seat before they both convulsed with laughter.

"Well, that was an interesting evening," Viv remarked when they finally stopped laughing.

"For you maybe. I would have preferred a date with Harriet than that moron Adam. Would you believe, he says he thinks the site attracts the wrong sort of woman because they all leave early!"

Viv burst out laughing once again. "Well, you win some, lose some. There's always the next date."

"Gosh, I'm not so sure I want to go on another one."

"Don't tell me you're going to give up at the first hurdle? We have to kiss some frogs before we find our prince."

Claire shuddered. "Can you imagine kissing Adam? *Yeuch!*"

As they pulled into the driveway, they saw that Sarah's car was parked outside.

"Good, she's home, I'm just in the mood for her now," Viv declared.

"Oh no," Claire wailed, knowing that a massive row would ensue.

Sarah was in the living room watching MTV when Viv strode in.

"You're home early," Sarah remarked, surprised to see her. "Not such a hot date then?"

"You bitch! How dare you take my suede jacket without my permission and then spill wine all over it!"

Sarah was taken aback. She'd forgotten all about the jacket. Claire hovered behind Viv, afraid to interfere.

"Hold your horses. I was going to ask to borrow it but you were out."

This was a blatant lie and they both knew it. In fact, Sarah blamed Viv for Claire's new hard streak and had taken the jacket to spite her.

"You are most selfish, obnoxious person I've ever had the misfortune to meet and I feel sorry for poor Claire being related to you," Viv spat out furiously, her voice rising a few decibels.

"Oh, shut it, you bitch!" Sarah shrieked and went to grab her hair.

"Stop it, Sarah!" Claire cried out. Terrified, she stepped in between them and Sarah's hand connected with her face. Claire stared at her, shocked.

"Oh, go to hell, the two of you!" Sarah cried. "I'm leaving right now. I wouldn't spend another minute in this house. And don't bother contacting me again, Claire. You're dead as far as I'm concerned."

She stormed out and up the stairs. Minutes later, while Viv was still comforting Claire, she came down again, carrying bags and a suitcase.

"Good riddance!" she yelled at them as she flung the key into the living room. Then she stormed out, banging the door behind her.

Claire was shaking. "Oh God, that was awful! She's really horrid, isn't she?"

"As she said herself, good riddance!"

Sarah had just left when Ben called Claire. He sounded distraught.

"Have you spoken to Sarah?" he asked.

"Not really. She's just had a row with Viv and then stormed out. Why?"

"Did she tell you she's not coming home? She wants us

to separate. She's got it all worked out. She's moving in with a friend and she's also got herself a job."

"Oh, she never told me any of that." Claire hoped she hadn't precipitated this move by telling Sarah she had to leave. "I'm so sorry, Ben. Have you told the kids?"

"Yes. She came round to talk to them. Tash is angry as hell and Owen, well, you know him. It's hard to know what he's thinking. She says she'll have them for weekends as soon as she gets her own place."

Claire didn't know what to say. She was completely lost for words. How could Sarah leave her kids? It was unthinkable. All she could say to Ben was "I'm sorry, I'm so sorry, Ben."

Sarah booked herself into the Stillorgan Park Hotel. She needed a little pampering after the stressful day she'd had. She ran a bubble bath and opened a snipe of champagne from the mini-bar. She resisted the urge to call Mark, having heeded Orla's warning, but as she luxuriated in the big bubble bath she imagined what it would be like making love to him. She sighed with pleasure. Could life get any better?

# Chapter 25

Things returned to normal after Sarah had left and the girls were relieved that she had not fractured their relationship. It had been a close call. It was a relief to all of them that the Sarah saga was over. It was like old times as they slipped back into their easygoing relationship. Claire was happy, though she couldn't help but worry about her sister. She did try calling her but Sarah's phone was always off. Claire wondered if she had in fact changed her number. She called Ben but he had not heard from his wife either though she had been back to the house on Thursday morning and cleared out all her clothes. She obviously meant business.

Meanwhile Richard had been pressurising Claire to meet him and she eventually agreed to do so. They arranged to meet on Saturday night in the Leopardstown Inn. Viv and Megan agreed to be there too just in case it turned into a disaster. Viv made the same arrangement as before, to follow Claire into the ladies' if things weren't going well.

Then she would call her, giving her an excuse to leave. Otherwise, if it was okay, Claire would give Viv a sign and they could leave.

Sarah moved into Orla's apartment on Saturday morning. It was a penthouse in Ballsbridge and very luxurious. She loved it and couldn't believe her luck. She had wanted to call Mark on Friday but Orla had insisted it was still too soon. Reluctantly, she refrained from doing so, though she was aching to see him.

"Trust me. I know Mark. He'll be panting for you by now."

Sarah hoped she was right.

Claire was a bit apprehensive once again as she got dressed to meet another stranger. She hoped it wouldn't be a disaster like the last time. He appeared to be very nice, according to the messages he'd sent, but then Adam had seemed nice too. If this guy turned out to be a jerk she knew she would give up on this online-dating lark.

She was pleasantly surprised when she met him. He was quite good-looking and was dressed neatly – and expensively, she guessed. He had exquisite manners and, to her surprise, she found that he was as shy as she was. He was also new to this dating game and not at all sure about it.

"You're only the second girl I've been out with. The first date was a disaster."

"Mine too," she grinned and then told him about her date with Adam.

"Oh gosh, that sounds pretty bad all right," he agreed, wrinkling his forehead.

He was interesting company and told her that he'd grown up in Dun Laoghaire. He was an only child and both his parents were dead. He had inherited the family chain of up-market, fast-food restaurants but he didn't involve himself in the day-to-day running of the business. He employed very good managers to take care of that side of things.

"I'm not very good with people," he admitted, "so I prefer to oversee the business from my office."

He handed her his business card and Claire was suitably impressed. She knew the chain well and had often eaten there. He seemed very pleased when she told him so.

He was also a good listener and coaxed her to talk about her life. She surprised herself by opening up to him and she was enjoying herself so much that she forgot all about Viv and Megan who were having a drink nearby. It was only when her phone rang that she remembered she should have given them a sign.

"I take it it's all going well?" Viv said sarcastically.

"Yeah, absolutely. Talk to you later."

"I suppose that's a friend of yours calling to give you an excuse to leave," he remarked.

Claire blushed.

"Actually, I've asked a friend to call me too. He should be ringing me at any moment," he admitted bashfully. As he said it, his phone rang.

"No, everything's great." He grinned at Claire as he spoke. "No, I don't need rescuing tonight. Quite the opposite, in fact."

He and Claire were laughing about it as Viv and Megan left the bar, giving her the thumbs-up.

If he had one fault, it was that he seemed very intense about everything. Claire guessed that he didn't relax very much. Everything about him was controlled. She was surprised, when they stood up to leave the bar, to find that he was quite a bit shorter than she was. Although Claire was only five-foot four, she found herself looking down at him. It felt weird. Of course she *was* wearing very high heels. She guessed she'd be in ballerina flats around him from now on. After all, if it hadn't stopped Nicole Kidman from marrying Tom Cruise, or that very tall model from marrying the teeny, tiny Formula One guy, Ecclestone or something, then it shouldn't affect her either. If those successful women could accept a small man, surely she could do it too? Still, she wished Richard was a bit taller.

She was impressed when he led her to his car which turned out to be a Porsche. As she'd suspected, he was wealthy.

Viv happened to be out front, putting something in the bin, as the car pulled up at the gate.

"*Verrrry* nice car," she whistled as Claire walked in.

"How was it?" Megan asked.

"Great. He's very nice. I really liked him. There's only one problem. He's smaller than me."

"Well, you know what they say. He'll look taller standing on his money," Viv sniggered and both she and Megan roared with laughter at the old joke.

Claire used to laugh at it once but it didn't seem so funny any more.

Conor rang Viv that night from Edinburgh and from the sound of things he and his friends were having a good time.

"We're having a great time but I'm missing you," he said.

Viv's heart skipped a beat. She was thrilled to hear him say that. "I've been missing you too," she told him, which was certainly true.

"Look, I was wondering," he said. "I have two hours to wait at Dublin Airport tomorrow evening, before my flight to Galway. Is there any chance that you could come out there and meet me for a drink?"

Viv didn't tell him that she'd have flown to Edinburgh in a flash if it meant seeing him again.

"Yes, I could do that," she replied.

"Could you? That would be great. I'll have a friend with me though."

Viv wanted to see him so badly that she didn't care. If she took the M50 it wouldn't take too long. She laughed as she heard his friends calling out to her in the background. They'd obviously had a great time and she was over the moon that he seemed to be missing her. She couldn't wait to see him.

# Chapter 26

Orla and Sarah were having brunch in Maia's on Sunday when Orla's phone rang. It was Mark. She listened to him for a minute then grinned, giving Sarah the thumbs-up.

"Well, she's with me at the moment. Hold on and I'll ask her."

"It's Mark Flynn," she said to Sarah, trying not to giggle. "He wants to talk to you."

Sarah's hand was shaking as she took the phone.

"Hello, Mark," she said, as coolly as she could, although her heart was hammering in her chest.

"I thought you would call me, you little minx," he greeted her, in his deep sexy voice.

"Oh, I've had a busy week."

"Seriously, I've been waiting for your call, Sarah. When can we meet? Can you see me tonight?"

"I'd like that," she replied, her voice husky. There was no point in playing hard-to-get when she was simply dying to see him.

"You sound so sexy on the phone," he said. "You're giving me a big problem here. And I mean *big*!"

Sarah laughed sexily. "Will it hold till tonight?" she asked.

"I doubt it," he replied. He was laughing too.

"So, say we meet in The Schoolhouse at nine. That suit you?"

"Grand, I'll be there."

"I'll be counting the hours, *chérie*."

Sarah almost squealed with delight when he'd hung up.

"Yesssss!" she cried, pumping the air.

Orla laughed at her exuberance and high-fived her.

"I told you, he's crazy for you now."

Sarah had to agree that Orla's strategy had worked. She spent the rest of the afternoon getting ready for what she hoped would be a thrilling night. She had butterflies in her stomach just thinking about it.

On Sunday Claire met Ben and the kids in the afternoon and they all went bowling and then to Eddie Rocket's afterwards. Tash was quieter than usual but nobody mentioned Sarah. It was as if she didn't exist. Richard had texted Claire twice to say how much he'd enjoyed their night out. While they were bowling she got another text from him, asking when he could see her again.

"New beau?" Ben asked, smiling, guessing that it was a man who was texting her this often.

"Sort of," Claire replied, blushing.

She texted him back: 'I enjoyed meeting you too but I'm afraid I'm not free any time next weekend.'

'How about this coming Wednesday?' Richard replied. 'I can't wait to see you again.'

Claire smiled. He certainly seemed keen and wasn't letting the grass grow under his feet.

'Okay', she agreed. **'I'll call you Tuesday evening to arrange a time and place.'**

Daphne had invited Megan to have lunch with her on Sunday. Megan would have preferred not to go but her mother's invitations were more like Royal Commands. They were meeting in Fitzpatrick's – where else? Daphne would never dream of meeting her halfway. "Dublin city has become so common. All those foreigners," was her refrain. So Megan found herself in Killiney, waiting for Daphne to make her entrance.

There was no doubt about it: her mother did look years younger than the last time they'd been there together. That plastic surgeon was damn good, Megan thought as Daphne pecked her on each cheek.

"I really miss Luis," her mother said after they'd ordered. "I still don't understand why he left like that. Are you sure you didn't say anything to him?"

"No, definitely not," Megan replied, wishing her mother would drop the subject.

"I just don't understand it," her mother said, shaking her head. "What about you? Any boyfriend on the scene?"

Megan sighed, "No, though Viv has met a great guy and Claire too."

"If they can meet someone, why can't you? You're prettier than either of them."

"They met these guys through an online-dating site. That is *not* for me."

"Really?" Daphne leaned forward, her eyes alight. "Tell me about these sites? I know nothing about them."

Megan told her the little she'd picked up about them from Viv.

"How fantastic!"

"I don't think they are the ideal place to find a husband," Megan said petulantly.

"Husband? Who said anything about looking for a husband? I've had three of those and that was enough, trust me."

Megan looked at her mother, horrified. "You're not thinking of joining one of those sites, are you?"

"Why not? Sounds fun."

Megan shook her head, sorry now that she'd mentioned anything about them.

"You're such a prude, my dear," her mother stated as their order arrived.

They didn't discuss the subject further.


Conor seemed very pleased to see Viv when she walked into the Airport Bar on Sunday evening.

"I appreciate you coming all this way to meet me." He smiled as he kissed her cheek. He introduced her to his friend, Ultan, who greeted her warmly.

"The others are all Dubs so they've headed home. This was the only culchie among us." Conor grinned as he punched his friend playfully.

"How many of you were there?" Viv asked as Ultan went to the bar to order a drink for her.

"Eight in total."

"That must have been good craic," she said, smiling.

"It was brilliant. We played some wonderful courses and Edinburgh is a beautiful city."

"Great pubs," Ultan chimed in, as he returned to the table.

"Just as well we don't have to drive back to Galway," Conor laughed. It was obvious the two were close friends.

The barman brought her drink and Conor told her about their trip. He asked her what she'd been up to during the week and when she told him about Harry/Harriet, they both roared with laughter.

"I didn't know you were still messaging guys," Conor said then, frowning.

Viv hoped it meant he was a little jealous.

"No, I had made the date the week before, when you hadn't called," she said pointedly, "and didn't like to cancel it." She didn't add that she'd been afraid that he might not contact her again.

"You were lucky so to find such a great guy as this fella here," Ultan said, clapping him on the back. "You don't cross-dress in private, do you, buddy?"

"Get outta that!" Conor grinned.

Viv was happy as Conor stroked her arm while they talked and, when he went to the loo, Ultan leaned closer to her.

"Conor's told me about you. I'm so happy that he's met you, all his friends are. We've been very worried about him. No doubt he's told you all about Adele and how much she hurt him."

"Mmmm . . ." Viv said non-commitally, hoping that Ultan would continue. Thankfully, he did.

"She was a bitch, a ball-breaker, but he couldn't see that. They were engaged to be married but that meant nothing to her. She treated him very badly and he was devastated when she left him. You're the first girl he's gone out with since. Having met you, I can see you're not like that. It would destroy him if it were to happen again."

"I'm extremely fond of him and I don't plan on hurting him," Viv assured him.

"I can see that. He's pretty fond of you too."

She was hoping he'd say more about Adele but unfortunately Conor came back just then.

She enjoyed their company and Conor kept his arm protectively around her for the rest of the time, which passed too quickly. She was disappointed when the flight to Galway was called and they had to go. Ultan gave her a big hug and Conor kissed her warmly as they took their leave.

"I'll call you during the week," he said as he let her go. "Thanks for coming over."

She drove home, wondering what exactly had happened between him and Adele to cause their split. She would definitely ask him the next time they met.

Sarah spotted him the moment she walked into the bar. Mark stood head and shoulders above the other men there. He was even more gorgeous than she remembered. He ordered a glass of wine for her and the spark between them was palpable. She barely knew what they spoke about, so aware was she of his body touching hers.

The moment she'd finished her wine, he took her hand and stood up.

"Let's go," he said huskily.

She didn't demur and willingly went with him. She was very impressed when she saw the Bentley he was driving. Settling back in the luxurious leather seat, she knew without doubt that they would make love and tingled with anticipation at what was to come.

She thought he would take her to a hotel but instead they pulled up at an apartment complex on Baggot Street.

He parked in the underground car park and once inside the lift they couldn't restrain themselves any longer and fell upon each other. He kissed her and fondled her breasts, driving her wild with desire. She was so hot for him she thought she would explode. Once inside the apartment, he led her into the bedroom and started to undress her. She couldn't wait, throwing off her own clothes and opening his shirt with fumbling fingers. When they were both naked he drew her down on the bed and she lost all reason as he kissed her neck, then breasts, as he made his way down her body.

She gave herself up to the pleasure, moaning as she moved under him and, just when she could thought she might come, he entered her. Her orgasm exploded almost instantly and he came with her. But he didn't stop and, slowly moving inside her, his mouth on her nipples, he brought her to orgasm yet again. He was insatiable but she kept pace with him. He made her feel incredibly sexy and alive again. He was too good to be true.

She figured that at last she had found *the one*.

# Chapter 27

Sarah started work for Orla on Monday and was very impressed when she saw the modern hi-tech office on Fitzwilliam Street where she would be working. She was on a high after her night with Mark and nothing could have dampened her spirits. He'd dropped her home at six that morning, on his way to the airport. He had business meetings in the UK all week but asked her to keep Friday night free for him. At that stage Sarah would have kept her whole life free for him but instinct told her not to let him know that. She didn't know how she'd survive without him for a whole week but he promised he'd make it worth her while. Her imagination took flight as she thought of what he might have in mind. She could hardly bear the suspense.

Thank goodness she had her new job to keep her occupied. She was amazed by Orla's professionalism and her vision for the company. This girl sure knew her stuff! There was no doubt the business would be a big success. Sarah immersed herself in learning everything she could and Orla was surprised by how quick she was to pick it up. Yes, life was looking good!

On Tuesday, Megan finally finished the edit on Gloria's book and sent it back to her so that she could make the changes she'd proposed. Gloria promised to work on it non-stop till it was done. It was looking good and Megan was busy presenting it to the bookshops and drumming up publicity for it. It looked like they might have a winner on their hands. She hoped so, as much for Gloria's sake as for her own.

She had avoided Davy's company since that fateful night but found herself alone with him at the gym that evening, which was rather awkward.

"Er . . . about that night . . ." she blurted out, unable to meet his eye. She knew she was stammering but she had to go on. "Can we just forget it ever happened?"

She was blushing furiously and kept her eyes trained on the floor. When he said nothing, she looked up and saw a strange expression on his face. It was a look of disdain and made her feel very uncomfortable, but the sooner they both forgot about that night the better.

She caught him looking at her with that same disgusted look while she was on the treadmill but she looked away immediately. Luckily, other people had joined them so she didn't need to speak to him again. He obviously hadn't said anything to any of the others, otherwise they would have teased her unmercifully. She was grateful to him for that. She would die of mortification if anyone else got wind of it.

They were all geared up and looking forward to the marathon which would take place on the Bank Holiday Monday. Megan had done the necessary training and was now saving her energy for the big event itself. The girls and her colleagues at work had all promised to turn out on the big day to cheer her on. There was a party planned for the night but she didn't think she would go. She didn't want a repeat of her night with Davy.

Richard took Claire for dinner on Wednesday evening and, although she was wearing ballerina pumps, he was still smaller than she was. This bothered her and she thought it probably meant that she was a very shallow person, but she couldn't help it. He took her to a very nice restaurant in Monkstown which had been garnering rave reviews lately. She was taken aback when, out of his inside pocket, he took a cloth and proceeded to clean his glasses and cutlery with it.

"You can't be too careful these days," he explained, when he saw Claire's shocked expression.

She didn't comment and declined to have him clean hers. There was a snow-white tablecloth and sparkling glasses and cutlery on the table. Everything was pristine and there was absolutely no need for him to do what he just had. Oh no, she thought, reminded of how Jack Nicholson behaved in one of her favourite comedies, *As Good as It Gets*. It looked like Richard might also be suffering from Obsessive Compulsive Disorder. It was terribly funny in the film but she knew OCD was not funny in real life. Still, nobody was perfect and she tried to make allowances. After all, he was good company and she certainly wasn't perfect herself.

He confided in her that his parents had been very strict and demanding and, as an only child, he'd borne the brunt of it. He'd also been bullied as a child and Claire felt great empathy with him.

As he dropped her off later he took her hand in his.

"I really like you, Claire," he said. "You're a very special girl."

She blushed. "Thank you. I enjoy your company very much."

"We make a good couple. Can I see you again on Friday?"

"I'm sorry, Richard, but as I told you, this weekend is a bit crazy. I'm going to be very tied up. It's my birthday on Friday and I'm going out with Viv and Megan that night."

"Well, how about Saturday night and you can celebrate your birthday again with me?"

"No, Saturday is out too. I've already made arrangements to go out with my friends from work and Sunday I'm with family." He looked very downhearted so she added, "I would like to see you next week though, if you're free."

"I'll always be free for you," he replied. "I'll call you Sunday."

She half-expected him to kiss her goodnight but he didn't. Well, it made a nice change from guys who tried to jump you on the first date. There was no doubt that her social life had picked up lately. She was having fun. There was something to be said for online-dating after all.

Claire was in the canteen on Friday having lunch with her friends when the young porter approached her, his face almost hidden by an enormous bouquet of yellow roses.

"These came for you, Claire," he said, grinning cheekily as he handed them to her.

"Wow!" her friends cried when they saw them.

She read the card: *Happy Birthday to a very special girl – With love, Richard.*

"Who's it from?" the others chorused, vying with each other to read the card.

"Richard! Who's Richard?" Angela, who had managed to read the card, asked.

Claire blushed. "Just this guy I've met."

"Oh, you *are* a dark horse," another girl cried.

At that very moment Jamie and his girlfriend passed the table. As usual, Hannah blanked Claire but Jamie smiled, raising his eyebrows when he saw the huge bouquet.

She was back in her office when he poked his head in.

"It's your birthday today, isn't it?" he said. "Sorry, I should have remembered."

"Don't worry."

"I see you have an extravagant admirer. Nice bouquet."

Claire found herself blushing but didn't reply.

"Happy Birthday anyway," Jamie said. "Hope you have a nice evening."

"Thank you, I will."

She didn't enlighten him further although it was obvious that he was curious. He shrugged as he left.

She called Richard after work to thank him for the beautiful flowers.

"I'm glad you liked them. I don't suppose you'll change your mind about meeting me this weekend?" he asked.

"I'm sorry, Richard. I'd love to but honestly I can't."

He sounded dejected as he said goodbye and she knew he was peeved that she wouldn't cancel her friends but she was damned if she'd let him bully her. She'd had enough of that in her life.

Megan and Viv eyed the huge bouquet of roses as Claire struggled in the door that evening.

"*Woooo-hoooo!* What's this? They're beautiful," Viv cried, burying her nose in the bouquet.

"Who are they from?" Megan asked.

"Richard," Claire told them, blushing.

"My, my, I'm impressed," Viv said admiringly.

"Very nice," Megan observed. "He's obviously keen."

"Give over!" Claire laughed as she went to find a vase to put the roses in water.

When she came back into the living room she found that the girls had opened a bottle of wine and they toasted her before they gave her their presents. Megan presented her with a soft cashmere sweater and Viv had bought her delicate La Perla lingerie.

"They're beautiful, thank you so much," Claire cried, hugging her two friends. "They're so luxurious. I feel very spoilt."

"About time," Viv remarked, pleased that Claire liked their gifts.

"I don't suppose Sarah remembered your birthday," Megan queried.

"No," Claire said sadly, "but I did get cards from Ben and the kids and he's invited me to lunch there on Sunday."

"Silly bitch," Viv muttered under her breath.

They finished the wine and Claire ran upstairs to change before the taxi arrived to collect them. Megan had reserved a table in Beaufield Mews in Stillorgan, a place Claire had often heard about but had never been.

The food was fabulous and she declared it was the best birthday she'd ever had. But she and Megan had a problem getting Viv to talk about anything other than Conor. Every time she started to wax lyrical about him, they rolled their eyes and starting humming 'Falling in Love'. It was obvious to them both that Viv was, most definitely, falling in love.

While her sister was celebrating her birthday, Sarah was on tenterhooks waiting to hear from Mark. Her first week working for Orla had been a great success but now all she could think of was seeing him again. Eventually, just before ten o'clock, he called her.

"Sorry, I'm late. I'm on my way from the airport. Can you meet me at the apartment?"

She was so relieved she would happily have agreed to meet him on the moon.

He looked pleased to see her as he let her in and once inside the apartment Sarah kissed him, sliding her hand down inside his trousers.

"Hey, hey, not so fast," he said, staying her hand. "I thought we'd have a little treat first. It will make things even better, I promise."

She looked at him questioningly, wondering what he had in mind. Some sex game perhaps? Instead he took out a small plastic packet of white powder and she watched, fascinated, as he emptied a small amount of the powder onto a small mirror he'd produced and used a credit card to separate it into two lines. Then he took out a euro note, rolled it up and handed it to her.

"What do I do with this?" she asked.

"Sarah, don't tell me you've never taken coke before?" he asked disbelievingly.

She shook her head.

"A coke virgin! You don't know what you're missing, honey."

He showed her what to do.

"Your turn now," he said, handing the note back to her.

She did as he had done and felt the tingling in her nose as she sniffed the coke in.

"Welcome to heaven, babe," he grinned as he started to undress her slowly.

By the time they were both naked, the wonderful feeling hit her. It was amazing and she felt more sexy than she ever had in her life. She was euphoric and he smiled lazily at her as he lifted her and carried her into the bedroom.

The sex that followed was even better than the first night. She let him take complete control and surrendered herself to him totally, sensing that this was what he wanted.

When they'd both climaxed, he took her hand and led her over to a full-length mirror. Standing behind her, he caressed her breasts as she watched in the mirror.

"You are so sexy," he whispered, nuzzling her ear.

She felt the heat rise inside her once more. Then he was inside her again and she watched, fascinated, as he thrust into her. It seemed to go on and on and, by the time they both climaxed, they were soaked in perspiration and panting. This was the exciting life she'd wanted. This was what it was all about. Satiated at last, he led her back to bed and she fell back on the pillows, her body bathed in sweat.

"You liked that?" he asked, leaning on one elbow and smiling at her.

"Oh, yes," she whispered.

"It's only the start," he replied, stroking her hair. "We'll have lots more good times like this."

She shivered with delight at the thought.

# Chapter 28

Viv met Conor on Saturday night and felt they were getting closer with each meeting. She knew she was falling in love and, although he hadn't said anything, she suspected he might be too. She wanted to ask about Adele but they were having such a wonderful evening that she didn't want to spoil the mood. Again, he dropped her off in a taxi and when he kissed her goodnight it was with more passion than before. She knew he wanted her and she wanted more than anything to make love to him. She would have to try and plan something where it could happen spontaneously, but it was difficult what with him staying with his mother every weekend and the 'no-guys' rule of Claire's house. It would be difficult but she was desperate to find a way.

"I'm taking my mother to a family lunch tomorrow," he said, "but I'd really like to see you tomorrow evening. Are you free?"

"Nothing I can't cancel," she smiled in reply.

On Saturday night Claire was out with the girls from work, celebrating her birthday with them. It was a hilarious evening that ended up in Bad Bob's at two thirty in the morning. This was turning into one hell of a weekend.

Sarah was furious. She'd called Ben to say she'd like to see the kids on Sunday, but he'd said it wasn't possible because he'd invited her sister to lunch. She'd also expected to see Mark over the weekend but, when he'd dropped her home on Saturday morning, he'd mentioned nothing about a future date.

As she made her way to the 37 bar with Orla on Saturday night, she prayed that he'd be there. As it was a bank holiday weekend, Evan and all the usual gang were there, ready to party. There was no sign of Mark, however.

"Where's Mark?" Sarah couldn't resist asking.

"His kids are home from boarding-school this weekend," said Evan, "so he's playing Happy Families. I spoke to him earlier and he said to say hello."

Sarah was a bit peeved that Mark hadn't told her. Her disappointment was a good excuse to get pissed – on Harvey Wallbangers this time.

It was after two when the taxi dropped them home.

"How about a nightcap?" Orla asked.

Sarah agreed readily but was surprised when, instead of opening a bottle of wine, Orla laid out two lines of cocaine on the table.

"I didn't know you did coke," she said.

"Of course I do. Everyone does," Orla replied before she snorted and handed the rolled-up note to Sarah.

Sarah followed suit and sat back, waiting for the lovely carefree feeling to take hold. Shortly it hit her and she felt exhilarated, her mind as clear as a bell. This stuff was way more effective than alcohol. What a discovery!

It was with great difficulty that Claire struggled out of bed on Sunday morning to go to lunch in Ben's. Tash was delighted to see her and hugged her warmly. Owen surprised her by succumbing to her hug too instead of shying away as he normally did. Claire guessed it must be because he missed his mother. Poor little fellow.

It was strange being in Sarah's house when she wasn't there.

Ben was a great cook and Claire stood in the kitchen, sipping a glass of wine, as he put the finishing touches to the lunch. He had refused absolutely to let her help.

"Any word from Sarah?" she asked him.

"Yes, she called to say she couldn't have the kids this weekend, as she hasn't got her own place yet. She wanted to take them out today, but I told her you were coming to lunch. That annoyed her, not that Tash would have wanted to go anyway."

"Me neither," Owen piped up. He had been sitting at the kitchen table engrossed in his Game Boy and they hadn't realised he was listening.

Ben threw Claire a helpless look and for the hundredth time she thought what a fool her sister was.

The lunch was delicious and after Claire and Tash had cleared up they went for a walk in Marlay Park. Then they watched *Parental Guidance* which had them all rolling around laughing. She was very touched when, at teatime, Ben brought out a birthday cake and he and the kids sang 'Happy Birthday'. They each had a present for her and Claire felt very emotional as she hugged the three of them, thinking how much she loved them. Sarah was a moron!

Richard had texted her throughout the weekend. He wanted her to go out on Monday night.

'**Please, Richard, I told you I'm busy. I have to go to a party in The Goat on Monday for Megan's running club.**'

She sighed, exasperated. He just didn't take no for an answer, did he? Talk about determined!

Sarah woke with a raging hangover on Sunday and couldn't understand how Orla appeared to be as fresh as a daisy.

"How do you do it?" Sarah moaned, holding her throbbing head.

"My little miracle cure," Orla laughed, shaking a bottle of pills in her hand.

"What are they?"

"Here, take one. They're my magic pills. You'll feel right as rain in ten minutes."

Sarah couldn't believe it. It *was* a miracle cure. Within ten minutes her headache had gone and she felt marvellous.

"Wow! They certainly are effective. What are they?"

"Vicodin. They're my lifesavers. I couldn't survive without them."

"I didn't know such things existed. My God, they're marvellous! Where can I buy some?" Sarah asked, intrigued.

"They're on prescription only but PJ, my supplier, can get anything for me. He's bringing me some coke this evening. I'll ask him to bring some Vicodin for you."

"Brilliant! Maybe he could bring me some cocaine too?"

"Sure," Orla said, laughing at her enthusiasm.

Viv was excited and apprehensive as she went to meet

Conor in The Goat. As she'd been to Sunday lunch with her parents and he'd been to the family lunch, they intended to just have a light snack.

Viv had decided that she had to know where she stood and felt that they were far enough along now for him to talk about his past relationship. Surely he trusted her enough to share it with her now? Once they could get that out of the way they could hopefully move on. Viv planned to ask him to spend the following Saturday night with her.

They had just finished their sandwiches when Viv decided to broach the subject.

"Conor, I'd really like you to tell me about your last relationship. Don't you think it's time?"

"That's something I don't want to discuss," he said quietly, looking away from her. He seemed to go into himself and fell silent, refusing to meet her eyes.

Viv could have kicked herself. She'd known not to rush him but that was exactly what she had done. Now she'd created a gulf between them, one she didn't know how to bridge. Why couldn't she have kept her big mouth shut? No doubt he'd have told her when he was ready. *Oooooh!* She was furious with herself.

Things were strained between them after that and she didn't dare mention the possibility of spending the night together the following week. She was worried he might not even want to see her again. She couldn't bear if that was to happen.

He walked her to the door as he always did but his kiss was cooler than usual.

"I'll call you," he said, as he walked away.

"Damn!" she said as she watched the taxi pull away. "Why couldn't I just have shut up and had patience?" She was terrified that she might have lost him forever.

Megan was excited and apprehensive about the marathon which was only a day away. She'd received cards from people she'd never expected, wishing her good luck. Gloria Rivers, her new author, had sent a lovely card saying that she and her daughters would turn out to cheer her on. She hoped she wouldn't let them down.

Nothing from Daphne, of course, not that she'd expected anything.

Sarah was missing Mark. She especially missed the sex. Thank God she had cocaine and the magic pills to help her through. When Orla's guy arrived around ten o'clock with the supplies they'd ordered, she introduced him to Sarah.

"I have a new customer for you, PJ," she told the attractive young man.

"Cool," he said, shaking Sarah's hand as if it was a social introduction. "Just let me know your poison and I can get it for you."

When they'd completed the transaction PJ gave her his phone number and welcomed her as a new client.

"I sell only the best shit. Call me anytime. I'm available 24/7," he grinned.

He left whistling, hands fingering the cash in his pockets.

The two girls snorted the coke and in good spirits, decided to go clubbing. They were both on a high and had a fabulous night. They even snuck into the ladies' later and, giggling, did two more lines, taking care that no one saw them. Then they continued partying till after four thirty in the morning. Sarah was exuberant, flirting with the guys who hovered around them and plied them with drinks.

"I work hard and play hard," Orla laughed as they rode home in the taxi.

"You sure do, girl," Sarah agreed, admiringly.

Orla had the world at her feet and Sarah was on her way.

# Chapter 29

The day of the Dublin City Marathon dawned bright and sunny as fifteen thousand people made their way to the start on Fitzwilliam Street. Megan was filled with excitement as she joined her running group at the gym, from where a bus they'd hired would take them to the city centre.

Claire and Viv had got up at seven that morning to see her off, promising to be in Bushy Park to cheer her on and then at the finish line to congratulate her on her achievement.

"What happens if I don't make it to the finish line?" she asked, her voice apprehensive.

"Of course you will," Claire assured her.

"If not we'll come and physically drag you over it," Viv said, causing Megan to laugh, which relaxed her somewhat.

Viv had decided to be upbeat today and not spoil Megan's day. She would worry about Conor if he didn't contact her again. She prayed that wouldn't happen. She insisted on going with Claire as she drove Megan to the gym. They both wished their friend good luck and waved her off.

Later Viv and Claire took their places with other spectators on the route, just past the halfway mark.

Claire couldn't believe the crowds that flew past her, young and old, every shape and size imaginable. They all seemed in good spirits even though they had already run fifteen miles, more than half the twenty-six miles they had to do.

"I'd really love to try this next year," she remarked to Viv.

"I'd never manage it," replied Viv who was in awe at the sheer number of people running past them. Most of them were ordinary people too, not athletes, at least not after the first hundred or so had passed.

Megan had given them a rough idea of what time she would pass that point and they scanned the faces of the runners, terrified that they would miss her.

Suddenly they spotted her, long legs flying, ponytail swishing, and they roared, "Go on, Megan! Go, girl!" waving and jumping to catch her attention. She saw them and waved, a big grin on her face as she gave them the thumbs-up. All the people around them had taken up the chant, "Go, Megan!" and she laughed, waving at them all. Claire had never been so proud of anyone in her life and said a silent prayer that Megan would make it to the finish line. They then drove into the city centre, having to detour as many roads were closed, but they'd planned it well and reached the city centre in plenty of time.

Megan was surprised to see Viv's parents on the sideline, waving and calling her name. She waved back at them.

Shortly after that she saw a big banner being waved by kids which said GO MEGAN GO! She thought it was for another Megan until she spotted Gloria Rivers, and what were obviously her daughters and grandchildren, standing under the banner, cheering and calling her name. She was touched and really grateful to them all.

It was the best experience of her life and she was so happy to be a part of it. Half of Dublin seemed to have turned out and it made her very proud to be one of them. Her group had all started out together but she lost sight of most of them early on, as they were all seasoned marathoners. Tom stayed back with her although she told him to go ahead.

"No, it's your first marathon, I'll stick with you. I don't run much faster than you anyway," Tom, who was fifty, assured her.

Despite her pleas he stayed running beside her and it was only when she hit the dreaded 'wall' after twenty-one miles, just as they turned onto the Stillorgan Road, that she appreciated his support. Her legs started to feel heavy and her breathing became laboured. She was terrified she wouldn't be able to continue but Tom encouraged her to keep going and saw her through it.

"Only four more, you're doing great," he told her.

It was then she saw Simon, Emily and the gang from the office waving and yelling her name and she waved back at them. It was the lift she needed and she felt her energy return as the last four miles flew by.

Then, with the finish-line in sight, amidst all the din, she heard Viv and Claire screaming her name and she realised she'd done it. It was with huge relief that she crossed the finish line and saw her time flashing above it. It was better than she'd expected and she crossed the line, hands over her head, before she bent over, taking in big gulps of air.

When she could breathe normally again she looked around for Tom and saw him grinning at her, looking as fresh as if he'd been out for a quiet stroll.

"You did it, girl!" he said, as he came to her and hugged her. "And in a great time too."

"I can't believe it!" she exclaimed, eyes shining. "It wasn't so bad."

"Wait till tomorrow and you might feel differently," he laughed. "See you later."

The medics gave her water and a plastic poncho and then she received the precious medal that she'd worked so hard for. She picked up her bag, slipped on her tracksuit and went to meet Viv and Claire at the spot they'd arranged.

They hugged her, jumping up and down excitedly.

"You were fantastic!"

"Awesome!"

Exhausted but happy, Megan went home with them and, after a quick lunch, sank into the warm bath Viv had run for her. It was so delicious that she was tempted to doze off but she resisted the urge and after half an hour soaking dragged herself out and into bed, where she was asleep within seconds.

It seemed to her she'd only been asleep for five minutes when Claire was shaking her awake.

"Come on, Marathon Girl, time to party."

"Oh no," Megan wailed, wanting to go back to sleep, but Claire persisted and, aided by Viv, managed to get her awake.

After a quick shower she felt better and was ready to get dolled up. They were meeting the others at seven and all three girls were looking forward to the evening ahead.

Viv had asked Conor to the party but he'd had to take his mother to dinner. She wished he was there but was determined to enjoy the evening anyway.

They could feel the buzz immediately when they entered the bar of The Goat, where they were meeting up. Thirty people had signed up for the buffet which would be served in a private room upstairs. There was an air of exhilaration as the runners compared times and stories with each other. They had all run this marathon before, some of them the London and New York ones too. Megan was the only first-timer in the group and when she came in they all cheered loudly. She blushed as they congratulated her with kisses and hugs and then she introduced the girls to them.

"Where's lover boy?" Viv whispered to her and with a shock Megan realised she was referring to Davy.

She looked around frantically, hoping no one had overheard. Thankfully they hadn't. "He's over there by the bar. The guy in the pale blue jacket," she muttered under her breath.

"Mmmm . . . dishy!" Viv grinned. She didn't blame Megan one bit for hopping into bed with him. She'd have done the same. "You'll have to introduce us."

"Please," Megan whispered with a strained look, "don't say anything and don't let Claire hear you."

She had invited her colleague, Simon, to the party and was relieved to see him arrive at that moment. She waved to him and beckoned him over and introduced him to the girls. Viv and Claire had heard her speak of Simon often and they were surprised to see that he was only in his late thirties. Somehow they'd expected him to be older and not this attractive sexy man.

"I think Megan's achievement calls for champagne to celebrate, don't you?" he said, smiling.

"I told you she didn't need online dating," Viv whispered to Claire as they followed him over to the bar. "Imagine working with a gorgeous guy like that! And he's single to boot."

To Megan's dismay she found that Simon had taken a place next to Davy, who congratulated her on the race. She had no option but to introduce him to Simon and the girls.

Viv threw Claire a look as much as to say, 'What did I tell you? She's surrounded by gorgeous men.'

"I think I have to sit down, my feet are killing me," Megan declared. Simon, who was chatting to Davy, spotted a free bar stool and went to get it for her. He had noticed that Megan was uncomfortable in Davy's presence and so he placed it away from him.

"I take it Davy is the lucky guy?" Simon whispered to her as he handed her a glass of champagne. He had brought another glass for Davy, who he thought seemed like a very nice fellow.

They toasted Megan and as they drank she was surprised to see Claire and Davy chatting animatedly. They appeared to be getting on very well. She trusted he would not mention anything about their night of passion. Megan still blushed when she remembered it.

Simon was asking Viv about her job and she had him laughing with her usual witty anecdotes. She found him charming and Megan was surprised to hear them discussing various designers. She'd never imagined Simon would know anything about fashion.

Claire was in mid-sentence when she stopped talking and her hand flew to her mouth. "Oh goodness!" she cried, looking across the room.

"What's the matter?" Megan asked as they all looked at her, wondering what was wrong.

"It's Richard," Claire murmured. "He's just come in. What is he doing here? It's miles from where he lives." She looked very anxious.

"Did you tell him you were coming here tonight?" Megan asked.

Claire had gone pale. "I guess I mentioned it."

"Some nerve that guy Richard has," Viv remarked. "He's obviously besotted."

"Who's Richard?" Simon and Davy asked simultaneously.

"An admirer of Claire's," Megan explained.

Richard had moved to the other end of the bar and was now in Claire's direct eye-line.

"I'd better go and say hello," Claire said.

"I'd love to meet him, Claire," Viv declared. "Do bring him over and introduce him." She stared over at Richard, unabashed.

Claire left the group to go over to him.

"Hi, what are *you* doing here?" she greeted him.

"I was just passing and decided to drop in for a pint." She doubted that.

"Can I get you a drink?" he asked.

"No, thanks, I have a drink over there." She nodded in the direction of her friends.

"Who's that big guy you're talking to?"

She thought she heard an accusing note in his voice. She hoped she was wrong.

"He's a friend of Megan's. He ran the marathon today also."

"Hmmm . . . I thought maybe you were with him."

"No, I'm not. I'm with my two girlfriends. Look, I have to get back to them. Do you want to come over and meet them?"

His face lit up. "I'd love to meet them."

She hoped he didn't expect to be invited to the dinner. Well, she would not be blackmailed into that.

He followed her over to the girls and she introduced them.

They made small talk for a few minutes and Claire was relieved when they were asked to go up to dinner.

"Sorry, I have to go, Richard," she said.

He looked crestfallen. The others moved off upstairs and he put a hand on Claire's arm to detain her.

"Claire, I'm sorry if I've annoyed you but I was really worried you were with someone else. Forgive me."

He looked so contrite that she felt sorry for him.

"I'm not like that, Richard. I wouldn't do that to you."

"I know that. It's just that I couldn't bear to lose you."

He looked like a Little Boy Lost. "Can I see you Wednesday night, please?"

She smiled at him. "Yes, I'd like that."

He beamed at her. "Great! I'll pick you up at seven – and wear something glam. I'm going to take you somewhere very special."

Viv and Megan were waiting for her upstairs, agog to know what he'd said.

"He was a bit worried that I was meeting another guy," Claire explained.

"I still think it's a bit rich – coming here when he knew you were otherwise engaged," Viv remarked.

Megan had a worried look on her face. "He does seem a little possessive," she observed. "I suspect he's very insecure."

"Aren't all men? Probably was hoping you'd invite him to the party," Viv said disgustedly.

"Well, I didn't," Claire replied firmly but she guessed Megan was right about him. "He's just like a little kid really. He says he's taking me somewhere special next Wednesday."

Claire found herself beside Davy at dinner which pleased her. When she told him she was a children's nurse in Crumlin, he was amazed.

"I work in Crumlin too, two days a week. What a coincidence! I'm a paediatric physiotherapist," he said. "Strange we've never met."

"I work on the cardiac ward, that's probably why. My kids are too sick for physiotherapy."

"That figures."

Megan watched in alarm as Claire and Davy became engrossed in conversation. There was definitely a chemistry there. She felt a little out of it, to be honest, as Simon and Viv appeared deep in conversation on her other side. Simon obviously found Viv amusing as he threw his head back and let out a loud laugh every so often. Viv was in sparkling form tonight.

Megan's euphoria had passed. Tiredness was setting in and she felt somewhat down. Tom's wife, who was across the table from her, told her that he was always quite down for a few weeks after the event so it was natural to feel as she did.

The buffet meal was great and, after it, as the DJ tuned up, Megan excused herself.

"I'm just so bushed, girls, I have to get to bed. I feel like I could sleep for a week."

"We'll come with you," Claire offered but Megan could see that both she and Viv were having a ball and wanted to stay.

"No, no, you guys stay on here. I'll feel bad if you leave."

"Well, if you insist," Viv said, relieved.

"I do."

"Why don't you take the morning off tomorrow? I guess you've earned it," Simon suggested.

"Thanks, maybe I will," Megan replied tiredly. "Goodnight, everyone."

# Chapter 30

Mark finally rang Sarah on Monday evening.

"How nice of you to call," she greeted him coolly. "Where have you been?"

"Sorry, honey, it's complicated. Can you meet me in the apartment at nine? I've missed you."

Despite being determined to play it cool, Sarah melted. "Sure," she replied, butterflies in her tummy as she anticipated what lay ahead.

Mark opened the door for her, with only a towel around his waist. He drew her in and held her close as he slowly opened the wraparound dress she was wearing and let it slip to the floor. She was naked except for her red high heels and he moaned as he touched her voluptuous breasts.

"Fucking beautiful!" he said hoarsely.

Taking her hand, he led her into the bathroom. She looked at him quizzically as she stepped out of her heels. He ran the shower, kissing her breasts as he waited for it to be hot enough and then drew her into the shower with him. Soaping her body, he caressed her as the hot water streamed over them both. She was so excited she thought she would explode with pleasure. He kissed her deeply, his erection pressed against her stomach. Then he lifted her up and she wrapped her legs around his waist as he entered her. Thrusting rhythmically together, they both climaxed at exactly the same moment and afterwards, panting, he eased her down and held her close, only the water between them. It was the most erotic thing she'd ever experienced.

Afterwards, he towelled her dry and then himself, and wrapped a fresh towel around her waist.

She giggled. "What about my boobs? You're not going to cover them?"

"No way," he said as he wound a towel around his waist. "I want to look at those beauties all night."

She laughed as she followed him into the living room where he laid out four lines of coke.

"Four?" she exclaimed.

"Sure. I think we've earned it."

Afterwards they relaxed on the couch.

"So, tell me about your weekend," she said.

"Not much to tell. My kids were home from boarding-school for the long weekend. I don't see them often enough so it was good to spend time with them."

"What age are they?"

"Christian is eight and Jessica is ten."

"And they're at boarding-school? So young?" Sarah exclaimed, shocked.

"My wife's decision. She's busy with her career. That's her priority."

Sarah saw the look of disgust on his face.

"Do you still live with her?"

"Only when the kids are home. She lives in the family home in Killiney, I mostly stay in town. We lead separate lives."

Not much of a marriage, Sarah thought to herself.

They made love again when they went to bed and she fell asleep, wrapped in his arms, gloriously happy and contented. Sometime before daybreak, she was awakened by his lips on her body and, half-asleep, she made love to him again.

At around seven she felt his lips on hers and woke to find him fully dressed.

"I have to go, hon. It's been a great night. Go back to sleep. I'll call you."

She felt bereft. She curled into a ball, hugging his pillow to her as she sniffed the scent of his body from it. She couldn't get enough of him and knew she would just be existing until she saw him again.

Megan had slept for twelve hours straight and felt better when she arrived at work after lunch on Tuesday.

"You missed a great night afterwards," Simon said as she poked her head around his door.

"I'm sorry, but I was bushed. I couldn't keep my eyes open. I'm glad you enjoyed it."

"Best night I've had in ages. We ended up in Club 92. Your friends are great fun. I really like them."

"Yes, they are. Eh . . . who went to Club 92?" She tried to keep her voice casual.

"Just Viv, Claire and Davy. How that guy danced until two in the morning after running a marathon, I'll never know."

271

Oh no, Megan thought. Please don't tell me Claire got off with Davy. I couldn't handle that. Simon's next words seemed to indicate that she had.

"He was trying to persuade Claire to join the gym and the running club."

Megan didn't want to hear any more. If Claire became involved with Davy she would have to confess that she'd had a one-night-stand with him. There was no doubt that if they became an item, he would tell her. Megan would have to 'fess up first. She didn't know how she could tell her best friend that she'd slept with her boyfriend first. She didn't want to go there!

In fact, Claire had enjoyed herself immensely. Davy was such fun and he made her laugh and she felt like she'd known him forever. He was also the best-looking man she'd ever met. He had a great sense of humour and was easy-going and relaxed. However, she was still going out with Richard and she wasn't the kind of girl who cheated.

To Viv's relief, Conor rang on Tuesday morning.

"Sorry if I upset you. I just find it hard to talk about . . . you know . . ."

"I'm sorry. I shouldn't really have asked. I know you find it difficult."

He cut her short. "No, you have a right to know. I have to travel to Dublin tomorrow for a meeting. Could you meet me for a drink when you finish work?"

"I'd love that," she replied, her heart singing. It looked like everything was going to be okay.

Megan rang her mother that afternoon to invite her out to

dinner for her birthday. Saturday would be Daphne's fifty-sixth birthday, although she professed it was only her forty-sixth. In fairness, she could almost have passed for that after the latest work she'd had done.

To Megan's chagrin, her mother informed her that she was busy on Saturday.

"Sorry, sweetie, but I'm completely booked up every night until Thursday week."

"Booked up with whom?" Megan asked, a little piqued. Good grief, even her mother had a better social life than she had.

"Oh, a different guy every night. I'm so glad you told me about those dating sites, darling. I've had a whole new lease of life since I joined them. It's simply fabulous, darling. You should try it."

"I don't think it's quite the place to find a husband, Daphne," Megan said sardonically.

"As I've told you before, I am *not* looking for a husband. I'm thinking more toy boy. You'd be amazed how much fun I'm having and how many young men are interested in an older woman." She hooted with laughter.

Megan squirmed with embarrassment.

Disgruntled, she agreed to take her mother out the Thursday after. She was beginning to think that *she* was out of step. Was the whole world meeting the opposite sex online? Was she the only one who still thought that you met someone and, if you clicked, then you started dating. Seemingly, she was.

Later, sitting in alone watching TV, Megan wondered if maybe she was just being old-fashioned. Claire, Viv and her mother were all going out with men they'd met online. Maybe she was the one missing out.

# Chapter 31

Viv felt closer to Conor than ever before as he held her hand and haltingly told her what had happened between him and Adele. She stroked his hand as he recounted how he'd ignored rumours over the years that she was cheating on him. Then he arranged a special dinner and proposed to her on their fifth anniversary together. He'd presented her with a beautiful diamond ring he'd had designed specially and she'd laughed in his face.

"I have no notion of getting married," she'd told him, laughing. "My modelling career is just taking off and I don't want to be tied down. The world is my oyster now. I'll have millionaires and celebrities queuing up to take me out." She'd turned the knife cruelly. "You didn't seriously think I'd want to marry you? I considered us more as housemates."

Conor was devastated. He'd really believed that they had a future together.

"She then admitted that she'd been sleeping with other

men all the time we were together. I needn't tell you how that made me feel." He put his head in his hands. "It has taken me a long time to get over it."

Viv put her arm around him and kissed him gently. "How awful for you," she said softly.

"And the funny thing is, her modelling career never really took off," he said bitterly. "The European girls came in and took over."

Viv felt bad for him but was happy that he'd shared it with her. When they parted, he kissed her with more intensity than ever before. She felt confident that they'd turned a corner and felt it was time to take their relationship to the next level. She desperately wanted to make love to him and decided she'd book a hotel for the following Saturday night and hopefully take it from there.

When Viv got home, Megan was sitting forlornly on the sofa, listlessly watching TV. Viv barely noticed, she was on such a high.

"I'm so happy," Viv said, and told her about the meeting with Conor and what she'd planned.

"I'm glad for you," Megan replied. "God, everybody seems to have a boyfriend except me. Even my mother has joined that goddam dating site and is out every night with a different guy."

"Why not let me join you up? They allow us to join our friends and write their profiles ourselves. Some people are saying it's actually more honest than people doing their own. What have you got to lose?"

"Nothing, I suppose. Oh, do it if you want!"

Viv couldn't believe her ears and gleefully set about it before Megan could change her mind.

"This doesn't mean that I will necessarily go out with any of the guys who reply. That's if I get any replies," she added doubtfully.

"Of course you'll get replies, and you don't have to go out with anyone you don't like," Viv assured her.

Richard had taken Claire to what was probably the most expensive restaurant in Dublin. The food was out of this world with waiters dancing attendance on them. It was the best meal she'd ever had which was not surprising as it had two Michelin stars. That hadn't stopped Richard taking out his napkin to rub the cutlery and glasses however. She guessed he would do this even in Buckingham Palace.

"That was simply wonderful," she told him as she dabbed her lips.

"Nothing is too good for my girl," he replied as he slid a gift-wrapped box across the table.

"What's this?" she asked with a frown.

"It's your birthday present. Open it," he ordered, smiling.

"But your roses were more than enough," she protested.

"Nonsense! Go on, open it." He was beaming broadly now.

Reluctantly she opened it and gasped when she saw the beautiful rose-gold watch, surrounded by diamonds.

"Oh, no, this is far too much. I couldn't accept this," she stammered.

"Of course you can, my dear."

"No, honestly, this is far too extravagant," she protested yet again.

"It's my pleasure. Let me put it on."

He took her wrist and fastened the watch on it. It was the most exquisite watch she'd ever seen.

"Honestly, Richard, I really appreciate the thought but I couldn't accept this. We barely know each other."

"I feel like I've known you all my life and I know that you'll be in my life forever. I'll be very hurt if you don't accept it," he insisted and she could hear the determination in his voice.

Claire had never been in a situation like this before and didn't know what to do. She didn't want to hurt his feelings and the watch *was* exquisite but she had an uneasy feeling.

"It's beautiful," she said, turning her arm this way and that so that it caught the light. She was beginning to suspect that he was a control freak. This was the last thing she needed right now. She had just started living her own life and had no intention of handing over control of it to anyone, no matter how many extravagant presents they bought her.

"Honestly, Richard, it's too much. I can't."

"Take it!" he said, grabbing her wrist and cutting her off.

His eyes were steely and his voice brooked no argument. Suddenly she felt frightened and stopped protesting.

"When can I see you again?" he asked as he pulled up outside her house.

"Let's leave it for the moment and I'll call you," she suggested.

She could tell he was annoyed but she didn't care. She turned to say goodnight to him and at that precise moment he leaned over to peck her on the cheek. His kiss landed on her lips instead.

"*Aaaargh!*" he cried out, pulling away from her.

"What's wrong?" she asked, wondering if she'd hurt him somehow.

He took his handkerchief out of his pocket and wiped his lips.

"I never kiss on the lips," he said, rubbing them furiously with his hanky. "It's very unhygienic."

"Sorry," she mumbled, bolting out of the car and hurrying inside God, he had some weird ideas!

Viv was sitting in the living room when Claire burst in, all flushed.

"What's wrong?" Viv asked when she saw the look on her face.

"Are you okay?" Megan asked, coming into the room with two hot chocolates.

Claire showed them the watch.

"That watch is to die for!" Viv exclaimed as she and Megan admired it.

"I know but I don't think I can keep it. I don't want to be under a compliment because of it."

"*What?*" Viv shrieked. "You can't be serious."

"Yes. I told him it was too much but he wouldn't take it back."

"Thank God for that!" Viv cried.

"He spooked me a little. He's very intense."

"I could put up with intense for a beautiful watch like that," Viv commented.

"He's obviously very keen," Megan said to Claire.

"I don't know . . ." Claire mumbled, wondering what she should do.

"You see, Meggie," said Viv, "I've met a wonderful guy and Claire too may have met her Mr Right – Mr Right *and* Rich. Like I said, there are decent guys out there, decent rich guys, just waiting to meet Mrs Right online. It's the way to go. Aren't you glad I signed you up?"

Megan rolled her eyes and made a face as she went out to make Claire a hot chocolate too.

"Megan signed up?" Claire asked Viv with surprise.

"Yeah, well, I signed her up. As we've both been lucky enough to meet nice guys there, she agreed she has nothing to lose."

After that, Claire hadn't the heart to tell them what Richard was really like. How he polished the cutlery, his fear of kissing, but most of all how scared she'd been of him when she said she couldn't take the watch. One thing she did know: Richard was *not* her Mr Right.

Sarah found an apartment on Thursday. A friend of Orla's had been transferred to London urgently and wanted someone to take over her apartment immediately, for a year, maybe more. The rent was manageable on her salary and it was only five minutes' walk from the office. It was perfect. It wasn't nearly as luxurious as Orla's, of course, but it was very comfortable with all mod cons. Sarah snapped it up right away. She could move in on Saturday, her new landlady said.

Mark had called her on Tuesday to say he had to go to the States on business and might not be back till after the weekend. She was missing him desperately and was glad she would have the move to occupy her.

Claire was extremely worried about Richard and on Thursday night she made her decision. She wrote a polite but firm letter to him, saying that it was too early in their relationship to accept such an extravagant gift and she thought they should take a break. Then, on Friday morning, she called a courier service and handed the courier the package with the watch and letter and strict instructions to deliver it to his office and to get a signature of receipt.

She didn't have to wonder long whether Richard had received it or not, as one hour later her phone started hopping. She never took calls when on duty and by lunchtime he had rung fifteen times and left eight texts. She couldn't bear to listen to his voice-mails and it was with dread that she opened his texts. The first few were aggressive and disbelieving and then the tone changed to wheedling and begging. They left her quite shaken. She had a feeling he would not let go easily. She didn't reply and turned her phone off completely. She just couldn't face him right now.

Claire collected Viv from her work as her car had had to go into the garage for repairs. As they pulled up outside the house she was horrified to see Richard parked outside.

"You'd better talk to him," Viv advised, "or he just won't leave you alone. Why don't you ask him in? I'll be in the house all the time."

Nervously Claire approached Richard's car, determined to be firm.

"What are you doing here, Richard?" she asked in through the open window.

"Please sit in, Claire." He opened the passenger door.

"No, Richard, if you want to speak with me you'll have to come in the house."

He looked annoyed but closed the passenger door and got out of the car. She hurried into the house and he followed her. She showed him into the living room, keeping her coat on. She could hear Viv pottering about in the kitchen.

Richard reached for her hands. "Please, Claire, come out with me and we can sort this out," he pleaded.

"No, Richard, I'm sorry. You read my letter: I think we should cool it a bit."

"You don't mean that," he wheedled. "I'm sorry if I was insistent about the watch. I wanted to please you. Please, Claire, please reconsider!"

He had tears in his eyes and she didn't know how to respond. She even felt a little sorry for him but stood her ground.

She shook her head and, when she said nothing, without warning he turned angry.

"It's that guy you were with at the party, isn't it?"

He grasped her arm roughly and she cried out.

Viv, who had been earwigging at the door, came running in.

"What the hell do you think you're doing?" she cried, advancing on him.

He dropped Claire's arm immediately and backed away.

"Get out!" Viv yelled at him so fiercely that he almost ran out of the room.

As he reached the front door he called out in a loud voice, "You haven't seen the end of me, Claire, I warn you!"

She sank down on the sofa as she heard the door bang after him. "Good heavens," she said, her hands shaking as she covered her eyes.

Viv sat beside her and put her arm around her. "Don't mind him. He can't force you to do anything you don't want."

"I hope not. I don't trust him, he scares me." Claire admitted fearfully.

# Chapter 32

Megan was in bad form. She'd been feeling down all week, probably because she'd been training and working towards the marathon for months which had given her a purpose in life. Now suddenly it was all over and she felt flat. Nor did she hold out any hope, unlike Viv, that she might meet someone online.

She went out for a drink with the gang from the office after work on Friday instead of heading for the gym or a run, as she usually did. She only had one drink as she was driving and was just leaving the bar when she was stopped dead in her tracks. Coming in the door was her ex-fiancé, Paul. He seemed rooted to the ground also.

"Megan!" he said softly. "How are you? You look great."

She thought he looked pretty great too. "Hello, Paul. I'm fine, and you?"

"I'm okay. Still missing you, of course. Do you have time for a drink?"

Megan's heart was racing and her legs felt weak. Even though he'd hurt her so badly, she still had some feelings for him. She knew it would be dangerous to spend any time in his company.

"Sorry, but I have to run."

"Please, Megan. I really want to talk to you. I'm leaving for Australia next week. Without you, there's no reason not to go."

"It's too late for talking, Paul," she made herself say. "Good luck in Australia." Then she ran out the door before he could say anything else or she might change her mind.

She was shaking as she got into her car. Memories came flooding back and she put her head on the wheel and sobbed. No matter what she felt for him, she would never be able to trust him again, so there was no point in it. The only good thing about the encounter was that she would not be bumping into him again if he was on the other side of the world.

Pulling herself together, she drove home slowly.


Viv was very worried about Claire and the situation with Richard. What a mess that was turning out to be, and he had seemed so perfect at first. She thought Claire should go to the police but she was reluctant to do so. When Megan came home and Viv told her what had happened, she added her voice to Viv's.

"He's dangerous, Claire. You really should report him," she advised.

All that evening Richard bombarded Claire with texts and calls, which she ignored, but each one made her more nervous than the last and, after three hours of this, she was a nervous wreck.

"What can I do?" she wailed. "He won't leave me alone."

"Give me your phone," Viv ordered. She tapped on a few buttons. "There, I've blocked his number. Deleted! He can't bother you any more."

At least Claire's problems had given Megan something to think about besides her own concerns but Viv was worried about Megan too. Her friend was more down than she'd been since Paul had walked out on her and she'd had to cancel her wedding. Meeting him again had reawakened old feelings. Damn him! Thank God he was moving to Australia. Viv tried to jolly her out of it, but it was an uphill battle.

Megan had received quite a few replies on the dating site but was not interested in reading them. Viv, however, was monitoring them and answered in her place. There were some nice men among them. It was fun pretending to be Megan and Viv did it with glee. She wished Megan would take an interest and hoped that she would eventually agree to go out with some of them.

With all that was going on, Viv knew how lucky she was to have found Conor. Her life was going swimmingly while her friends were suffering and it made her feel guilty. She tried to hide her happiness but it was difficult.


Orla helped Sarah move into her new apartment on Saturday.

"I wish Mark were here to christen the bed with me. I really miss him," she admitted to her friend.

"Honey, you're not falling for him, are you?" Orla asked, a little perturbed. "Mark is fine for a fling but not for anything more serious. Trust me, I've known him a long time. Mark does *not* get involved."

When Orla had left, Sarah mulled over what she'd said. She *was* falling for Mark. What woman wouldn't? Feeling forlorn, she snorted more coke than usual and took two Vicodin, then knocked back the best part of a bottle of wine before collapsing into bed.

Conor had insisted on picking Viv up on Saturday evening. He was a little early and Megan answered the door to him.

"Hi, you must be Conor," she greeted him, inviting him in. She liked him instantly. There was something solid and reassuring about him and he had kind, honest eyes. Viv was lucky.

"And you must be Megan," he smiled, holding out his hand and giving her a firm handshake.

"Let me call her for you." Megan went to the bottom of the stairs and called up. "Viv, Conor's here!"

"Coming!" Viv yelled back and they could hear her feet racing down the stairs. Her face was flushed as she flew into Conor's arms.

They walked out to the waiting taxi, arm in arm, and Megan felt a pang of envy as she watched them. She had been that happy once, with Paul, and she wondered if she ever would be again.

Meanwhile, Claire was sitting in Ben's house, listening in dismay to what he was saying. He had called her a little earlier, sounding upset.

"I'm very worried about Tash, Claire," he had said. "Something's bothering her but she won't tell me what. Could you have a talk with her? You two have always been very close."

She'd dropped everything and gone around there.

"She has been very withdrawn lately," he told her, concern in his voice. "She doesn't go out with her friends any more and spends all her time in her room. I'm worried she's being bullied in school or it might be a reaction to Sarah leaving. You know she hasn't seen her mother since she left. I'm at my wits' end. Maybe you can find out what the problem is," he appealed to her, running his fingers through his hair in agitation. "She's in her room."

Claire knocked on her niece's door and, when she entered, saw immediately that Tash had been crying. She had dark circles under her eyes and the haunted look in them almost broke Claire's heart.

"Hi, sweetie," she said, taking the young girl in her arms.

"Oh, Auntie Claire," Tash said in a stricken voice, burying her head in her aunt's chest.

Claire held her as she sobbed quietly, stroking her hair, murmuring words of comfort – "There, there, it will be okay" – over and over.

Eventually the sobs subsided and Claire gave Tash a tissue to wipe her eyes. "Okay, now tell me the problem."

"It's all my fault Mum left," Tash said, her voice stricken.

Claire was shocked. "Of course it wasn't your fault! Whatever gave you that idea?"

"One of the girls at school said it was. She said it was because I'd been so horrid to Mum that she'd left." She started to cry again. "And now Dad is upset and I've ruined everything."

Claire took her into her arms again. "Of course it was not your fault. Your mum wasn't very nice to you either. She couldn't help it. She was unhappy, with your dad, with her life. She wanted an exciting life and that's why she left. It had nothing to do with you."

"You think not?" Tash asked, looking at her hopefully.

"I'm certain of it. And if I get my hands on that girl at school, I'll throttle her," she said angrily.

"She's always been horrible to me," Tash admitted.

"Well, you tell her that if she's nasty to you again, I'll come and sort her out."

Tash giggled.

"Come on now, let's go down and tell your dad that everything is okay. He's been awfully worried about you."

"Poor Dad!"

Ben was surprised to see them come back into the kitchen, both smiling.

"I love you, Dad," Tash said, giving him a kiss. "I'm going round to Karen's house now. Is that okay?" she asked as she hugged him.

Ben's eyes met Claire's over his daughter's head. 'Thank you,' he mouthed.

He was shocked when Claire told him how Tash felt guilty because Sarah had left.

"Christ, the poor kid! How did she ever think that? What can I do to convince her that's not the case?"

"Sarah is the one to do that. She needs to talk to Tash and clear the air."

"Funny, she texted me today to say she has moved into her own place. She gave me her address so that I can redirect her post."

"Can you give it to me? I'll try and talk to her and explain how Tash is feeling." She put the address into her phone.

Claire had planned on telling Ben about Richard and

asking his advice but she reckoned he had enough on his plate without having to worry about her too.

Conor had booked a table in Roly's, a popular restaurant in Ballsbridge for eight o'clock. First, he took Viv to the Ice Bar in the Four Seasons for a cocktail. Viv was brimming with happiness as she sipped her margarita and greeted many of her clients, who she guessed frequented the bar regularly. She felt quite chic, perched on her high stool as she sipped a second cocktail. She waved at quite a few women clients as they left.

"Hey, you know everyone," Conor remarked admiringly.

"Oh, I get around," she replied impishly.

Roly's was only a short walk away but, as it was raining, Conor insisted they take a taxi. Viv was grateful as she did not want to end up with a pile of frizz on her head. She had been to this restaurant before and loved the buzz of the place. They had a lovely meal and Conor seemed in sparkling form. The cocktails had gone to Viv's head a little and the wine on top of them made her quite giggly. It also gave her the confidence to propose that perhaps they book a room in a hotel for the following weekend.

"Why not?" Conor said, entwining his fingers in hers. "It's time, I think."

She was ecstatic.

He was holding her hand as they waited for their dessert when she felt him tense.

"Oh no," he said in a low voice and she saw his face pale as he snatched his hand away.

Viv turned to see that a stunningly beautiful girl, who appeared to be on her way from the ladies' room, had stopped and was staring at them. For a moment Viv thought it was Nicole Scherzinger but, as she made her way to their table, Viv saw that this girl was taller than the celebrity, but just as stunning and sexy. She vaguely recognised her face. She was sure she'd seen her on the telly, and guessed she was a model.

"Does she know you?" Viv asked Conor who was looking panicked.

"Yes. It's Adele – my ex-girfriend," he replied, his voice a whisper.

"Well, well," the beautiful brunette addressed Conor, bending down to kiss his cheek. "Fancy meeting you here."

She was smiling but Viv noticed that the smile never reached her eyes.

"Aren't you going to introduce us?" the girl asked, nodding towards Viv.

Conor stammered as he introduced them and Viv was aware that Adele was looking her over, taking in every detail.

"I gather this is my successor?" Adele commented, laughing sexily and tossing her silky mane back as she did so.

Conor mumbled something that Viv couldn't hear.

"I'm so happy to see you again, Con. I've really missed you." She laid her hand on Conor's in what was almost a caress. Her soft brown eyes were moist with emotion.

Viv longed for Conor to say something or to reach for *her* hand but he sat motionless as if mesmerised.

"Well, I'll leave you and love you," Adele said, bending low and leaning towards Conor, shutting Viv out completely. "Why not give me a call, Con? It would be lovely to get together again, for old times' sake. We had such wonderful times together." She sighed. "You still have my number, don't you?" She smiled coquettishly at him and, with a flick of her beautiful long black hair she was gone, leaving Conor a quivering jelly.

Viv was absolutely furious. What a bitch, she thought. How dare she? She was very upset at Conor for not saying something and for letting Adele block her out like that but he seemed incapable of action or thought. Viv was frightened at the effect Adele had on him. He appeared to be under her spell.

The rest of the evening was a disaster and Viv knew that Conor was mentally absent and couldn't wait for it to end. Adele had knocked him for six. Viv wondered if he was still in love with her. When she suggested she get a taxi home alone, Conor shot her a grateful smile.

"You don't mind?" he asked in a relieved voice.

"Of course not," she lied, with as much dignity as she could muster. "No point in you coming all the way to Dundrum."

"I'll be in touch," he said as he kissed her on the cheek.

Viv wondered if he would and if she'd ever see him again.

Megan was in her dressing-gown watching the *Saturday Night Show* when Viv came in. She was surprised to see her back so early. The moment she saw Viv's face she knew something was wrong.

"What happened?"

Viv sat down beside her and burst into tears.

Megan put her arm around her, wondering what had caused this.

"It was just awful," Viv confided when she'd stopped crying. "His ex, who is a model and simply gorgeous by the way, was in the restaurant and came to our table. He was very upset to see her and she was obviously put out to see him with me. She acted like such a bitch. She asked him to call her so that they could get together for old times' sake. He never said a word but was obviously very affected by seeing her. Anyway, the night went downhill after that and I knew I'd lost him. I could tell he couldn't wait to get away so I offered to get a taxi home by myself. I could see that he was relieved about that."

"I'm so sorry," said Megan.

"So much for taking it to the next level," said Viv, her voice wobbling.

"Poor Viv! I know you really liked him." Megan patted her back sympathetically.

"I did, I do," Viv sniffed. "I was sure he was *the one*. I guess I was wrong. I've been an awful fool."

"Love makes fools of us all," Megan said quietly. "Look, why don't I open a bottle of wine? It might help."

"I think I need something stronger than wine. Any vodka in the house? I'll need something lethal to drown my sorrows." Viv laughed hollowly.

"Sure. Orange juice okay with it?"

"Perfect! What would I do without you?"

"I could say the same. We'll drink to that."

Claire came in, feeling down after her conversation with Ben. "What's up with the vodka?" she asked, seeing the bottle on the coffee table.

Viv started crying again. "It's over with Conor, I think," she said through her tears.

Claire sat down heavily. "Oh, no, what happened?"

Megan told her and Claire put her arms around Viv. "Maybe it will be okay, when he has time to think about it."

"I don't think so," Viv sniffled, wiping her eyes.

"I need a vodka too," Claire said, going into the kitchen to get a glass and ice. When she sat down again, she recounted what had happened with Tash.

"Crikey, that's dreadful," Viv remarked, forgetting her own problems for a moment.

"Poor Tash," Megan said sympathetically.

"And Ben," Viv added. "I suppose that puts our problems in perspective."

"I really need to go and check on Sarah," Claire said sombrely. "I don't know what's happening to her. I want to make sure she sees Tash and tells her that she wasn't to blame."

"Life is so bloody difficult, isn't it?" Viv remarked.

"I'll drink to that," Claire said.

"Me too," Megan agreed.

"Well, at least we have each other," Claire observed as they clinked glasses.

# Chapter 33

Megan's mother rang her the following morning.

"Hello, Daphne," Megan greeted her listlessly. She was really missing her Sunday runs.

"Helloooo, darling," Daphne's chirpy voice rang out. "I can't thank you enough for recommending that dating site to me. I've been having the most marvellous fun *and* I've met the most wonderful man. I'm dying to have you meet him," she cooed.

Megan sighed. It was bad enough that her two friends were having problems with guys they'd met online, but now her mother was starting down the same path. She tuned out and only half-listened as Daphne went on.

"You know, maybe I was a bit rash saying I didn't want to get married again. Wayne is simply a darling, and so good to me. I can't tell you how happy I am. You absolutely must meet him! He's dying to meet you." She giggled like a schoolgirl and Megan had visions of just what Wayne might be doing to her mother at that very moment.

Hang on a minute. What was it her mother had just said? Something about being rash when she'd said she didn't want to get married again? Oh Lord! What next? Megan groaned. She didn't want to think about it. She promised to come and meet Wayne on Tuesday evening.

At midday on Sunday, Claire rang Sarah's bell. Sarah struggled out of bed and answered the intercom, hoping it might be Mark.

"Hi, it's Claire. I need to talk to you."

"I have nothing to say to you," Sarah muttered.

"It's important. It's about Tash."

Sarah hesitated, then pressed the buzzer to let her sister in.

It was obvious to Claire that Sarah was very hungover. She looked a mess.

"What's wrong with Tash?"

Claire explained and saw that she had got through to her sister at last.

"Of course it's not her fault I left," Sarah said sullenly.

"You need to tell her that. Can I bring her around this afternoon?"

Again Sarah hesitated. "Okay," she said finally. "And can you bring Owen too?"

"Of course. Maybe you could get this place tidied up by then."

"I see you haven't changed," Sarah observed drily.

Claire bit her tongue as she left to give Ben the good news and arrange to pick up the kids later. God, if her mother knew what was happening, she'd be turning in her grave.

Claire couldn't believe the change in her sister when she

returned with the kids that afternoon. Sarah looked great, was beautifully made up and welcomed them as if they were royalty. She even beamed at Claire which was a bit of a shock. She had bought in pizzas and ice cream for the kids and had made a big effort to tidy the place. Claire could see she was nervous as she greeted them and, after hellos, left them alone so they could talk. When she came back two hours later, the three of them were all smiles and playing a game of Gin Rummy.

"Mum explained everything to me," Tash told her happily as they drove home. "She wants us to come and stay next Saturday."

"She has cool games on her iPad," Owen said.

Claire was relieved, as was Ben when he heard that all was well.

"I can't thank you enough," he said, hugging her tightly. "I don't know what we'd do without you."

All day Monday and Tuesday Claire worried about Richard. Thankfully she hadn't had to put up with his endless texts and calls since Viv had blocked his number from her phone. She hoped he'd got the message and would leave her alone now.

On Tuesday she went straight from work to her Italian class which was located in Fitzwilliam Square in the city centre. She met up with Pippa there and they enjoyed the class even more than they had the first few weeks.

But, as they came down the steps after class, Claire noticed Richard's car parked on the other side of the square.

"Oh *no!*" she cried, putting her head down and turning up her collar.

"What's wrong?" Pippa asked, concerned.

"Just keep walking and don't look around," Claire instructed her, quickening her step as she walked towards her car. "That guy I told you about, Richard – the one who gave me the watch – is parked across the road. He's been stalking me." She sounded nervous.

"You're not serious? Wow, that's scary."

"I know. He turned up in the place where Megan's party was last week and then he was outside the house last Friday. He's making me nervous."

"What are you going to do about him?"

"Viv thinks I should report him to the police. I don't know what to do. I'm hoping he'll tire of it when he sees he's getting nowhere."

They sat into her car and Claire locked the doors, then drove off nervously.

"You met him online, didn't you?" Pippa asked.

"Yeah.

"My cousin met some right weirdos too, dating online. But then she met a lovely guy and they're now engaged. I guess you have to kiss some frogs before you meet your prince."

"That's what my friend Viv always says – but some frog Richard has turned out to be!" Claire said wryly. She tried to make it a joke but it wasn't funny.

She dropped Pippa off and drove the few yards home, looking nervously in her rear-view mirror, afraid he had followed her. She gave a sigh of relief to find he hadn't. She was relieved to find the house empty when she got in. Viv was having dinner at her parents' house and Megan was visiting her mother. She knew if she mentioned it to Viv, she'd go on about contacting the police again. Claire felt that was a bit drastic. After all, although he was spooking her out, he hadn't actually done anything to hurt her. He just seemed a bit over-the-top about her. The police would probably think she was paranoid.

Meanwhile Megan was in Killiney, meeting her mother's new paramour. She was pleasantly surprised by the suave, charming American who Daphne introduced as Wayne. She'd expected another thirty-year-old, which was the age-group her mother was into recently, but to Megan's surprise he looked to be around fifty. It made a nice change. He was dark-skinned, of mixed race Megan guessed, and extremely handsome. He was very pleasant and good company and it was obvious that Daphne was head-over-heels in love with him. How had that happened so quickly? Megan wondered. If she had to have one reservation about Wayne, it would be that he was a little too slick. He certainly had a way with women, born of experience, Megan suspected.

He had businesses in the UK and the States and had come to Ireland to establish one here. He was an entrepreneur, he told her, a job description that she didn't have a lot of faith in. Still, his clothes were expensive and he had impeccable manners so she decided to reserve judgement until she got to know him better. It appeared her mother was not so reticent.

"Wayne has asked me to marry him, and I've said yes," Daphne announced, giggling as she leaned into him.

"*Whaaaat?*" Megan squealed, horrified. "But you barely know each other."

"I know this must come as a big shock to you," he said gently, taking Megan's hand. "But we're not youngsters any more and we love each other, so why wait? I hope you understand," he appealed to her, looking earnestly into her eyes.

He was quite mesmerising and Megan began to understand how her mother had been so quickly swept off her feet. He was *very* persuasive.

"Well, I just think it's all so sudden –"

"Oh, don't be such a fuddy-duddy," Daphne cut her short. "Life is for living, daaarling, which is something you should be doing." She turned to her fiancé, and threw her eyes to heaven. "My daughter has always been a bit of a stick-in-the-mud."

Megan was hurt by her words and Wayne saw that immediately.

"I'm sure she's not and I think she's just concerned about your welfare, dear," he assured Daphne, patting her hand as he smiled at Megan. "If I was lucky enough to have a daughter, or son for that matter, I'm sure they'd be very cautious too."

Megan wanted to hug him then. Maybe he would be good for her mother and keep her grounded. He certainly appeared to be an utter gentleman. Still, it was way too fast.

"When do you plan to get married?" she asked.

"Friday week," Daphne trilled, beaming.

"*Whaaat?*" Megan shrieked again. "You can't get married that quickly in Ireland."

"No, we're eloping to Gretna Green," Daphne cooed. "Isn't that romantic?"

Megan was flabbergasted. Her mother seemed oblivious to her shock but Wayne spotted it immediately.

"I know this is very sudden and a big shock for you but we're hoping that you'll understand and be happy for us," he said, looking at Megan anxiously.

"Yes, of course," Megan mumbled. What else could she say?

"How did it go?" Viv asked, as Megan came in and plonked down on the sofa without taking off her coat.

"What's up?" Claire asked, alarmed.

"You won't believe this. She's getting married next week."

"*Whaaat?*" Claire and Viv cried in unison.

"That's exactly how I reacted to the news." Megan shook her head in disbelief.

"Gosh, that's rather fast, isn't it?" Claire said sympathetically. "You must have got a shock."

"Shock doesn't begin to describe it!"

"Nothing your mother does could shock me," Viv grimaced. "What's he like, her fiancé?"

"Suave is the way I'd best describe him, and very, very charming. He's about fifty. He seems really nice but I'm worried that it's all happened too fast."

"Well, at least he's nice and about her own age," Claire remarked.

"Your mother never was one to let the grass grow under her feet," Viv said pithily. "He's not after her money, is he?"

"Gosh, I hope not. He looks pretty affluent. He's an entrepreneur."

"Huh! That could be anything." Viv wasn't too impressed.

"I'm sure it will work out fine," said Claire, hoping to reassure Megan. She threw Viv a warning look which shut her up.

Sarah was on a high. She was happy that she'd cleared the air with Tash and was looking forward to having her and

Owen stay over at the weekend. It was a good decision, getting her own place. On the other hand, she was equally happy that Ben would have them all week.

Mark had stayed with her in her new place on both Tuesday and Wednesday night and the sex had been as great as ever. So much so that she could hardly sit or walk on Thursday morning. Orla teased her unmercifully about it but Sarah didn't mind.

"I called PJ to buy some more stuff," she told her friend.

"Hey, girl, be careful. You got to take it easy. These things are addictive," Orla exclaimed.

"Yeah, well, a lot's been happening. I'll be fine," Sarah assured her.

She could have kicked herself for mentioning PJ. She didn't want Orla to know that now she couldn't get through the day without some coke and Vicodin. Who wouldn't when they made you feel so wonderful?

Viv was not herself all week. She was on tenterhooks, praying that Conor would call. So far she'd heard nothing from him and she got more despondent with each day that passed. Her iPhone lay idle. She had no interest in Facebook or Twitter and certainly not in the dating site.

Finally, on Friday night she saw Conor's name come up on her phone. With fingers crossed she answered it, her heart in her mouth. She knew from the moment he started to speak that it was not good news.

"I'm really sorry, Viv, but Adele wants us to get back together again. I said I'd give it a try. I think she's changed. It's the least I can do. I hope you understand."

Viv couldn't remember afterwards what she'd replied because her whole world had collapsed. She was shaking as she told the girls what he'd said.

"Men!" Megan said bitterly. "They don't know what they want."

"It may not work out," Claire said. "These things seldom do."

Viv hugged her body with her arms as the realisation hit her. Conor, the man she loved, was gone. The thought of him with the beautiful Adele was more than she could bear. She felt like someone had pierced her body with a sword. She sobbed as her two friends looked on helplessly. There was nothing they could do.

Megan had got out the vodka bottle again and poured a good stiff one for Viv.

"Thanks," she sniffed as she took it from her, her sobs subsiding. "I'm only beginning to understand now how you must have felt when Paul left, Megan."

"I know, sweetie. It's pure hell."

# Chapter 34

Megan and Claire took Viv out to lunch the following day in an effort to cheer her up. They were both coping with their own problems but they understood Viv's need was more urgent at the moment. She was grateful for their support and wondered what she would have done without them. She still could hardly believe that Conor was gone from her life.

Megan had offered to drive to the restaurant and, after a few minutes, she remarked, "I think we're being followed," with an eye on her rear-view mirror.

Viv and Claire both swivelled around and saw a Porsche, exactly like the one Richard drove. The driver was wearing a hat and large sunglasses, even though it was a dull rainy November day, but Claire could tell that it was Richard.

"Oh, no!" she cried, growing pale. "It's Richard."

"Christ, the nerve of him! Has he been following us since we left home?" Viv asked, furious.

"I think so," Megan replied.

"Can you lose him?"

"I'll try."

Megan put her foot down on the accelerator and treated them to a driving display that would have been worthy of a spot on *Top Gear*. She knew the area a lot better than he did and she was a better driver. As she sped through an amber light, they saw that Richard had been caught by the red one and had to stop. Claire saw him bang his fist on the steering wheel in frustration.

"*Yippee!*" Viv whooped. "We lost him. This is like something from a movie."

"This is serious, Viv," Megan said. "You absolutely *have* to make him leave you alone, Claire."

"He's a sicko. Do you really think he'll listen?" Viv scoffed. "You should report him to the Gardaí. I would."

"What can they do? I don't think he means to harm me," Claire replied, more bravely than she felt. "I need to talk to him and get him to understand that it's over, that there is no future for us. There *is* no 'us'. I'll do it this week."

"He's obviously stalking you, Claire. That's illegal," Viv said seriously. "The Gardaí have an obligation to do something about it."

"I suppose there *are* a lot of weirdos out there," Megan mused, making Claire even more worried than she already was.

She knew she'd have to deal with him, and soon.

She was also worried about Sarah. She had rung her one evening during the week and it was obvious Sarah was on a high.

"Have you been drinking, Sarah?"

"Leave me fucking alone!" Sarah had shrieked, before cutting her off.

Claire prayed the kid's visit wouldn't be a disaster.

Ben dropped the kids off to Sarah on Saturday as planned. He was pleasantly surprised by Sarah's apartment and hoped the visit would be a success. She was more nervous than they were and, as soon as Ben left, piled them into the car and took them to Burger King for lunch. Then they went shopping, much to Owen's disgust, but he cheered up somewhat when she bought him the latest Irish jersey. Tash was thrilled when Sarah offered to buy her the pair of Converse trainers she'd been hankering after.

"Gosh, Mum is nicer than when she lived with us," Owen whispered to Tash while Sarah was paying for the shoes.

Tash had to agree. She's never seen her mother in such great humour.

After that they went to see the latest *Hobbit* movie and then Sarah took them to Tesco where they chose pizzas for dinner. They threw a box of Magnums and some bars of chocolate into the basket when Sarah wasn't looking and, to their surprise, she said nothing at the checkout but scanned them and bagged them. Tash and Owen looked at each other in wonder. Before, she had always freaked out whenever they tried this. Yes, Mum seemed to have changed, and for the better, they agreed.

After dinner, she let Owen play games on her iPad while Tash watched E News. Her mother had changed completely. Maybe she really was happier now.

Sarah allowed Owen to stay up until Tash was going to bed and he whooped and gave Tash the finger behind Sarah's back.

Then, just as they were about to retire, Sarah's phone rang. Tash heard the change in her mother's voice when she answered. She knew she was talking to someone she really liked.

It was Mark on the other end and Sarah's heart lifted.

"I'd love to see you. Can I come around?" he asked.

"No, no, not here. I'll meet you in Baggot Street."

"Great! I can't wait. Don't be long."

"Listen, Tash, I have to go out for a little while," Sarah explained to her daughter. "You'll be able to keep an eye on Owen, won't you?"

Tash wasn't at all sure about that but didn't want to anger Sarah when she was being so nice to them. "Okay," she replied. She wondered where her mother was going at this hour.

After lunch on Saturday, Viv, Claire and Megan went shopping and then to see the film, *Gone Girl,* that was getting rave reviews. Viv tried to concentrate on the movie but all she could think of was what Conor and Adele might be doing at that moment. She was torturing herself but she couldn't help it. They went to Eddie Rocket's after the cinema and when they arrived home that evening, Claire warily kept an eye out for Richard's car, half-expecting him to be parked outside. She breathed a huge sigh of relief when there was no sign of him.

Tash was worried when she woke the next morning and Sarah wasn't there. She tried calling her but her phone was turned off. Tash was scared. She hoped nothing had happened to her mother and tried to stay calm and not worry Owen who had started to cry. Frightened, she then rang Ben and told him that Sarah hadn't come home.

"She left you alone last night?" Ben asked, furious.

"Yes," Tash admitted in a small voice. "Owen is scared. I don't know what to do."

"I'm leaving right now to pick you both up. Get your things together."

Tash could hear how angry her father was. She did as he asked, hoping there wouldn't be more rows between her parents.

Sarah, exhausted from her night of sex, woke with a start to see it was past eleven. "Jesus!" she cried, jumping up in the bed. "Look at the time!"

"What's your hurry?" Mark asked languidly, rolling over to pull her to him.

She could feel his big erection pressing against her belly.

"I have to go," she cried.

"I have to come," he grinned, straddling and entering her.

She knew she should leave but she couldn't resist his urgency and found herself moving with him. Another ten minutes wouldn't make any difference. In fact, it was almost an hour later that she dragged herself from the bed.

"What's the hurry?" he asked. "It's Sunday."

"I know but my kids are staying with me this weekend."

He looked at her, disbelief on his face. "You didn't leave them alone last night?"

"It's okay. Tash is fourteen."

"Oh, for God's sake, Sarah," he exclaimed, his face contorted in anger. "What kind of a mother are you? How could you do this to your kids?"

It was the first time she had seen him angry and it scared her. She dressed hurriedly and left.

She was shocked when she got back to her apartment to find the kids gone. She checked her phone and saw the missed call from Tash and then took the angry message from Ben. Oh, God, she'd blown it! Screwing up her courage, she called him.

"Never, ever again, will I put my children at risk in your care," he said coldly, before hanging up on her.

He called Claire to give her the bad news. She couldn't believe that Sarah would have left the kids alone.

What was she thinking? Claire sighed. She just did not understand her sister.

Viv had Sunday lunch with her parents and afterwards they were all going to visit her grandmother in the nursing home. Megan had been invited by Gloria Rivers' daughter to a surprise party she was throwing for her mother to celebrate her sixty-fifth birthday and also the fact that her book was being published.

Alone in the house, Claire took her courage in her hands and called Richard.

"Claire, I'm so happy you've called me," he said, his voice excited.

"Richard, we need to talk."

"Any time, my dear. Just tell me where and when."

"Can you meet me in The Orchard at five?"

"I'll be counting the hours," he replied. "Are you at home? Do you want me to pick you up or can one of the girls drive you so we can have a drink?"

"No, they're both out for the day. I'll drive myself. See you there."

For Sarah, the rest of the day stretched out before her, empty. Even the coke and magic pills did not lift her mood.

She tried calling Mark several times but he didn't answer. Eventually, she rang Orla and asked her to meet up for a drink.

They met in the Schoolhouse Bar in Ballsbridge. `

"I've had an awful day," she told Orla, as she recounted what had happened.

"You didn't leave the kids alone all night?" Orla asked, sounding shocked.

Sarah hadn't expected this. God, why was everyone overreacting?

"I'm worried that Mark is annoyed with me," she said, appealing to her friend to understand.

"Can't say I blame him."

"Please don't say that!" Sarah said, panic in her voice. "I have to sort it out with him. He won't take my calls. Will you call him, Orla?"

Orla looked at her pityingly. "I warned you not to get involved with him, Sarah. Have fun, fuck him, but don't expect anything more. You won't get it." She saw Sarah's panic-stricken face. "Oh, girl, please don't tell me you've fallen for him."

Sarah sat there feeling numb, unable to reply.

"Christ, what a disaster!" Orla mumbled to herself.

"Please come to the 37 with me tonight," Sarah pleaded. "Maybe Mark will be there and I can talk to him." She looked at Orla hopefully.

"No way. I have a big account to sign up tomorrow and two more this week. Sorry, but work comes before fun. I expect you to put your problems with Mark aside and be in top form tomorrow to help out."

Sarah saw the ruthlessness in Orla's eyes. She didn't know how she could bounce back but now her job depended on it. She'd have to pull herself together.

Claire rehearsed what she would say to Richard over and over as she drove to the Orchard.

He was waiting for her, drumming his fingers nervously on the table. When she walked in, his face lit up and he reached out to embrace her. Neatly, she evaded him and sat down opposite him rather than on the banquette he indicated.

"What would you like to drink?" he asked her.

"Nothing, thank you."

"I was so afraid you'd change your mind about seeing me. I brought you a gift," he said, smiling as he pushed a bag towards her. She saw the name Boodles, the most expensive jeweller in Dublin, on the bag.

"No, Richard," she said, pushing the bag back towards him. "No more gifts, please. I came here today to talk seriously to you. I don't think it's a good idea to keep seeing each other." Although she was shaking inside she kept her voice firm.

She saw the colour drain from his face and his eyes narrowed. "But we love each other, Claire. How can you say this to me?"

"Richard, I don't love you. I barely know you. We barely know each other."

He stared at her in silence, clenching and unclenching his fists, then buried his face in his hands.

"You don't mean that," he said when he finally looked up at her, his eyes pleading.

"I'm sorry, Richard, but I do." She leaned forward, trying to impress upon him just how serious she was.

In a flash his eyes turned angry. "You're making a big

mistake, Claire," he said abruptly.

"Richard, you have to stop following me. Please, you're scaring me."

He said nothing, just looked steadily at her. The look in his eyes spooked her. She felt she was getting nowhere with him.

"That's all I have to say. Goodbye, Richard."

With more courage than she felt, she got up and walked away from him.

Claire was in the living room when she heard the door open.

"Megan, is that you?" she called out.

When Megan didn't reply, she got up to check. She opened the door to find Richard there, brandishing a gun.

"You didn't really think I'd let you go, did you?" he asked, his eyes manic.

She opened her mouth to scream and that was the last thing she remembered.

Megan came home from Gloria's party with her spirits lifted. Gloria always had that effect on her. She helped Megan appreciate that being young and healthy with a good career and great friends was actually not a bad hand to be dealt in life.

"I believe everything happens for a reason," Gloria had said. "So I'm certain Paul was not the man for you. Was he really so perfect?"

"Mmmm . . ." Megan paused to think. "Not really. He had no ambition whatsoever. That bothered me a lot. I used to worry that I might not be able to handle it if he stayed unemployed and feckless, happy to just doss around every day."

"That would have been very difficult for you. So you see, it probably wouldn't have lasted and you'd have been much worse off than you are now."

Megan realised Gloria was right and all of a sudden everything was clear. She'd had a lucky escape and it was time to move on with her life. Gloria had a great perspective on life. She was like the mother Megan yearned for.

Humming to herself, she let herself into the house, thinking that it was time she got back to the gym.

She was surprised to find that Claire was out although her car was in the driveway. She had said she wasn't going anywhere.

Viv came in an hour later. "Where's Claire?"

"Don't know. She didn't leave a note to say she was going out."

When she hadn't returned home or called by midnight, Viv tried ringing her. Claire's phone was turned off.

"That's strange," Viv said. Claire only turned her phone off when she was working.

"Gosh, I hope she's okay," Megan speculated, frowning.

"Maybe she went to baby-sit Tash and Owen," Viv suggested.

"Then her car would be gone. And I don't think Ben would stay out this late on a Sunday night." Megan bit her lip. "He has school tomorrow. Anyway, Claire would have called us if she was there."

They both went up to bed but neither of them could sleep, listening for the sound of Claire's key in the door.

Megan was first up the following morning and hurried into Claire's room only to find that her bed had not been slept in. Panicking, she ran in to wake Viv.

"Viv, I'm really worried. Claire hasn't come home."

"Don't panic. There could be a reasonable explanation for it."

"But she would have called us."

"I suppose. I'll try her number again." Viv speed-dialled Claire with the same result as the night before. Not turned on. Now she was really worried too. "I'll give Ben a call to see if she's there."

Ben answered on the first ring. No, he hadn't heard from Claire since they'd spoken on the phone early yesterday. When he heard she hadn't come home or called the girls, he was troubled.

"This is pretty out of character for Claire, isn't it?" he observed in a worried voice.

"Do you think we should report it to the Gardaí?" Viv asked.

"Let's wait and see if she turns up for work," Ben suggested. "There could be an innocent explanation. Maybe she spent the night with that guy she's been seeing. She wouldn't thank us if that is the case."

Obviously Claire hadn't said anything to Ben about Richard stalking her, so Viv stayed mum, not wanting to worry him further.

"That's my biggest worry," Megan admitted when Viv repeated what Ben had said. "I do hope she didn't go to meet Richard. She did say something about talking to him." She was biting her thumbnail now which was a sure sign that she was anxious.

"I'll call the hospital at nine and if she hasn't turned up there, I'm contacting the police," Viv said.

"Good idea. Let me know what happens."

# Chapter 35

When Claire came to, she felt disoriented as she tried to figure out where she was. Her head felt woozy as she tried to remember what had happened. The last thing she recalled was the shock of seeing Richard standing in the door of her living room, a gun in his hand. She tried to move her right arm but she couldn't, as metal chaffed her right wrist. She was frightened when she realised her arm was tied to something. As her eyes adjusted to the dark room she could make out a figure, sitting in a rocking-chair at the side of the bed. Suddenly terrified, she was reminded of the film *Psycho* and the rocking chair in the attic. Was this just a nightmare? She struggled through the fog in her mind as she tried to wake up. It was then she realised that this was not a dream, this was really happening to her.

"Who are you? Where am I?" she asked, her voice trembling.

"You're okay, my darling. Don't worry, I'm taking care of you," a voice said and with horror Claire realised that it was Richard sitting there.

He got up out of the chair and came towards her.

"You're safe, my angel. It's just the two of us now."

"Richard, why are you doing this?" she asked, cowering away from him.

"You have to understand that we are meant to be together, Claire. I love you, I want you to be my wife," he murmured softly, caressing her hair.

She shrank away from his touch, trembling.

"I won't hurt you, Claire. Don't be afraid."

"Please, Richard, untie me. You can't do this to me."

"Oh, Claire, Claire, you don't understand. You're mine now."

She saw the manic look in his eyes and had to try hard not to panic.

"Please, Richard, untie me and we'll talk."

"Naughty, naughty," he wagged his finger at her. "I can't do that until you promise to be my wife."

"Please untie me or I'll shout for help."

He gave a high-pitched laugh as he turned on a lamp.

"Go ahead. There's no one to hear you. We're in the cellar of my house in the mountains and look," he gestured around the room, "there are no windows. I've thought of everything." He looked at her slyly and she started to whimper.

"Please, Richard, please," she begged.

"Hush, hush, my little one," he said, trying to soothe her. "You're safe with me. Richard will take care of you, my angel."

Terrified, Claire closed her eyes.

Viv, Megan and Ben had all tried calling Claire's number

early on Monday morning. When there was no reply Megan then called the hospital at ten to nine in the hope that Claire had arrived early at work but was told she hadn't come in yet. All three of them called the hospital from nine o'clock on and when Claire hadn't made an appearance by nine thirty, they really started to panic.

Viv insisted on calling the police, but they weren't much help.

"Sorry, Miss, but she's an adult woman. We can't treat her as a missing person until she's been gone for twenty-four hours. She's probably with friends or she met someone . . . You've no idea how many young women disappear for a day or two," he chuckled, "and it turns out they met some guy in a bar and went off with him."

"Claire is not like that!" Viv practically screamed at him.

"Now, Miss, no need to behave like that. Are you her next of kin?"

"Well, no, I'm her friend."

"We will need her next of kin to report her missing, I'm afraid."

Viv banged the phone down. She rang Ben and reported what the garda had said to her.

"Maybe he's right and she'll turn up today," Ben said hopefully. "If not, I'll contact them at lunchtime."

Viv wondered whether she should tell him about Richard but decided to wait and see if Claire surfaced.

There was nothing any of them could do then but wait and pray.

By noon, nobody had heard from Claire and they were all seriously worried now. She had never before been known to miss a day at work without informing the hospital. The staff there were clearly worried too.

Viv asked to leave work and met up with Megan and Ben at the house. There they decided that Ben should contact the Gardaí.

"Ben, there's something you should know," Viv said fearfully, as he took out his phone. "That guy Claire was seeing – well, she tried to finish with him two weeks ago but he's been stalking her ever since." She felt terrible giving him this news, certain now that Richard had something to do with Claire's disappearance.

Ben paled at this information.

Megan, who had been biting her thumbnail, now started to wring her hands. "He was beginning to spook her out and she said she would talk to him and get him to leave her alone," she stated uneasily, feeling guilty that she hadn't realised he might be dangerous.

"I tried to get her to report him to the police," Viv added, her voice trembling, "but Claire was convinced he'd never hurt her."

"Now we're not so sure," Megan whispered hesitantly, tears in her eyes.

"Who is this guy?" Ben demanded. "Do you have his name and address? We'll have to tell the Gardaí immediately."

Ben made the call and was eventually put through to Inspector Staunton, who was responsible for missing persons in the area.

"Are you her next of kin?" he asked Ben after he had explained the situation.

"Not strictly speaking. My wife is her sister."

"We do need her next of kin to report her missing, I'm

afraid. Could you ask your wife to call us?"

"Okay." Ben realised that he hadn't even thought of contacting Sarah to tell her that her only sister was missing.

"In the meantime, if you could gather together for me all details of your sister-in-law – name, date-of-birth, address, place of work, car registration etc – that would be a great help. I will also need a recent photo and her passport and any information whatsoever you can give me about this bloke who was stalking her. If you could drop them in to me at the station asap, then we'll get the ball rolling. Needless to say, if you hear anything from your sister-in-law, I want you to call me directly."

Inspector Staunton gave Ben his extension number and told him that they would do everything possible to locate Claire.

"I know you must be very worried," he said sympathetically, "but try not to panic. There could be a simple explanation for her going missing."

Ben thanked him but didn't really believe that. It was not like Claire to do something like this.

The girls were relieved to be able to do something to help and Megan went to get Claire's passport while Viv went on to Claire's dating account to find info on Richard. She also found the business card he'd given Claire in her room.

"Richard Walsh," she read out. "I never actually heard his surname before."

"Me neither," Megan remarked, thinking once again how dangerous this online dating actually was.

While they were doing that, Ben called Sarah.

"What?" Sarah answered the phone belligerently.

"Sarah, Claire is missing. Have you seen her?"

"No, though I'm surprised she hasn't been on to me, bollocking me because I left the kids alone for a couple of hours."

"Sarah," Ben said, trying to stay calm, "this is serious. Claire didn't come home last night and hasn't turned up to work today. Her friends are desperately worried and so am I."

"She probably just took off for a few days," Sarah suggested.

"That's not like Claire. She would never just take off like that without telling anyone," he replied, irritated that she wouldn't take this seriously. "The Gardaí need you to report her missing as you're her next of kin," he said firmly.

"Do I have to? Are you not overreacting a bit?""

"Sarah, this is important," Ben continued, his jaw clenching as he spoke. "Did she ever mention a man who was stalking her?"

"Claire?" she laughed. "Are you serious? What man would bother with her?"

"Will you please call Inspector Staunton in Dundrum Garda Station and report Claire missing?" Ben said angrily.

"I suppose I'll have to," she replied sullenly, "but I think it's all a storm in a teacup."

Ben gave her the number and then called the Inspector.

"I've just spoken to my wife and she'll be calling you to report Claire missing," he said. "I've gathered all the information you requested and I'm leaving for the station right away."

"Great, just ask for me at the front desk. The quicker we act the better chance we have of finding your sister-in-law."

Sarah contacted him shortly after and reported Claire

322

missing. It started the wheels turning.

Viv and Megan went with Ben to the station as he thought they could give more insight into Claire's movements than he himself could. The Inspector questioned them at length about Richard and his stalking.

"There are not too many Porsches in Dublin so that narrows our search. It would also help if you could contact all her friends and colleagues and let them know she's missing," he advised. "Someone just may know something."

Inspector Staunton was efficient and professional and Ben and the girls were relieved that he would be in charge. He was also sympathetic and seemed quite positive which gave them hope.

Ben left the girls then to go and collect Owen from school. Viv and Megan returned home and started calling around Claire's friends. They left the landline and both their numbers with everyone, asking them to call if anything occurred to them. Viv went on Facebook and Twitter with the bad news and, within the hour, thousands of people were spreading the news via social network.

Claire was struggling to open her eyes but she was so terribly tired that she couldn't stay awake and kept falling back asleep. No matter how hard she tried, sleep overcame her before she could rouse herself. She had an ominous feeling that something was wrong but she couldn't figure out what.

Richard sat beside her bed, smiling contentedly. He knew he couldn't keep her asleep forever, but for now he was happy to sit looking at her as she slept. He thought about how wonderful life would be once she realised that they were meant to be together. The thought excited him and he savoured it, imagining the happiness they would share.

Claire had been so sweet and kind to him, not like some of the women he'd met previously who wouldn't even go out with him a second time. Claire was different. She understood him, she loved him, he was certain of that. He just had to make her see it and everything would be perfect.

One of the first to call Viv and Megan was Jamie, Claire's ex-boyfriend, who was distraught.

"I can't bear to think that something might have happened to her," he said, tears in his voice. "If there is anything I can do, anything at all, please call me."

Viv was touched. She knew that Claire was still carrying a torch for him. She prayed that her friend would return home safe and she could tell her how upset Jamie had been.

Jamie's girlfriend, Hannah, who had overheard his conversation with Viv, was not so happy. Things had been going very badly between them lately and she suspected that he still had a thing for Claire.

"I wish you were as interested in me as you are in your old girlfriend," she remarked when he came off the phone.

"Oh for God's sake," he snapped at her.

"It's Claire this and Claire that. I'm sick of hearing about her to be honest."

He looked at her coldly. "Have you no heart? Someone I care about is missing and all you can do is think about yourself."

With a start, Hannah realised that she'd never seen

Jamie as upset as he was right now, not even when her dog had gone missing.

With tears in her eyes, she looked at him sadly. "It's still Claire, isn't it?"

When he didn't reply, she gathered up the few things that she kept in his apartment and quietly let herself out.

He barely noticed her leaving. All he could think of was Claire and where she might be now.

# Chapter 36

Ben had to tell the children that Claire was missing before the news hit the media and they might hear it from one of their friends. Owen didn't quite understand but Tash certainly did. She sat, her face white with fear, as Ben explained it. Then she started sobbing and Ben wrapped his arms around her.

"The police are looking for her – it will be okay, I'm sure."

"I'll die if anything happens to Auntie Claire," she sobbed. "I love her!"

When Owen saw her reaction, he too started to cry, and Ben tried to hold back his own tears as he held his children close. He prayed this nightmare would soon be over and that Claire would be found safe and well.

As the word spread via Twitter and Facebook, more and more people contacted the girls. Many of Claire's colleagues from work contacted them and it was obvious that she was very well-liked in the hospital. Even the parents of some of the patients she'd cared for called. One couple, the parents of little Amy, for whom Claire had thrown the party, were very upset and asked if there was anything at all they could do. They offered to have posters printed and organise their friends to distribute them. The girls and Ben were very touched by their offer.

Viv and Megan became more emotional with each call that came in.

Megan was surprised when Davy rang her mobile.

"Hi, Megan, I just heard about Claire. I'm terribly sorry. You must be desperately upset. I know what great friends you are and she's such a nice girl. I really enjoyed her company the night of the marathon."

Megan was touched. She remembered how well he and Claire had hit it off that night. "Thank you, Davy. It's a nightmare, to be honest."

"I can imagine. Have the police any idea where she is? I presume they're looking for her."

"Yes, they are but so far there are no clues as to where she might be. We're going crazy with worry," she confessed, her voice soft. She could tell he was genuinely upset.

"Well, if I can do anything at all to help, please let me know. Do you have my number?"

"I'll get it from this call and, Davy . . . thanks."

"I'm here if you need me," he replied.

She felt the tears prick her eyes again. People were all so kind, which was a measure of the high esteem in which they held Claire.

While Megan was talking to Davy, Viv answered her phone

and was shocked to see it was Conor. To her amazement she realised that she hadn't actually given him a thought all day.

"Hi, Viv, I just saw on your Facebook that your friend Claire is missing. Are you okay? What happened?"

Viv was overcome with emotion at the sound of his voice and felt tears threatening to choke her.

"Hello, Conor. We're sick with worry. We have no idea where she might be but the police are now looking for her."

"That's terrible. Are you sure you're okay? Can I do anything?"

Viv had to pull herself together not to start bawling. Her voice was trembling as she answered him.

"Thanks, Conor. There's nothing any of us can do at the moment. The Gardaí are doing all they can." Before she could stop herself she asked, "How are you?"

She heard him hesitate before he replied, softly, "I'm doin' okay . . . well, actually I'm not that great. I miss you."

Viv caught her breath. Did he really say that? Did he mean what she thought? She couldn't trust herself to ask.

"Well, I'd better go and keep the line free, in case we get news," she said.

"Of course, I'm sorry . . . Do you mind if I call you again?"

"No, of course not."

"And if I can help, well, you have my number."

"Sure, and . . . well, thanks for calling, Conor, I appreciate it."

She was shaking and her heart racing when she hung up. Was he really missing her? He was obviously checking her Facebook still. Maybe it wasn't over after all.

Before she could tell Megan, her phone rang again. It was Ben.

"Inspector Staunton just called and they can find no trace of Richard. His phone is turned off and he hasn't been home since Sunday. None of his neighbours have seen him. It appears that he is a loner and not very well liked."

"Oh God! It must definitely be him so," Viv cried, looking at Megan.

They were more worried than ever now.

"Poor Claire," Viv said, breaking into tears when Ben had hung up. "It's all my fault. I made her join that dating site."

"Don't be silly," Megan said, putting her arms around her best friend. "You couldn't have known she'd meet a crazy man." Still, she knew that Viv was racked with guilt, blaming herself for Claire's disappearance. "They'll find her, I just know it," she tried to console her.

"Oh, God, I hope so, or I'll never be able to forgive myself."

Claire was desperately thirsty when she woke and turned to see Richard still sitting in the rocking chair, smiling serenely at her.

"Please can I have some water?" she whispered. Her mouth was so dry that her tongue was sticking to the roof of her mouth.

"Of course, my little one," he replied, getting up and opening the bottle of water which was on the small table beside him. He came to her with a plastic beaker of water and reached out to help her sit up.

She shrank from his touch but she was desperate for the water so she pushed up on her side and took it from him. Her right arm was still tied to the bedpost which made it very awkward and the water dribbled down her chin.

"How long have I been asleep?" she asked him warily.

"A long time. I gave you something to help you sleep. You look so beautiful and peaceful when you're sleeping, just like an angel."

"Richard, why are you doing this?" she asked, her voice wobbling.

"Because I love you and I know you love me too. You just don't realise it."

With a shock she realised that her own clothes were gone and that she was now wearing a white silk negligee.

"Where did this nightie come from?"

"I went out and bought some pretty things for you while you were sleeping," he smiled.

Claire pulled the sheet up to her chin with her free hand, horrified at the thought that he had undressed her while she was unconscious. Mortified to find that he had taken off her underwear, she slid even lower beneath the sheet. It felt like an invasion of her person and made her feel very vulnerable.

She tried to gather her thoughts and think clearly although she was shaking with fear.

"Why have you got me tied up, Richard?"

"I love you, Claire. I want you to be my wife and for us to live happily ever after."

She saw he was deadly serious. Did he really think that was a possibility? Looking at him sitting there serenely, smiling, it hit her that he was a psychopath. How had she not realised that before? She'd thought that he was harmless, just a little OCD, but now she saw that he was mad, quite mad. She should have seen the signs.

As he sat unconcerned, still smiling at her, she closed her eyes and racked her brain, frantically trying to remember what she'd studied about psychopaths in Nursing School. One thing she knew, calm as he appeared, he could turn nasty at the slightest provocation. She had to avoid provoking him at all costs. She had to stay calm and use all her wits to keep him sweet. It would not be easy, terrified as she was. She wondered how long she had been in this room? It could have been days. She knew she'd been sleeping for a long time. Surely her friends would be worried and have raised the alarm. But how could anybody find her in this place?

"You must be hungry. Would you like something to eat?" he asked solicitously.

Playing for time, she nodded her head.

He left the room then, locking the door after him.

Why had he locked the door? How did he think she could escape when she was tied to the bed, with what she now saw was a handcuff?

She looked around the room, seeking anything that might help her, but it was hopeless. There was a door on one wall and she hoped it housed a bathroom as she badly needed to go. She started to whimper softly but stopped when she heard him returning. Instinctively, she knew he would be angry with her if he found her crying and she dare not risk that. She figured that she would have to go along with this charade if she was to survive.

He came in, locked the door, and laid a ham sandwich on a plate beside her on the bed. He held a cup of milk for her as she ate ravenously. When he raised the cup to her lips she looked up at him tremulously and smiled. She knew she had to keep him amiable.

"That's my girl," he said softly. "We're going to have such a wonderful life together."

Claire continued to smile despite her terror. After she'd eaten she told him that she needed to use the bathroom. He undid the handcuff and she rubbed her chaffed wrist. She needed his help to walk to the tiny bathroom that was through the door she'd spotted earlier. She wanted to cringe at his touch but managed to disguise her reaction.

Inside, she wanted to break down crying in the privacy of the loo but the door was very thin and she was afraid he would hear. So she bit her lip to stop herself from venting her feelings.

He had left some wash-things there for her and she tried as best she could to clean herself up. She wished she could have her underwear back. She felt naked without it.

Afterwards, he helped her back to the bed and when he went to tie her wrist again, she pleaded with him.

"Please, Richard, there's no need to tie me up. I'm not going anywhere and my wrist is sore – look." She showed him the abrasions. "Please, it's very sore. You'll be here with me, won't you?" She was quaking inside but knew she had to make a huge effort to sound normal and not let him see how terrified she really was.

He smiled a deeply satisfied smile. "Of course, my angel. I knew you'd see things my way." He took her hand to his lips and kissed it.

At least the awful handcuff is gone, Claire thought, but she was still his prisoner.

What Claire didn't know was that it was now Monday night and she had been incarcerated in Richard's cellar for over twenty-four hours.

He was very pleased with himself and how he had manoeuvred the whole thing. Now it looked like his plan had worked and she was realising just how much he loved her.

Meanwhile, Inspector Staunton and his team had been busy. Not for the first time he thanked God for social media. It had certainly made police work a lot easier these days. The first piece of luck came just after ten on Monday night. The station had put through a call to him at home from a barman in the Orchard Inn who had spotted Claire's photo on Twitter. He remembered seeing her in the bar, with a man, on Sunday afternoon. Inspector Staunton thanked him and arranged to come and talk to him right away. He called the station and instructed them to have Detective Kiely meet him at the bar in fifteen minutes.

"I was checking my tweets during my break," the young barman told them when they met up with him, "and someone had retweeted a photo of the girl who is missing. I recognised her. She was here in the lounge on Sunday afternoon with a guy. She didn't have a drink and I could see things were tense between them. I didn't pay much attention but I noticed that he was very angry when she left after only a few minutes."

The Inspector was excited, thinking this was the break-through they were looking for. He asked to see footage of the security cameras from Sunday and, sure enough, the man in question was Richard Walsh, and the woman with him was Claire.

From the car-park footage, he saw that Claire had arrived and left in her own car. Richard had come out immediately after her, looking tense, staring straight ahead. He got into a Porsche and drove in the direction Claire had taken.

The Inspector thanked the young barman again for his help and wondered what had transpired at that meeting. Had Claire finished their relationship as she'd planned?

Most likely, he thought, which is probably why he'd abducted her.

"Now we know for sure that he's our guy," Detective Kiely said.

"Yes, indeed," Inspector Staunton agreed, rubbing his chin.

He called Ben on his way home and gave him the news. Ben was naturally distraught.

"We'll launch an urgent appeal tomorrow morning asking anyone with information," he assured Ben, "or anyone who may have seen either Claire or Richard since Sunday, to contact us or any Garda station. The public are very good about coming forward so I'm sure we'll get some leads from that."

Ben rang the girls with the news. They were distraught to hear it, although they'd known Richard was behind it.

"The bastard! I hope they hang him!" Viv cried.

"I just hope he doesn't harm Claire," Megan said sombrely.

Sarah knew Orla was angry with her. Unfortunately, she'd caught her snorting a line on Monday, during her lunch-break. Maybe she shouldn't have done it in the office but she'd been terribly upset about Mark and then all that hassle about Claire. Was it any wonder she'd needed something to lift herself?

She'd come home from work on Monday night, feeling down, and after a few drinks decided to go to the 37 bar in the hope that Mark might be there. She desperately wanted to patch things up with him. He was there all right – with a stunning, twenty-something girl draped over his arm. She was so shocked she could barely speak. He nodded briefly to her and Evan asked if she would care for a cocktail.

"No, thanks, I was just looking for Orla."

"She never comes in during the working week," Evan told her, looking at her oddly.

"Right! I'll push off so," she said, exiting with as much dignity as she could muster.

She'd cried all the way home and then took two sleeping pills to knock herself out. She hadn't thought much more about Claire and guessed that she was probably home by then. No fear any of them would inform her. Typical!

On Tuesday morning every newspaper and all the TV and radio stations carried the news of Claire's disappearance. Richard's photo was also splashed all over the media which quoted him as a 'person of interest' in the case.

The Inspector was unprepared for the sheer amount of information that this appeal provoked throughout the day. He fielded calls from quite a few young ladies who told him that they'd dated Richard, but only once, because he was weird and he had scared them. When they refused to go on another date with him, he had starting stalking them.

"This was obviously his modus operandi," Detective Kiely opined.

"Yes, we're dealing with a nasty piece of goods here," Staunton replied. "A psychopath, I reckon."

It was very strange, he thought, but other than the girls he'd dated once not one other single person had come forward with any information on Richard Walsh. Was the man invisible? Had he no friends or family? It was very unusual.

Then a stroke of luck. The Inspector received a call from the owner of a lingerie boutique in Wicklow to say that she'd had a very strange customer on Monday afternoon. She'd seen the photo in the newspaper of the man the police wanted to interview in connection with that girl that was missing and she thought he could be their man. He had purchased quite a lot of lingerie, all of it white, which had surprised her a little. Her customers were mainly women and when men did patronise her shop they invariably purchased black or red sexy lingerie. She had tried to engage him in conversation but he was pretty monosyllabic and obviously uneasy. He'd paid in cash. She *had* wondered about him and thought he was a little weird.

Inspector Staunton felt a flutter of excitement after hearing her story. His gut instinct told him that this was Richard and it looked like he was in Wicklow. Of course, Wicklow was a big county but it was a starting point. He contacted Ben to say that they were making good progress and could hear the relief in the other man's voice.

"I'm sorry that I can't give you details but we received a good lead and I have a great team working on it, 24/7."

Ben thanked him and not for the first time said a prayer that Claire would be found safe and well.

Sarah slept out on Tuesday morning and Orla was furious with her when she turned up two hours late. She couldn't concentrate on her work and needed four Vicodin just to function normally. She somehow managed to get through the day and, as soon as she got home, she collapsed on the couch and did a line of coke. She was relaxing with a bottle of wine when her friend Kay called her.

"I've just been watching the news and a girl called Claire O'Dowd is missing. Is that your sister?"

Between the drugs and the drink Sarah could hardly get

her words out and Kay could barely make sense of what she was saying. But she was sure that it was her Sarah's sister and was shocked that Sarah didn't seem in the least bit worried.

Ben was also disgusted that Sarah had shown no interest whatsoever in helping find her sister. Despite their differences he had thought that, at a time like this, she would put those aside. He'd called Sarah on Tuesday afternoon but she'd appeared disinterested and was still convinced it was all much ado about nothing. He couldn't understand how she could be so heartless. Had she no feelings for her poor sister at all?

# Chapter 37

Claire woke feeling drowsy and guessed she'd been out again for a long time. She lay there, trying to focus on what had happened. Slowly it came back to her. She turned her head and was shocked to see that Richard was lying, sleeping, on the bed beside her. She was relieved to see that he was at least fully dressed. She said a quiet prayer of thanks to God.

She pulled away from him but the movement woke him.

"How are you, my sweet?" he asked, stroking her hair.

She shuddered, but he seemed to think it was with pleasure.

"I feel so sleepy," she said.

"That's probably because of the pill I gave you in your milk, my angel."

"How long have I been asleep?"

"About twenty hours. You look so angelic when you're sleeping. It makes me love you even more."

Claire was horrified that she'd slept so long and

wondered what day it was. Why had nobody found her yet? She bit her lip, trying to quell her fears.

Richard started to caress her arm and turned toward her on the pillow.

"Isn't this heaven?" he asked.

She gave him a watery smile and nodded. It took a massive feat of will to pretend, but she had to make him believe that she agreed with him.

"Richard, I think I'm going to be sick. It must be those pills you gave me."

Like a flash he was out of the bed.

"Please wait, Claire. Don't get sick in here. Come, I'll take you to the bathroom."

She sensed his panic as he practically pushed her in there. She remembered how fastidious he was about cleanliness and how he hated dirt of any kind. Thank God for that! Maybe this was a way to turn him off. She had no problem throwing up and felt a grim satisfaction knowing how distasteful it would be to him. She stayed in the loo a long time, trying to figure out how she could escape from this nightmare. Then she had a brainwave. Of course, this would only give her four or five days' respite.

"Have you washed yourself thoroughly?" he asked when she returned to the bedroom.

"Yes, but I still feel sick and I'm afraid I've just got my period. I'll need some tampons."

"Ugh," he said, wrinkling his nose in distaste. He didn't lie on the bed again but sat back in the rocking chair while she lay down on the bed.

"I'll get them for you shortly. Let me just give you a little sedative first."

"I'm fine. I don't need anything, honestly," she replied.

"I'd just like some water and then I think I'd like to go back to sleep."

He handed her the beaker of water and, after drinking, she lay down and closed her eyes.

"My poor baby," he crooned. "Don't worry, I'll take care of you." he said gently as he handcuffed her to the bedpost again.

Thankfully, Claire sank into oblivion.

Richard sat looking at her tenderly and then left to get those things she needed. This was true love indeed, he thought. He would never have considered doing this for any other woman but Claire was not just any woman. Even so, he found the whole thing quite disgusting.

Inspector Staunton had requested a room in Wicklow Garda station to direct the search for Claire and Richard. Richard's Porsche had gone to ground, just like the man himself. The Inspector thought someone would surely have spotted it in Wicklow town on Monday afternoon, but no one had come forward with a sighting.

Once the appeal had hit the airwaves and newspapers on Tuesday, Viv and Megan were inundated with calls from people offering to help. They were both exhausted but kept going in the hope of finding Claire.

Amy's parents had been as good as their word and by noon on Tuesday they'd turned up with a van, full of posters with Richard and Claire's photos, asking for anyone with any information to contact the Gardaí. Megan co-ordinated the campaign in her usual, efficient manner, and on Tuesday afternoon, a convoy of volunteers, including Megan's co-workers, Viv and her parents, Ben

341

and the kids, Jamie, Davy, Pippa and a host of other friends, including some parents of children Claire had nursed, descended on County Wicklow and started putting up the posters on every available surface. Ben and the girls were amazed and grateful that so many of them had taken leave from their work to help them.

By seven that evening they were done and every town and village in County Wicklow had a poster, or quite a few, asking if people had seen Richard or Claire.

Viv and Megan were a little discouraged when their efforts brought no response at all.

"I really thought the posters would jog somebody's memory," Viv fretted.

"They will. We have to give it time," Megan assured her.

"Time is something we don't have," Viv replied hollowly.

Inspector Staunton and his team worked tirelessly all day Wednesday but despite many calls from the public, they were no closer to discovering where Richard might be holding Claire. He was just about to get into bed in his hotel when he got the call. It was from an elderly farmer called Seán Griffiths from outside Laragh. He had a strong Wicklow accent and although he spoke in slow, measured tones, the Inspector had to strain to catch his words.

"I jus' saw tha' poster ye put up about a lassie what's missin' on the way home from de pub," he said.

"Yes," the Inspector replied, feeling his pulse quicken.

"Well, da fella on the posters looks awful like me neighbour, a verra strange man."

"What's his name?" Staunton asked.

"No idee. He don' talk to the likes of us. As I say, he's a strange wan."

"Tell me about him."

"He owns de big house next to my place, in from the road, up a long drive. He only ever comes in de summer but I saw him goin' in an' out dis week, which is awful strange."

"What kind of car does he drive?" the inspector asked, holding his breath.

"Wan a dem big four-wheel tings. Don' know the name," the farmer said.

"He always arrives in one a dem fancy cars but when he's here he drives de big Range Rover kinda thing. Ya know, dem fancy cars ain't no good for Wickleh roads!" he laughed.

Inspector Staunton was exultant and got Seán Griffiths' address from him. He would need a search warrant to check out the neighbour's place so he contacted the superintendent of the station.

"Luckily the local judge is a friend and neighbour of mine, though he won't take too kindly to being disturbed at this hour of the night," the Super chuckled.

"I understand, sir, but as you know time is of the essence in this case."

"Of course I know that. I'll contact him right away and get back to you."

Thirty minutes later the Inspector had the warrant in his hands. He kissed it, hoping that it would be the means by which he would free Claire. Her friends and family were so dedicated to her that it had touched a nerve in him. He could only imagine how he would have felt if it was his daughter who'd been kidnapped. The Inspector quickly rallied a team together and set off for the address Seán Griffiths had given them.

"Be careful, he could be armed," the Super had advised.

Staunton was well aware of that and had no intention of taking any chances with a psychopath like Richard Walsh.

They drove through the heavy rain and arrived at Griffith's house an hour later. He directed them to his neighbour's house and stealthily they made their way there, silently making their way up the long driveway.

Inspector Staunton directed the team into their places. They had to cover all exits, back and front, in case Walsh tried to escape with Claire as a hostage.

Richard had come back with Claire's tampons and woke her to give them to her. She smiled gratefully at him, knowing she had to go through with this charade if she wanted to keep him at a distance. She was afraid to think of what might happen when her supposed period would be over. Please God she'd have been rescued by then.

He freed her again and helped her into the bathroom.

"Thank you, Richard. You're so kind," she said, forcing herself to sound genuine.

"I was thinking," he said when she came back, "that we should exchange wedding rings and make our vows to each other. Isn't that a good idea?"

"Yes, I'd like that," she replied, and could hardly believe that he swallowed the lie.

"Great! I'll buy the rings tomorrow, and maybe even a beautiful wedding-dress for you." He beamed at her.

"You're so thoughtful, Richard. That would be wonderful!"

She was very close to breaking down but steeled herself to stay calm. If she broke down, he might get angry and hurt her – even possibly kill her, if he suspected she was lying.

It was then she heard the noise. It was muffled but there was definitely something there. Richard heard it too. He jumped up and rushed to the door. As he opened it, the noise became louder. It came from somewhere upstairs.

Please, God, please, Claire prayed silently, let it be someone to rescue me!

Richard bounded up the steps and Claire, seeing her chance, made for the door. Her heart was in her mouth as she tripped on the long negligee but, hiking it up, she climbed up the steps after him. That was when she heard an almighty crash.

"Who are you?" she heard Richard ask in a squeaky voice. "What's going on here?"

"I might ask you the same thing," a male voice replied coldly. "Richard Walsh, we have a warrant to search your premises. I hope for your sake that we find Claire O'Dowd alive."

Claire gasped as she entered into the hallway and stumbled against the big man.

"Cuff him!" he said to one of his companions as Claire fell into his arms.

Richard was handcuffed in a flash as the older man tried to calm Claire who was heaving great sobs of relief.

"You're safe now, my dear," he said gently. "I'm Inspector Staunton and we'll take care of you. Mr Walsh will not be bothering you again."

"Thank you, thank you!" Claire gasped.

"Take him away, John," the Inspector ordered another policeman.

"You don't understand!" Richard cried in a girlish voice. "Claire is my fianceé. We love each other. Tell them, Claire." He looked at her imploringly.

"No, Richard, we do not love each other," she managed to voice, through her sobs. For a brief moment she felt pity for him as she saw the desolation in his eyes and then he was gone. "He's mad, quite mad," she said to Inspector Staunton as he handed her over to a female Garda who had been sent to find Claire's clothes.

"We need you to make a short statement and then, Claire, we'll take you home." Inspector Staunton was greatly relieved to hear that Richard had not raped her or hurt her in any way, physically at least.

"He's a psychopath and he needs help," Claire said, her voice breaking. Then she starting crying again, just thinking of the enormity of what had happened to her.

"It's thanks to your brother-in-law and your friends that we managed to find you when we did. They've been wonderful. Let's go and I'll call them on the way and tell them you're safe. They'll be mightily relieved. Maybe you'd like to talk to them."

Claire smiled through her tears and nodded her head.

He called Ben first. "I have someone here who'd like to talk to you." The Inspector was smiling as he spoke, and then he handed the phone to Claire.

"Hi, Ben, it's me, Claire."

"Oh thank goodness, thank goodness you're safe, Claire! We've been so dreadfully worried about you. Are you okay? Where are you?"

She told him briefly what had happened.

"Thank God you're all right. Can you call Viv and Megan? They've been out of their minds with worry too.

346

I'll go around to the house now so that I can be there when you arrive. And thank the Inspector for me. Wow! I'll go and wake the kids with the good news. Poor Tash has been worried sick about you. We all have."

Claire smiled at his exuberance and realised that it must have been pretty awful for them too.

Next the Inspector called Claire's house. Viv answered and he handed the phone to Claire.

When Claire spoke, Viv burst into tears. Megan took the phone from her.

"Is that really you, Claire? Are you okay? Where are you? What happened? We've been going crazy with worry here."

Claire laughed. "I'm fine and I'm on my way home. I'll tell you all then."

Viv grabbed the phone back from Megan. "Claire, I'm so relieved. I was afraid you were dead. He didn't hurt you, did he? Or do anything . . . you know?"

"No, nothing like that. He just wanted to marry me. He's totally insane, Viv."

"You poor thing! We can't wait to see you."

"I'd better go now. The Inspector has to call some people. See you soon."

"Kisses and hugs from us," Viv said and Claire could hear the two of them whooping with joy as she hung up.

# Chapter 38

Meanwhile Sarah was oblivious to all the brouhaha surrounding Claire's disappearance and rescue. After the cocktail of drugs she'd imbibed the night before, she slept out again, till noon, on Wednesday also.

It was the persistent ringing of her mobile phone that woke her. Orla was on the line and she was livid.

"Sarah, I'm running a business here and I need my staff to be reliable. I can't put up with your irresponsible behaviour any more. You're fired!"

Sarah could not believe it. Orla was supposed to be her friend. How could she do this to her? What would she do now, with no job? Her new exciting life was in tatters. Mark was gone and now her job was gone too. How had it all gone wrong? She blamed Mark, she blamed Orla, she even blamed the kids. If they hadn't called Ben and had only waited for her to come home on Sunday, none of this would have happened. She was distraught. Feeling very sorry for herself she spent the afternoon snorting coke, drinking vodka and popping her magic pills.

It was her friend Kay who found her later that evening. Kay had been worried about Sarah after the conversation of the previous night. She tried for three hours to get Sarah on the phone and had an ominous feeling when Sarah wasn't answering, On the spur of the moment she decided to call around to her apartment. There was no reply and when she looked through the window of the downstairs apartment, she saw Sarah slumped half-on, half-off the sofa. She called 999 and within minutes the ambulance had arrived.

They had to break down the door and the paramedics were very gentle as they put Sarah on the stretcher and lifted her into the ambulance. She had a deep gash on her head where she must have hit it on the coffee table as she fell.

As expected, a crowd of gawkers had gathered outside the apartment when they'd heard the ambulance siren. Kay shooed them away, wondering if it was just an Irish trait to be drawn to gory scenes and disasters. Accidents were always guaranteed to draw a crowd.

Kay went in the ambulance with Sarah and held her hand as the paramedics attended to her.

At the hospital, Sarah was whisked into A&E and Kay waited nervously, praying that her friend would pull through. After what seemed like a lifetime, a doctor came and told her that Sarah was okay but that they'd had to pump her stomach out.

"Have you any idea what drugs she's been taking?" he asked.

Kay shook her head, shocked. She knew Sarah was very fond of the drink – but drugs? As she waited to be allowed in to see her, Kay vowed that when Sarah came round she would try to persuade her to contact her husband and see if they could work things out. Maybe he could stop this downward spiral that Sarah had been on. She figured it was Sarah's only hope. Kay hated to see that happen to anyone and she would do everything she could to stop it. She had listened to Sarah's boast about how exciting her life had become but look where it had got her. She shook her head sadly.

While she waited she checked her phone for news. Sarah's sister was still missing. Gosh, one sister unconscious and rushed into hospital and the other kidnapped, all at the same time. It was the stuff of novels!

She was allowed in to see Sarah for five minutes but she looked so bad that Kay refrained from saying anything about Claire. Sarah had enough to worry about now.

"You're a very lucky girl to be alive," the doctor said to Sarah. "You know, if your friend hadn't found you when she did, you might have died. How are you feeling?"

"Terrible," she replied wanly. "My throat is very sore."

"Yes, well we had to pump all those opiates out of your stomach. Did you mean to overdose or was it accidental?"

Sarah shuddered at the word *overdose*. Is that what had happened?

"It was an accident," she mumbled, looking away.

"You have a nasty cut on your head. I had to put a few stitches in it. Do you have any headache?"

"No, it's just a little sore," Sarah replied, touching her head gingerly.

"That's good. I'd like to keep you here for a couple of days, just for observation."

She had nowhere to go, so acquiesced readily.

"Your friend would like to come in and see you now. I've told her she can stay only a few minutes. You need to rest. You're a very lucky girl."

Sarah didn't feel lucky. She felt ashamed and embarrassed and half-wished Kay had never found her. She just wanted to die but instead she now had to face everyone and explain her actions. Her throat was sore and she longed for something to make her feel better but the nurse looked at her in disbelief when she called her and asked if she could have a Vicodin.

"Absolutely not!" was her indignant reply.

Claire's homecoming was a joyous affair and after much hugs and kisses and a million questions, it was obvious that everyone was over the moon to have Claire home safe and sound. Ben was there with Tash and Owen. When he'd wakened them to tell them that Claire was safe, they'd insisted on getting up and going with him to see Claire. They hugged her and wouldn't let her go. She was overwhelmed to discover that, if it hadn't been for her friends, things might have turned out differently.

When Ben and the kids left, Claire went up to take a long hot shower. She scrubbed herself vigorously in an effort to wash away all remnants of Richard and his horrible cellar. She felt better after that and, wrapped in her dressing gown, came downstairs where Megan had rustled up something to eat. The three girls talked into the small hours until, exhausted, they retired, for the first proper sleep any of them would have since Claire had been abducted.

Claire had thought that she would not be able to sleep

after all the excitement but in her old familiar bed, safe and sound, she fell asleep as soon as her head touched the pillow.

Claire had hoped to be back at work the next day but the Inspector had said she would need to be medically examined and she would also have to make a formal report at the station the following morning. Richard was due to be charged that afternoon.

Viv had wanted to stay home with Claire but she'd already missed two days at work and had a lot of appointments scheduled for that day. Much as she wanted to support Claire, she couldn't risk losing her job. Megan insisted that she go to work and said she would stay with Claire.

News of her release had hit the media and it was Megan who fielded the calls that came in non-stop from them. They were all looking for interviews with Claire but she refused to speak to any of them. To her horror, some of them were parked outside her house and followed as Megan drove her to the station to meet with Inspector Staunton. Claire was wearing a hoodie and pulled the hood up over her head, just like she'd seen numerous criminals do on TV. It felt surreal to her and she wished the reporters would go away.

"Don't worry – if you don't talk to them they'll get tired and leave you alone," the Inspector advised when she told him. "As we used to say when I was young – *Today's news is tomorrow's fish-and-chip paper* – not any more of course, health regulations wouldn't allow it."

He laughed and Claire joined in. She was incredibly grateful and indebted to this kind man who had rescued her and she told him so.

"I'm only doing my job," he replied modestly, but he was very happy that he'd been able to help this sweet girl. She was every bit as lovely as her friends had said. This particular job had given him great satisfaction.

Claire would be forever grateful to her friends who had worked tirelessly to try and find her. She spent the afternoon contacting them all to thank them for their efforts. She was also inundated with good wishes from people she barely knew. The goodwill she felt brought a lump to her throat.

On Thursday morning Kay read about Claire's release with relief. She wondered if Sarah knew that her sister was safe. Probably not. Kay had tossed and turned all night, worrying about her friend and the mess she was in. By morning she had made her decision. She couldn't stand by and watch Sarah destroy herself, so she called the only one who might be able to help her: her husband.

"Hello, Ben. You don't know me. My name is Kay. I'm a friend of Sarah's."

Ben braced himself for what he was sure would be bad news. He listened in horror as Kay told him what had happened the previous night.

"Oh my God," he groaned. "Where is she?"

"In St Vincent's. She needs your help, Ben. She's in a bad way."

"Thank you, Kay. I'll call the hospital right away."

He called and was told that Sarah was comfortable but was being kept in for observation. The Sister also told him that the doctor would like to discuss her condition with him and Ben arranged to meet him at twelve thirty.

When the Sister told Sarah that her husband had been

on the phone, enquiring about her, she became very agitated.

"How does he know I'm here?" she asked, panic-stricken. The thought of Ben and his accusatory 'I told you so' look was more than she could bear.

"I've no idea but the doctor has requested a meeting with him."

Sarah paled. Ben would be furious when he heard what she'd done. How could she face him?

Ben was shocked when he heard what the doctor had to say.

"I don't know how this could have happened. We separated only recently. She wanted more excitement."

"Well, she certainly found it, though not the kind any of us would welcome."

"She's always been fond of her drink – but drugs?" Ben was flummoxed.

"We see it all the time. Young women who get in with a fast set, for whom drugs are a way of life. They try to fit in, think it's cool and exciting, but they can't handle it. It's a shame."

"What happens now?" Ben asked.

"She needs to go into rehabilitation. She's been on a cocktail of various drugs and needs to come off them. Do you think you can persuade her?"

"I'll certainly try. Thank you, Doctor."

They had moved Sarah to a ward that morning and it was there that Ben found her. He was shocked when he saw how bad she looked. She was pale and wan and her normally glossy black hair was limp and dull. She had also lost weight.

"How did you know I was here?" she whispered, not able to look him in the eye.

"Kay called me," he said simply.

She waited for him to vent his anger and bawl her out but instead he just took her hand, his eyes sad.

"I've been talking to the doctor," he said gently. "He said it was an accident. You didn't mean to end it all, did you, Sare?"

She could see he was very upset. She shook her head and saw the relief flood his face.

"Thank God for that!" he said.

The kindness is his voice surprised her and she started to cry.

"Don't cry. You're safe now," he said, bending and taking her in his arms.

Sarah sobbed against his shoulder as he rubbed her hair tenderly.

"I'm sorry," she said, between her sobs.

"It's okay. You're going to be fine. We all make mistakes."

This made her cry even harder. He handed her his handkerchief.

"You rest now and we'll talk about things tomorrow. Tash and Owen send their love."

"Did Claire come home?" she asked, wiping her eyes.

"Yes, she's fine." He didn't think now was the time to burden Sarah with what had happened to her sister. She was too fragile. It could wait.

"Tell her I'm sorry," Sarah whispered.

Ben didn't know what she was sorry for but it wasn't important. There would be time for that later. He could see she was tiring. He kissed her on the forehead and fixed the bed-cover over her.

"Try and have a good sleep now," he said gently, "and we'll talk tomorrow."

He decided that he would not tell anyone about Sarah just yet. Claire didn't need this right now and the kids didn't need to know until things were sorted. He sighed. What a week it had been. Enough drama to last a lifetime.

Richard was charged that afternoon with kidnapping and false imprisonment. His lawyers put in a plea of insanity, although Richard, when charged, insisted he was not insane and that he and Claire loved each other. This convinced the judge that he actually was insane and he remanded him in custody to the Central Mental Hospital for psychiatric assessment. Richard was removed from the court yelling that he and Claire loved each other.

Claire refused to watch the news that night. She really never wanted to set eyes on Richard again. That chapter of her life was over and she wanted to forget all about it.

The best thing that had come out of the whole terrible saga was hearing how upset Jamie had been. He called her that evening to say how relieved he was that she was safe. Her heart lifted as she heard the concern in her voice.

"I'd really like to see you. Could I take you out to dinner some evening?" he asked.

"What about Hannah?" Claire asked.

"Past tense, I'm afraid," he admitted. "We're finished."

"Oh, well in that case I'd very much like to go to dinner with you."

"Great! How does Saturday night suit you?"

"Fine," Claire answered, her stomach doing somersaults.

"I'll pick you up at seven thirty and we'll go somewhere quiet and unpretentious."

Claire twirled around after he'd hung up. Was this really happening? Was it possible that Jamie still had feelings for her? She was afraid to believe it.

Conor too had been calling Viv regularly on the pretext of his concern over Claire but Viv had a feeling that he wanted to get back with her. Still upset with him, she acted as though things hadn't changed. Let him cool his heels for a bit, she decided. She was still smarting at the way he had gone running back to Adele. She was very curious as to how the reunion with his ex had gone but restrained herself from asking.

On Thursday night she was in her bedroom when he called to say how relieved he was that Claire had been found safe and well.

"I . . . em . . . was wondering if . . . em . . . you could see me any time at the weekend?" he finally managed to ask.

"What about your girlfriend – eh, what's-her-name? won't she mind?"

"Oh, that didn't last, I'm afraid. She hasn't changed and besides I couldn't get you out of my mind." He sounded sheepish.

Let him sweat, Viv thought. "Actually, I have a date on Friday night and I'm busy on Saturday night too." She grinned to herself as she heard his intake of breath.

"Oh, I understand."

She could tell by his voice that he was a bit put out.

"Maybe the following weekend then. Could you see me on the Friday?"

Ah-ha! This was a change. Normally he went out with his friends on a Friday night when he got to Dublin.

Viv had given a lot of thought as to how she should have handled Conor last time round and she knew she'd been too keen. Playing it cool and letting him do all the running was the way to go and, although she was anxious to see him again, she replied nonchalantly.

"I think so, let me just check my diary." She pretended to be doing that and then came back to him. "Sure, I'm free that Friday. Give me a call sometime during the week and we'll arrange a time." She hung up before she might give herself away and flew down the stairs to tell the girls.

"Looks like you're all back on track with your loves now, except for me," Megan remarked, making a face.

"There's always online dating. Your profile is still up there."

Both Claire and Megan jumped on her, wrestling her to the ground.

"Don't dare mention that word in this house again," Megan cried.

"Not evvvvver!" Claire agreed.

The following day Sarah agreed to go for treatment to the clinic that her doctor recommended. Ben was surprised that she'd agreed so readily. She knew it wouldn't be easy but she'd thought about it carefully and, really, what choice did she have? The life she'd craved had turned out to be an illusion and now she wanted to get back to real life. She owed it to Ben and the kids and couldn't bear to think how stupid she'd been and how much she'd hurt them.

She couldn't believe it when she heard what Claire had been through and felt extremely guilty. She'd been so wrapped up in her own stupid problems that she had not been there when Claire needed her. What a lousy sister I've turned out to be, Sarah thought ruefully. She vowed to make it up to her – to make it up to them all.

"How can you forgive me for everything I've done?" she asked Ben as he drove her to the clinic.

"When you love someone, it's easy to forgive," he replied, smiling.

# Chapter 39

Claire took extra care getting ready for her date with Jamie on Saturday night. She was even more nervous than she'd been years ago, when she went out with him for the first time. She smiled, thinking how much she'd changed since then. For the better, I hope, she thought, and laughed aloud. She was no longer the timid little mouse she'd been then. She hoped Jamie would like this new Claire.

He was as kind and considerate as ever and took her to a small bistro in Sandyford. She looked around nervously, afraid someone might recognise her, but nobody did.

"Do you want to talk about your ordeal?" Jamie asked gently, after they'd ordered.

She shook her head.

"Okay then, we won't. I just hope he didn't hurt you."

"No, he didn't, honestly. He was just delusional. He thought we were in love."

"You weren't, were you?" Jamie looked at her, his dark eyes anxious.

"Of course not, silly," she laughed as she smacked him playfully on the hand.

He held on to her hand and stroked it gently.

"I'm very happy to hear that."

"What about you and Hannah? What happened there?"

"Well, things were over for quite a while but you know how it is . . . you kind of hang in there. Then when you were missing, she was annoyed that I was so concerned. She was always jealous of my feelings for you and it came to a head then. It's for the best."

Claire was amazed that anyone as pretty and smart as Hannah should be jealous of *her* but she was secretly pleased that they'd broken up.

She and Jamie quickly settled back into their easy-going relationship and it was as if they'd never been apart. She still loved him and hoped that he still felt something for her.

As he was saying goodnight to her, he leaned forward and kissed her and it was as sweet and gentle as before.

"Can I call you tomorrow?" he asked and when she nodded yes, he kissed her again. "And you'll see me again?"

She smiled as she nodded once more.

"Oh, Claire, Claire," he murmured into her hair as he drew her close.

At that moment she knew that their love was still alive.

Megan was sitting in alone on Saturday night, watching TV and feeling down. Claire was out with Jamie, and Viv was meeting with Gilles, the gay French guy she'd met online. They'd kept in regular contact via Facebook and Twitter and had become good internet friends. He was in love once more and was anxious for Viv to meet his new boyfriend.

Megan's life seemed to be at a standstill, her social life at any rate. She hadn't been to the gym or out running since the Dublin City Marathon.

Just then the phone rang. It was Davy and she was pleased to hear his voice on the other end of the line. The embarrassment of the night they'd slept together had dissipated somewhat, thank God. He had called quite often while Claire was missing and she guessed he was interested in Claire. Still, she enjoyed talking to him and was grateful for his support. It surprised her to discover that he was a sensitive soul and had sensed that she was down in the dumps. He had been trying to persuade her to get back running and to the gym.

"Hi, Megan – how's Claire doing?"

"Great. She's out to dinner with an old boyfriend tonight."

"That's good news. I hope he can help her forget the nutcase who kidnapped her. Tell her I said hi."

He sounded quite pleased to hear that Claire was out on a date. Did that mean he wasn't interested in Claire himself? Megan was relieved. That meant she wouldn't have to admit to Claire that she had slept with Davy herself. Thank God for small mercies!

"Hey, I was wondering if you would like to join us for a short run tomorrow morning?" Davy asked. "All the gang are coming and we're going out to lunch afterwards."

"Oh, I don't know, Davy. I'm not in a great mood right –"

"Oh, come on. It's going to be a lovely day tomorrow and I know everyone is dying to see you again."

Megan sighed. "Okay. I suppose as I'm not doing anything else . . ."

"Great! I'll see you at the gym at eleven. Wear something warm – even though it will be sunny, it could be a little chilly."

"Sure. See you then."

Thirty minutes later, Megan's phone rang again. This time it was her mother. She groaned. She really wasn't in the mood for her mother's drama right now.

"Helloooo, dahhhhling! I thought you might have called to congratulate me." Her mother sounded a little drunk.

Megan wondered what she was on about.

"You are now speaking to Mrs Wayne Jackson."

Megan realised that she'd completely forgotten that her mother had planned to tie the knot in Gretna Green yesterday. With all the fuss over Claire, it had completely slipped her mind.

"Sorry, Daphne. Things were quite hectic here this week. Congratulations! How was it?"

"Simply divine, darling. The best wedding night I've ever had." Her mother giggled.

Still on the champagne, Megan guessed.

"Wayne and I would like to take you to dinner on Wednesday night, to celebrate our union."

Megan had no option but to agree. Trying to argue with her mother would be a total waste of time. It wasn't as if it was her mother's first or second marriage – it was her fourth! Who could blame her for losing track?

Megan met up with the guys on Sunday morning and was grateful that Davy had persuaded her to start running again. It felt wonderful to be flying along like the wind, your mind free of all thoughts, enjoying the sheer exhilaration that running produced. Afterwards she was exuberant as she went to lunch with her old friends. Davy was delighted to see that she was having a good time and he was determined to get her back to the fitness regime that he was certain would help her. He knew she'd had a rough six months, what with her wedding scuppered and then Claire's kidnapping. It was enough to bring anyone down.

Davy understood more than anyone. He'd had his share of heartbreak when his fianceé had died of breast cancer, seven years previously, and it was his running and workouts that had helped him survive. He admired Megan enormously and hoped they could be friends but he feared that their single night of passion might have put an end to that possibility.

Megan was happier than she'd been since the day of the marathon. She needed this. The lunch had gone on all afternoon and she promised that she would join them again the following weekend.

"What about working out on Tuesday?" Davy asked her as they sat having a drink after the lunch.

"*Aaaargh!* You're a slave-driver," she replied, swatting him. They all laughed but she knew she'd be happy to get back into her old routine. She'd moped for long enough. Davy was being very sweet and she felt a bit guilty at the way she'd treated him after their night of passion. She recognised that she'd been as much to blame for that night as he was, but she didn't want to think about that.

Meanwhile Ben had invited Claire out to Sunday lunch as the kids were both busy elsewhere.

"I have something to tell you," he said to Claire as they

sipped their wine in La Dolce Vita in Sandyford. "It's about Sarah."

Claire looked at him anxiously. "Have you heard from her?"

"Yes. I didn't want to tell you earlier as you'd been through so much, but on the night you were rescued she was rushed into hospital."

"Oh my God! What happened? Was it an accident?" She'd always worried about Sarah's drinking and driving.

"Sort of," he replied, before telling her, haltingly, what had happened.

Claire's eyes opened wide with shock. "My God! I never thought she'd touch drugs."

"No, well, she just got in with a fast crowd. She realises that now and is really trying to turn her life around. She asked after you and asked me to tell you she's sorry."

Claire felt the tears prick her eyes. "Poor Sarah. When can I see her?"

"Let's leave it till she's stronger. She's still very fragile."

"The poor thing. Please tell her I love her."

"She knows that. I haven't told the kids yet. I want to wait till she's well enough to see them. She's changed, Claire. I think we'll work this out."

"I'm so happy, Ben. You've been very patient."

"I still love her, Claire. She's worth fighting for."

# Chapter 40

Viv had been up to her eyes at work for weeks now as her clients stocked up on their glamour wardrobes for the Christmas party season. She was counting down the hours to her meeting with Conor the following Friday. Things had changed subtly between them and he was now calling and texting her every day. It took all of her willpower to stay cool, but stay cool she did. It appeared the cooler she was the more keen he became. Men! She'd never understand them. She just hoped she could keep this up yet in a way she enjoyed that he was the one doing the chasing. She was anxious about seeing him again and was grateful that she was so busy at work that she didn't have time to worry about it.

On Monday evening Megan rang her dad in Spain.

"Hi, Princess, how are you?" She could hear the smile in his voice as he greeted her.

"Fine, Dad. I started running again yesterday. I'm really glad to be back at it."

"That's good. I was getting worried about you, moping around the house. That's not the girl I know. And how is your friend Claire?"

Megan had been in touch with him all during the kidnapping and he had been very concerned, although he'd never met Claire.

"She's fine. Relieved that her kidnapper is behind bars. She was out with an old boyfriend on Saturday night, someone she's mad about, so it's not all bad."

"That's good news."

"Have you heard from Daphne?"

"No, what has she done now?"

"She got married in Gretna Green last Friday."

"What?" he exclaimed, laughing. "I thought she was through with marriage. How old is this new husband?"

"About her own age."

"Well, thank God for that. Recently her men have usually been half her age as opposed to her second two husbands, who were double it."

They both laughed.

"I spoke to her last month and she never said a word about getting married," Megan's father remarked.

"I don't think she knew him last month. It was very sudden."

"Oh Lord! I hope he's not a gold-digger."

"I've met him and he seems nice. A bit suave maybe."

"I hope he's above board. Keep an eye on things, will you, sweetie?"

That was one of the things Megan loved about her father. Although Daphne had treated him dreadfully, cheating on him with his friends, he didn't hold it against her and still looked out for her. He was a true gentleman and Megan loved him dearly.

"When are you coming out to visit us?" he asked. "It's been too long."

"I was thinking of coming for Christmas," Megan told him.

"That would be wonderful although Betsy and I are going skiing for the New Year. Any chance you'll come with us?"

Megan shuddered. Her father was a keen skiier but she'd broken her leg while skiing when she was ten years old, and had steadfastly refused to go ever since.

"Not a chance in hell," she replied, laughing.

"No change there then," he laughed with her. "But you will come for Christmas?"

"Yes, I'd love to spend Christmas with you."

"Wonderful! Betsy will be so pleased. Why don't you bring some friends with you? You know we have plenty of space here."

"Yeah, that's an idea. Kisses to Betsy, and big hugs to you."

"To you too, Princess," he said lovingly.

Megan went to the gym on Tuesday, as she'd promised. Davy had a big grin on his face when he saw her and some of the other members came over to say hi and that they'd missed her. She had a great workout and felt wonderful after it.

"Care to come for a drink?" Davy asked when they'd finished.

"Sure," she replied, as she went to shower and change.

They went into the pub next door to the gym and he had a beer while she had a Spritzer.

"I'm so glad you bullied me into coming back," she said.

"I didn't bully you, I coerced you," he laughed.

"More like seduced," she retorted as they smiled knowingly at each other. "You're good at that."

He knew she was referring to the night they'd made love.

"I prefer to think I encouraged you," he said.

"I didn't need much encouragement, I'm afraid."

They both laughed then, realising that they'd put that night behind them.

"To friendship!" Davy raised his glass to her.

"To friendship!" Megan replied, thinking how very sexy his eyes were.


Claire went to her Italian class as usual on Tuesday evening. She got a rapturous welcome from the teacher and the other students who had all read about her kidnapping. She thanked them all but said she'd rather not talk about it. It had been the same in the hospital the day she'd returned to work.

People were fascinated with crime. She couldn't understand it. She supposed all those CSI-type programmes were to blame and now they had a real-life victim in their midst. She wished this notoriety would go away. She was not enjoying it in the least.


Megan met up with Daphne and Wayne on Wednesday night, bringing the Waterford crystal candlesticks she'd bought them as a wedding present.

"What can I buy a couple who have everything    I mean *everything!*" she'd said to the salesgirl in BT's.

370

"You can never have too many candles," the girl had replied, obviously familiar with this query. So candlesticks it was.

"How lovely, darling," her mother said, opening the gift. "One can never have too many candles."

Megan grinned at her.

Wayne had insisted they travel into Dublin to Patrick Guilbaud's for dinner.

"That's a first," Viv had said when she'd heard where they were taking her. "Usually you have to drag out to Killiney to meet your mother. Maybe her new husband has put manners on her."

Megan had laughed. "I doubt it."

They had a lovely meal and Daphne seemed madly in love. Megan wasn't so sure about Wayne. He was very charming and courteous but Megan had the feeling that she was watching an actor in a play. He was too slick. It gave her an eerie feeling and she remembered that her father had said "Keep an eye on things". She certainly intended to.

Towards the end of the meal, Daphne announced. "Now for our big news. Wayne is starting up a new company in Dubai and I am going to be on the board of directors. Can you believe it? Me a company director?" Daphne giggled like a schoolgirl.

"Oh, I thought you were expanding here," Megan said, looking at Wayne.

"Yes, I was looking into that but it hasn't worked out and now this great opportunity in Dubai has arisen."

"What does a directorship entail exactly?" Megan asked.

"Oh, it's just a title," Daphne broke in. "He assures me I won't have to bother my little head with the mundane, day-to-day business. He'll take care of that. I'll just fly out there for receptions and corporate functions." Daphne smiled lovingly at him and giggled again.

"Are you investing in this company?" Megan enquired of her mother.

"Maybe. As a director, I probably should have a stake in it."

Wayne said nothing throughout this exchange and Megan was aware of his eyes silently studying her. She felt suddenly afraid for her mother. Did she really know anything about this man she had married?

"What's the name of this company?" she asked him.

He told her and she memorised the name, making a mental note to check it out. She left them shortly afterwards, feeling a certain disquiet. She hoped her mother had not made a dreadful mistake.

Life was returning to normal for the three girls after all the drama of Claire and Sarah. It even looked as if their love lives had all taken a turn for the better. Claire and Jamie, now that they'd found each other again, wanted to be together every moment possible. They met every night but neither of them had dared to suggest making love again although they both wanted to. They were closer than ever and on Thursday evening, after a very romantic dinner, Jamie reached over and stroked her face gently.

"Let's go back to my place," he suggested.

She knew from the look in his eyes that the time had come.

"I'd like that," she replied, her heart racing.

It was wonderful to be back in his arms again and their lovemaking was even better than the previous time they'd been together.

"Funny, you only really appreciate someone when you lose them," he murmured in her ear as they drifted off to sleep, wrapped around each other. "Thank God I found you again."

Viv's romance was looking hopeful as Conor called and texted her every day. She couldn't help smiling at his texts. Conor hadn't quite got the hang of texting shortcuts and so used words spelt fully and perfect grammar with full-stops and commas. She guessed they must have taken him hours to write. He kept saying how much he missed her and how he wished he was living in Dublin so they could see each other more often. However, Viv was still piqued that he'd dropped her like a hot potato, to go back to Adele.

Life was also picking up for Megan and she was back going to the gym every evening. Viv and Claire suspected that it was Davy who was the attraction, rather than the workouts.

Megan felt happier than she had been for a while and it came as a shock to her when she realised that she had stopped thinking of Paul every day. It was almost six months since he'd walked out on her although it seemed like a lifetime ago.

The only fly in the ointment now was her mother. Megan was uncomfortable about Wayne and not convinced he was what he seemed. She had tried to check out that company that he had mentioned but could find no trace of it. She didn't know what to do next. She tried to get more information about it from Daphne who told her not to be so suspicious. She was in love and trusted her husband, she informed her daughter. So Megan dropped it, hoping she was wrong.

# Chapter 41

Davy asked Megan if she'd like to go for a Chinese after training the following Friday night and she readily agreed. The others in the group had started teasing her but she laughed it off.

"What's he got that I haven't?" one of her former suitors asked.

"Do you really want to know?" she'd replied teasingly and Davy had grinned while the others had laughed and cheered.

She and Davy laughed about it afterwards as they waited for their order.

"They're all jealous of me, you know," he'd smiled. "They used to call you the Ice Queen."

She roared with laughter. "Well, you know that's not true!"

"I sure do, lucky for me," he replied, looking at her, his eyes serious.

They locked eyes and she felt that same chemistry that

she'd felt on the night she'd slept with him. He reached over and touched her hand and it felt like an electric shock running through her body. She realised then that she wanted him as much now as she had then and she knew he wanted her too.

"You know, I was in love with you before we got together that night," he admitted, his voice low.

Megan was shocked. "In love with me?" she asked.

"Yes, and I'd hoped you felt something for me, but then you ignored me after that night."

Megan was ashamed. "I'm sorry. I was afraid you thought I was a slut," she mumbled.

He looked at her disbelievingly. "How could you think that? I'd hoped it was the start of something between us."

"It's not too late, is it?" she asked shyly.

"It's never too late," he smiled at her before he reached over and kissed her softly.

It was the sweetest kiss Megan had ever experienced and she kissed him right back.

Meanwhile Viv was having dinner with Conor who was obviously trying to make up for his misdemeanor. He had booked a table in JD's in Terenure, reputedly the best steakhouse in Dublin and had ordered a bottle of Pol Roger Champagne in advance, which had the desired effect of impressing Viv. She had to agree that her steak was the best she'd ever, ever eaten. Scrumptious! Conor was as touchy-feely as she remembered and she basked in his attention as he told her again and again how much he'd missed her.

"And what happens if your ex decides she wants you back again? Will you drop me and go running back?" she asked him pithily.

He winced. "I know I hurt you but I promise that will never happen again. Please forgive me and give me another chance?"

Viv smiled but didn't give him an answer. She wasn't being cruel but he would have to show her that he meant what he said.

"Let's just see how it goes," was all she would say.

On Saturday, Claire and Jamie took Tash and Owen out for the day. They went bowling at noon, then they took them to Eddie Rocket's for lunch and, finally, to a movie. It was great for Claire to see how the kids loved Jamie. He had a great way with them and she couldn't help thinking what a great father he would make. She stayed with Jamie again on Saturday night.

"This is getting to be a habit," she laughed, as he brought her breakfast in bed the next morning.

"I wish it was permanent," he said, looking at her seriously, making her pulse race.

Sarah had settled in well to the clinic although it had taken her a little while to adapt to the group sessions she had to attend. She particularly found support from others who had been in her situation and had come through it. She even made some new friends.

Ben was delighted with her progress as were her doctor and counsellors. Finally, she felt strong enough to see the kids and became very emotional when Tash and Owen walked in. She explained that she'd been sick and had done some really stupid things for which she was truly sorry, but now she was getting better and was looking forward to going home soon to look after them.

Ben looked at her to make sure he'd heard right. She nodded and he joined in the hug she was giving Tash and Owen. She wanted to see Claire too.

It was an emotional visit and Claire was shocked when Sarah broke down in tears when she saw her.

"I'm so sorry," she said, sobbing. "I've been so terrible to you. I really don't know what was wrong with me. Can you ever forgive me?"

"Of course I can. I do. I'm just happy that you're okay." Claire hugged her.

"I've learnt a lot about myself in here. They strip you bare, you know, and then you have to build yourself up again." She dabbed at her eyes with a tissue. "It's been a real learning curve. I behaved like an awful bitch, didn't I? To you, to Ben, to the kids and just about everyone, I suppose."

"Well, you weren't the nicest, I have to admit." Claire grinned.

"And you've been through so much. Was it awful?"

Claire recounted what had happened with Richard as Sarah listened quietly.

"I wasn't much help to you then, was I? Some sister I've turned out to be." She sounded so downcast that Claire gave her another hug.

"Well, we can start afresh, can't we? Things will be different now. I'm so glad you're going home."

"Ben has been wonderful, and the kids too. I'll make it up to all of you, I promise."

To Claire's amazement Sarah said she'd like to see Viv so, the following Sunday afternoon, Claire and Viv made their way to the clinic.

"I'm so glad you came," Sarah greeted Viv. "I just want to say I'm sorry for being such a bitch when I stayed in Claire's. And for ruining your suede jacket."

"It wasn't ruined. Claire got it cleaned and it's good as new." Viv took Sarah's hand and squeezed it. "I'm really glad you're okay."

"I envy Claire her friends," Sarah said hesitantly. "I guess I was jealous but I hope maybe we can be friends after all this. I *have* changed." She looked hopefully at Viv.

"Of course, I'd like that," Viv replied, touched.

Claire was pleased that they'd made up. Sarah certainly had changed. They went to the coffee shop and Sarah explained about the treatment she'd been through.

Viv couldn't believe how humble she'd become. Wonders would never cease.

"Thank you so much for coming, Viv. I really appreciate it," Sarah said, smiling as they took their leave.

"I'm really glad to see you and hope you'll be okay. We'll have a night out when you're better. Okay?"

"I'd love that," Sarah replied wholeheartedly.

The three girls had been like ships that pass in the night since Claire's release. Sarah's hospitalisation and their budding romances were also keeping them busy and now, as December arrived, the Christmas parties would begin. It was all go. They agreed to stay in together on Monday night so they could catch up on each other's lives.

They had a lot to talk about on this first Monday night.

Megan cooked a spaghetti bolognese and she opened a bottle of Barbera d'Asti to go with it. All three were delighted to have this night together and they were all in high spirits.

"Well, shoot, Claire! We'll allow you to go first, seeing as how it's your house."

Claire laughed and told them all about her week. When they quizzed her about Jamie, she blushed and got embarrassed.

"I hear wedding bells," Viv sang out.

"Oh, I think it's a bit early for that," Claire protested.

The others were not convinced. They knew that Claire had never stopped loving Jamie. They just hoped he felt the same and would get on with it.

"And what about you?" Claire asked Viv. "How did the date with Conor go?"

"Okay. He went out of his way to make it a great night and I had a good time, but you know, I'm still pissed with him for what he did."

"I don't blame you," Megan said, "but you should give him a chance to make up for it."

"I will, I will," Viv replied, "but he needn't think I'm going to fall into his arms with gratitude."

Claire and Megan exchanged glances. This didn't sound like the madly-in- love Viv of a month ago.

"And how's *your* love life?" Viv turned to Megan, anxious to change the subject.

Megan blushed but couldn't stop smiling. "Great! I'm seeing Davy a lot. He's asked me to go to the hospital Christmas party with him."

"Brilliant, Jamie and I will be there too. I knew he was crazy about you that night of the marathon party," Claire told her.

"You did?" Megan exclaimed, surprised. "I thought you and he were getting off together that night."

Claire laughed. "Gosh, no. He spent the whole night

talking about you."

"Are you serious?"

"Absolutely! That guy has it bad."

Megan was over the moon to hear this.

"Okay, I think it's safe to tell Claire about your night of passion, now that she and Davy are not an item."

Megan threw her an agonised look. "Do I have to?"

"What night of passion?" Claire asked, mystified, looking from one to the other.

"You tell her," Megan muttered, embarrassed. "I'm going to open another bottle of wine." She escaped into the kitchen.

When she came back into the table Viv had finished.

"I think you guys are perfect together," Claire said. "He's a darling."

"You don't think I'm a slut?"

"Don't be daft! Of course not."

"We've all been there," Viv stated, as Megan poured the wine. "To one-night stands!" she cried as she raised her glass.

"To one-night stands that turn to love!" Claire toasted her.

Megan grinned as she clinked her glass with theirs. "To the best friends anyone could have!"

They drank and then Megan put down her glass and said, "By the way, what are you guys doing for Christmas? I'm going to Spain to visit Dad and he told me I could bring some friends with me. Any takers?"

"Gosh, I'd love to go," Viv said wistfully. "I asked Conor what he was doing, thinking we might do something together, but he said he's taking his mother to a hotel for three days. So that's me told." She made a face.

"Why not come to Spain so?"

"Maybe I will. I've got holidays to take or I'll lose them. Mum and Dad have been invited to Dad's sister in Galway for Christmas but they're worried about leaving me alone."

"They needn't worry any more. That's settled. España, here we come! What about you, Claire?"

"No, I don't think so. It all depends on how Sarah's doing and whether she'll be out of rehab. Whether she is or not, I guess I'll have them all here for Christmas Day."

"Of course. Still, it would have been great craic, the three of us together in Spain."

They decided that they would keep every Monday night free for a girls' night in until then. Otherwise they would never get to see each other. Life had certainly gone up another gear for all three of them since they'd moved in together. They all agreed that it was the best thing they'd ever done.

# Chapter 42

The following Saturday, Jamie took the kids bowling while Claire and Ben went shopping for their Christmas presents. With Christmas only three weeks away, they were hopeful Sarah would be out for it, but it was by no means certain. Claire was busy planning to make it a wonderful occasion after all they'd been through. Jamie was also coming so it would be a very special Christmas for her. She had never been so happy and she hoped that the following year would be even better.

Megan realised that she was falling in love with Davy and it was nothing like what she had felt for Paul. It was way better. Sometimes, she was close to a panic attack to think that she had almost married Paul. What a travesty that would have been! Somebody up there must have been looking out for her. Once she knew that her feelings for Davy were real, she was ready to make love to him again.

It happened on the following Sunday. They'd been for a

run and had lunch afterwards and the chemistry between them was electric. She could feel the excitement mounting. When they left the restaurant he pulled her close.

"I want you so much," he murmured softly into her hair before he kissed her.

She could feel his hardness against her body and her own desire rose to match his. Suddenly she could wait no longer. "I want you too, very much," she told him, after they'd pulled apart.

"Let's go," he said, taking her hand.

They ran to the car and drove to his house.

Once he'd closed the door they became locked in each other's arms. They left a trail of their clothes as they made their way to the bedroom, unable to wait another minute. The sex had been great the night she'd spent with him previously but tonight it was out of this world.

The first coupling was frantic with their desire but the second time he made love to her it was slow and gentle and, when they'd both climaxed, tears of emotion rolled down her cheeks. He kissed her tears away, understanding what she was feeling.

"I love you so much," he murmured as he held her head tenderly.

"I love you too," she replied shyly. She meant what she said and his smile lit up her world.

"I'm so happy," he told her and then it was he who was crying.

They stayed in bed, dozing and making love, late into the evening. Megan was blissfully happy and never wanted to leave. She promised she would stay the night on Tuesday. It was midnight when he drove her home.

"This has been the best day of my life," he said as he

kissed her goodnight. "I can't wait to see you again." She felt the same way.

Megan had booked the flights to Spain for herself and Viv and now she was wondering how she would survive without Davy for a whole ten days.

The more Conor chased her, the more annoyed Viv became with him. It was hard to explain but she'd been so crazy about him and then so hurt when he'd left that she was finding it hard to forgive him. And it seemed that the cooler she was towards him, the more keen he became.

When she confided this to Megan and Claire on Monday night, Megan threw her eyes to heaven and said, "You were mad about him."

"Exactly, and he knew that but he still walked away."

"I really thought he was *the* one for you," Claire said.

"So did I," Viv agreed, "but I'm afraid to trust him now."

"I suppose I can understand that."

"He's a fool," Megan remarked. "I'd die if Davy did that to me."

"When I see you two and how you are with Davy and Jamie, I realise that my relationship with Conor is lacking something. Well, who knows, maybe I'll meet a gorgeous señor in Spain."

As they talked of men and love, none of them could have anticipated what was about to happen.

Claire was surprised to be called to the Matron's office on Tuesday afternoon.

"Claire, sit down. I have some bad news I'm afraid. I've just had a call from Beaumont Hospital. I'm afraid your sister has had a seizure and is undergoing tests at the

385

moment. It's not looking good, I'm afraid."

"Oh, no!" Claire cried, burying her face in her hands.

"I'll have someone drive you there right away, if that's what you want."

"Yes, of course. What about her husband?"

"He's been told and is on the way there now."

"Oh my God, poor Sarah!" Claire started to cry.

Matron put an arm about her shoulders. "Come on, we'll go get your things."

Claire allowed herself to be led out and once in the car she called Ben.

His voice was stricken and she could tell he had been crying.

"They say she's had a massive seizure, Claire, and she's had a CT scan and is having an MRI as we speak. We'll know more when we get there."

"What about the kids?"

"My mother is picking them up from school. She won't say anything to them until we have more information."

Claire could remember nothing of the rest of the journey until she found herself hugging Ben tightly at the hospital.

"They've found bleeding in the brain," he told her. "A subdural haematoma, the doctor called it. That blow she got on her head the night she collapsed probably caused it. They're preparing her for surgery but we can see her for a moment before that." Then he added, his voice breaking, "He warned me that it would be an uphill battle."

They were allowed in to see Sarah shortly afterwards and she opened her eyes and smiled wanly at them. Ben took her hand and stroked her brow as Claire held her other hand.

"You can come through this, Sarah. You're a fighter,"

Ben said. "We need you, the kids and I."

Claire choked back tears as Sarah tried to speak but her words were jumbled. They made no sense.

"I love you," Ben said as the nurse came to wheel her away.

"We all love you," Claire said, her voice wobbling.

Sarah smiled and squeezed their hands as the nurse said sympathetically, "I'm sorry, it's time."

They watched her being wheeled away, praying that everything would be okay.

Ben broke down then and Claire put her arms around him as he cried and cried.

"Just when we had a chance to start anew," he sobbed.

Claire had tears in her own eyes but had to stay strong for him.

The wait seemed never-ending but eventually the surgeon came out and they knew immediately that it was bad news.

"I'm so sorry. We did everything we could but she had another seizure as we prepped her. The bleeding and damage were just too much. I'm sorry."

Ben was stricken but now it was Claire who broke down as he comforted her.

"It's so unfair," she cried.

"Who ever said life was fair?" Ben replied bitterly.

They were allowed in to see Sarah and were surprised to see how peaceful she looked.

"She'd have hated to have her beautiful hair all shaved off like that," Claire remarked hollowly.

"I don't know. She had changed. I think she wouldn't have minded as much as before," Ben said and kissed his wife goodbye.

Now he had to break the news to the children.

The following days were a blur to Claire as they arranged for Sarah's funeral. It helped that they had the experience of her mother's funeral behind them but still there was so much to do.

Tash and Owen were shocked and distraught, but children are more resilient than adults and it was Ben and Claire who felt it most. She thanked God she had Jamie to comfort her and spent most nights with him, curled up in his arms.

The funeral was moving as they huddled together for comfort. Ben's mother, a widow, had moved in with him and the kids and was a great support. His two sisters had come with their families, one from London, the other from Limerick. After the funeral he invited the mourners for drinks and a buffet in The Goat. Claire remembered that the last time she'd been in this room was for the marathon party.

She and Viv had been as solid as a rock all week, helping with the arrangements and lending moral support. Sarah's friend, Kay, had also been a rock, clearing out Sarah's apartment for them. Claire had become very fond of her. She'd been a true friend to Sarah.

Ben rallied throughout the funeral, surrounded by family and friends, but Claire knew that when everyone was gone, Sarah's death would hit him. It would be tough for him and the kids but luckily he had his mother and Claire would also always be there for them.

Viv had told Conor about Sarah's funeral but he had not offered to come. That had pissed her off, especially as it was on a Friday and he was coming to Dublin that afternoon anyway. He could at least have offered to come later but he'd said he had promised to take his mother shopping. When she saw Davy and Jamie so loving and supportive of Megan and Claire, she felt really left out and more annoyed with Conor than ever.

Megan's friend and colleague, Simon, had come to the funeral out of respect for Claire and she'd insisted he come to The Goat afterwards. When he saw Viv there, sitting glumly by herself, he came over to her.

"Are you okay?" he asked, sliding into the seat beside her.

"Oh, I'm okay. It's all been a shock and poor Claire is heartbroken but I didn't really know Sarah that well." She wasn't about to tell him that she was feeling a bit out of it with all the loved-up couples. "I guess I'm not feeling too great recently anyway."

He seemed to hesitate and then said, "I thought Megan said you had a new boyfriend?"

Viv turned down the corners of her mouth. "Not much of a boyfriend if he wouldn't make the effort to come today, or even later."

"Well, let me offer my services as your boyfriend for the evening."

Viv laughed. She remembered how much fun he had been at the marathon after-party. "Offer accepted!" she said with a laugh.

And so later, when the funeral party broke up, they joined Megan and Claire and their boyfriends and went out for a meal together.

Claire had offered to go back home with Ben but, with his sisters and family there, he had a full house.

"You've been a rock through all this," he told her. "Go out with your friends tonight. I'll be needing you when they're all gone."

Claire was grateful to have a few hours with her dearest friends and Jamie.

Megan nudged her when they got a few moments together.

"See what I see? Viv and Simon are really hitting it off."

"Yeah, they got on great together the night of the marathon."

"Gosh, wouldn't it be great if they got together?" Megan said wistfully.

"Yes, they're very well suited," Claire agreed. "Our Viv is such a whirlwind and he's so quiet and calm, just what she needs. Yin and Yang. Of course we never really got to know Conor."

"No. Well, she did meet him online. He can't be normal."

"Don't mention that word," Claire cried.

They both laughed.

"Let's have a dinner party next weekend and get Viv to invite Conor. Then we can decide for ourselves," Megan suggested.

"Great idea. How about the Saturday."

"Perfect! We'll make it an Italian night. Everyone loves Italian."

Daphne called Megan on Saturday morning, sounding very peevish.

"I'm very upset, darling. We're only just married and now Wayne says he has to go to Dubai for a week to take care of this new business he's starting. Can you believe it?"

Megan threw her eyes to heaven. "Well, I suppose he will have to spend a lot of time there," she pointed out. "Maybe you could go with him?"

"No," her mother sniffed. "I suggested that but he said he'd be too busy to spend much time with me."

Megan privately agreed that was a bit Irish. Nobody worked 24/7 but there was no point in riling her mother even further about it.

"I'm sure he'll make it up to you," Megan said

"I should bloody well hope so."

Megan told her about Sarah's death but as usual Daphne was so wrapped up in her own petty problems that it went over her head.

"When am I going to see you?" she demanded.

"Well, I was hoping to bring someone to meet you next week."

"A boyfriend, I hope."

"Yes. Davy is his name. He's a physiotherapist."

"God! Could you not have found someone rich, like a surgeon, or better still a plastic surgeon?"

Megan gritted her teeth. "Does next Friday suit you?"

"Okay. Wayne will be home by then so we can both vet him."

Poor Davy, Megan thought. She'd better prepare him well for this encounter.


Her father, when he called her shortly after, was much more sympathetic when she told him about Sarah.

"Poor Claire. It must have been a shock for her and for those poor children."

Megan could have hugged him. He could always be relied on to make her feel better.

"Well, how many friends are coming with you for Christmas?" he asked.

"So far, just Viv."

"What about that new boyfriend of yours? I'd like to meet him and make sure he's good enough for my princess," he said.

"Oh, he is, Dad. You'll love him."

"I get the feeling that you do too," her father observed.

"Well, yes, I do actually. He's wonderful."

"Well, bring him out here so we can get to know him," he said, his voice booming across the line.

Megan felt a flutter of excitement. Ten days in Spain with Davy! The very thought made her pulse race. She wondered if he'd come.

She need not have worried. He was thrilled when she asked him that afternoon as they lay in bed after making love.

"I was dreading Christmas without you, to be honest," he admitted, curling her hair around his finger. "I'll be very nervous meeting your father though."

"Don't worry. He'll love you," she assured him. "He'll be a doddle compared to my mother. I hope you don't mind but I said I'd take you out to meet her next Friday."

"The Divine Daphne – I can't wait!" he laughed. Megan had spoken often of her mother and now he was keen to see if she was as bad as Megan claimed. "Bring it on!"

"God, I'm dreading it but at least Wayne will be there so she won't be throwing herself at you."

"I only have eyes for one woman," he stated, pulling her close.

She felt her desire rise again and straddled him, amazed at his appetite for her. They finally dragged themselves from the bed, and while Davy showered, she went online and booked his flight. Then she called her father to say Davy would be delighted to come.

"Great! I love to have the house full of young people at Christmas."

# Chapter 43

Viv met Conor in the Orchard on Saturday night but things were very strained between them.

"I really wish you had come last night to be with me and my friends after the funeral."

"I told you, I had to take my mother shopping."

For the first time Viv noticed the whine in his voice. Had that always been there, she wondered.

"Couldn't you have taken her today?" she enquired.

"No, today I had to take her to the hairdresser's and the beauty salon."

"Please, spare me," Viv muttered under her breath. "Couldn't she go to these places alone?" she asked aloud, curious as to what he would say.

"You don't understand. She depends on me. My father did everything for her and now it's fallen on my shoulders."

Great! Just what I need, a Mammy's Boy, Viv thought.

"That's why I think I really should move back to Dublin. My mother needs me here."

"Oh, I thought you wanted to be nearer to me."

"Of course I do. This way I can kill two birds with the one stone," he pointed out smugly.

Viv was furious. How dare he put it like that! He reached over for her hand but she snatched it away.

"Megan has invited me to Spain for Christmas," she informed him.

"You're not going, are you?"

"Of course I am. Why not?"

"What about me?"

"What about you? You'll be with your mother."

"Only for three days. I'll be in Dublin till the second of January. I had hoped we'd spend New Year together."

"Well, I'm afraid I'll be in Spain with my friends for it. It should be great fun."

"Well, I must say that's a bit selfish."

She looked at him, shocked. "You're calling me selfish?" she cried, her voice rising angrily. "Selfish is dumping me for your ex-girlfriend without considering my feelings. Selfish is not discussing Christmas with me first. Selfish is not making an effort to be with me at my friend's funeral!"

She was aware that the people at neighbouring tables were earwigging so she lowered her voice. "And you're not killing two birds with one stone because this bird is finished with you. So there!"

Gathering her things, and her dignity, she walked, head high, out of the bar, aware of his shocked face and the admiration in the eyes of some of the women who had witnessed this exchange.

Claire and Megan had both stayed in and were surprised to see Viv home so early. When she recounted what she'd said they tried to keep straight faces but by the end of her narrative, they were both in stitches.

"Boy, you told him!" Megan said, holding her sides with laughter.

Viv grinned. "I did, didn't I?"

"You sure did," Claire spluttered, and then all three were falling around the place laughing.

Claire opened a bottle of wine and they made Viv tell them again, word for word, what she'd said.

"And you're not killing two birds with one stone . . ." Claire finished for her but couldn't continue, she was laughing so much.

"Because this bird is finished . . . with . . . you!" Megan giggled uncontrollably.

"So there!" Viv finished it for them and pealed with laughter herself.

She took her phone and deleted Conor's number from it.

"Another one deleted," Megan cried, wiping the tears from her eyes.

"What will we do now about the dinner party next Saturday?" Claire asked. "You hadn't asked Conor, had you?"

"No, thank God. I guess it will be just you four now. I don't want to feel like a gooseberry."

Megan had an idea, but didn't say anything.


Claire and Jamie had called in on Ben almost every night and he was very grateful for their company.

"A loved one dying at this time of year is particularly hard on everyone," he admitted on Tuesday night. "Would you mind, Claire, if I take the children away for Christmas? I know we'd made other plans but now with Sarah gone . . ."

"Of course not, Ben. You do whatever you think is best."

"My sister has invited us to London for the holidays and I think the break might do us all good. Tash and Owen have cousins their own age so it would take their minds off Sarah's death."

"I think that's a great idea. It will be good for you too."

"So many memories of happier Christmases here," he remarked sadly.

When Claire told Megan this, she was hoopla. "Fantastic – maybe you and Jamie can come to Spain with us."

Jamie had planned to go to his brothers' for Christmas but assured Claire that he would much prefer to go to Spain with her.

"I won't be missed – they have hordes of friends in over the holidays. I think this is what you need after all you've been through. Book it straight away."

Megan was delighted that they would be joining the party. An idea had started simmering in the back of her mind.

The following morning at work, she said casually to Simon,

"Are you doing anything special for Christmas, Simon?"

"No, I hate Christmas now since Miriam left. I'll probably go to visit my aunt on Christmas Day, that's about it. Friends have invited me but all these happy families just make me sad." He sounded glum. "Christmas goes on forever here in Ireland. I hate it."

"Yes, it's really got out of hand, hasn't it?"

"I generally go racing in Leopardstown on Stephen's Day and every day after that. More to pass the time really.

I'm usually glad to get back to work." He grimaced.

"Mmmm . . ." Megan replied nonchalantly, her plan escalating.

The hospital dinner took place on Wednesday night and Claire and Megan had a ball. Davy and Jamie were fast becoming friends which pleased the girls. Megan lost count of all the people who approached Claire to say how happy they were when they'd heard she'd been rescued.

"God, it seems like months ago since it happened," Claire confided to her friends.

Many others sympathised with her over Sarah's death.

"Gosh, everyone knows you here," Megan exclaimed.

"My girl is the most popular nurse in the hospital," Jamie said proudly, beaming.

"Go on outta that!" Claire swatted him playfully. "You're embarrassing me."

"It's true," Davy added.

"We've decided to make Saturday an Italian evening. Does that suit you guys?" Megan asked.

"Brilliant! I love Italian food," Jamie enthused. "How about you, Davy?"

"My favourite cuisine," Davy chipped in.

"What about Viv?" said Claire. "Will she come, now that Conor's a thing of the past?"

"I'm going to invite Simon," Megan winked.

"Great idea!" Claire exclaimed.

"He's a great guy," Davy said and Jamie agreed.

On Thursday morning Megan asked Simon if he was free on Saturday night. When he said he was, she invited him to the dinner.

"We're having an Italian night."

"Great! Who else will be there?"

She told him and saw his eyes light up when she mentioned Viv.

"What about her boyfriend?"

"No, that's finished. They broke up."

At that snippet of news, the smile on Simon's face could have lit up the entire building.

Megan returned to her own office, rubbing her hands with glee.

She chose her words carefully when she told Viv that evening that Simon would be coming.

"I hope you don't mind but, since Conor is off the scene, I took the liberty of inviting Simon to dinner on Saturday night so you won't be a gooseberry. We didn't want you to miss the evening and he gets on great with Jamie and Davy."

Viv's face brightened up. "No, that's fine. He's great craic."

First step of my plan accomplished, Megan thought gleefully. Now let's hope the second part goes as smoothly.

Megan took Davy out to Killiney on Friday night to meet her mother. She had prepped him well so he knew what to expect of Daphne but she hadn't prepared him for the luxurious mansion where she lived.

"Dahhhling, how lovely to see you," Daphne trilled as she air-kissed her daughter, looking over her shoulder at Davy. "And this is the physiotherapist. I'm *sooo* happy to meet you." She kissed Davy on the cheeks and stood back to admire him. "He's so cute," she cooed. "Where on earth did you find him?"

Megan threw her eyes to heaven. You'd think her mother was talking about a baby! She looked helplessly at Davy but he just smiled and shrugged his shoulders. He did look gorgeous, she thought lovingly. The blue jacket he was wearing made his blue eyes look bluer than ever. He was divine and she was crazy about him.

Her mother obviously thought so too as she proceeded to flirt outrageously with him, despite being newly married. Davy ignored it and held Megan's hand all evening, occasionally bringing it to his lips. Daphne's flirting didn't seem to bother Wayne, which Megan found strange.

He was his usual charming self but Megan detected a strain between him and her mother. The reason for this surfaced during dinner, which was being catered for by her mother's usual caterers and was, as always, delicious.

"Darling, will you talk to Wayne and tell him that leaving his new bride after ten days of marriage is just not acceptable. I'm sure Davy would never do that." Her mother spoke in a girlish voice as she looked at Davy from under her eyelashes.

Megan looked at him helplessly, wishing her mother would give over. She was also embarrassed for her new stepfather and didn't know how to respond.

"My sweet," Wayne spoke gently to his wife, "I've explained to you that I want more than anything to be with you, but business sometimes requires my attention elsewhere."

Daphne sulked despite his explanations, making for a very uncomfortable atmosphere. Megan couldn't wait to make their excuses and leave.

"I warned you," she said to Davy as they drove away.

"You weren't exaggerating," he grinned, holding her

hand as he drove. "It's hard to believe that she's your mother. It must have been very difficult for you growing up. You're way more mature than she is. She's so insecure."

Megan wanted to hug him. At last someone understood.

"Trust me, Dad is way different. He's very grounded. I can't wait for you to meet him."

"It won't be long now," he smiled and kissed her hand.

The girls went shopping after breakfast on Saturday morning and then spent the afternoon preparing for the dinner. Megan was making a lasagne and for dessert Claire was making a tiramisu. Viv's contribution was to be an antipasti platter which suited her down to the ground, as it entailed no cooking whatsoever. Finally, all was ready and they stood back to admire their efforts. The house looked lovely with a fire blazing in the hearth and candles flickering all around the room.

Davy and Jamie arrived together, brandishing bouquets of flowers and two bottles of Italian wine. Simon came in with a bottle of sambuca and a beautiful orchid plant. Viv greeted him warmly and the party got under way. It was a terrific success and Simon gelled very well with Davy and Jamie. Viv was having a great time and, not for the first time, thought how glad she was that Conor wasn't there.

It was one of those magical evenings that happen rarely. Everything was perfect, from the food to the wine, the company and the ambience. Simon prepared sambucas for them all after the dinner and placed two coffee beans in the top of each glass. Then he lit them and the girls ooohed and aaahed as the lovely blue flame rose up. They giggled as they drank them, loving the taste.

"It's a shame Simon isn't coming to Spain with us,"

402

Claire remarked as she licked the sweet liqueur from her lips.

Megan shot a jubilant look at Claire.

"Are you doing anything special for Christmas?" she asked Simon innocently.

Simon was about to reply that he'd already told her no, but then he twigged. "No, nothing special. I hate Christmas in Ireland, to be honest."

"Then you must come with us. It'll be fun. All six of us there together."

"Please say yes," Viv implored him. "Otherwise, I'll feel like a gooseberry."

Simon blushed with pleasure. "I don't know what to say . . ."

"Say yes!" they all chorused together.

"Well, yes, thank you. I'd love to come." He beamed around the table.

Megan took out her iPhone to book Simon's flight. Luckily there was still one seat left. She booked it.

"*España, vamos!*" Megan raised her glass as Davy started singing, '*Y viva España!*' and the others joined in,

"As we'll be restricted with luggage, can I suggest that we do a Secret Santa right now?" said Megan. "We'll put all our names in a hat and then each of us will buy a Christmas present for the name we pull out. That way we buy just one decent present instead of five smaller presents. What do you say?"

"Great idea," Claire said.

The others all agreed so they did that.

"What about a present for your dad and his wife?" Davy asked.

"Well, if you like we can all band together and get him

some cigars or whiskey. He's very fond of both and Betsy loves Newbridge silver."

"We can get them at the airport," Simon suggested.

"Okay, all agreed?" Viv asked.

"*Yessss!*" they chorused.

"It's going to be a great Christmas," Megan said happily, after the party broke up and the girls were alone.

"Yes, it's all working out great," Claire agreed.

"I'm delighted Simon can come," Megan said. "I hope you don't mind my saying, Viv, but I'm kinda glad you deleted Conor recently."

"Who's Conor?" Viv asked mischievously before they all dissolved with laughter.

# Chapter 44

The following week was a hectic one as all of the friends Christmas-partied and met with family to exchange Christmas gifts.

Claire and Jamie took Ben and the kids out for dinner on Thursday evening as they were flying to London on Friday. It was an emotional evening but the kids were excited about their trip and delighted with their presents. Claire had bought a Samsung Galaxy 4 for Tash and a PlayStation 4 for Owen. Jamie had surprised her by arriving with presents for them too and Owen was delirious with excitement when he unwrapped his present and found the new FIFA 14 game to go with the PlayStation.

Tash squealed with joy when she saw the voucher for €100 for Abercrombie and Fitch.

"Oh wow!" she cried. "This is *sooo* cool. All my friends will be madly jealous." Then she threw her arms around Jamie and gave him a kiss as Ben and Claire looked on smiling.

"I hope you have a great time in Spain," Ben said as they hugged goodbye.

"Take care of yourself." Claire held him tight. "I know it won't be easy."

Ben sighed. "The break will be good for us all. I'm so grateful to have these two. They're my priority now."

He stood at the door with his arms around the kids as they left.

"I'll keep in touch by Skype," Claire promised, waving goodbye.

On Saturday morning, the three girls were in high spirits as they made their way to the airport. Viv's parents drove her, Jamie and Claire there and Simon, who was leaving his car in the long-term car-park, picked up Megan and Davy.

The airport was mental with crowds coming and going for Christmas but eventually they were on their way.

Megan's father, Trevor, welcomed them warmly and was obviously delighted to have them there. Betsy had pulled out all the stops and had cooked up a storm before they'd arrived.

Davy had been very apprehensive about meeting Megan's father but, when Trevor wrapped him in a bear-hug, he knew it would be okay. He instantly liked the man and it was obvious Trevor approved of him too.

Davy had been concerned that he and Megan would have to sleep in separate rooms and sneak about at night, but when Betsy showed them to their room which had a huge kingsize bed and a jacuzzi shower, he wanted to hug her.

"You're mature grown-up people," she remarked, seeing his relief. "We're not judgemental here."

Then he did hug her as Megan laughed.

Simon and Viv were given single rooms but Simon hoped that might change before the holiday was over.

The fabulous house overlooked the sea and had a heated infinity pool. It was twenty-four degrees as opposed to the six in Dublin. The sun was shining and the sky was blue, a big improvement on the grey, wet, cold weather they'd left behind.

They swam, they walked, they sunbathed and played ball games on the beach where Megan and Davy ran every day. Every evening there was fun and laughter as the men barbequed while the girls drank cocktails on the terrace. From time to time Jamie and Claire went off alone, as did Megan and Davy. Everyone understood this occasional need for privacy and respected it. It was perfect.

The only fly in the ointment where Megan was concerned was her mother's complaining phone calls. Daphne had been annoyed when Megan told her she would be spending the holiday with her father.

"What about me?" she'd demanded.

"You have Wayne."

"Hmph! I hardly ever see him. He won't be home from Dubai till Christmas Eve, can you believe it? All those parties I have to attend on my own! I'm furious with him."

Then on Christmas Eve night, just as they were leaving for Mass, Daphne called in hysterics. "Wayne missed his flight from Dubai and now he says he can't get home till Stephen's Day. How could he do this to me?" she shrieked.

Megan didn't know what to say. Her father, who could hear Daphne's voice screeching over the phone, threw his eyes to heaven.

"*Plus ça change . . .*" he murmured.

"He probably got delayed and –"

"Bullshit!" Daphne shrieked. "He'll pay for this, you can be sure."

Megan didn't doubt it for a minute.

"I don't know what's going on with them," Megan confided to her father as they drove to church. "He's very charming but there's something about him . . . I just don't trust him."

"It does seem strange. I think I'll hire an investigator to look into this guy."

Although Daphne had remarried three times since they'd divorced, Trevor still felt a sense of responsibility towards her, because she had given him Megan.

"Thanks, Dad. I *am* worried about him."

"And I trust your instinct."

After Mass, they gathered for cocktails and sang carols around the piano as Betsy played. Then after some delicious tapas, the party really took off and they sang and danced into the small hours.

"God, I miss a good old Irish hooley," Trevor announced as they finished singing 'The Fields of Athenry'. He smiled around at the six youngsters as he put one arm around Betsy and the other around Megan.

"We are so happy that you've all come to celebrate Christmas with us. It's the best Christmas I remember."

"So say all of us!" said Viv. "Thank you for having us."

The others murmured their agreement.

"And to have Megan here and to see her so happy has made it extra special." Trevor squeezed his daughter.

"Thanks, Dad," she said, as she kissed his cheek, then

exchanged a smile with Davy. She thought she would burst with happiness.

On Christmas morning they breakfasted on the terrace, the girls drinking Mimosas and the men Bloody Marys. Then they exchanged presents under the huge Christmas tree. Trevor was thrilled with his Cuban cigars and Jameson Gold Reserve whiskey and Betsy loved the Newbridge silver pendant they'd given her.

Megan had bought a Montblanc pen for Davy but hadn't put it under the tree. She would give it to him later.

After a lavish Christmas dinner, Irish-style, at four, Davy suggested to Megan that they should take a walk on the beach to see the sunset.

He and Megan set off, hand in hand but the sea was very calm and soon they couldn't resist skimming stones across its surface.

"Do you remember that Specsavers ad where they were skimming stones and a guy handed the girl a box with an engagement ring in it," said Davy, "and she skimmed it into the water, thinking it was a stone? It was brilliant!"

"Yes, I remember it," Megan laughed. "It was so funny. All their ads are."

"Yes, well, you don't need Specsavers, I hope," Davy said seriously, handing her a small velvet box.

Megan looked at him and saw he was serious.

"Open it," he said.

She did, and gasped at the beautiful diamond ring sitting there.

"Oh my God!" she cried, putting her hand to her mouth.

Davy then went down on one knee in the sand. "Megan Ross, will you marry me?"

Megan started to cry. "Oh, yes, yes, Davy. Oh yes!"

He smiled at her, stood up, then kissed her. "I love you so very much," he said, picking her up and twirling her around.

"Careful, careful," she cried, afraid the ring might fall. He put her down.

"Put it on," he said, taking the ring from the box. It fit perfectly.

"It's beautiful," she whispered. "It's exactly what I would have chosen myself. Oh, I love you so very much too."

Arm in arm they walked back up the beach, Megan still in shock.

"My goodness, my father and friends will be surprised."

"Not your dad. I asked him for your hand last night," he grinned.

"And he never hinted to me."

"I asked him not to," Davy said, smiling happily.

When she walked in flashing the ring at Viv and Claire, they squealed with excitement. Her father produced champagne and a hooley started up again. Viv had never seen Megan so happy. Maybe there is a silver lining in every cloud, she thought, thrilled for her friend.

"Maybe we should think of getting engaged too," Jamie suggested to Claire as they walked on the beach later, the moon making a path on the sea.

"We have plenty of time," Claire replied.

"Yes, but I want to spend the rest of my life with you," Jamie told her.

Claire was touched. "Me too."

He pulled her to him and kissed her passionately. She responded and they fell down on the sand, hungry for each other.

"We don't have a condom," Claire observed.

"Who cares?" Jamie replied huskily, as he lifted her skirt.

Megan's engagement had lifted the party spirit even higher and the rest of the week was a blast. On New Year's Eve, Trevor and Betsy left for their skiing holiday amidst much kissing and hugging. Megan and Davy had decided to stay on alone for an extra five days but the others were due to return to Ireland the following day. They went to a restaurant that last evening and at midnight they ate twelve grapes each, as was the Spanish custom, then kissed and sang 'Auld Lang Syne' as the fireworks exploded. It was a fitting end to a wonderful week.

That night Viv slept with Simon for the first time. They had slowly come to know each other over the week and she knew that she was falling in love with him. He was already deeply in love with her.

Megan called her mother to tell her of her engagement but Daphne hardly reacted. All she could talk about was Wayne and his insensitivity.

"I will never, ever forgive him for leaving me alone on Christmas Day. Can you imagine how embarrassing it was for me with my friends? Our first Christmas together, and he's missing."

Megan threw her eyes to heaven as Daphne ranted on.

"Well, you did marry him in rather a hurry," she reminded her mother.

"What's that got to do with it?" Daphne demanded.

Megan didn't reply but her unease about Wayne increased. She texted her father to remind him to hire that guy to investigate Wayne and his business concerns. She received a text back to say that it was already done. However, before they heard anything back from the investigator, Daphne received a phone call from a woman with an English accent.

"Hello, is this Mrs Wayne Jackson?"

"Yes," Daphne had responded. "Who is this?"

"My name is Lucy Jackson. I'm also Mrs Wayne Jackson."

"I beg your pardon?" Daphne asked in her best hoity-toity accent.

"I am married to your husband. We've been married for eight years and we have three children together."

"I don't believe you," Daphne exclaimed, shocked.

"No? Believe me, it's the truth. Ask him."

"What is it you want?" Daphne asked suspiciously. This must be some kind of hoax, she thought.

"I don't want anything. I just want you to know that you're not married to Wayne because he is still legally married to me. He's a liar and a cheat and I see he's duped you too."

Lucy spoke in an educated, well-modulated voice, but Daphne could not believe what she was saying.

"He spent Christmas Day with me and the kids but when he said he had to leave on Boxing Day, I got suspicious and checked his mobile phone. I thought he was having an affair as he's been away so much on business lately."

Daphne felt weak. Shaking, she sat down, clasping the arm of the armchair.

"I found your number there and then a photo of the two

412

of you in Gretna Green. I put two and two together. Seemingly, he conveniently forgot to mention to you that he was married already, to me."

Daphne was flabbergasted. "Is this some kind of hoax?"

"I wish it was. When did this wedding take place?" the other Mrs Jackson asked.

"It was . . . November," Daphne replied haltingly.

"Well, I hope you haven't given him any money for his fictitious business because there is no business. I fell for that too. Now I'm penniless. Wayne lives off his wits."

Daphne gasped.

"Look, I know this is a frightful shock for you, I'm sorry. And I know how charming and seductive he can be, but he can't be trusted. Here's my number if you want to contact me."

With a shaking hand Daphne wrote it down.

Wayne, of course, denied it all when he came home, claiming that Lucy was a deluded woman with whom he'd had a brief relationship, five years previously. He sounded so sincere that Daphne wanted to believe him but there was a niggling doubt at the back of her mind.

The following day he presented her with a diamond bracelet and begged her forgiveness for missing Christmas Day. She wanted to forgive him, but the woman's voice was still ringing in her ears. She rang Trevor and told him about the phone call.

"Leave it with me," he told her. "I'll have him checked out." He didn't dare tell her that he already had somebody on the case. Daphne would have blown a fuse.

Before he left Meribel, Trevor had the report in his hand.

Wayne was not only a bigamist, he was a polygamist. He had a wife of eight years and three children living in Bristol and also a wife and four children, all teenagers now, back in the US. Even Trevor was shocked at the man's ingenuity. How could he have got away with this for so long? There were no business ventures. He lived off his wealthy wives. Trevor knew Daphne was not going to like hearing this.

She took it amazingly well, given her penchant for histrionics. In fact, Daphne was seething with anger at the duplicity and nerve of her soon-to-be ex-husband. She corrected herself. He'd never been her husband. She asked Trevor to fax her the report. It was all there, the marriage licences and the children's birth certificates. She thanked her lucky stars she hadn't yet invested in his non-existent company.

Calmly, she rang the Gardaí.

"I'd like to report a polygamist, please," she stated.

When she'd finished, she went up to Wayne's closet and calmly tossed all his clothes and things out the window, on to the front driveway. It gave her a sense of satisfaction as she hurled his lovely suits into the rain. She'd always admired women who did things like that and followed their maxim: *Don't get mad, get even*. Then she called a locksmith and had all the locks changed. She also got a certain satisfaction calling Lucy back to tell her that *she* was not actually the first Mrs Jackson, but the second. She promised to fax the report to her.

Wayne texted her to say he'd be home at six that evening. When he arrived, the Gardaí were waiting for him. He knew the game was up.

# Chapter 45

*6 Months Later*

"You look amazing," Viv said emotionally as Megan stood before them in her dream wedding-dress, the one she'd intended wearing ten months previously.

"Absolutely beautiful," Claire agreed, close to tears as she saw the radiance on Megan's face.

Megan was indeed glowing with happiness as she smiled at her two bridesmaids.

"Life is so strange, isn't it?" she remarked as she took their hands in hers. "Who would ever have imagined, one year ago, when Paul walked out on me and I thought my life was over, that I would be standing here in my wedding-dress today?"

"God works in strange ways," Claire observed, smiling.

"He sure does, and what a year it's been!" Viv exclaimed.

"If it wasn't for you two, the best friends any girl could have, I wouldn't be here," Megan said emotionally.

"Don't you dare cry, you'll ruin your make-up," Viv cried.

"Okay, okay," Megan replied, taking a deep breath.

There was a knock on the door.

"Ready to go, Princess?" Megan's father called out.

Viv opened the door and Trevor gasped as he saw his darling daughter glowing with happiness.

"Oh my, my," he exclaimed with an intake of breath. "I have never seen a more radiant bride. You look very beautiful and blissfully happy, a real-life princess," he said, obviously very moved.

"Thank you, Dad. I *am* blissfully happy."

He took her arm and Viv helped her down the stairs.

"Here goes, girls," Megan said nervously, taking another deep breath.

"It's going to be wonderful," Claire whispered as she kissed her cheek.

"The happiest day of your life," Viv said hugging her best friend while trying not to crease her dress. "See you in the church."

Viv and Claire walked to the car that was to take them there. Daphne had come to the house earlier but had made Megan even more nervous than she already was, fussing about how she herself looked, rather than being concerned with her daughter. Viv felt like strangling her but stayed quiet, not wanting to upset Megan. It was a great relief when Daphne had finally left and they could calm Megan's nerves.

Five minutes after her bridesmaids left, it was time. Megan's hands were shaking as she took her father's arm and walked to the limousine that was waiting to take her to marry Davy.

The past six months had been hectic but Megan had

enjoyed every moment. This would be a much lower-key wedding than the one she'd planned with Paul. Davy was happy to go along with that and so they were keeping it simple. Daphne of course had kicked up a stink, wanting to have a huge wedding so she could impress her friends.

"She's one to talk!" Viv had said disgustedly. "She eloped to Gretna Green and look how that turned out. Not too well."

"That's an understatement," Claire giggled.

"Oh Lord, don't remind me," Megan had sighed.

Megan had asked Viv and Claire to be her bridesmaids and had initially planned the wedding for September but when Claire announced in March that she was pregnant, with her baby due at the end of September, Megan brought the date forward. Claire's baby had been conceived Christmas Day, on the beach in Spain. Both she and Jamie were overjoyed that they were going to be parents.

"No, no," Claire had protested. "Don't worry about me. Just stick with September."

"No, I absolutely want you for my bridesmaid," Megan insisted.

"She doesn't want you spoiling her wedding-day in September by going into labour during the ceremony," Viv teased.

"That's not it," Megan swatted her. "You know I want you there with me, Claire."

So the wedding was brought forward to July, although Claire was a bridesmaid no longer but a matron of honour. She and Jamie had got married in a quiet, small ceremony in April. There were only fifteen guests and Ben had given her away. It was the happiest day of Claire's life and she only wished Sarah had been there to share it with her.

As they drove to the church Claire and Viv talked of what a tumultuous year it had been since they'd moved in together.

"To think now that we were looking for love online. How crazy was that?" Claire remarked.

"Yes, I will never forgive myself for that," Viv confessed, sadly. "You really suffered because of it."

"Don't blame yourself. I might never have got together with Jamie if it hadn't been for my kidnapping."

Richard was now confined to the Central Mental Hospital undergoing treatment. Wayne had been deported and was awaiting trial for polygamy in the UK. Daphne had moved on, of course, and now had another younger man on her arm. She was not a happy bunny when Megan told her that she and Davy wanted to start a family right away.

"*Whaaat?* You can't be serious! I'm too young to be a grandmother," she'd shrieked.

"Frankly, Mother, I don't care," Megan had replied, grinning at Davy.

It was the most beautiful wedding any of them had ever been to. Not just because it was simple and classy with none of the extravagances that were the norm at weddings today, but because the love between Davy and Megan touched everyone's heart. This one was a keeper.

Gloria Rivers was a guest and something of a celebrity now since her book had topped the bestsellers list and been snapped up by UK and US publishers. There was even a bidding-war starting over the film rights. Megan was very thrilled for Gloria and delighted that she was here to share her big day with her.

She had also invited Ben to her wedding. He was beginning to get his life back together and was now focused solely on his children who were coping well now with Sarah's death, as kids do. Tash was becoming quite the young lady and they were all very excited about Claire's baby.

As Simon and Viv watched the happy couple take their first dance, Simon, who had been very moved by the ceremony and the whole day, whispered to her, "Do you think we should be the next?"

"What?"

"To get married."

"Is this a proposal?"

"Well, yes. My divorce will be through shortly, so why not?"

"That's very sweet of you," Viv stroked his face, "but I don't need a piece of paper to prove we love each other."

"No, but maybe you'll think about it."

"Okay, let's see how living together goes first," she suggested.

They'd moved in together in April and so far it was going wonderfully well but two weddings this summer was enough. She could wait.

Later, after all the guests had departed, the six friends sat having a last drink.

"You're next, Viv," Megan said, grinning at her.

"I have asked her," Simon pointed out, "but she's keeping me on tenterhooks."

"Ah, Viv, can't you see how wonderful marriage is?" Jamie commented.

"We'll see," she murmured. "Beats online dating, I

419

suppose," she grinned mischievously.

"*Aaaaaargh!* No more!" Megan cried and Claire descended on Viv, shaking her as she laughed.

"Meet and Delete is dead and gone!" Megan exclaimed.

"We'll drink to that!" The three men, who had heard of their online-dating antics, raised their glasses.

"Okay, okay, *finito*! I promise!" Viv said, laughing.

"Or else we'll delete you," Megan admonished her.

"If I don't get there first," Simon declared, smiling lovingly at her.

### The End

If you enjoyed
*Meet and Delete* by Pauline Lawless
why not try
*The Birthday Girls* also published
by Poolbeg?
Here's a sneak preview of Chapters One and two


# *The*
# *Birthday Girls*

# The
# Birthday Girls
# Chapter 1

"I absolutely refuse to be forty," Angel declared, her voice strong and determined, "so I won't be taking part in any fortieth celebrations next year. Please don't be angry with me, Lexi, but I have always said that I planned on staying thirty-nine forever." She reverted to her normal little-girl-voice as she continued. "I'm truly sorry, honey, but this coming November will be my very last birthday."

Angel was a diva – a full-blown, over-the-top, Hollywood-style diva. She had been for as long as Lexi had known her, which was all of thirty-five years. She was almost thirty-nine now and as dramatic as ever as she made her announcement. The emotion in Angel's voice was palpable on the other end of the line. Lexi sighed. Angel had often said her thirty-ninth birthday would be her last, but no one had really taken her seriously. Now it was apparent that she had indeed meant it, thereby wrecking Lexi's plans for a fabulous slap-up fortieth, the following year, in Guatemala.

"Well, if you're really serious –"

"Oh, I am," Angel insisted. "I'm sorry, sweetie, but I just can't go there. I hope you understand. It would be the death knell for my career. God, if word got out that I was forty, I'd never be offered another part." She sounded appalled.

Lexi thought she was overreacting. Lots of Hollywood actresses were still working well into their forties.

"Well, in that case the four of us had better try and get together for our thirty-ninth as it will be our last birthday together," she responded glumly. "Doesn't leave much time though – it's only six weeks away."

"I know, but I was thinking that we could all come to Florida, to your place," Angel suggested breathlessly. "That would be just fabulous. Could you arrange it, Lexi?"

Angel had been born with that knack of being able to wind everyone around her little finger and Lexi, as always, was unable to deny her anything.

"Okay," she reluctantly said. "As Thanksgiving falls the Thursday after our birthdays, maybe we'll make a week of it. What do you think? Do you think Mel will be able to come?"

"I'll make sure she does," said Angel. "Could Brenda get over for it, I wonder? Seeing as it is our last?"

"I don't know. Leave it with me. I'll see what I can do."

"You're a pet – I love you!" Angel cried, blowing kisses down the line.

Lexi rang off with a heavy heart, disappointed that her plans for Guatemala were dashed, unless Angel changed her mind by next year, which was possible, but unlikely. Ah well, she thought sighing, things could be worse.

\* \* \*

She rang Brenda right away but it went to voicemail. Lexi hated those bloody things. She found it hard enough to talk on the phone without talking to a disembodied voice. She hung up without saying anything and decided to wait until 1 p.m. to call, which would be 6 p.m. in Ireland and a good time to get Brenda in. She had intended going to her studio to paint but Angel's phone call had scuppered that. She was too agitated now to produce anything worthwhile so decided to go for a walk on the beach instead.

\* \* \*

Brenda was very surprised to hear her old friend on the other end of the line.

"Lexi, is that really you? Is everything okay?"

"Fine, sweetheart, just fine. How are you?"

"I'm grand. There's nothing wrong, is there? I'm just surprised to hear you. I know how much you hate the telephone."

Lexi laughed. "There's nothing wrong but it is an emergency of a sort, I suppose. Angel has decided that this will be her last birthday so it looks like we won't be having a fortieth, at least not all four of us together. She's asked me to have everyone here to Florida for our thirty-ninth. Is there any way that you could get over for the third week in November?"

Brenda hesitated. "Well, the kids are all away so that wouldn't be a problem but . . ."

"I would like to offer you your flights, as a fortieth birthday present – seeing as how we won't be having one – if you'd accept. It just wouldn't be the same if you weren't here."

"Oh, Lexi, that's very generous of you! I would so love

424

to go. I'm feeling very down at the moment, suffering from empty-nest-syndrome I suppose. Carly, my baby, went away to college in Limerick last week. I can hardly believe it! I'd love to get together again with all of you but I'm not sure Bob will agree to my going."

"Oh I'm sure you'll be able to persuade him." Lexi smiled to herself. "It's Thanksgiving so we can have a whole week here celebrating and maybe you and I could have a few days in New York the following week. We could stay with Mel. What do you think?"

Brenda could hardly believe her ears. She'd always longed to visit New York and to visit Florida would be heaven. This was an amazing opportunity. She'd have to manage it.

"Leave it with me. I'll see what I can do," she said excitedly.

"Let me know as soon as you can. It would be wonderful if you could come, Brenda. I'd so love to have you here."

Brenda's heart beat wildly as she replaced the receiver. How generous of Lexi, who knew that there was no way on earth Brenda could afford to pay for the trip herself, to offer her the flights as a gift. Money had always been tight and now with the economic crisis and three of the children still at university, it was a struggle to make ends meet, let alone take off on a holiday to Florida. She desperately wanted to go. It would be great to get together with Lexi, Angel and Mel for a whole week. If only she could persuade her husband, Bob, to agree to it. Unfortunately, she wasn't at all sure that he would.

\* \* \*

She made Bob's favourite dinner and even bought a bottle of wine – a rare occurrence these days – hoping to soften him up. After they'd finished eating she broached the subject of a possible visit to the States to meet up with the girls.

"Florida? Are you serious?" He looked at her aghast. "You know we can't afford that."

"It won't cost us anything. Lexi is giving me my flight as a birthday present and I have some money saved from my Avon sales." Brenda had started selling Avon cosmetics when the children were little so that she could make a few bob to buy those little extras they needed. To her surprise she'd enjoyed being an Avon Lady and had built up a loyal clientele over the years, many of them becoming her friends. She'd continued with it even when the kids were gone and, although her earnings were not huge, she'd managed to put a little by each week. She'd been saving it for a rainy day – now she was hoping to spend it on a sunny one in Florida. "I really want to go," she persisted, determined not to give up without a fight.

"For how long?" he asked sullenly.

Brenda decided to go for broke. "Two to three weeks. There's no point going all that way for just a few days, is there?" She held her breath, waiting for his response.

"I suppose not," he muttered, finding no reason to oppose it. As long as it wouldn't cost him anything!

She breathed a huge sigh of relief and didn't dare mention a possible jaunt to New York. She knew he'd never agree to that. She felt bad deceiving him, but she wasn't really. It wasn't definite yet anyway, just a possibility.

\* \* \*

On a high, she tried later to initiate lovemaking but as usual Bob wasn't interested and turned away from her, feigning sleep. She lay awake, wondering where it had all gone wrong. They'd been married for twenty-two years and, with five children to raise, they'd never had much time to think about themselves or worry about their marriage. But now, with the kids gone, Brenda had begun to question her life. She had given unselfishly to others all of her life: as a daughter, sister, wife and mother. She loved them all, naturally, but she felt badly in need of some TLC herself now. She'd been so busy taking care of them all that she felt as if she had lost herself. She longed to find herself again and she hoped this holiday might help her do that.

Being on their own since the last of the kids had flown the nest had also brought home to her just how much she and Bob had grown apart. Maybe a break from each other would be a good thing. She turned her thoughts to the forthcoming trip, unable to sleep with excitement.

\* \* \*

The four women went back a long way, back to their very first day at school, in fact. It was a day that would be etched in Brenda's memory forever. The teacher had put the new pupils together according to their birth dates and, as the four of them had birthdays within days of each other, they were all put sitting at the same small table. They were excited but a little nervous and shy, as most kids are on their first day of school, except for Angel of course, who was in her element with this new audience of admirers.

Brenda had felt dowdy and plain beside the other three and was quite in awe of them. She was particularly drawn to Lexi who was quiet and gentle and had a sweet, kind face. Her hair was a halo of unruly red-gold curls which hung down her back and she had soft brown eyes which lit up when she smiled, which was often. Brenda was fascinated with her and her accent which she later discovered was because her mother was American and Lexi had been born in the States and had lived there for the first three years of her life.

Angel was exceptionally pretty with long silky blonde hair and blue eyes and a cute nose that turned up at the end. She was outgoing and extrovert and a right little chatterbox. Brenda could still recall every detail of the beautiful blue dress Angel wore on that first day and the blue ribbon that tied back her hair. She was the prettiest girl Brenda had ever seen and she longed to be her. Even back then, Angel had acquired the knack of batting her eyelashes and using her big blue eyes to get whatever she wanted. And she did! No one could resist her – not the other pupils and not the nuns. She was adored and petted and the envy of the whole class.

Mel was another kettle of fish entirely. Her hair was jet black and tied back in pigtails. Her eyes were so dark that they appeared almost black, or maybe they just gave that impression because of the scowl she continually wore. She could have been pretty, if only she'd smile. For a long time Brenda was almost afraid to talk to her. Lexi was the only one who seemed to see past that and had taken Mel under her wing, otherwise it is doubtful that she would have made many friends.

Brenda remembered how ugly she'd felt in her cousin's hand-me-down dress which was way too big for her. She was also as timid as a mouse and felt overwhelmed by the others. Lexi understood this and reached over and took her hand, squeezing it gently. Brenda smiled gratefully at her as her fears receded. She loved Lexi from that moment on.

Strange but, thinking about it now, Brenda realised that their characters really hadn't changed all that much since that first meeting.

Angel was still a chatterbox and was a famous actress in Hollywood. She was as vivacious and beautiful as ever – with a little help now from the best plastic surgeons in LA.

Mel was still unhappy even though she was now a very successful businesswoman in New York. She was still driven and never satisfied despite the fact that she was now a partner in the most prestigious law firm in New York and highly respected in the legal world. Brenda suspected that Mel regarded her as a failure and thought that she hadn't achieved anything. Raising five children would not be considered an achievement to Mel's way of thinking.

As for Lexi – well, she was still gentle and loving and the glue that held them all together. She was still happy in her own skin and had a wonderful outlook on life. She only saw the good in other people and was loved by everyone who met her. When any of them were in trouble it was Lexi they ran to and somehow it never seemed quite as bad when seen through her eyes. She reached out to people and spread sunshine wherever she went. Her three old school friends would have been lost without her over the years.

\* \* \*

Brenda was dying to call Lexi first thing the following morning but had to wait impatiently until one o'clock due to the five hours time difference. With shaking hands she dialled the Florida number.

"Hi, Lexi, it's Brenda."

"Calling with good news, I hope?" Lexi sounded apprehensive.

"Yes, yes, I can come." Brenda's voice was high with excitement. I'm so thrilled."

Lexi whooped with glee. "Brenda, it's fantastic that you can make it. I'll book your flights right away. I was thinking of bringing you via New York so that you can fly home direct from there. You'd like to visit New York, wouldn't you?"

Would I what? Brenda thought. "Oh, Lexi, that would be heaven," she squealed. "I've always longed to visit New York. Are you sure Mel won't mind my staying with her?"

"Course not. I'll fix it with her," Lexi replied confidently. "You won't have a problem staying those extra few days, will you?"

"No, I told Bob it would be two to three weeks."

"That's decided then. Hopefully Angel will persuade Mel to come and we'll all be here together for Thanksgiving which will be wonderful. I'll contact my travel agent now and have the tickets sent on to you. It will be great to get together again – like old times."

"It sure will. I'm really excited about it. This thirty-ninth birthday is going to be the best birthday I've ever had."

Lexi laughed. "Well, I'll do my best to make it so. You coming is the best birthday present I could have."

# Chapter 2

Angel knew that Lexi was disappointed when she'd told her that there was no way she would consider having a fortieth birthday but Lexi, true to form, had rallied round and agreed to organise a party in Florida for their thirty-ninth. A party was just what Angel needed right now. The very thought of approaching forty was depressing her as she peered in the mirror to check for any new fine lines around her eyes.

She had called Mel as soon as she'd come off the phone from Lexi but as usual it went to voicemail.

When she wasn't working, Angel's day usually started around noon with a mug of coffee – not decaf, she couldn't stand that stuff – or more likely, especially if she was hungover, a glass or two of champagne with orange juice. That always lifted her as she checked her iPhone for messages. She lived in hope that one would be from her agent offering her the role of a lifetime – a fabulous script with her in the starring role. She constantly cited other actresses such as Jennifer Anniston, Sandra Bullock and

Halle Berry, who at the same age were still hot and even winning Oscars. If they could do it, so could she. Anything was possible in Hollywood!

Then she would settle down at her computer to read her emails. Most of them were rubbish but this could just be the day she would hear of some project coming up with a part for a thirty-something blonde. Hollywood ran on rumour so it was important to keep one's ear very close to the ground.

With a second mug of coffee in hand, the next thing she did was check her dating site to see if any eligible blokes had winked at her. She had not dared put a real photo of herself up there as there was a good chance she might be recognised so she'd put one of another blonde up instead.

If she liked the look of any of the men who winked at her she might flirt back and forth in the hope that one of them might turn out to be the gold nugget amongst all the mud and sand. She knew it was unlikely but she was always optimistic. She had met some nice guys on there though unfortunately most of them were married at the time. But, as she was fond of saying, "How long do marriages last in this town? Whoever is married today could be available next week!" She did meet her third husband on a dating site and my God, what a tosser he turned out to be! She refused to think about him. It would only bring her down for the whole day.

She did have a live-in boyfriend at the moment, Will, who was about to become live-out very shortly, although he didn't know it yet. He was sixteen years younger than Angel, which was nothing in Hollywood, but she'd discovered that, hot as it made her look, pandering to the whims of a penniless twenty-three-year-old could be very tiring, not to mention expensive. He wanted to party all night, drinking champagne that she paid for, and then stayed in bed all day. She regularly bemoaned the fact that unfortunately there was only one Ashton Kutcher! Will hadn't worked a day in his life and she knew he probably never would, as long as there were foolish women like her around to support him.

After she checked the dating site, it was more coffee and then she went on Facebook to see what all her friends were getting up to. She had hundreds of friends – too many, she often thought – but it just wasn't possible to drop them. She knew that people got very upset when you did that. She did. Then it was on to Twitter to catch up on all the news there. She only read the @connect now – the tweeters who had mentioned her. She doubted there was anyone on earth who had the time to wade through 375 tweets every day. She knew that she should unfollow some of them but then they'd unfollow her and she was trying hard to reach 5,000 followers. She was very nearly there. If she just followed another forty people or so, they'd follow her back and she'd make it. If by any chance she should land a plum role then that would go up to gazillions, just like Demi Moore, whom she followed. People loved to follow big stars.

Angel sighed, thinking back to the time when she'd been a mega star, famous all over the world. She was twenty-four then and newly arrived in Hollywood when she'd landed a major role in the most popular TV show of the day. Those were halcyon days when she'd been an A-lister and feted wherever she went. The show had lasted for eight glorious years and she'd been bereft when it had ended. She'd landed a plum role in a movie about Marilyn Monroe shortly afterwards, thanks to her resemblance to the famous star, but unfortunately the movie had bombed. She'd worked pretty constantly since then but only bit-parts. A further big movie role had eluded her but she never gave up hope. Sadly, there'd been no Twitter around when she'd been a star.

Sometimes she wondered if maybe Lexi had the right idea shunning all this modern technology. One thing for sure, Lexi would never find the time to paint if she were to try and keep up with the social network.

All of this took until about four thirty every day when, if she was lucky, Will might condescend to put in an appearance. She had lunch then which was usually an egg-white omelette or some salad leaves. Angel was a serial dieter, like every other actress in Hollywood. Of course, she drank the best part of a bottle of wine with it. She read somewhere that there were no carbs in white wine and carbs were the real enemy.

She was excited at the thought of hanging out with the girls again. They'd been best friends all of their lives but it had been a while since all four had met up together. The last time was three years ago and then only for a night. She, Lexi and Mel all happened to be back in Ireland at the same time and they'd met up with Brenda. What a night that had been! Even though they hadn't all been together since their combined thirtieth birthday, six years before, it was as if they'd never been apart.

Both she and Mel had been down to stay with Lexi for quick breaks, but never at the same time. Lexi sometimes travelled to New York in connection with her art and met up with Mel but as she hated Los Angeles – Shallow Town, she called it – Angel didn't see as much of her as she'd like.

Brenda was a little out of the loop, being the only one left in Ireland and of course it wasn't easy for her, with five children like steps of stairs. When they last met she seemed happy enough but her life was a constant struggle. Bob had a taxi and Brenda said he now earned less than he did seven years ago. So much for the Celtic Tiger! Three of her children were at university and living away from home which took every cent they had. Angel could never live like that, no matter how much she loved a man. She thought Brenda was a saint!

\* \* \*

Mel rang back an hour later.

"Sorry, missed your call, I was in a conference."

Angel threw her eyes to heaven. When was Mel ever not in a conference?

"What's up?" Mel asked impatiently.

"Well, as you know, I will not be having any more birthdays so Lexi has agreed to host our last birthday party in Florida. You absolutely have to come."

Mel laughed. "So she's finally accepted that you plan to stay thirty-nine forever?"

"Yeah. Can you make it?"

"Gee, don't know if I can. We're crazily busy here. When is it?"

"Thanksgiving week."

"Hang on a sec while I check."

Angel heard her turning the pages in her diary.

"Well, I can make a couple of days – but a week? I don't know. Leave it with me."

"She's invited Brenda to come over for it."

"She's what?"

Angel heard the surprise in her voice before a huge clatter almost deafened her.

"Sorry, I just dropped my phone," Mel explained. "Can Brenda afford it? I thought they were struggling financially."

"Don't worry – Lexi will find a way. Anyway, isn't it

fantastic? The four of us together again for a whole week!" Angel squealed excitedly.

"Well, I could certainly do with the break. I'll call you when I get home around nine. Okay?"

"Jesus, Mel, you're working yourself to death. What time did you start this morning?"

"Six thirty. Why?"

"You'll kill yourself." Angel shook her head in disbelief. "Mel, you have to come. I need you there."

"Okay, okay," Mel said resignedly. She knew Angel would keep at her until she gave in. "But only for a couple of days. Have to rush now, sorry. I've got another meeting. Byeee!"

"Bye," Angel started to say but Mel had already hung up.

"What a life!" Angel said aloud as she replaced the receiver. Mel had sounded stressed. She would kill herself working. Hopefully she could make the party. It wouldn't be the same without her. She obviously needed the break and a week in Florida would help her relax and chill out. Angel knew that once she got her there she would convince Mel to stay the whole week.

\* \* \*

Lexi rang Angel the next day. "Wonderful news! Brenda is coming for the party."

"That's great. I'm looking forward to seeing her again."

"What about Mel? Did you talk to her?"

"She said she'd come but maybe only for a couple of days. But I'm sure once we get her there we'll be able to persuade her to stay the week."

"That girl works far too hard."

436

"She's nuts. She never takes a holiday and for what?"

"I know, but that's Mel. She's always been like that," Lexi remarked dolefully.

"Isn't it great that Brenda can come?"

"Yes, I'm really looking forward to having her here. God love her, she's earned it. I must give Mel a call. How was she today? She was very stressed out the last time I spoke to her."

"She still is. It looks like we all need this break."

It amused Angel that Lexi had never lost her Irish accent which was even more accentuated over the phone. Both she and Mel had embraced the American way of life with open arms and could now be mistaken for natives, but not Lexi. She had been almost paranoid about keeping her Irish identity. Angel sometimes regretted that she had been so quick to lose her Irish accent. Colin Farrell – what a dish – hadn't, and what success he'd had, Dublin accent and all! Well, too late to do anything about it now, Angel sighed.

\* \* \*

Mel was thinking about Angel's phone call as she rode a taxi home that night. She doubted she could take a whole week off although she'd had no holidays at all this year. She was feeling so very tired and stressed and had begun to wonder if this was all life had to offer. She had no love in her life – heck, she didn't even have a dog or cat to welcome her home at night. She couldn't remember the last time she'd had sex and sometimes feared that she was turning into a dried-up old prune. Sure, she had a fantastic job and a fabulous apartment on the Upper West Side of New York. She was now a partner in the most prestigious law firm in New York and made pots of money but what good was that if she had no time to spend it and nobody to spend it with?

Arriving home, she reheated one of the soups from the 2nd Ave Deli that substituted for dinner most evenings and had just finished it when Lexi rang. To Mel's surprise, she appeared to be as excited as Angel about the forthcoming birthday party. Lexi was usually very laid back about things. Mel supposed it was probably because Brenda was coming. Those two were always as thick as thieves. It would be nice to be together again for a whole week but she honestly didn't think she could take that much time off. However, she'd certainly make it for the party.

She felt that old fear in her stomach again, thinking back on her childhood. She was unfortunate in that both her parents had been teachers and had very high expectations for her. They were teachers first and foremost and could never leave their teachers' hats behind them at school. They saw Mel and her brother more as 'pupils' than as their own offspring. They were brilliant teachers but as parents they sucked. Everything was geared towards academic success, which was very tough on Mel and her older brother. He rebelled against their Dickensian regime and ran off to London after his Inter Cert. Mel wasn't sorry to see him go as he'd always teased her unmercifully but it did mean that she was now unfortunately the sole focus of her parents' attentions.

Her teen years were miserable. Her parents exerted constant pressure on her to be the best which was difficult for her as she was only an average student – certainly not as bright as Brenda or Lexi. Even Angel, who was much more concerned with boys and how she looked than with studying, sailed through all her exams without a worry.

Mel watched longingly as the others went to parties and

discos, wishing with all her heart that she could join them. "There will be plenty of time for partying when you've finished your education, young lady," her parents would say, setting her some more Irish or maths tests to do. It was then that she started to hate them. She didn't have her brother's courage to up and leave. If it hadn't been for her friends, Mel knew that she would have committed suicide. She'd often considered it but somehow Lexi and Brenda had managed to see her through the bad moments. They were both very supportive and, if they hadn't been there for her, she was sure she would not be alive today.

Angel had scarcely been aware of Mel's misery. She was too busy having fun. The ease with which she attracted boys fascinated her friends. Watching her flirt and tease them left Mel feeling more inadequate than ever. She was always tongue-tied in their presence and never knew what to say. Things hadn't changed much since then! Angel still had every man she met falling in love with her and Mel still had a problem connecting with them on any level or letting any man close. She had done so once but it had ended disastrously.

By contrast, Angel had sailed through life petted and pampered by one and all. She'd been christened Angela but by the age of three months she was such a beautiful baby that her besotted, doting father started calling her Angel and the name stuck.

They lived in a beautiful big house on Kenilworth Square, which was the posh end of Rathmines, and they all loved going to Angel's house for tea. Her mother was very beautiful but aloof and not very friendly. It was always Angel's father who was there at parties and who seemed to be in charge. They had lots of servants who did all the cooking and cleaning so her mother could go to lunches and dinners, so Angel told them. Her father was very wealthy – a developer, Angel informed them – although none of them knew exactly what that was.

Everyone adored Angel. She was so pretty and lively and all the other girls wanted to be her friend and be invited to her parties. To Brenda, in particular, Angel resembled a princess who lived in a world that was a million miles from hers.

Brenda's world was a three-bedroom council house in the poorer part of Rathmines where she lived with her parents and seven siblings. All through secondary and even primary school, Brenda had had it tough because she was the eldest of the eight children and had to shoulder a lot of responsibility. Her mother was lazy and very fond of the drink and so Brenda had practically raised her younger brothers and sisters. In spite of this she found the time to study and was the brightest student in the whole class. How she had ever managed to get straight A's in her Leaving Cert and win a university scholarship was a miracle. The others couldn't help but admire her for that. She certainly got no help at home.

Lexi's home life was the most balanced of them all. Her father was a doctor and they lived in a lovely house on the Rathgar Road. Her mother was forty when Lexi arrived and her parents called her their miracle baby. Lexi was very laid-back and easy-going and a bit of a dreamer. Nothing fazed her and she took everything in her stride. Her parents were very nice and down-to-earth which was probably why Lexi was so grounded. She was very artistic and excelled in art class and it was no surprise to any of them when she went on to be a successful artist.

She still painted and regularly had exhibitions in New York and London. Her paintings now sold for exorbitant amounts and she was quite famous.